D1269503

LEGEND

DRAGONRIDER LEGACY

Book 3

BESTSELLING AUTHOR OF THE DRAGONRIDER CHRONICLES

NICOLE CONWAY

Month9Books

Books By Mail
Palm Beach County
Library Annex
4289 Cherry Road
West Palm Beach, FL 33409-9808

This book is a work of fiction. Names, characters, places, and incidents are either products of the author's imagination or are used fictitiously. Any resemblance to actual persons, living or dead, business establishments, events, or locales is entirely coincidental. The author makes no claims to, but instead acknowledges the trademarked status and trademark owners of the word marks mentioned in this work of fiction.

Copyright © 2019 by Nicole Conway

LEGEND by Nicole Conway
All rights reserved. Published in the United States of America by Month9Books, LLC.
No part of this book may be used or reproduced in any manner whatsoever without written permission of the publisher, except in the case of brief quotations embodied in critical articles and reviews.

Trade Paperback ISBN: 978-1-948671-36-1
ePub ISBN: 978-1-948671-56-9
Mobipocket ISBN: 978-1-948671-57-6
Hardcover ISBN: 978-1-948671-58-3

Published by Month9Books, Raleigh, NC 27609
Title and cover design by Danielle Doolittle
Cover illustration by Tatiana A. Makeeva
Map illustration by Nicole Conway

Month9Books

To all the readers that have been following
The Dragonrider story since the very
first release of FLEDGLING.

I have been continually humbled by your
patience, support, and generosity!
Thank you so much for
believing in me—and Jaevid!

Now let's get to it, shall we?

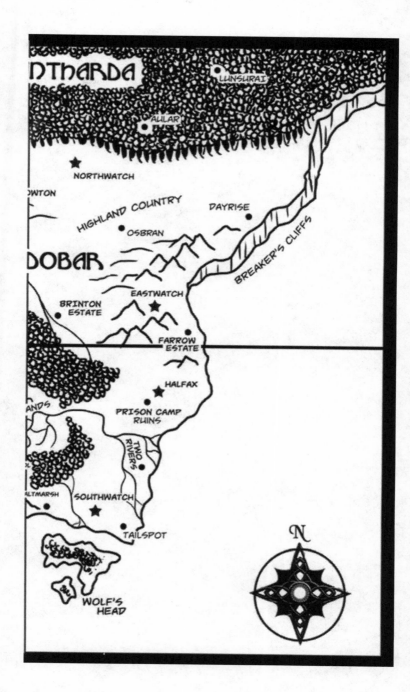

LEGEND

PART ONE

REIGH

ONE

There's a fine line between heroic and insanity—so fine it barely exists. Based on my experience, whether or not you succeeded in your mission was usually what determined which side of that line you wound up on. You succeed, and you're a hero. You fail, and you were a fool for even trying.

I was in dangerously deep "insane" territory.

Granted, this wasn't exactly a new problem for me. I couldn't even blame Jaevid. I'd been winding up in these kinds of life and death situations long before I ever roused him from his divine slumber. The only difference now was—thanks to his explanations about my powers and Noh giving me an impromptu tour through the horrifying secrets of my past—I had more of an understanding of just how screwed I actually was.

It was astronomic, by the way, even by my usual standard of reckless stupidity.

Storming a highly fortified tower crawling with hundreds of furious Tibran soldiers? Idiotic. Splitting up with Jaevid to do this on my own? Insane. Trying to rescue Aubren from this mess and getting us both out alive? Impossible. Thinking I could actually pull this off by myself? Hah! Let's just say, somewhere beyond the Vale, Kiran was probably rolling his eyes. If I did die this time, I was willing to bet good coin he would greet me with a smack to the face and a long lecture—which was something that made a smile tug at my lips.

Gods, I missed him.

Collapsed in the middle of the freight elevator of Northwatch tower, I listened to the ominous symphony of battle all around as the wooden platform made its slow descent. The metal mechanics and gears groaned. Iron chains rattled. The wooden frame creaked. All of it nearly drowned out the distant shouts of the Tibran soldiers, who were now thoroughly aware of our presence in the fortress. The call to arms was blaring in the night. They'd be waiting for me at the bottom of this elevator, ready to cut me down as soon as I showed my face.

But that didn't mean I wasn't going to make them work for it.

Besides, somewhere in this abyss, Aubren was waiting for a rescue. We'd gotten lucky and gained the help of a gray elf kid named Aedan, who'd been secretly slipping information to the scouts in Luntharda under the alias Lamb. Thanks to him, Jaevid and I had been able to get inside Northwatch tower easily enough. Well, considering what we were up against, anyway. We'd sprung my older sister, Jenna, from her cell, but that's where things started going off track.

Apparently, Duke Phillip Derrick been captured at Barrowton, too, which was not something we'd planned for. He was somewhere in this tower, probably praying for his own miracle, and we couldn't leave him here to die. So, I made the hard choice. I sent Jaevid, Aedan, and Jenna away to find him while I stayed behind to find Aubren.

It had sounded good at the time. Good enough to convince Jaevid, anyway. There was just one small problem ... I'd used a *lot* of my power just getting us into the tunnels, so we could access the tower. Now I was clinging to consciousness, fighting the swirling spots in my vision while I tried to figure out what to do. Somehow, I had to pull myself together. I wouldn't fail Aubren, even if that meant he was the only one who got to walk away. He was my brother. I would save him.

I stumbled and staggered as I got to my feet, my head swimming and my vision still spotting. Jaevid hadn't been exaggerating when he said that valestepping would drain me. This, I imagined, must be how an insect felt after a little kid shook it up in a jar. I was on the brink of losing it, clinging to consciousness and control.

My mind raced, scraping together a plan. I had to keep it small, make my hits count, and string out my last bit of strength until I could reach Aubren.

Then I'd unleash pandemonium—otherwise known as Noh. I'd go down, and I'd take as many of these Tibran thugs with me as possible to carve a clear path so Aubren could escape. It would work. It *had* to.

As the elevator clattered and shook toward the bottom of the shaft, I took in a deep breath. My lungs burned. My body screamed in pain, like someone was splitting my head open, as I called more power to my command. I could feel it rising—a deep chill that quivered through every part of me—as though I were being slowly immersed in freezing water.

Darkness gathered around my open hands, swirling and taking the shape of two long scimitars. I closed my fists around the hilts, gritting my teeth and opening my eyes as the elevator came to a shuddering halt.

There wasn't time to count them, but at first glance, I figured there were about thirty angry Tibran soldiers standing between the hall to the left and me. That was where our new ally, Aedan, had advised me Aubren was being held in the solitary confinement cells. Right. Time to get to work.

A Tibran commander shoved his way to the front of the ranks, shouting the order for the archers to open fire. The twang of a dozen bowstrings filled the air with iron-tipped arrows all aimed straight at me.

I dropped into a crouch, gritting my teeth against the sharp pain in my throbbing brain as my blades flickered in my hands, their jagged tips leaving lingering trails of streaking black smoke that hung like dark ribbons in the air. I spun, dancing through maneuvers and feeling the hum of every arrow as though it were a part of myself. Two to the right. One dead center. Six more straight for my head. I cut them out of the air, bringing my blades down in perfect synchronization as my pulse roared in my ears.

My body hummed with dark energy. My nerves blazed. Every movement, every second, brought me closer to the edge.

But there was no stopping now.

"Noh," I whispered. Just the mention of his name sent another wave of chills through my body. "I'm going to need some backup."

"*At your command, master.*" His voice hissed in my mind an instant before I saw him materialize next to me, taking his favorite shape as a black, shadowy canine with tall pointed ears, eyes like red bog fires, and a wide, toothy maw. "*Let us teach them what becomes of those who stand in the way of the Harbinger.*"

His smile was as wicked as it was disturbing, and the sight of him made the front ranks of the Tibran soldiers hesitate. Some of them stopped dead in their tracks, their eyes wide as though considering an immediate retreat.

"Don't get scared now." My mouth twisted into a menacing grin that probably looked a lot like Noh's. "We're just getting started."

It was a mad sprint. I had minutes left, maybe less. I couldn't feel my feet as I ran, hurtling headlong down the narrow corridors and torch-lit halls of the tower's solitary confinement cellblock. Every step sent a surge of fresh agony up my spine. My vision swerved in and out of focus, sometimes dimming until I couldn't see at all.

"Aubren!" I wheezed and gasped, barely able to croak out his name. "Aubren, you better answer me!"

I blitzed past cell after cell, the shouts of prisoners calling to me with haunting, desperate voices through the tiny barred windows on the doors. Sometimes I caught a glimpse of their eyes catching in the dim light, or their fingers reaching out desperately.

I couldn't stop. I couldn't save them all.

"Noh, find him!" I rasped.

His voice whispered in my brain. "*Of course, master. Right this way.*" He materialized like a phantom, trotting along ahead of me, and then vanishing. He appeared again, further down the corridor, taking a sharp right.

The sudden strain of his pull on my power again made both my legs go numb. I fell, barely catching myself before my face cracked off the cold stone floor. My head swam as I lay listening to my own ragged breaths and the sound of Tibran soldiers in hot pursuit. They weren't far behind me.

I set my jaw and willed my legs to work, dragging them into place when they tingled and threatened to buckle again.

"*They are coming.*"

I looked up into Noh's flickering red eyes, burning like hot coals in the dark. "Thanks. I had no idea."

"*We must hurry.*"

"On it," I growled as I heaved myself up again. "How far is he?"

Noh's shaped blurred, the edges of his gaunt, canine body wavering like flame. "*Not very. But his life is waning. He may not be able to flee on his own.*"

"Great." I leaned against the wall of the corridor for a moment and stamped my feet, trying to bring some feeling back to my calves. "Any more good news?"

"*The dragonriders have come. I feel their presence. They are descending upon the roof.*"

"Evacuating?" I guessed. I had no doubt that bringing the dragons here was Jaevid's doing. His divine power allowed him to communicate with any animal with his thoughts, so his plan of calling in an aerial rescue to get all of us clear of the tower was our best option.

Noh's pointed snout dipped in a nod. "*They'll soon be clear of the tower.*"

"Well that's no good. Who's going to stand in captivated horror and awe when we raze it to the ground?" I pushed away from the wall and started limping forward again.

Noh's laughter crackled in my head. "*The thousands of Tibran soldiers encamped outside, perhaps?*"

I smirked. "Good enough for me." At the very least, maybe they'd give it a second thought before they challenged the force of Maldobar again.

The further I ran through the labyrinthine halls of the tower's lowest levels, the less frequent the torches lighting the hallways became. It was nearly total darkness now, and all I could see of Noh were his glowing eyes lighting my path in the gloom. Behind us, the sound of the soldiers grew louder and louder. They were gaining on us.

"H-how much further is—?"

"*Here!*" Noh stopped so suddenly, I nearly limped right past him.

I approached the solid iron door of a cell. It was on the opposite side of the hall than all the others. I could only guess it was an extra special, deluxe solitary suite especially for royal guests. Yeah, right.

"Aubren," I shouted and beat my fist on the door. "It's Reigh. Can you hear me?"

No answer.

"You better not be dead in there! So help me, I will drag your soul back through the Vale if I have to."

Still nothing.

My body burned with a surge of adrenaline and panic. How bad off was he? Would he be able to get out of here, even if I carved a path for him?

Bringing the door down with my power wasn't the problem—it was what came after. I'd be a breath away from losing it, or dying, or collapsing. None of those were good, especially if Aubren couldn't walk out by himself.

This called for a change of plan.

Help. I needed help.

Whirling around, I went to the cell door directly across the hall and banged on it. "Anyone home in there?"

A pair of shimmering, vivid eyes appeared in the tiny window. They stared at me, wild, desperate, and strange. They had rings of golden yellow around the outside of the irises that faded gradually into an electric shade of green. I'd never seen anything like them.

"Who are you?" a feminine voice asked. It was a soft, breathy sort of voice twanged with an accent I didn't recognize. Was she from outside Maldobar and Luntharda?

"Someone who can get you out of here. But only if you do something for me in exchange."

I waited, staring in silence as those strange eyes studied me for a moment. Something about them gave me a swirling, nauseating feeling in the pit of my stomach. Or maybe that was Noh sucking away more of my soul. Who could tell? It was hard to concentrate on anything when I was nodding in and out of consciousness.

"Okay," the voice answered at last. "What do you want me to do?"

"I'm going to open the doors to your cell and the one across from you. The man inside there is extremely important. You have to help him get out of this tower—even if that means leaving me behind. I will make a path for you, so the soldiers don't follow. But he *must* survive. Understand?"

"But where will we go? There must be Tibrans everywhere."

She had a point. "I'll send you as far away from here as I can. Head north, toward the jungle of Luntharda. Once you get there, climb the first tree you can and wait. Gray elf scouts will find you—they're running frequent patrols and will probably be watching you long before you even reach the jungle. They'll take you somewhere safe."

"They won't try to kill me?"

I shook my head. "Any enemy of the Tibrans is a friend of theirs. Just tell them Reigh sent you. You'll be fine."

"Very well, Reigh," she answered faintly. "I will do what I can."

That would have to do.

"Step back from the door," I commanded as I hobbled to the middle of the hall.

"*Master, the Tibran soldiers will be here in minutes,*" Noh warned.

It didn't matter. I only needed one to get this done.

Widening my stance, I set my jaw and spread my arms, a hand aimed at both doors on either side of me. One quick burst. That's all I needed. The mere touch of my power would turn the iron to brittle heaps of rust and ash—the same way I'd freed Jenna from her cell—then Aubren would be free. I could get him out of here. Then I could die knowing I'd at least saved my family.

Jaevid would just have to find a way to save the rest of the kingdom without me.

I squeezed my eyes shut, pressing my will out into both of my hands. The pull was instant, like someone had snatched me under the surface of that freezing water so suddenly I didn't even have time to scream or take a breath. The temperature dropped as the shadows swelled and filled the air with whispering voices. Then again, those might have been just in my head. I couldn't tell. And as my vision tunneled, my lungs constricting like someone with icy cold hands was squeezing the air out of them, it didn't matter.

I was out before I even hit the ground.

TWO

"Reigh!"

The sound of Kiran's voice jolted me awake. I blinked, squinting up into the brilliant rays of sunlight breaking through the vast green canopy overhead. I breathed in deeply, filling my lungs with the sweet, humid air that smelled of moist soil and wild jungle flowers.

Home—I was home.

"Reigh, you're all right." Kiran's face appeared over me, drawn into a look of pasty concern. He seemed … younger, somehow. It didn't make any sense. "Just lie still," he said in the calm, deep tone he used whenever he was dealing with a frantic patient. His hands shook as he started poking at me, searching my chest and arms for signs of broken bones. "Can you feel this?"

I bobbed my head.

He let out a shaking breath of relief.

I wanted to ask what happened. How could I possibly be back home? Was this some strange manifestation of the Vale? Or was this the paradise that awaited me after death?

"Your leg is going to feel strange. It will hurt. But you have to sit up for me, all right?" Kiran's expression faltered, flickering between panic and relief. With one hand under my back and the other supporting my neck, he helped me sit up.

That's when I realized … I was *smaller*. Too small. Something wasn't right. It was as though my body had shrunk. Glancing down at my leg, which was lying limply on the ground, I realized why he was so upset. I had a compound fracture. The bone was sticking through the skin of my shin, pearly white against all the blood.

The sight made my body flush and my pulse launch into overdrive. But I didn't feel it. It didn't hurt at all. How was that possible?

"You fell a long way. Your leg is broken. I can fix it, but right now we have to get you back home," he said as he slid his arms under my body and lifted me easily off the jungle floor. "Does anything else hurt? Your neck? Your back?"

"N-no, Kiran." My voice came out small and childish, muffled by sobs.

Suddenly, I remembered. This wasn't paradise or some kind of trick of the Vale. It was a memory. I'd fallen out of a tree when I was little, broken my leg, and once again dodged an early death. After lying helpless on the jungle floor for hours, Kiran had finally found me.

The instant I recalled that distant memory, the world around me seemed to get clearer. I could hear the calls of the birds and feel the coolness of my tears against my flushed cheeks. The familiar scent of medicinal herbs—Kiran's smell—was so close, it brought all my pain, grief, and shame exploding to the surface. I wanted to scream, to put my arms around him, to apologize.

But I couldn't. I couldn't say anything.

"I was so worried, Reigh. You know better than to go off climbing on your own. You're not ready yet." Kiran started in on a lecture even with his face still blanched with worry as he jogged past trees heavily laden with moss and flowering vines. "What if a tigrex had found you first? Or what if you had broken your back? You keep pushing yourself too far and someday you might break what I cannot fix."

"I just wanted to see it again," I whimpered against his shoulder.

"What?"

"The lapiloque's tree. I thought I could get to the top."

Kiran blinked in surprise. "Why didn't you just ask me to take you?"

"You were busy with the scouts. You said you would take me climbing again. You promised. But you never did. You went to train them instead."

"Oh, Reigh," Kiran sighed, the tired lines around his eyes seeming to deepen.

"Do you like them better?" I asked. "Because they're elves, too?"

He halted, staring at me in bewilderment. "Why on earth would you think that?"

"That's what Lurin said. He said you only took me in because you wanted a human pet. He said I'm too stupid and slow to be a scout and that's why you won't let me train with them."

Kiran's multihued eyes seemed to spark and smolder with anger as he started jogging again, faster than ever. "None of that is true. Lurin is an idiot. I will handle him."

"Can I tell him that?"

"What?"

"That you said he's an idiot."

I nearly missed it. Kiran turned his face away, probably so I wouldn't see. But the instant before, one corner of his mouth twitched upward into a smile. "No. I'll tell him myself," he replied. "And if he doesn't listen, then life will eventually teach him that the hard way."

We continued in silence as he carried me through the jungle. All I could do—all I wanted to do—was lie there and stare at him. I wanted to memorize every feature, every detail.

"Kiran?" my tiny, childish voice spoke again.

"Yes?"

"I'm sorry I went climbing alone," I mumbled.

He smiled again, looking down at me with the warmth and parental affection I'd almost forgotten. Gods, it had been years since he smiled at me like that. Not that I'd given him much reason to, but it had almost seemed like the older I got, the colder he became. I wondered if that had something to do with Noh, if he'd somehow known what was in store for me.

"It's all right, Reigh. You're safe now," he replied. "Just promise me you won't do it again. You're always so eager to prove yourself. But a scout must always be careful. He must always remember Luntharda is not forgiving to the naïve and unprepared—nor is the rest of the world, for that matter. There are dangerous things out there, things that will want to kill or hurt you."

"Animals? Like the tigrex?"

"Yes, some are animals," he answered quietly. "But some are men, who are often far worse than any hungry tigrex. They are cruel only for the sake of cruelty."

The memory began to fade, crumbling around me as Kiran lifted his gaze to look back at the road ahead.

"You cannot be like that, Reigh. If you must be cruel, if you must kill, let it be for a good reason. Let it be for something good." His voice was fading fast, growing more distant as his image wavered. "Let it be for something you love more than yourself."

Little by little, it all dissolved away—back into darkness. Back into hell.

A warm, rough-palmed hand patted my cheek, almost comfortingly. It felt nice. Right up until it gave me a hard smack.

My cheek stung and immediately my eyes flew open, staring up into the eerie, yellow-green gaze of a young woman stooping over me. "Wake up, boy! You cannot die yet. You promised to get me out of here."

I groaned. My head pounded; the pressure inside making me wonder if I was bleeding from the ears. Groggily, I rolled over and coughed. The numbness had reached my lungs. I could barely get a good breath.

"You must hurry. The soldiers are nearly here," she urged in her weird accent.

I raised my head enough to glare at her. "Working on it," I wheezed.

"Perhaps you have overestimated your talents?" She arched an eyebrow, her deep ebony skin gleaming flawlessly in the faint light. With slender pointed ears peeking out through her long, loosely curled locks of black hair, the woman studied me, tilting her head to the side slightly.

She looked like an elf—but not any I'd ever seen before. Her lithe frame was petite but muscular, and there was a bizarre mark on her face. A thin, curved line crossed her forehead and vanished into her hair like a circlet with a small crescent shape right in the center. When she moved, the light shimmered off those markings as though they'd been painted there with liquid silver. Strange—but beautiful.

"What? Melting doors wasn't impressive enough for you?" I rasped as I dragged my tingling, aching body upright. When I stumbled, she quickly darted forward to grab my arm and steady me. Her grip was surprisingly strong for someone who probably didn't stand a single inch over five feet.

"I've seen such tricks. But I take it you've never seen a Lunostri before," she quipped, stepping away again with one of her eyebrows arched.

"How'd you guess?"

"Because you're staring at me like I've got a second head.

I suppose it can't be helped. From what little I've seen, the elves in your lands seem quite different. And my people are not explorers. We prefer to keep to our own and let the rest of the world squabble amongst itself. It wasn't until the Tibrans landed that many of us had ever set foot beyond our borders." The young woman crossed her arms and stood farther back to observe me from a cautious distance. I guess she didn't quite trust me yet. Fair enough.

"Is that how you wound up down here?" I asked.

She gave a stiff nod. "Argonox took many of my people into his ranks after he conquered our land. No doubt he plans to do the same here. Don't let him see your power—he's rather fond of adding *special* individuals to his private collection."

I resisted a laugh. Too bad it was a bit late for that.

"Does that include you?" I flashed her another look, studying her ragged clothes and bare feet. It was impossible to tell anything more about who she was or where she'd come from. The Tibrans had likely stripped away anything she owned when they took her prisoner.

Her lips bowed into a secretive little smile. "You could say that. But now is not the time for introductions. I checked on your friend. He is unconscious and severely beaten. It seems Argonox was very thorough with his interrogation. I will have to carry him. But first, you must show me you can get us out of here."

"Go get him, then." I slurred a little as I let my shoulder rest against the closest stone wall. "And hurry."

I closed my eyes as the elf woman disappeared into Aubren's cell. I had to get it together—I had to finish this. A few deep breaths, that's all I needed. Then I could finish killing myself so Aubren would be safe.

Attempting to valestep again was probably beyond idiotic. I'd only done it once to get us into the tunnels, and it had immediately brought me to my knees with a pain like a dragon was doing a tap dance on my head. I wouldn't survive it this time, and yet I knew it was the only way to get them out of here. I'd send them as far north as I could. Hopefully it would be far enough.

Then I would die.

Taking Aubren myself or going along with them wasn't an option. Assuming I even survived the effort of creating the portal, I wouldn't be able to make the journey to safety in Luntharda on my own, let alone carrying Aubren. We'd both die somewhere in the snowbound prairie. So, sending this mysterious elf girl in my place was better. She looked capable. Gods, I prayed she was trustworthy.

Once they were clear of Northwatch, if I was still alive, I would use whatever remained of my power to bring this place down and kill as many Tibrans in the process as possible. If I could make any dent in Argonox's forces, it would be worth it. I'd carve my name into his memory with blood, and he would *never* forget it.

Sounded good, anyway.

Down the hall, the voices and footsteps of the Tibran soldiers grew closer, mingled with the baying of hounds. No wonder they were able to track me so easily.

"*Shall I slow their progress?*" Noh offered with a gleeful laugh. At least one of us was enjoying this.

I shook my head. "Not worth it. Let them come. I need every last drop of power I have left to open the portal."

"Who are you talking to?" The elf woman reappeared from the darkness of the cell with Aubren's limp body over her shoulders. He was easily twice her size, but she didn't shake or waver as she strode out to meet me.

"Death." I chuckled. Maybe that was a bad joke, but it wasn't exactly a lie.

"I hear them! This way!" someone shouted. The soldiers were nearly upon us.

"Well?" The elf woman's bright eyes flashed with urgent panic.

"Get ready." I sucked in a few final breaths and pushed away from the wall.

The hounds were coming. Their claws clicked off the stone, and their snarling and growling echoed off the ceiling. We had seconds.

Widening my stance again, I pushed both of my arms forward with my palms pressed together and squeezed my eyes shut, calling forth every lingering fragment of my power from the furthest corners of my mind and gathering it between my palms. My body twitched, resisting the pull, as my breath caught, my heartbeat thundered in my ears, and everything went numb and cold. Focus. I had to keep calm. This was my last chance, and it had to count.

Slowly, I pulled my hands apart like I was opening a curtain.

I couldn't see it—not with my eyes closed. But I felt it just as clearly as if it were a part of me. The fabric of the living world split, opening to reveal what lay beyond. The Vale. A portal of churning, swirling darkness that led into the realm of the spirits.

"By the goddess," the elf woman gasped. "You … you are—"

"G-go!" I roared. She could be mystified by my awesome power later. I couldn't hold the portal open forever. With every passing second, my pulse slowed, and my body shook under the strain. My lungs constricted. I couldn't breathe anymore. Something warm drizzled out of my nose and eyes, streaking my face and dripping off my chin.

Blood.

"Go *now!*"

Peeling my eyes open, I stole one last look at her as she darted past, lugging Aubren over her shoulders like a giant, man-shaped sack of flour. Her jaw was set, vivid eyes flashing with a resolute determination I had to admire. She ran straight for the portal without hesitation.

This was it. She was going to make it.

Something whipped past my head, humming through the air. Too late, I realized what it was.

Oh no.

The arrow caught the elf woman right in the back of the calf. She stumbled. Aubren's large frame rolled off her back as she fell forward, arms flailing wildly as though trying to catch herself and hang onto him at the same time.

It didn't work.

The last thing I saw was her long black hair disappearing into the portal as Aubren flopped onto the ground right before it. She'd gone through the portal—or fallen into it, rather—but Aubren hadn't been along for the ride.

No … *No!*

Something inside me snapped.

My body jerked suddenly, pitching wildly as the coldness under my skin exploded through every part of me. I was finished. I felt my heart stop with one final, desperate thump.

Then nothing—just a strange silence in my ears where my pulse and breathing should have been.

Dark energy hummed through my veins, vibrating through every part of my brain. The world spun around me, smeared with the light of torches blurring in and out of focus. The sound of the approaching soldiers was muffled chaos. My body suddenly went slack as the portal closed, and I hit the floor right next to Aubren.

I barely recognized him, lying only a foot or two away. His entire face was purple and swollen, and there was dried blood crusted around his nose and mouth. One of his eyes had practically swollen shut. Some of the bruises were a deep, angry, fresh shade of purple, while others were turning yellow and green—they were older and already healing. He'd been beaten many times, probably interrogated and tortured. Gods and Fates, was he even alive?

Thoughts swirled through my mind, tossed amidst the churning whirlpool of thrumming power as everything went dark. I'd failed him. I'd failed Jenna, Jaevid, and Enyo, too. We were both going to die here in this putrid hole, far away from the people we loved.

"Sorry," I croaked, not knowing if he'd hear me.

Aubren's brow twitched. Slowly, his eyes opened just enough that I could see him staring back at me. "Reigh?" he groaned. "W-why? How?"

There were a thousand things I wanted to say. He was right about everything. I was his little brother, albeit a lousy one. I shouldn't have left them after that first battle. I was a coward. I'd run away like a sniveling child and hid because ... because I was embarrassed and ashamed. Maldobar deserved better. I should have been there to fight for Barrowton. Maybe if I had, none of this would have happened.

It was too late for all that now, though.

As soon as I opened my mouth to try to speak, someone grabbed a fistful of my hair and yanked my head off the floor. I dangled, delirious and defenseless, staring groggily into the sneer of a Tibran soldier dressed out in elaborate bronze armor. He wore a matching sloped helm with a mane of light red feathers down the middle, the visor raised so he could wrinkle his nose at me.

"We've got you now, Maldobarian rat."

Under any other circumstance, I'd have snapped back with a clever, witty one-liner. I was good at those. Maybe something about how nice he looked in that fancy *pink* helmet. Did they give those to the lousiest fighters in the Tibran armies? Or just the ugly ones?

But I couldn't speak. My lungs squeezed and spasmed for want of just one tiny breath.

"Lord Argonox! I've found him!" The solider dropped me like a rotten apple, sending me face-first back into the floor. Then he used the toe of his boot to poke me in the ribs. "I think he's dead."

As if I would ever be that lucky.

"Turn him over," a deep, smooth voice spoke over me.

Immediately, the soldier roughly rolled me onto my back. It took every ounce of strength to suck in one, short, desperate little breath. Just enough to keep me conscious a few seconds more. I couldn't move. I was helpless, sprawled out in the most undignified way possible, as I stared up at the stone ceiling overhead.

Then an unfamiliar face eclipsed my view.

A man about Aubren's age peered down at me, his slate blue eyes narrowing as he grabbed my chin and turned my face to the side long enough to look at my ears. "My, my. The Fates have smiled upon me today after all." The smile that curled over his lips was nothing short of disturbing. "He's not dead. This is the boy Hilleddi discovered, the one from Luntharda. He turned the tide during our first siege at Barrowton. He's human, although he dresses like one of those elf savages from Luntharda."

"T-the one who serves the dark goddess?" the soldier stammered. "The angel of death!"

Wait—the Tibrans *knew* about Clysiros? And the Fates?

"None other. No wonder your men have had such a difficult time containing him."

"Yes, My Lord. He slaughtered everything on the ground floor. Even the two dread-hounds." The soldier paused as he leaned over me again, trying to peek around his master's head. He swallowed hard. "If he truly is not dead, then perhaps we should take precautions in case—"

"He is no longer a threat, Captain. He obliterated two legions of my finest soldiers at Barrowton—after that, sieging a tower should be elementary for someone playing with that kind of power. He must have drawn out too much of it in an effort to save that shoddy excuse for a prince. A convenient mistake for us. And here I thought today would be a waste." Argonox's smile widened. "Pushed it right to the brink didn't you, boy? A pity no one in this kingdom seems to know anything about divine power."

"What shall we do with him, My Lord?"

"Bind him and take him to the experimental wing. Phoebe will have much work to keep her occupied."

"And the prince?"

Argonox's face disappeared from my view. He sighed as his heavy footsteps began to retreat. "Put him back in the cell." The footsteps stopped abruptly. "No … wait."

"My Lord?"

"Hilleddi said this boy broke the Mirror of Truth. That he was able to defy it with his dark power." Argonox's voice drew closer again. His eyes narrowed slightly, brow creasing as though he were trying to read my mind. "Coming down here was utter madness. There is no exit from this portion of the tower, and he must have known he was already pushing his abilities to their limits. But rather than escaping with the rest of his cohorts, he came down here. He must have known he would be risking death."

"We have seen such efforts from Maldobarian troops on behalf of their royals before," the captain offered. "They are nothing if not fiercely loyal."

"True, but this goes beyond mere loyalty to the crown." A hand grabbed my chin again roughly. Argonox turned my head, forcing me to make eye contact with him. "And you are no mere soldier. It was not your power that spared you from the mirror, was it? You spoke the truth to it."

Bright spots swam in my vision as I started to lose it. Air—I needed air!

"King Felix has been keeping a dark little secret hidden

in that wild jungle." Gleeful realization sparkled in his eyes. "You *are* a Prince of Maldobar."

A greedy, endless darkness dragged me under, snuffing out everything as my mind reeled, whirling with panic at that last glimpse of sheer excitement and delight on Argonox's face. I didn't want to imagine what that meant. Would he torture me? Kill me?

Or something worse?

THREE

"*Reigh? Reigh! Wake up!*"

A loud shout startled me awake, as though someone were bending right over to yell down into my face. But when my eyes flew open, there was nothing. Only empty air. What had happened? Where was I?

I still couldn't move to find out. My whole body was numb and limp, nothing but an itchy, tingly, dead weight. Lying on my back, my vision gradually adjusted to the dimness of the prison cell where I was sprawled on the floor. It was essentially a windowless stone box with one heavy iron door. The smell of cinders, ash, and something else—like scorched metal—wafted past my nose. Each one of my shuddering breaths turned to white fog in the cold air.

"*Reigh? Can you hear me?*" the voice spoke again, so clear it seemed as though whoever was talking should be standing right over me. But there was nothing.

"W-who?" My voice scraped hoarsely through my raw throat.

"Oh, thank the gods," she replied. *"I thought I was too late. It's Hecate."*

Hecate? But where? I forced my aching eyeballs to roll around, searching as far around the cell as I could without being able to move my head.

"I'm here, in your head. It's hard to explain. Noh let me in," she explained quickly. *"But I can't do this for long. It's still difficult. I'm trying, though. I've been practicing, just like Jaevid said. Soon I can help."*

"W-with what?"

"Hush now. Don't waste your strength trying to talk. Just listen. I may not have much time," she cooed gently. *"I was able to find out where you are. The foundling spirits are much easier for me to talk to, so they've been helping me search,"* she said. *"The Tibrans have taken you away from Northwatch, further to the south. My grandfather believes you're in Solhelm, at the old estate that used to belong to King Felix when he was still a duke."*

Solhelm? Why would Argonox want to bring me here? Surely Northwatch was more defensible. It was a tower built for war.

"He's been searching for something," Hecate went on, as though she could read my mind. Maybe she could, if she was taking up Noh's usual spot buried somewhere deep in my semi-conscious brain. *"At first, I assumed it was the crystal. But I was wrong. Reigh, he's been combing the estate's cemetery. He's opened almost all of the crypts, even the one where Jaevid was supposedly buried during the Gray War."*

I got a bad feeling about a second before she confirmed my worst fear.

"He's exhuming the bodies of fallen dragonriders. He's even collected the remains of several of their mounts. I think he's planning something terrible. We must find a way to get you out of there before—"

Her voice went silent, as though someone had snuffed her out of my brain like a candle in the night. It didn't matter. She'd said enough. Argonox was digging up old dragonrider graves and raiding them for their bones? That did not bode well for anyone, especially me. I didn't know exactly what he intended to do with them, or me for that matter, but if the past was any clue, I was willing to bet it was going to be something horrible.

Lying alone in the depths of some duke's dungeon, I tried to think of anything I could do to end this before it began. In this state, I couldn't even try to kill myself to prevent Argonox from being able to use my power against my friends and family. I was helpless, cut off from everyone who might have been able to help me. I might as well have been sitting on the dark side of the moon.

No matter what I did, a persistent flicker of hope remained burning brightly in the back of my mind that maybe Jaevid would come for me. He was probably the only one who could at this point. My better sense knew otherwise. Coming here would be suicide.

Tears welled in my eyes until I squeezed them shut, clenching my teeth against the sharp pain constricting my throat. Maybe the end, *my* end, would be quick and painless.

"Enyo." I rasped her name into the dark. With my eyes

still shut, I could almost picture her face. "H-Hecate, if you can still hear m-me. Tell Enyo I'm sorry. Tell her I love her. Tell h-her ... it's all going to be okay."

I'd just begun to get the feeling back in my fingers and toes when the cell door banged open. Propping myself onto my elbows, I raised my head shakily to see a company of armored Tibran soldiers file in, surrounding a ... little girl? I blinked a few times just to make sure I wasn't hallucinating.

She couldn't have been more than fourteen, with ginger-orange hair pulled into two wildly curly pigtails right behind her ears. Her face was mottled in freckles, and a long leather apron and soot-stained dress were draped over her scrawny frame. She stared down at me, her wide eyes as blue as birds' eggs, and nibbled on her bottom lip.

She turned to one of the soldiers beside her. "How long has he been like this?"

He shrugged, making his bronze shoulder pauldrons clank.

The girl frowned and rubbed the bridge of her nose. "Bring water right away. If Lord Argonox wants this to work, then it might be in everyone's best interest that he doesn't die of dehydration first."

The soldier obeyed, disappearing back into the hallway. Interesting. Since when did a scrappy-looking teenage girl give marching orders to Tibran soldiers?

"Hello there." She spoke softly as she approached and knelt at my side. "I'm Phoebe. We're going to be … working together."

I furrowed my brow into the most threatening scowl I could muster. "T-Tibran scum," I growled hoarsely. It sounded more menacing in my head.

Her expression dimmed. "I guess so. I'm sorry we're meeting this way, but Lord Argonox has already given orders." Her lips thinned as she looked away, her delicate brows crinkling with distress. "I'll try to make it as painless as possible."

Painless? What was she going to do to me?

Reaching into one of the pockets of her apron, Phoebe withdrew a strange device—a glass cylinder tipped with a long, thin needle. It was filled with a black substance, and she held it up to the dim light that bled in from the doorway, giving the glass a few taps before turning back to me.

No way! I had to get away from her and that needle.

Floundering backward, I struggled to crawl away over the cold, gritty stone floor. I only managed a few steps before my body gave out, still too numb and weak from hunger and thirst to attempt an escape.

She shook her head. "It'll go much easier if you cooperate, I promise. I just need to—"

"I'll die before I cooperate with a Tibran," I shouted.

Suddenly, a deafening roar shook the cell around us. The stones rattled like chattering teeth, and the soldiers at the door flinched for their weapons.

"Can't you do anything to steady her?" Phoebe barked at the soldiers.

"I'm sorry, Miss Artificer," one of them replied. "She's strong. Even with the bridle in place, she continues to resist."

She? That beastly cry sounded so familiar. Why? Where had I heard it before? Oh, gods, no! They had *my* dragon.

The word left my lips like a scream. "Vexi!"

Another bellow made a shower of dirt spill from the ceiling. I coughed and wiped my eyes, body beginning to quake under the strain of pushing myself upright once more. Everything hurt. My head swam in and out of consciousness. Through the haze, I spotted Phoebe coming closer with the needle poised.

I kicked away wildly, scrambling into the furthest corner of the room, gritting my teeth. If she wanted to stick that in me, she was going to have to fight me first—however pathetic and brief it would be.

"I guess I will need some help restraining him." Phoebe sighed. She motioned to the guards at the door, and two stepped forward.

My pulse thrashed, making my vision tunnel as I staggered to my feet. I barely made it there before the guards grabbed my arms and wrenched me around, crushing my body against the wall.

All I could do was scream. And every time I did, Vexi roared and the room shook, as though she were pitching and fighting to get to me. As the cold pinch of the needle sank into the skin of my neck, I realized what that meant: Vexi had come back. My dragon had tried to rescue me.

And now it was going to cost us both dearly.

PART TWO

JENNA

FOUR

The sight of the black dragon perched atop the keep, its decaying hide rotted away in places to reveal white bone, stopped us in our tracks. Standing on the frozen lake of Cernheist, we gaped up at the undead monster as it let out a shattering cry and spat a burst of burning venom into the frigid air. It was a creature of pure nightmare. It shouldn't have been alive. How? How was this possible?

And the rider ...

The figure seated in the creature's saddle wore armor like polished obsidian. Even from a distance, I could pick out the shapes of golden wings painted onto the shoulder pauldrons and breastplate. How many times had my father described those markings to me during our bedtime stories? More than I could ever count.

But it couldn't be. It was impossible. Beckah Derrick was

dead. She'd died a hero's death forty years ago at the end of the Gray War. I'd seen the place where her body was buried on my father's family's land in Solhelm.

"Jenna."

Startled, I turned to glance at Jaevid. Standing tall beside me, his scimitar firmly in his grip, his whole face flushed as his expression closed. His glacier-blue eyes smoldered ominously, and his jaw went rigid. There was no mistaking it. He recognized that beast and rider, too.

"You must take the others away from here," he commanded softly. "I will draw their focus. Make for the mountain pass and do not stop until nightfall."

My body shook with a sudden surge of adrenaline. I couldn't fathom what he must be feeling. Did he remember her? Did he know who and what she'd been to him before?

According to my father, Jaevid and Beckah had been ... much more than close friends. They were not just lovers; their bond went far deeper than just a mere attraction. They were like two halves of the same brilliant spirit. In fact, Beckah had died protecting him. She'd sacrificed herself so that he could complete his mission to destroy the god stone.

So why, by all the Fates, would she come here to challenge him?

As he stepped away, I lunged to grab his arm. "Wait, Jae, you don't have to do this alone. My men and I—we are ready to fight with you. We are dragonriders. We should stand together."

"No." His voice cracked over me like the punishing bite of a whip. "This is not open for debate. You evacuate the city. Defend the people. Protect them at all costs. Their safety is all that matters."

I didn't believe it. Not for a single second. Perhaps he did want to make sure everyone got out safely—but there was more to it. This wasn't duty or heroism. He wanted to fight her alone. This was contrition.

Biting down hard, I seized the front of his breastplate and jerked him down an inch or two, so I could look him squarely in the eye. Demigod or not, he *would* hear me. "You need to remember your place in this mess. If you go out there and get killed over some grand gesture of atonement, then all of Maldobar falls with you. So, fight her, if you think you have to, but don't kill yourself doing it. Please, Jae. We—Maldobar—still needs you."

Jaevid's eyes went round. He blinked a few times, mouth hanging slightly open. Then a thin, sad smile spread over his handsome face. "You sound like him."

I didn't have to ask whom. Once again, he was comparing me to my father, King Felix. "As long as you listen, I don't care who I sound like. Do whatever you think you have to, but come back. Swear that you will."

He nodded once. "I swear."

Throwing my arms around his neck, I squeezed him as tightly as I could. I buried my face against his shoulder, biting against the curses that stung my throat. Then I had to let him go.

Jaevid started for his dragon at a sprint, climbing into the borrowed saddle fixed to the beast's spiny back. Mavrik was an impressive specimen, able to match the undead king drake pound for pound in size. He crouched, powerful legs rippling as his black claws gripped the ice. His wing arms flexed to spread their leathery membranes wide in the freezing wind. With the sunlight dancing off scales of royal blue, he launched skyward with a booming roar. The frozen surface of the lake shuddered, sending out cracks like growing strands on a spider's web.

I watched, captivated by the sight of Jaevid Broadfeather forging headlong into battle as the opposing black drake also took to the air with a screeching cry. My pulse thrashed in my ears, racing so fast I could scarcely breathe. Never in my wildest childhood dreams did I imagine I would see this in person.

But I couldn't waste any more time gawking.

"To work, boys!" I shouted as I whirled back to face my dragonrider brothers. Calem and Haldor were already mounted on the backs of their dragons, waiting for orders. Aubren, after trying to murder me while under the control of foul magic, was now bound and thrown over the back of Haldor's saddle like a prisoner. He kicked and pitched against his bonds when I strode past, as though whatever dark power Argonox had infected him with was driving him to kill me by any means necessary.

I'd deal with him later.

"Easy, girl. I know it hurts." Phillip spoke soothingly to the sleek green dragoness who hunkered before him.

I had not seen Reigh's dragon, Vexi, since Barrowton. The sight of her without that redheaded troublemaker on her back made my stomach turn. Their initial bonding was rocky; Reigh hadn't seemed convinced that the dragonrider path was one he wanted to take. I was willing to chalk that up to him not fully understanding what it meant to be chosen. He'd grown up in Luntharda, after all, so despite being human, the dragonrider culture was foreign to him. He probably didn't understand that Vexi would be loyal only to him for the rest of her life—regardless of how he felt about it.

Still, I couldn't envision Reigh doing anything to hurt her. He wouldn't have muzzled her like that. No, all of this *had* to be Argonox's doing.

What on earth was happening at Northwatch?

Either from terror or fatigue, Vexi didn't resist as Phillip inspected the contraption that had been clamped around her head. Her wide blue eyes panned between us as her emerald hide shivered and her ears drooped. It was a metal bridle, sort of like the kind you might put onto a horse, only with a pinching bit far at the back of the jaw that was angled so it would dig into her sensitive tongue if she rebelled. My blood pressure spiked to think of what sort of person would do this to a dragon.

There had been a time when the Dragonriders of Maldobar had fallen far from our original calling. We'd bred dragons like cattle and treated them as dumb animals. My father had done much in his reign to begin rectifying that. Under his rule, wild dragons could no longer be captured or taken from their natural environment, and it was illegal to steal their eggs or cut wing tendons. But never in our history had we ever stooped this low. This was torture.

Closing his fists around a heavy iron chain at the back of the muzzle that ran behind Vexi's ears and horns, Phillip's thick arms bulged as he gave a swift jerk. The chain snapped like a thread. I blushed and looked away. Phillip's new strength would take some getting used to.

"There we go," he crooned as he slowly started to slide

the rest of the device off her head.

Vexi gave a weak, low murring sound and pressed her snout against his chest like a frightened puppy wanting comfort.

Phillip chuckled and ran his hands over her scaly head. "You're welcome, girl. Stay with us, all right? We'll watch out for you."

She chittered sadly in response.

"You can talk to her?" I asked as I stopped next to him, bending over to get a better look at the iron and steel muzzle that had been fastened to her head. It was a crude looking thing—with rough edges and unpolished finishes, as though it had been slapped together quickly and without much forethought.

One glimpse of the marking engraved onto the very top of it, right where the center of her head would have been when she wore it, made my stomach turn. It was a single symbol etched deep into the metal, and it was one I knew all too well. It was the same mark Argonox was fond of branding into the necks of his captured slave-soldiers.

"In a way," Phillip replied, rubbing at the back of his neck. "I suppose it's some kind of mutual animal understanding. I wouldn't say we're ready to start debating politics, though."

"Maybe she can help us figure out what's happened with Reigh," I murmured as I lifted a glare to Aubren. He had gone quiet again and hung limply over the back of Haldor's saddle. I sighed. "But that will have to wait. Jaevid is right. We need to secure the mountain pass and get the city evacuated."

As I stood straight again, the rest of my companions gathered in to listen. "Phillip, you ride with Calem and take point. I'll have the townspeople follow you to the beginning of the pass. Haldor, you guard the rear and make sure we don't leave anyone behind. Keep eyes on Eirik. We'll be counting on him to let us know we've got everyone. Meanwhile, Phevos and I will circle and make sure nothing else interferes. If another one of Argonox's surprises turns up, we will intercept and hold it off as long as possible."

One by one, my riders responded with a dragonrider salute. Phillip nodded in agreement, his arms crossed and long tail flicking anxiously. Behind us, the air shuddered under a sudden burst of green light, flame, and roaring chaos. Everyone turned to look.

Jaevid and Mavrik had reached the keep.

My pulse throbbed in my fingertips as I watched the two king drakes collide midair. With their wings spread and hind legs outstretched to attack with talons, they snarled and snapped as they grappled. They plummeted toward the earth together, only to break apart at the last second and begin another bout of aerial pursuit. It was a deadly dance that reminded me of two eagles battling for territory.

Another burst of green light made me jump back, bouncing off Phillip's chest. He grasped my shoulders to steady me, and together we watched, frozen in silent awe. Standing in his saddle, Jaevid cast his earthen magic with concussive force, conjuring blasts that sent the wicked undead dragon reeling every time he got too close. It was a game. Jaevid was baiting them—leading them further and further from the city so we could get away without being caught in the crossfire.

Or so I hoped.

"He'll win," Phillip rumbled earnestly.

"He has to," I whispered back.

Every second seemed like an eternity as we worked to get the townspeople and refugees safely out of Cernheist. Eirik and Aedan lead a group of soldiers going door to door as fast as they could to be sure that no one was left behind. Unfortunately, progress was agonizingly slow due to the number of injured, who needed time to get onto wagons, so they could be taken out of the city. There were many women, children, and elderly, too.

Cernheist had become a place of sanctuary for many fleeing the Tibrans. However, it was not a fortress meant for battle. Wheeling far above the frozen lake, Phevos and I watched the surrounding wilderness for approaching Tibran forces, but so far there was no sign of a cavalry or support. Had Argonox really sent just two agents to take the city? I didn't understand that. Then again, a king drake was a considerable force—especially pitted against an unfortified city. There were no city walls or ramparts to guard it or legions of soldiers to defend it. It was vulnerable and Argonox must have known that. He didn't need an army to raze it—just one monstrous king drake and a few good sprays of its burning venom.

We could not afford to give him that chance.

Good thing we had a king drake of our own to match him.

Jaevid and Mavrik pressed in hard, bringing fire and a hailstorm of that glowing green magic whenever the undead mount got in close. So far, they seemed evenly matched. Standing in her saddle, Beckah brandished a strange golden bow. I only assumed the rider was Beckah. The rider's stature seemed petite, but dressed out in full battle armor, it was impossible to tell for sure if it was a man or a woman in that saddle.

Still, that did look like her armor from all the stories and paintings. No one else had ever worn black armor adorned with paintings of golden wings like hers. The helmet was new, however. It hid her face behind a visor painted to resemble a pair of eyes weeping golden tears. None of the stories or paintings referenced anything like it.

Beckah moved on Jaevid with a ruthless precision I tried not to envy. Her aim was deadly, and she fired arrow after arrow with unshaking accuracy. The only thing sparing Jaevid from each strike was his ability to cast some sort of deflective shield with his power. He blocked blow after blow, firing back and snarling out words I couldn't understand over the roar of battle. As far as I could tell, she never answered.

Landing on the top of Cernheist's keep, I let Phevos take a quick breather while I took account of all my men. Perish, Calem, and Phillip made low passes back and forth, guiding the people out of the city toward the mountains. Aedan and Eirik were galloping down the streets on horseback, trying to organize efforts to get everyone moving. Haldor and Turq, with Aubren still in tow, made low circles while they waited to take up the rear position behind the crowd of refugees.

So far, so good.

Suddenly, the keep shuddered beneath us. Phevos flapped wildly, nearly losing his balance and letting out a yowl of panic. I gripped the saddle handles and brought him around, looking toward where Jaevid and Beckah had been dueling in the sky. They were gone. But there was a brand new, dragon-sized hole in the ice of the frozen lake.

Oh gods.

"*What happened?*" Haldor signaled as he and Turq landed next to us.

I shook my head. I hadn't seen it. My heart thumped with wild panic as I watched the surface of the lake and waited.

The keep shuddered again as the two dragons burst up through the ice, so close I could feel the force of their blows like a shockwave in the air. They were locked in combat, clawing and snapping as they rolled like two feral cats. Mavrik snagged the monstrous black dragon by the back of the head and began trying to get enough leverage to break his neck. Would that even work on a dragon that already looked like it should be dead?

Then their riders emerged from the water, as well.

Jaevid came out first, sputtering and coughing as he heaved himself back onto the solid ice. He lay flat out on his back for a second or two, catching his breath, before staggering back to his feet.

Not twenty yards away, Beckah emerged, too. She leapt out of the water, bow still in hand, and strode directly for him without missing a beat.

Reaching back to draw another arrow from her quiver,

she stalked toward him with smooth, even strides.

My stomach dropped.

Jaevid was still reeling, wiping water out of his eyes as he turned to her. His face twisted with a look I wished I hadn't seen. Agony. Sorrow. Rage like the surface of the sun. It was as though he were burning from the inside out as he walked forward to meet her. His whole body tensed, shoulders hunched, and hands clenched as he shouted at her, although I couldn't make out the words over the dragons snarling.

In one smooth, beautiful, lethal motion, Beckah drew back her arrow and fired. Jaevid stopped, his body jerking on impact. Without full armor to protect him, the arrow caught him right in the shoulder above his breastplate.

That was an easy shot. No way she had missed on accident. What then? Was it a warning? Or was it really her under that helmet?

Jaevid grabbed onto the shaft of the arrow and snapped it off, tossing the feathered end aside. He started walking toward her again, still shouting.

"*What is he doing?*" Haldor signaled.

I didn't reply—but I knew. Deep down, I understood not wanting to imagine someone you loved would try to kill you. I'd felt the same way when Aubren had me pinned, ready to land the final blow. Jaevid must have been struggling with that, as well. He wanted to believe that—if it really was Beckah under that helmet—some part of her spirit was in there, fighting to get control over whatever dark power had brought her back into this world. He was gambling on that hope just like I had.

And he was doing it with all our lives—not just his own.

FIVE

Standing less than five yards apart, Jaevid and Beckah stopped. She slid another arrow from her quiver and snapped it into place, drawing the string back to take aim with shoulders braced and firm. At that range, she could pierce his skull easily. She could end it with one shot, and there was nothing any of us could do to stop her.

Jaevid never moved.

Blood dripped from his injured shoulder, leaving a trail of pink splotches and smears across the ice where he'd walked. He faced her, upright and tense, his mouth moving but his words lost to the chaos of their brawling dragons. His eyes closed as he dipped his head slightly. Surrender?

My heart hit the back of my throat. Jaevid, gods, *no!*

Her grip on her bow trembled. She faltered.

My mouth fell open. Was it actually *working?* Was she

listening to him? Did she ... remember?

With no warning, Jaevid lunged at her.

Her bow went flying, skittering across the ice and far out of reach. They rolled, wrestling for control. Jaevid wasn't holding back. He worked her into a hold, pinning her down on her back with his knees on her shoulders so she couldn't get up. He grabbed her helmet and tore it off with one quick yank.

Fluffy bangs and a long, messy braid of dark hair framed the face of the beautiful young woman lying beneath him. She stared up with a defiant sneer, though inky tears smeared across her ashen skin and her eyes were stained as black as pitch, just as Aubren's were.

The helmet rolled out of Jaevid's hands. Eyes wide and expression eerily blank, he stared down at her and didn't move a muscle for what felt like an eternity.

Then he threw his head back and yelled skyward. It was a broken, horrible sound that broke over the two dragons still clashing nearby.

My heart shattered as tears blurred my vision.

It was Beckah.

Slowly, Jaevid's shaking hand went to the hilt of his scimitar. He drew it, knuckles blanching as he squeezed the hilt. Gods, was he going to—?

No. I couldn't let him do it. Regardless of what Argonox had made her into, I knew Jaevid loved her. If this had to be done, if there truly was no other way, I would *not* let him be the one to do it.

I owed him that much.

Nudging Phevos, I urged him forward and we leapt from

the top of the keep, surging toward them as fast as possible.

Jaevid raised the scimitar, angling it over Beckah's chest. Then he hesitated. I couldn't see his face. Part of me didn't want to. But I had a feeling I knew what I might see.

We were only seconds away. Just a little further. We could make it.

Something exploded to my left and heat scorched the side of my face, singeing my eyelashes. I turned to look, but Phevos whipped over into a desperate roll, angling himself between a burst of burning dragon venom and me. His scales would protect him. Dragon venom doesn't burn through their own hides.

I hugged myself against his neck and hung on as we dropped into an evasive dive just as Beckah's enormous, undead mount hurtled past. Phevos was barely able to flare his wings in time for a rough landing on the surface of the lake. The undead dragon cut in low with Mavrik in hot pursuit, barely skimming the surface of the ice as he sped toward where Jaevid still had his rider pinned.

I screamed—anything to try to warn him—but they were too far and going too fast.

The sound of their approach made Jaevid turn, causing his focus to break. With a twist of her body and a swift kick to his already injured shoulder, Beckah launched herself out of his pinning hold. She left him staggering on the frozen ground and ran to intercept her dragon. The massive beast plucked her up in one fluid motion, and the two sped skyward in full retreat.

Mavrik landed next to Jaevid, taking up a defensive position over his injured rider as he went on snarling at their enemies. Beckah and her black dragon circled once, the beast roaring and breathing a few more plumes of burning venom nearby. Warning shots?

I twisted my saddled handles and Phevos darted forward, taking up a position beside Mavrik with his teeth bared and his tail flicking. If they came back down for seconds, they'd have to contend with two of us this time. She was no longer the only woman worthy of a dragon's loyalty.

And I would end her without hesitation.

After another pass, Beckah turned her mount away to the east—back toward Northwatch. In minutes, they were gone, disappearing into the gathering dusk like phantoms. When the booming wing beats faded, the silence squeezed at my already frayed nerves. It didn't make any sense. Why had she come here? To kill Jaevid? Or just to taunt us? Was this some kind of test to see how easy we would be to kill?

I had no answers, and at the moment, none of it mattered. Jaevid was hurt. He needed help.

Scrambling down from Phevos's saddle, I ran to Jaevid as fast as I dared on the slick ground.

Mavrik's massive head appeared in my path so suddenly I nearly crashed right into the end of his snout. He bared his jagged teeth, ears slicked back and yellow eyes as bright as moons. I'd seen this before. Dragons were extremely protective of their riders—especially the ones who had chosen them voluntarily. Sometimes they didn't even bother to discern friend from foe. Mavrik was still on edge from the battle, seeing red, and ready to roast anyone who got too close to his injured companion.

Behind me, Phevos gave a protective growl and snapped his jaws. He fumed a long string of popping, chirping sounds that made the king drake hiss.

"It's all right." I raised my hands in surrender. "Jaevid is hurt. I'm sure you can smell his blood. Please, let me help him."

Mavrik studied me with those huge, yellow eyes. They seemed to stare straight through me with intelligence I could hardly fathom. With a heavy snort, he licked his chops and moved out of my path.

I took that as permission to go.

Jaevid sat on his rear, the snow and ice around him splotched with blood. His scimitar lay only a few feet away, so I picked it up as I knelt down beside him. Only an inch or two of the arrow's shaft was still sticking out of his shoulder, through fabric and flesh. I prayed it wasn't poisoned.

Words failed me as I searched his face for some sense of how he was. Catatonic was putting it far too lightly. He stared straight ahead with his broad shoulders slumped and jaw slack. His eyes were empty, expression blank, even when I started probing at the wound on his shoulder to see how deep the arrow's head had lodged into his body.

We would talk about it. We needed to. But not here—not now. There was still work to do.

"Can you stand?" I asked softly.

No response.

Touching my fingers to his chin, I carefully turned his face to look at me. "Jaevid?"

His brows snapped together, mouth skewing. "I-it was … did you see?"

"Yes," I whispered gently.

He spat a string of curses under his breath, fists quaking as he gnashed his teeth.

"Jae, I can't imagine what you must be feeling right now. But we can't stay here. The others are counting on us. We have to get everyone safely into the mountains."

He drew in a deep, rattling breath and nodded. "Lead on."

"You're all right to ride like this?"

"I've done it with worse."

I stood back as he got to his feet, waiting until I was certain he was able to sit securely in his saddle before I mounted up. Phevos shifted uneasily beneath me, his ears still perked in the direction Beckah and her mount had flown. He chirped and whined, hide shuddering.

I rubbed a hand along the back of his head. "It's all right, love."

Or so I hoped, anyway. We had no way of knowing what Argonox would do now that he had found us. Would Beckah come back with reinforcements? We were putting ourselves in a vulnerable spot. Deep in the mountains, our people would have nowhere to go for cover if we were attacked—especially from the air. It wouldn't take much of a force to overwhelm and destroy every last one of us. Only a small fraction of our company were soldiers. Most were ordinary townsfolk;

women and children. Bakers, blacksmiths, carpenters, and cobblers—people who had never once held a blade or had any reason to.

The thought made my throat constrict and my mouth go dry. Fates guard us; we were not in a good position to make any sort of stand. Not with so many innocent lives at stake. But we had no choice.

Together, Jaevid and I took off for the city to rejoin the others.

Cernheist was nearly empty. A long caravan of townsfolk and Maldobarian soldiers filed out toward the steep, rugged slopes of the Stonegap Mountains. The pace was slow. Merchants hadn't traversed this path in years, and this time of year, the ground was still slick and treacherous. The wagons, loaded down with people and supplies, frequently got stuck in the deep slushy drifts and it took an eternity to dig them out.

If Argonox did come for us, we would not be difficult to catch.

SIX

"We can't stay here with them," Haldor insisted as he rubbed his brow. "Every second we do puts these people in danger. Argonox wants us, not some band of refugees. The quicker we leave and draw his focus elsewhere, the better chance they'll have."

"If we leave them, they'll have no means of defense if Argonox sends someone else after them," Calem countered, his deep tone as cool and collected as ever.

Gathered around our tiny campfire, I watched the small pot of boiling water send wisps of steam into the frigid night air. We'd pushed the people as far as we could for one day. Less than twenty miles from Cernheist, we had set up a temporary camp under the cover of a sparse evergreen forest. It wasn't much, but it would do while we waited out the night and came up with some kind of a plan for our next move.

"Nothing has changed," Phillip murmured. "We were attacked, yes, but we were planning on departing anyway. All this has done is put more pressure on us to move quickly."

"Pressure indeed." Haldor snorted and rolled his eyes. "No one said anything about battling undead dragons and ancient war heroes. How do you kill something that's already dead?"

No one answered.

He sighed, head drooping as he let out a heavy breath. "Dead or not, I can't believe she would fight for that tyrant. Gods, how could she turn on her own?"

"You saw how it was with Aubren. You really think he would try to kill me if he were in his right mind?" I flashed Haldor a venomous glare. "That power does something to their minds. She may not have any sense of who she is anymore."

"Regardless, considering the state of Prince Aubren, I think it's safe to assume Argonox has already begun experimentation on how to weaponize Reigh's power," Aedan murmured through chattering teeth. He was burrowed so deeply into his fur-lined coat that only his multicolored eyes peeked out to catch the light of the fire. "We should assume we will meet more such monsters."

As much as I hated to, I had to agree. If Argonox was using Reigh to resurrect soldiers and dragons alike, then our advantage of being the only combatants in the air was gone. We would have to fight more of our own. That was something no dragonrider wanted—to have their own brothers-in-arms, dead or alive, pitted against them. It went against everything we stood for.

"It doesn't do any good to speculate on what we can't know. Let's focus on solving one problem at a time. We still have to make it to Halfax and hope my father will open the city gates to us," I said as I took the small pot off the embers and poured some of the boiling water into a small copper bucket. I'd mashed a collection of medicinal herbs, packed them into tea bags, and lined the bottom of the bucket with them. Then I'd taken my smallest, sharpest dagger and placed it inside, as well. As the bubbling water hissed into the pot, the mixture gave off a sweet, soothing, minty aroma. It would steep the medicinal herbs and sterilize the dagger. "We have to get to that crystal—the one that could quicken Reigh's power—before Argonox does. He cannot get his hands on it."

"Is he still up to it?" Phillip's gaze held mine for a moment, flickering with worry. Jaevid wasn't the only one with ties to Beckah. She had been Phillip's oldest sister, although he'd never known her. She'd died in battle long before he was born.

I shook my head. There were no words I could think of to describe Jaevid's state. I didn't know him well enough to even make a guess. It was impossible to imagine what he might be feeling, and I didn't want to insult him by trying.

"Just don't let any of the townspeople hear you talking about this," I warned as I got up and started back for our tent. "They're already terrified enough as it is. Let's not make it worse."

Phillip gave a forced smile, his pointed ears perked. He was the only one who didn't seem to mind the cold. I could only guess that was because of what the switchbeast venom had done to him.

Most of our group stayed huddled around the campfire, speaking quietly. Phillip, Haldor, Calem, and Aedan could speculate all they wanted. Until Jaevid was himself again, we had no idea what we were truly up against.

Ducking inside our one-room tent, I glanced over to where Miri and her aunt, Baroness Adeline, were huddled together in a corner. The baroness spoke to her in a quiet voice, stroking her hair affectionately as Miri lay propped up on a bedroll, covered with blankets.

Miri was rattled from the attack, but other than a bump on the head, she would be all right. I'd checked her over personally, if only to ease the baroness's concerns that she might have an internal injury. Miri had been lucky. But then again, we all had. It was a miracle none of us had died during that first assault on Cernheist's keep, let alone the events after.

Quarters were cramped in the tent. Not that it was small—it was probably twelve feet across, and it was tall enough that only Phillip had to stoop some to walk around in it. But there wasn't much in the way of privacy. We hadn't intended on staying the night, so there was barely room for all our bedrolls. Fortunately, it seemed not many of us felt like sleeping tonight. Not when there was an undead king drake lurking somewhere in our blind spot.

On the opposite side of the tent, Jaevid lay quietly on his own bed. He was staring straight ahead, eyes glazed and distant. Eirik sat next to him, fingers drumming on the long hilt of his two-handed longsword, which lay across his lap. He was busy gnawing on the inside of his cheek when I knelt beside them.

I didn't have to ask why he was here.

Sure, it might have looked like Eirik was keeping watch over Aubren, who was still bound like a prisoner and gagged in case he decided to start ranting and raving again. But that wasn't the real reason. Aubren had been quiet for a long time, lying perfectly still with his eyes closed as though he were sleeping. No, he wasn't what had my ridiculous best friend on edge.

With every other breath, Eirik's gaze darted to where Miri lay. His brow wrinkled, and he rubbed the back of his neck, muttering under his breath. I could have sworn I heard him giving himself a pep talk. Gods, I hadn't heard him do that since fledgling year. He must have really been worked up.

"She's going to be fine," I whispered as I wrung a clean linen rag in the herbal-infused water. "It's just a bump."

"She keeps shaking." He ran a jerky hand through his hair. "Is she cold? I can find another blanket. Or she can have mine."

I fought back a smile and passed the bucket and rag to him. "Here, give these bags a gentle squeeze. We need to draw out the oils in the leaves."

"What are you—?"

I didn't give him time to object. Getting up, I hurried over to where the baroness was seated right at Miri's side. She looked up with dark circles under her eyes. "Your Highness, is everything all right?"

"Yes. Things are quiet for now. But I've got to, um, dress Jaevid's wound. He'll need a new shirt when I'm finished. His old one was soaked with blood and now I'll have to cut it off him because of his injury. Could I trouble you to ask around some of the other campfires to see if anyone has a spare?"

It was a silly errand, sure, but it worked like a charm. The baroness nodded enthusiastically and left the tent without question. I guess she was eager to feel like she was contributing somehow. I could sympathize. Sometimes sitting still was hardest thing to do. Anyway, it would keep her busy for a few minutes.

As soon as she left the tent, I aimed a grin back at Eirik and gestured for him to come. He practically materialized out of thin air, zipping to Miri's bedside in an instant. I'd never seen him move that fast, not even during our dragonrider training. Silly man.

Returning to Jaevid's side, I tried my best not to eavesdrop or spy as Eirik and Miri began whispering to one another. I failed, of course. How could I not watch? Eirik's tone trembled as he took her hands in his and brought them to his face. Maybe it wasn't right to trick the baroness … but it was worth it.

"He cares for her a great deal." Jaevid's deep, quiet voice startled me.

I blushed as I went back to wringing the washcloth in the fragrant, herbal water. "Yes. He's an idiot—but a good one."

"You've known him a while?"

"We started dragonrider training together at the academy." I shrugged. "He was my roommate. A poor country boy from a forgotten dragonrider bloodline and the only girl stupid enough to test her luck as a fledgling student," I recalled. "I guess you could say we were destined to be friends. No one else wanted us."

A faint smile ghosted over Jaevid's lips. "Sounds familiar."

"You keep saying stuff like that and I'll be forced to smack you, injured or not." I sighed and gave the cloth one last hard twist. "It's bad enough hearing everyone else say it. But if it's coming from you then it must be true."

"Do you hate your father?"

I hesitated. "No. Of course not. He's my father—I love him. But that doesn't mean I like him right now. He's a hypocritical old fool to even imagine he could stop me from becoming what I was meant to be. He, of all people, should know better. You can't fill a child's head with stories of heroes and glorious battles and then act shocked and angry when she chooses that path. I wanted it even before Phevos chose me. I was not born to stand silently by, blushing and weeping while my kingdom burns. Destiny put a sword in my hand and a dragon's wings beneath my feet. I intend to use both— even if everyone in Maldobar despises me for it."

"A fair point."

"Yes, well, be sure to tell him that when you see him. He won't listen to anything I say anymore." Sliding my arms under Jaevid's good shoulder, I helped him up into a sitting position. He gasped and groaned whenever he moved his injured shoulder. No doubt it was hurting a lot more without the rush of adrenaline and battle to distract him.

I cut away his shirt and tossed the bloody rags aside. Underneath, he wasn't at all what the sculptures and paintings had suggested. He was muscular, yes, but more leanly built.

He didn't have any of the heavy brawn I was used to seeing on dragonriders. His deeply tanned skin was flecked with scars, telling tales of battles long past. We had that in common, at least.

Probing around his injured shoulder again, I tried to gauge just how serious this was. About a quarter of the arrow's shaft, plus the barbed point, was still lodged in the soft meat of his shoulder. Now I had to get it out somehow.

"How deep is it?" he asked hoarsely.

"Not far. Lucky for you, I've done this a few times. They made me choose field medicine as my secondary specialty. Little fingers and steady hands are better for stitching wounds, or so they claimed. Just thank that god of yours the Tibrans didn't dip this arrow in poison, otherwise you'd be dead already." Sitting back on my heels, I threw my hair up into a sloppy bun to get it out of my way before I rolled up my sleeves. "I've got to enlarge the wound, so I can pull it out. This is going to hurt."

He sucked in a breath. "Do it."

Taking off my belt, I handed it to him before I fished the sterilized dagger out of the pot of hot water. He put the leather strap between his teeth and gave a firm nod.

Here we go.

Jaevid's body went rigid as I started using the knife to cut a bigger hole in his shoulder. Trying to rip it out otherwise risked losing the arrowhead inside his shoulder. Unfortunately, it wasn't something I could do quickly. I had to be careful. He ground his jaw against the belt, eyes watering and head rolling back as he groaned. But I had to give him credit. He held steady.

When I finished, his whole body was shaking, so I

quickly poured him a cup of the herbal tea. "Drink this. It'll help with the pain."

While he drank, I cleaned the wound with the rest of the tea and washcloth. I wiped away the blood as gently as I could before applying a few quick stitches to close it. "It'll be tender for a while," I explained. "I'd say you should take it easy, but I think we both know that's out of the question."

He gave a weary sigh in between sips of tea. The shaking of his hand made it slosh, so I settled in beside him and held the cup. "T-thank you, Jenna."

I stole a quick glance over my shoulder at Eirik and Miri. They were still talking quietly, lost in their own little world. It was as good a time as any. I cleared my throat. There was no subtle or good way to approach this subject. I just had to ask. "Jaevid, are you okay? I know you said the memories were coming back, but this …"

His jaw went rigid again as his brows drew up. You would have thought I'd rammed my knife back into his shoulder. His pale blue eyes fell closed and he turned his face away.

"I don't expect you to be all right. No one does. We all know who she was and what she meant to you." I reached for his hand, lacing my fingers through his and giving a reassuring squeeze. "You can talk to me. Whatever you say stays between us."

"I-I know I should have ended it. That thing … it wasn't really her," he rasped through gritted teeth. "I thought I could handle it. I *should* have handled it. Paligno's essence demanded it. I felt his fury as my own. He commanded me to destroy her."

My heart sank at the brokenness in his voice. "Jaevid …"

His mouth skewed, grimacing between a smile and something anguished. "I couldn't sense her soul anywhere in that body. But her face—Gods. The sight of her underneath that helmet brought the memories back. I wasn't ready for it."

"What do you remember?" I whispered.

Jaevid squeezed his eyes shut again and clenched his hand around mine as though the words were agony on his tongue. "Her smile; that perfect smile lit by the sunrise over a calm sea. The freckles on her cheeks, so many you could never count them all. Her eyes, the same color as the ivy leaves that grow up the sides of my family's old house in Mithangol. Her fingers combing through my hair. The smell of the ocean on her skin. The taste of fresh peaches on her lips." His body relaxed slightly as he let out a trembling breath. "I thought I was meant to be hers forever."

"You don't think that now?"

Jaevid opened his eyes to stare up at the roof of our tent. "I believed she was gone, beyond my reach even as Paligno's vessel. Honestly, I don't know what to think about anything anymore."

He wasn't the only one. "If someone had told me a few years ago I'd be sitting here talking to the famous Jaevid Broadfeather and stitching up his battle wounds, I would never have believed it. We're all living to see things we never thought could be real." I gave his rough, leathery palm one more squeeze before letting go. "Is it destiny that she's been brought back into our world right after you were? Or is it just a cruel coincidence? Who's to say? All I know is, based on what I saw, she had a chance to kill you and she didn't. If that means there is even a tiny piece of her spirit left in that body, then you can't give up hope."

My gaze wandered back across the tent to where Miri was sitting on her bedroll, her petite body curled against Eirik's chest as he put his arms around her. I'd seen him joke, drink, flirt, fight, and cheat death many times in the years we'd spent as friends and comrades. But I'd never seen him like this before. There was a crinkle of subtle desperation in his brow as he held her, as though he were afraid someone might tear her away.

"Love is so much messier than they describe in the stories," I muttered. "Look at us—fighting like fools for it. Bleeding and dying for it."

"Yes," Jaevid conceded softly. "I suppose that's something I can say hasn't changed with time. Love is always messy. And it's always worth it."

Nearby, Aubren stirred and twisted against his bonds. The gag in his mouth muffled his groaning. It took everything I had not to look at him. I wasn't ready to. While I knew he hadn't meant to hurt me, part of me still felt betrayed.

"Do you think you can help Aubren?" I heard myself ask faintly. "Can you undo whatever Argonox did to him?"

Jaevid rubbed his jaw as he studied my older brother. "I'll certainly try. I think most of my memory is more or less intact now, but I don't recall ever encountering anything like Reigh's power before. What little I understand has come directly from Paligno, although it seems not even the god himself knows what to expect. He seemed so certain that this sort of abuse of Clysiros's power would be impossible before Reigh's ritual was complete. But maybe Paligno's divine sister is a mystery to him as well?" He shrugged and glanced my way with a grim frown. "During the Gray War, I saw a glimpse of what abusing sacred power could do. And yet, even at his most powerful, not even Hovrid was able to do things like this. What he began, Argonox seems to have perfected. Turning divine power we barely understand into weaponry that can be used by mortal hands is just … Gods, it's terrifying to think about."

"And now he's bringing people back from the dead," I murmured. "Does he even need the crystal or the ritual anymore? Is having Reigh enough to doom us?"

Jaevid's expression darkened. "No. Without the crystal, Reigh can only use so much power at a time. It was the same way for me until my ritual was completed. If he pushes it too far, he could kill himself."

"I wonder if Argonox knows that."

"He must. Reigh was already weak when we got to you in Northwatch. Valestepping is incredibly dangerous for him—especially now. But he's still alive to do these things to Beckah and Aubren, so Argonox must be monitoring how much he uses." He lowered his gaze, staring into his nearly empty cup of tea. "I've been thinking about it over and over, asking myself why he would send those two and no other forces. It's as if his goal wasn't to kill us, just to test what they could do."

"You really think *that* was a test?"

Jaevid nodded, gradually panning his eyes over to where Aubren lay. "He could have sent anyone to do this, but he picked two people with strong emotional attachments to us. They had both been poisoned with Reigh's powers in entirely different ways. Aubren was a live victim. Beckah wasn't." His mouth hardened, and his brow furrowed as he spoke in a deep, controlled tone. "I think he was testing to see which of them would make the most effective weapon against us."

SEVEN

When he was ready to deal with Aubren, Jaevid insisted that everyone except for Phillip and myself wait outside the tent. No one questioned him, and even the baroness seemed all too eager to get herself and Miri out of the way. Haldor and Calem spoke in hushed voices, lurking right outside the tent as though they were waiting to respond at the first sound of distress.

My insides squirmed and swirled like live fish were swimming around in my gut as I watched Jaevid take a seat next to Aubren's head. Phillip stood by, crouched with his pointed ears perked and tail slowly swishing back and forth. Every muscle in his powerful shoulders and corded back was drawn taut. I could only guess he was there to be our reinforcement if things went badly.

As if they weren't bad enough already.

Lying on his back, his arms still bound and mouth gagged, Aubren was completely still. Only his chest rose and fell in slow, even breaths. At first, I thought he might be sleeping. His eyelids were even flickering as though he were dreaming. But as I got closer, I could see that inky substance still leaking out like tears running down the sides of his face. His whole body shivered, vibrating ever so slightly.

I bit down hard. Aubren ... how had it come to this? Where was my big brother when I needed him most? Whatever he'd done, however wrong he might have been about trying to bargain with Argonox, he did *not* deserve this. He was and had always been a good person with a much gentler, softer heart than I'd ever had. He probably would have stayed in Halfax, following Father's orders, if I hadn't insisted on—

"Let him hear your voice," Jaevid coaxed, interrupting my thoughts as I scooted in closer. "That seemed to work before."

Work? I guess if you considered "stopped him from killing me with foul magic" as working, then sure—it had worked. I shot Jaevid a glare as I knelt down, careful not to touch Aubren where he lay. I didn't want to make it worse.

Aubren's right arm—the one Phillip had broken—was still in bad shape. The strange black mark on his hand spanned from his palm to his elbow like someone had splashed him with ink. Only, the splotches were not completely random. They seemed that way, at first. But when I looked closer, I could pick out the shapes of swirling, detailed glyphs and designs within the patches.

The sight made my throat grow tight.

"What is it?" The question escaped me in a breathless whisper.

Jaevid's frown deepened, putting stern lines across his forehead. "It's definitely Reigh's power, or some form of it. But there's something different."

Phillip leaned in for a closer look, sniffing the air around Aubren like a curious cat. "Different how?"

"I don't know how much you understand about the afterlife. It wasn't commonly taught when I grew up in Maldobar. Most regarded it as gray elven paganism or a ridiculous myth," he began to explain. "Our world is separated from that of the gods by a space, an in-between called the Vale. There, spirits await the judgment of the Fates before passing on into the afterlife. Those judged as worthy enter Pareilos, the kingdom of the old gods. Those who fail to meet that standard are condemned elsewhere." His eyes darkened as he studied Aubren's hand. "Desmiol, the prison of lights. We call them the stars."

"You're off it," Phillip balked. "You're saying the stars are some kind of prison of eternal damnation?"

Jaevid shrugged. "Of sorts. Clysiros is also there, banished away from the other gods. Just as Paligno represents life, renewal, and creation, Clysiros governs death, decay, and all that lurks in the darkest places of the world."

Chills prickled along my spine. "What does this have to do with Aubren?"

"Reigh got pulled into the Vale once before by accident. There was nothing I could do to stop it. Because of who he is, he can walk in both places and pass between the two at will." Reaching out, Jaevid brushed some of Aubren's hair away from his face so he could lay a palm against his forehead. "The sense I get from your brother now is similar to when Reigh went into the Vale. It's as though his spirit is trapped there, but every now and then he manages to claw his way back here, if only for a second or two, like someone gasping for breath while drowning."

A soft growl rumbled in the back of Phillip's throat. "If his soul is trapped in that Vale place, then what's keeping his physical body moving?"

Jaevid's head lowered, eyes closed tightly as though he were trying to focus. "I don't know. But it was the same with Beckah. Every time I reach out with Paligno's energy, I get nothing but darkness, anger, and chaos."

I tried to rationalize what this meant. Aubren's soul was gone? Trapped somewhere else? Did that mean he was dead? Could we even save him, or was it more merciful to just end this rather than let him continue to suffer?

The thought made my heart wrench in my chest. I had to look away.

"When this happened to Reigh, nothing I did could bring him back. It seems Paligno's influence ends at the Vale. He is a god of life; normally the realm of the dead is none of his concern. That's Clysiros's territory. So, unless I cross it personally, I don't know if I can help Aubren," Jaevid continued. "I can only think of one way to try. But it will be risky."

Phillip cocked his head to the side. "Riskier than usual?"

He gave a little chuckle. "No, I suppose not. But I'm not sure I'll be a welcomed visitor in the Vale. Still, if that's where Aubren's spirit is trapped, it stands to reason I could go there and set him free."

"And what if you can't?" I blurted. "What if you get stuck there, as well? What then?"

"I'll think of something." Jaevid gave a faint, despondent smile that made me want to jump over and throttle him.

Think of something? Was he joking?

"You can't do this," I protested. "I love my brother. I want him back. But we can't risk losing you over this, Jaevid. We need you if we are going to have any hope of stopping the Tibrans from taking what little remains of Maldobar. Your life, your influence in this war, means more than any of our lives."

"I'll come back, Jenna," he answered firmly. "One way or another, we need to know if this works. We have to find some way to fix it. If we don't, then anyone else infected with Reigh's power will be ... " His voice faded to a somber silence.

He didn't have to finish. I knew what he was thinking. This wasn't just about Aubren or anyone else Argonox might use against us. If Jaevid couldn't save Aubren, then he wouldn't be able to save Beckah, either. He had to experiment somehow.

This was the safest way to do it.

"All right," I sighed in defeat. "Then send me, instead."

Jaevid's eyes went wide. "What?"

"Send me into the Vale," I repeated. "I will find my brother and bring him back."

"*No*," Phillip snarled suddenly, lunging forward to seize my forearm. "Jenna, I will not let you do this."

I snatched my arm away. "I didn't ask for your permission."

"It's too dangerous," Jaevid agreed, his tone severe.

"Too dangerous? And yet you were ready to jump right

in? If this is about the fact that I'm a woman and I shouldn't be put in danger—"

"It's about the fact that I am the vessel of Paligno's essence," he interrupted. "I carry the spirit of a deity within my—"

"A deity you just finished saying would have no power or authority there," I fired back, cutting him off. "How does that make me any less qualified? He's *my* brother. He's never even met you. My voice brought him back once, and you said it might do it again. If he were able to see me, then maybe—"

"Guys?" Phillip whimpered.

Jaevid ignored him. "And just how are *you* planning on bringing him back? You have no idea what you might be facing in the Vale."

"And you do? How were you going to do it?" I snapped. "And another thing—"

"GUYS!" Phillip roared.

My mouth snapped shut. Jaevid cringed. Together, we fell silent and looked at Phillip. He was glaring at us; arms crossed and pointed ears slicked back. "If you're quite finished, he's awake."

Aubren lay calmly between us with his breathing slow and steady. His eyes were open, and he stared straight ahead listlessly. His skin was turning ashen, and dark circles had gathered under his pitch-black eyes. The sight made my chest go tight. Was he dying? Were we losing him to the Vale? What if we couldn't get to him in time?

"Aubren?" Jaevid leaned in closer, studying my brother's face. "Can you hear us?"

No reply.

Carefully, Jaevid touched Aubren's forehead. The contact made my brother's body go stiff and his eyes bulged. He writhed against his bonds and bit down hard on the gag in his mouth.

I covered my mouth and turned away.

"He's fading," Jaevid murmured. "We must hurry." Pivoting in his seat, the hero of the Gray War stretched his hand out to me, his expression firm and gaze steady. "It is not my place to deny you this. But you should know the risks. Every second you spend there will bring you closer to your own death. The spirits of the living aren't meant to linger there. You'll begin to fade, too. So, don't stop. Don't talk to anyone. Don't lose focus."

My heart kicked and pitched against my ribs, filling my face with a rush of warmth as I slid my hand into his while his other still rested on Aubren's forehead. "I'll come back."

He gave one stern nod. "I believe in you, Jenna." Then his brow twitched, mouth straightening. "I'll have to allow some of that dark power to touch you. It should pull you into the Vale, as it did Reigh." His eyes went steely. "One more thing ... should you see someone there who looks like Reigh, you must not engage with him."

"What? Why?"

"I'll explain later. Just promise me you won't speak to him. Try not to even look at him. Am I clear?"

I drew in a deep, shaking breath. My hands were clammy—something he was bound to notice. I set my jaw. Now was not the time to lose my nerve.

With one last, lingering glance toward Phillip, I let my eyes fall closed. If that was the last sight I ever saw in the mortal world, at least it would be a good one. At the last second, I decided I should tell him one more time. Phillip needed to know that I loved him.

But it was too late.

It felt like I was falling, only there was no end. No bottom. No crash. I tumbled end over end into the darkness, my head whirling with a desperate need for some fixed point to orientate by. But there was nothing—just me and a bitter cold that seeped through my skin, into my bones, and froze the air in my lungs. I kicked and flailed, groping for anything solid as my body twisted and tossed like a leaf in the wind. I tried to gasp, to scream, but the darkness swallowed everything.

A strong grip closed around my arms so suddenly, I tried to pull away. Fear tore through my body like a pang of cold lightning. Get away—whatever it was I had to get away!

Through the gloom, the hands looked like something sculpted from solid alabaster. Solid and strong, they pulled me out of the depths with one swift tug. My head broke the surface of a pool and I rattled and wheezed, drinking in frantic breaths as I was dragged the rest of the way out of the water.

I landed on my hands and knees on the bank, my clothes drenched and my body shivering. Soft grass squished between my fingers. It took me a few seconds of ragged breathing and coughing to realize the ground, my hands, and everything around me was entirely colorless. Miles upon miles of endless prairie was nothing more than a bleak grayscale. Drab stone buildings stood in the distance against a silver, featureless sky. Even my own skin and clothes had been drained of all color. Everything from my skin to my boots was the color of ash.

"W-what is this?" I yelped, glancing around for whoever had rescued me.

He stood a few feet away, eyeing me like I might be a threat. Shimmering somewhere between solid and transparent, the young man looked strangely familiar somehow. His sharp, sculpted features were undeniably human, and his appraising scowl seemed to pierce right through me. Gods, where had I seen that look before? My mind was a haze of confusion as I clamored to my feet.

"You saved me?" I guessed.

The man arched one of his brows curiously. With dark hair falling shaggily around his chiseled jawline, he stood straight and poised with his wide shoulders squared and his hands clasped behind his back. "I'm not sure that pulling someone into the Vale counts as saving them, my lady," he countered.

"It beats drowning in there," I replied, coughing again. "Who are you?"

"One of the many who linger here," he answered cryptically, his eerie, colorless eyes glinting with what I suspected was amusement—as if he knew that answer wasn't what I'd been hoping for. "I believe the more important issue is why you are here. You aren't dead, are you?"

I shook my head, wiping some of my wet hair away from

my eyes. "Not yet. I was sent here. I'm looking for someone."

"Someone who has passed?"

"No. My brother. He's not dead; not yet, at least. Something terrible was done to him in the mortal world. He's been touched by foul magic. Jaevid believes he might be here."

The man's expression blanked, eyes widening as he gaped for a moment. "Jaevid sent you here?"

My eyes narrowed. Wait—was this the person I'd been warned about? No, it couldn't be. This man looked nothing like Reigh. Jaevid had been very specific about that. "Yes," I replied at last. "To find Aubren. He's trapped here. I have to find him, and help him get back to the mortal world. I won't let him perish here."

His features tightened, lips thinning as he looked me over from head to foot. It was difficult to figure out how old he might be. Surely younger than Aubren. But did spirits age in the Vale? How did that work? Before I could ask, the man gestured to a white cobblestone path leading away from the pond. "I will assist you, if I can. The city ruins would likely be the best place to begin your search."

I took a wary step toward the path. "Why help me?"

He shrugged, following along with footsteps that made no imprint on the silver grass. "Seems the proper thing to do. It's been a long time since I spoke with anyone like this, even while I was alive."

"Why not?" I tried not to look back as he walked a few paces behind me.

"I was … ill for the latter half of my life." His tone softened, barely a whisper.

"So you remember your life before?" I couldn't help it; I stole a quick glance back at him. His handsome face was staring off into the distance, brow creased with intense focus.

"We all do. That's why some choose to stay. They know their mortal deeds will earn them condemnation," he explained. "That, or they await the arrival of loved ones to join them."

"Which is it for you?"

His brow creased, eyes going steely as they panned back to meet mine. "A little of both."

I tried to imagine a scenario that might have him both dreading divine judgment and waiting around for someone else to join him in death. "Let me guess," I thought aloud. "You betrayed your lover? Cheated on your wife? Both?"

"No, not quite." He chuckled, his tone so rich, deep, and infectious it made me glance back again. A smile spread over his face, curving across his mouth in a way that made my stomach flip wildly. Gods, he was handsome. I tripped over my own feet. Heat bloomed across my face and I quickly ducked my head, hoping he hadn't seen.

"How did Jaevid send you here if you did not die?"

I shuddered just thinking about it. "I don't know how to explain it. He goes on about gods, dark magics, and ancient powers and half the time, I've no idea what he's talking about."

"So, you know him well, then? Jaevid, that is." Something in his tone set off a warning in my head. Why was he so curious about Jaevid?

I hesitated and stole another quick look at him. "Yes. Do you?"

"No, not really," he sighed. "But I'm sure you can imagine how many of the spirits passing through here talk about him. The hero of the Gray War; chosen by a dragon and a god. It would seem he's earned many titles and no small amount of respect."

I frowned. His answer made sense, yes, but it sounded a lot like a weak attempt to dance around the truth. What was he hiding? Why wouldn't he tell me who he was?

Unfortunately, there wasn't time to sort it out now. I had to find Aubren and get out of this place before I wound up stuck here right along with him.

"Not to sound ungrateful, but really, why are you helping me?" I panted as we crested the top of a hill. There, many gray stone buildings clustered around a square with a fountain in the center. All about the square, sculptures stood tall in the shapes of faceless, winged women. Many were cracked or crumbling, and most were missing arms, wings, or even their heads. No water ran from the fountain—not that spirits needed it. Did they even get thirsty?

"A great many souls have been passing through the well lately. More than usual, anyway. I can only guess this means there is some sort of war being fought in the mortal realm again," he said evenly. "You emerged, but your spirit does not look like the others—or like mine. You are still solid, so that must mean you still live in the mortal realm. At least, that's what I guessed when I saw you floundering in there."

"What now? Hoping I will bring you back to the mortal world with me if you help me find my brother?"

"Gods, no. It's just ... nice to have a chance to help someone. I wasn't especially *helpful* during my own mortal life. I doubt anyone would celebrate my return to it."

"Ah, I see; you're hoping for some last-minute absolution?"

He laughed again. "Perhaps. Or maybe I'm just bored of standing around watching dead people crawl out of that well." That laugh, wonderful as it was, didn't do much to hide the touch of despair in his voice. "I'm not certain there is absolution for someone like me. But that's enough about my troubles. Let's find that brother of yours."

I had to stop and catch my breath for a moment as we wound deeper into the city, keeping a brisk pace. We passed more squares and courtyards that all seemed strangely empty. I only saw a few other figures lurking around, spirits with forms so translucent you barely noticed them at all. Gods, this place was enormous. How would I ever find Aubren here?

Then something on the horizon caught my eye—something standing off by itself on the wide-open grassland beyond the city.

A dark cloud, like a wisp of smoke or a lost fragment of a thunderhead, hung over some sort of small structure. It was so far away, I couldn't be sure what it was.

"What's that?" I pointed.

The man stood next to me, his presence as tall and commanding as a knight. His dark hair blew around his face as he narrowed his gaze upon the distant cloud. "I don't know. I haven't seen it here before."

A hard knot of fear twisted in my gut. "Let's go."

EIGHT

M y mysterious guide didn't protest and followed along as I jogged headlong toward the structure. The closer I got, the more I could tell that it wasn't a building at all—it was a monument. Seven stone arches stood around a central slab of stone like a platform. There, arranged in a perfect line, were four thrones made of solid black glass. Three had been shattered into crumbled bits and shards. The one on the end, its back adorned with a halo of spines like a sunburst, was still intact, however.

And lying before it … was my brother.

I broke into a wild sprint.

Overhead, the toiling dark cloud sizzled and popped, sending tongues of white lightning that snapped and occasionally struck one of the arches or the ground nearby. With each crack, my heart jumped, and I pushed for more speed, running to where Aubren lay.

Sprawled on his back, Aubren stared up at the thundering dark cloud with his mouth slightly open. His body wasn't translucent, just like mine, but his eyes were dark reflections of that cloud—just as they were in the mortal world.

Falling to my knees beside him, I grabbed his shoulders and began to shake him as hard as I could. "Aubren! You need to snap out it! We have to leave right now!"

He didn't move, not even to blink. I couldn't see him breathing. Was he dead? Was I too late?

Rearing back, I smacked his face as hard as I could. "Wake up!" His skin was bitter cold.

"W-what's wrong with him?" I shouted up at my strange, knightly companion as he stood nearby, watching with an apprehensive frown.

He shook his head, opening his mouth to speak.

"This is what becomes of one touched by the unbridled power of the Harbinger," a cold, menacing voice hissed suddenly.

Looking up, my whole body shivered with a rush of panic as I locked gazes with the very person Jaevid had warned me not to speak to. Gods and Fates. He'd found me.

Reigh—or some otherworldly version of him—reclined upon the only remaining dark throne. With his chin resting in his palm and a cruel smirk twisted upon his boyish face, he drummed his fingers on the glass armrest. "So, he sent my sister. Interesting."

"Reigh?" I gasped. It had to be. Every detail, even the scar across his nose, was the same.

"Hardly," he scoffed. "But don't worry, you're not the first to confuse us. I doubt you'll be the last."

"Who are you, then?"

"I have many names," he replied, his grin widening to show pointed canine teeth. "But Reigh likes to call me Noh."

My throat tightened. "You're that dark spirit, the one giving Reigh his power."

"More or less. The power belongs to both of us," he purred, leaning forward on his throne as his eyes flickered over me appraisingly. "But I doubt you came here for a speech on the specifics of divine magic."

A bolt of lightning snapped through the air, popping off the ground only feet away from us. It hit so close I could practically taste the current crackling over my tongue.

"What's happening?" I yelped, throwing myself closer to Aubren and dragging his head into my lap to try and shield him.

Noh rose from his throne, slowly descending toward us. "Using so much of *her* power without the completion of the ritual is forbidden. It's causing a rupture between Desmiol and the Vale," he said, pausing to tilt his head at us curiously. "Look at his hand."

I did, my breath catching in my chest as I spied a wide, open gash across Aubren's palm. It was as if someone had sliced a dagger deep into his flesh, but instead of bleeding, what oozed out of the wound looked like the same black, inky substance that had come from his eyes in the mortal world. It puddled on the ground and coated his arm all the way to his elbow, giving off a smell like molten tar. "W-what is that?"

"A defilement." Noh folded his arms, eyebrows drawing

together into a dissatisfied frown. "This is what becomes of those who try to implant her power into a mortal vessel. Unlike Reigh, his body cannot withstand it, so it consumes him. It burns him from the inside out, searing through flesh and devouring his spirit. Soon neither will exist ... in any world."

Oh Fates. No; this couldn't happen. There had to be something; some way to fix it! "Can you stop it?" I pleaded.

Noh's frown deepened. "Perhaps," he offered. "But it would require the use of spirit energy. A vast amount, I should think. The defilement has already fractured his soul. To repair it, I would need the soul of another."

Jaevid had warned me not to even speak to this spirit. He'd insisted I should stay away from him, and I had to wonder why. Was Noh lying? Could he really help Aubren? Or was he just trying to steal my soul?

Not that I had any choice. I would not let Aubren die like this.

Combing my fingers through his shaggy, dark-gold hair, I took a deep breath. Cruelty and violence had never come easily to him. He wasn't like me. Yes, he'd made mistakes. We both had. But he was softer, kinder, and a better person than I'd ever been.

He was worth saving.

I fixed Noh with a glare. "Can you use my soul to repair his?"

He blinked, his gaze darting between us. "I could. But you do realize this would mean surrendering your spirit entirely. There would be no afterlife for you—pleasant or otherwise. You would simply cease to exist. Not even Jaevid and all the power of Paligno could undo it."

I swallowed hard. "How do I know you're even telling the truth? How do I know this isn't a trick?"

One corner of his mouth twitched at a smirk. "I suppose you'll just have to take it on faith. What other choice do you have?"

Panicked, anxious heat flushed through me. He was right. There was no other choice. With Jaevid's warning still ringing in my head, I felt the words slip out. "Please save him."

Noh crouched down before us, his eerie eyes like two bottomless pits of eternal abyss as they studied me. I expected to see evil there. But there wasn't. His boyish face stared back at me with a look of pure confusion and something that might have been sympathy. Did he truly feel bad about this? Why? He wanted to kill people, right? I was giving him permission to do that in the most extreme way imaginable. So why did he look so … sad?

"You would truly give up your soul to save his?"

"I would." I brushed a hand over Aubren's stubbly jaw. "He'd do the same for me."

Noh's expression dimmed. "It is a shame we never met before now. Your spirit has always intrigued me. I am not pleased to see it end this way," he muttered as he began to reach out for me, as though he were going to take my face in his hands. "Close your eyes, Jenna."

I stole one last look at the mysterious stranger, who was still lurking nearby, watching us. Then I smiled down at my brother. Aubren would never understand this. He'd blame himself. But I had no other alternative. I shouldn't have left him at Northwatch. I should have made Jaevid stay or helped

Reigh—anything.

"Be strong, Aubren. They're going to need you more than ever," I murmured as I kissed his forehead.

Not wanting to see it coming, I squeezed my eyes shut as Noh's frigid fingertips brushed my cheeks. My breath caught, and I trembled, resisting the instinct to cringe away. Would it hurt? Would I feel anything at all? Gods, what was I doing? I didn't want to die. I hadn't even said goodbye to Phillip!

I held my breath and waited for the end.

"Stop," a deep voice spoke over us.

My eyes flew open, staring up at the strange tall man who had followed me here. His cryptic, disapproving frown reminded me of when my father caught me doing something I wasn't supposed to—like cutting Aubren's hair with a pair of sewing scissors when we were little.

"You really intend on going through with this?" With his arms crossed and jaw set, he glared down at us as though waiting for an explanation.

"Y-yes." My voice hitched. I scrambled to keep my nerve. Every second we put this off made me question it even more. I was trusting this being, Noh, but I had no proof he could even do as he'd promised.

The man shook his head. "Then you leave me no choice."

Grabbing my arm with surprising strength, he dragged

me away from Noh and Aubren and flung me aside. I clambered to my feet, shouting angry curses. What the hell was he doing? This was my decision, my responsibility to—

He seized Noh by the collar of his black robes and snarled, "You take me, not her. Understood? Use my soul to repair his. Do it now."

What? Why? Why would he do this?

"No! You can't!" I cried out.

The man shot me a silencing glare over his shoulder. "When you see Jaevid again, you must give him this message. Tell him that his father is sorry … for everything." His face screwed up and he looked away, back toward Noh. "It won't make it right. I know that. I can't describe what it felt like, to be trapped inside my own head, to see the monster I was becoming. I couldn't do anything to stop it. But I know that doesn't make it right. He deserved so much better. They all did."

"You're … " I gasped. "You're Jaevid's father?"

He didn't reply.

It didn't matter. He didn't have to say another word. I saw it—and it hit me like a punch to the gut. All the wind rushed out of my lungs as the realization settled in. That was why he looked so familiar. Jaevid favored him a lot, in spite of the elf ears and ash-gray hair. They had the same strong lines to their features, serious brows, and high cheekbones.

But this man was no hero, not according to Maldobar's history. He was the one who had started the Gray War, which had spanned more than twenty years and killed thousands of good people, both human and elf. He was a traitor, a thief, and, if my father's stories were true, he had been a cruel father to Jaevid, as well.

"I am truly sorry for what I did to him; for what that *thing* turned me into. Swear it to me," he rumbled under his breath. "Swear you'll tell him. You must."

My throat went dry. "I will," I promised.

Noh didn't say a word as Ulric Broadfeather surrendered. As soon as his hands brushed Ulric's face, the man stiffened and froze in place.

It only took an instant. Ulric's already translucent body shimmered, beginning to glow brightly. The light grew, shining like a white mist until his form had completely dissolved.

The light stung my eyes. It was too much. I had to look away.

The rumble of thunder and sizzle of lightning suddenly hushed. A tingling chill made every hair on my arms prickle. I held my breath and dared to look back.

Ulric was gone.

Overhead, the churning black cloud had dissipated. Now there was only more endless, bleak gray sky. Even Noh had vanished, leaving behind nothing apart from an empty throne.

But my brother—he was moving!

Noh had kept his word.

"Reigh!" Aubren shouted as he bolted up, shambling shakily to his feet. He turned in a circle, eyes wide and darting around frantically. His face blanched with panic as he seemed to notice the strangeness of the eerie, colorless world around us. "Reigh?"

Then he saw me. His mouth fell open.

Tears blurred my vision and I let out a shrill, desperate cry. "Aubren!"

"Jenna," he called back as he ran toward me. We met halfway, and I clenched my arms around his neck as tight as I could.

For a moment we stood still, holding one another. I couldn't remember the last time I'd hugged him like this. Maybe after Mother died?

"Are you all right? What happened?" He paused, looking around again. "Where are we?"

"I'm fine," I whispered, pulling back and sliding my hand into his. I didn't want to lose that contact. I didn't want to lose him again. "And there isn't time to explain now. We have to go back."

"Go back where?"

"Home." The word tasted bitter now. I couldn't understand why. I shivered, clinging to his arm as that chill lingered on my skin. My heart hardened, feeling like a heavy, cold stone in my chest. Ulric had almost destroyed Maldobar and Luntharda. I wanted to hate him. I should have—everyone else did.

But how could I?

Aubren gave my hand a firm squeeze. "Let's go then."

NINE

Passing back through the dark, churning waters of that well was no less terrifying than it had been the first time. It took some convincing to get Aubren to do it. But this time, the time spent whirling in that black chaos ended quickly. No sooner had I felt that constricting, crushing cold engulf me than a pair of strong hands reached out to take mine. Their warmth pulled me from the dark, and I awoke lying next to Aubren on the floor of the tent.

I was alive—I had made it back from the Vale.

The warm glow of candlelight and the gentle touch of a leathery palm against my face drew my gaze up. Jaevid and Phillip were leaning over me with similar expressions of mute astonishment. I could understand Phillip's surprise. But Jaevid? Really? Had he thought I wouldn't come back? Good to know he had no faith in me whatsoever.

"Jenna, can you hear me?" Jaevid asked quietly as he withdrew his hand.

I managed a drowsy grin. "Told you I could do it."

He cracked a smile and let out a relieved chuckle. "I'll never doubt you again."

"Good."

Phillip's eyes welled as he threw his arms around me, pulling me up into a desperate embrace. "Thank the gods!"

"Phillip! I-I can't ... you're squeezing too hard," I wheezed against his shoulder.

"Oh!" He let me go and sat back, ducking his head sheepishly. "I'm sorry. It's just ... you stopped breathing. Even your heart quit beating. But Jaevid said you weren't dead; he said he could sense you in the Vale."

I turned, my eyes tracking Jaevid as he skirted around us to kneel back down at my brother's side. Aubren had yet to stir from where he lay, eyes closed and expression now serene. His skin had regained its normal, sun-bronzed hue, but he wasn't moving. My pulse raced with worry. "Is he all right? Did it work?"

"Yes." Jaevid's shoulders sagged with relief. "The spreading of that power through his body has left him physically exhausted, but he'll be fine. He just needs to rest. He should be better by morning."

Jaevid reached for Aubren's arm, holding it up to get a better look by the light of the candle. The mark still stained my brother's palm and forearm with ominous black runes. My stomach soured. Why was the defilement still there? Hadn't Noh fixed it?

"It didn't work." My body drooped.

"No, it did," Jaevid corrected. "The mark seems to be stable now. It's no longer consuming him."

Phillip frowned. "But why isn't it gone?"

"I don't know. Think of it as a scar. Perhaps it will fade in time, or Reigh can remove it. We'll just have to wait and see. For now, let's just celebrate the fact that his life is no longer in danger. And it's all thanks to you, Jenna." He glanced up with a smile that made my insides scramble and my throat constrict like I might throw up. He looked *so* much like Ulric—the one who had *really* saved Aubren.

But how could I tell Jaevid that? I'd given my word, yes, but ... what would that news do to him? Did he even remember his father?

Thankfully, Jaevid didn't seem to notice my panic. "You should get some rest, as well. Dawn will be here soon, and then we'll have to make some decisions about what to do next. Your men will need you to be at your best."

"I'll stay with you, if you like," Phillip offered.

I nodded, easing back down onto the pallet next to Aubren's and curling up on my side so I could see him. When he did wake up, I wanted to be there. So much had happened since I last saw him. Jaevid was here, fighting with us. Reigh had been taken captive at Northwatch. Cernheist was lost. Now we had to find some way back to Halfax and pray our father would let us back into the city. Hopefully having Jaevid with us would help, but I honestly wasn't sure what to expect. There was so much I didn't know.

Suddenly, a pair of strong arms closed around my shoulders, pulling me back into a very warm and solid chest. "Jenna, it won't hurt to let it go for a few hours," Phillip's voice growled gently against my ear. His breath tickled along the side of my neck.

"How did you know I was—?"

He gave an amused snort. "We've practically known one another since birth. I can tell when you're overthinking something. Just rest, would you? The world won't fall apart in the next few hours."

"You don't know that. We have no idea what Argonox might have planned," I pointed out.

"Fair enough. But Jaevid is keeping watch. I doubt he'll sit back and spectate if that happens." His warm lips grazed the back of my ear.

Heat rose in my cheeks as he slid the collar of my tunic down to expose my neck. The sharp points of his canine teeth grazed my skin as he kissed me there, sending my pulse into a desperate flurry. Suddenly, Ulric, Argonox, and the end of the world were the last things on my mind.

"Phillip, stop, not here," I rasped. "Everyone's outside. What if Aubren wakes up? Not to mention Miri and Baroness Adeline will be back anytime."

"I thought I lost you, you know," he murmured, the words whispered softly against the nape of my neck. "Don't do that again. Don't go where I can't follow."

A hard knot caught in the back of my throat. Swallowing against it made my eyes water. I rolled over and hugged myself against him, hiding deep in his embrace. I wanted to tell him. I needed to tell *someone*. My thoughts scrambled, caught between keeping my word and the idea of what telling Jaevid about his father might do to him.

He pulled back enough to stare down at me, silver eyes

shining with streaks of gold that caught in the warm light. "What's wrong?"

I ran my hands over his cheeks, caressing slate-colored skin and lightly tracing the intricate little white flecks that mottled his cheeks and forehead, as though he were freckled by stars. The switchbeast venom had changed him. It had made him into something many would fear. But I couldn't look at him without amazement. Terrifying, powerful, monstrous—he was many things now. But more than that, he was beautiful.

And he was mine.

"Jenna?" He sounded worried.

"We've never danced, have we?"

He arched an eyebrow. "What?"

"At any of the balls and parties. We've known each other for so long, but we've never danced. Right?"

Phillip's gray skin went a little rosy around his cheeks and nose as his catlike pupils widened. "I-I ... uh, no. I don't believe we have. In my defense, however, you have a habit of snarling like a cranky dragon at anyone who approaches you for a dance."

"Since when has my snarling ever discouraged you?" I sighed and burrowed in closer against him. I let my head rest on his shoulder, right against his neck. "Promise me we will."

His heart was racing. It thumped wildly against my ear as he held me tighter, his chin resting on top of my head. Was he actually nervous? Interesting. He always acted so smooth and assured; I never would have guessed that anything I said would make him anxious.

"You honestly think I'll be invited to any more balls

looking like this?" he mumbled.

"Tail aside, you're still the Duke of Barrowton."

"Perhaps, if it's ever rebuilt. I'm sure the Tibrans did a fine job demolishing every square inch of it." He gave a snorting chuckle. "The entire noble court will need new underwear after I make my entrance. I suppose that might make an excellent party favor to hand out at the door."

"With Maldobar's emblem stitched on them?"

"Oh, of course."

I couldn't resist a smile. "So, does that mean you promise to dance with me?"

"Only if you can assure me there will be minimal snarling." I could hear the mischievous grin in his voice.

"I'll see what I can do."

My mind held me hostage in the dark, twisting and turning through everything that could possibly go wrong. The Tibrans attacking. Beckah returning. Aubren's defilement beginning to consume him again. Halfax falling to Argonox. My kingdom burning, forced to surrender to a foreign tyrant. My people becoming slave soldiers in his legions. Me, chained to his heel like a prize.

The memory of his face, his words, were scorched into my brain as though written there in molten flame.

"You would become legendary. A queen for the ages. A goddess."

My breath caught, and my chest seized as I jolted awake, barely able to stifle my own scream. Cold sweat clung to my skin. I shivered as I sat up and curled over, hugging my knees to my chest. I wasn't back there. It was a dream, nothing more. Argonox was miles away.

Or so I prayed.

Lying next to me, Phillip was stretched out on his back with his mouth open and his clothes rumpled. He snored softly, never twitching or stirring as I slid off the pallet and began lacing up my boots. I envied that—being able to sleep like nothing was wrong and the world wasn't about to come crashing down around us. It must have been nice.

Grabbing the heavy, wool-padded tunic I wore over my thin undershirt, I slipped it over my head. Then I grabbed my cloak and blades, swiftly buckling them around me before leaving the tent. It took a moment to pick out a safe path to walk so I didn't step on anyone's fingers or toes on my way out. Miri, Baroness Adeline, Aubren, Eirik, Aedan, and even Calem had settled in and were all sleeping soundly on their pallets. It filled the interior of the tent with the peaceful sounds of deep breathing and the occasional snore.

Outside the tent, the cold mountain air chilled my skin and numbed the throbbing in my head. The smell of crisp frost and fresh pine was soothing. My boots crunched over the snowy ground as I walked to where Haldor was still sitting up, keeping watch by the fire only a short distance from the tent.

"How is everything?" I asked as I stopped across from him, stretching my fingers to the warmth of the flames.

Haldor studied me, as though silently wondering why

I wasn't sleeping like the others. "Quiet," he replied at last. "Leaving on such short notice meant many of the supplies the refugees had gathered had to be left behind. There isn't much in the way of food for them, but we are making do. There are enough skilled hunters and trappers among us that no one will starve before they reach Luntharda."

"That's something, I suppose."

His mouth scrunched slightly, expression steeling into a look I knew all too well. "Permission to speak frankly, Your Highness?"

"You know you don't have to ask, Haldor," I said flatly. "Just as you know I *hate* it when people call me that, especially other dragonriders."

"In this case, I feel appropriate respect is necessary if I'm going to mention this," he muttered, his sharp features drawing into a tight, grim frown.

"Oh? So what you're saying is that this is something that will probably make me angry, right?"

His gaze met mine, eyes gleaming like warm amber in the light of the flames. "Undoubtedly. But it must be said." He paused there, combing his silky black hair out of his face as though to prepare himself for what was to come. "What happened at Cernheist was unacceptable. As a dragonrider, I am ashamed."

"Why?"

"Because we put every person in Cernheist at risk. All due respect to the one who ended the Gray War, but Jaevid Broadfeather is not fighting as a dragonrider. If we are to win this war, let alone survive, then we will have to stand together. Diving out after personal vendettas, forging alone like some sort of martyr for the cause, is not the dragonrider way. Our strength has always been in our unity. We train to fight and fly as one impenetrable force, but that is not what I saw today," he fumed quietly. "Did Jaevid come back to save Maldobar or to settle old scores?"

I crossed my arms. "You think we all should have fought her together?"

"No. The civilians did need our help. A few of us could have managed that. But Jaevid shouldn't have gone after her alone," he retorted. The faster he spoke, the more his accent slipped. It was the only time I'd heard it come out in such force—apart from a few incidents that involved a nearly lethal amount of ale. "You and I both saw what happened. You know he was not fighting to win. We've heard of his power, what he's truly capable of. He was just toying with her. Because of that, she escaped. She is still a threat, and now she is in our blind spot. The only thing more dangerous than an enemy we cannot see is one that the strongest among us doesn't have the stomach to kill."

"Point taken." I rubbed my chin, mulling it over.

"Answer me this, and think it over carefully, Jenna. The next time we meet some fragment from Jaevid's past that Argonox has dredged up from the dead and charged with foul magic, who is going to be the one to pay the price if he cannot bring himself to kill it? Innocent civilians? One of us? You?" He hung his head, turning his focus back to poking at the embers with a long stick. "I ask because I am not prepared to bear that shame. I am a dragonrider. I swore an oath, and I hold myself to it. As dragonriders, we are to leave our personal agendas at the doorpost and do what is necessary to protect Maldobar and its people. Now I must wonder if Jaevid remembers that, and if he doesn't, if he should even be called a true dragonrider anymore."

The crackling of the fire filled the heavy silence that hung between us. He was right—I didn't like hearing this. I didn't like the idea of questioning Jaevid or his intentions. But … Haldor had a point. We had been lucky this time. But if Jaevid hesitated at the wrong moment, if he couldn't bring himself to do what was necessary, we might not be so lucky next time.

Still, I knew why Jaevid had hesitated. I'd done the same thing when faced with Aubren under the same kind of control. The sight of him like that, ready to kill me because of that defilement, had hit me in a soft spot I wasn't expecting. I doubted Jaevid had been expecting it, either.

"Where is he?" I asked at last.

Haldor gave a slight shrug and gestured over one shoulder with a thumb. "With the dragons, of course. He said something about healing Vexi. I take it he meant that wild green one." He gave the fire a forceful poke, making one of the logs collapse and sending a shower of sparks fluttering up into the night sky like fireflies. "Jenna, please don't mistake my frustration for ungratefulness. I am glad he's here to help. I just don't like seeing innocent people put in harm's way, least of all by us."

"I understand. And I appreciate your honesty, Haldor. I'm not angry. Well, not about that, at least." Taking in a little more of the fire's warmth against my backside, I strode past him—but not before giving the back of his head a substantial smack.

He cursed at me in his mother's tongue, which he knew I didn't understand. That's the funny thing about profanity; you don't have to speak the language to know when you're being insulted.

I grinned and kept walking. "That's for using my noble title, by the way."

TEN

I found Jaevid a not far from camp under the shelter of a cluster of sturdy pine trees. He stood in the center of all our dragons like an old man feeding very large, scaly, fire-breathing pigeons. They gathered in close to him, pushing and muscling against one another as he ran his hands over Vexi's head. Her lime green scales were easy to spot, even if she was smaller than the rest of the flock. Occasionally, one of them would hiss and snap, and there would be a spat of nipping and growling before he broke them up with a few harsh words.

The only dragon that didn't seem enamored by Jaevid's presence was his own. Mavrik lay like a mountain of royal blue scales and leathery black wings, relaxing in the snow as he watched the younger dragons squabble. His body barely fit under the cover of the trees. He'd apparently dug himself a hole in the dirt right at the base of some of them to lie in.

"Aren't you supposed to be making them behave?" I asked as I stood beside his great horned head, picking out a few patches of my own dragon's purple hide amidst the crowd.

Mavrik gave an unimpressed snort, melting some of the snow in front of his snout with his hot breath.

"He's got no place to talk," Jaevid said, emerging from the group as though he were parting a curtain of writhing scales, spines, and horns. "When he was younger, he had a knack for mischief, too."

Mavrik snorted again and closed his eyes, smacking his chops indignantly.

"Oh yes, you did," Jaevid shot him a look. "That attitude is why the dragonriders were about to clip your wing tendons, if I remember correctly."

I tapped my chin. "I've heard this story. Ironically, it's one of the few my father didn't tell. I guess he didn't know you then. But Phillip's father used to tell it all the time."

"Sile Derrick," Jaevid recalled, his tone softening. Sadness flickered across his features so quickly I almost missed it. "At the time, I couldn't decide if he was trying to make me a dragonrider or offer me to this scaly monster as an evening snack."

Seeing that sorrow on his face was like a knife twisting in my gut. Haldor was right—those memories were affecting him, and whatever made his determination waver endangered our success and Maldobar's survival. I'd promised to tell him about Ulric. But now ... Gods, was that the right thing to do? If it shook his resolve even more, if it hit the wrong chords, I'd be risking the fate of my kingdom and all its people.

"You were supposed to be resting." Jaevid spoke up again, changing the subject.

"I've never been the sit quietly and rest kind of girl," I replied.

He laughed softly. "I see. Something on your mind, then?"

A jolt of panic shot through me. My mind raced for something—anything to say. "I-I just wondered how Vexi is."

He tipped his head in a slight shrug. "Upset. Angry. Afraid. They all are, really."

"The dragons are afraid? Of what?"

His expression darkened. "Something else is coming. It's a long way off, probably in Northwatch, but I can feel it like the gathering of a distant storm. Argonox is using more of Reigh's power."

I shivered at the thought. "To revive more of our dead? Or defile the living?"

Jaevid shook his head. "It's too far away to be certain."

Well that wasn't comforting at all.

Out of the group of dragons, my handsome, purple companion lumbered toward me, lowering his head, and chirping musically. I smiled, stretching my hands out to meet him as he pushed his snout against my chest. Tracing my fingers along the horned ridges along his cheeks and the teal stripes that mottled his dark violet hide, I let my head rest against his for a moment. The air was bitter cold, but his body was warm. It felt good.

"Your bond with him is strong." Jaevid regarded us with a strange little grin on his lips. "Much stronger than any other I've ever sensed. Well, apart from mine with Mavrik. I'm glad to see Mavrik's hatchlings have chosen their riders well."

Wait, what? "Mavrik's hatchlings?"

Jaevid nodded toward the other dragons, who were still sniffing Vexi over with tense curiosity. In their midst, she sank low, her ears pinned back, and tail curled in close in submission. "She and Phevos are his direct descendants. Phevos is older, hatched from an earlier clutch, but Mavrik is their sire. I suspect Turq is a relation, as well. Distant nephew, maybe."

"Oh." I looked at Phevos again, trying to pick out similarities between my dragon and the blue king drake snoozing nearby. Apart from their eyes and spines, there wasn't much to be found. "I didn't realize."

"Felix has been busy making the world a better place for them, it seems." Jaevid's tone softened, his expression tinged with sadness as he wandered over to stand next to me.

"Because of you," I clarified. "He dedicated a lot of time restructuring the dragonrider forces. He retired the title of Lord General permanently. Now, the station is called 'High Commander,' and he oversees all the dragonrider watches and reports directly to my father."

Jaevid's smile was cryptic. "And who is it that holds that office now? You?"

"Hah!" I shot him a look. Was that an attempt at a joke? "I've only been a lieutenant for three years—and against my father's will, if you remember. He'd never consider me for that office, and I wouldn't want it even if he did. I wasn't even a seasoned rider until this mess started. I've not earned that kind of authority, and there are much more qualified riders for it."

"More qualified, perhaps," he mused. "But better? I'm not sure your companions would agree with that."

I glanced down at the tops of my boots to hide my grin. "Fair enough."

"So, who rides as High Commander?"

"His name is Ruslan Morrig. A good man, by all accounts. I understand he comes from a proud dragonrider bloodline. His father was—"

"—an instructor," Jaevid finished for me. His brow creased, and he flashed me another one of those quick, haunted looks. What was he remembering now?

"You knew him?"

He nodded. "He taught me when I was a fledgling. Combat training, I think."

"Everyone says Ruslan is doing his bloodline proud. I admit, I've only seen him a few times at court, so I can't tell you that for certain. But my father was very selective with who he put in power after the war ended. He retired out many of the old officers and brought in new blood," I recalled. "Then he started enraging noble houses and merchants all over Maldobar by passing new decrees to protect the wild dragons. It was forbidden to capture them from the wild or harvest and sell their eggs. Dragons already in captivity could remain that way, since many of them would find it hard to return to their wild kin but clipping their wing tendons will now earn you a jail cell."

Jaevid arched a brow. "And that upset the nobility and merchants?"

I smirked. "Of course. Selling and breeding dragons has lined their pockets for hundreds of years. I'd expect you to remember that, old man."

His cheeks flushed, and he rubbed the back of his neck. "I wasn't exactly a noble before, you know. But yes, I suppose I do recall many of my peers being … more finely-dressed than I ever was."

"Except for my father, I'm sure."

"True," he added with a nervous chuckle. "I take it he still has no taste for silk or lace?"

"Gods, no." I rolled my eyes. "Not that I do, either. But he used to go straight from working with the infantry horses and dragons at the stables to court meetings without even bathing. He'd have bits of hay stuck in his beard. You could smell him from across the room."

Jaevid laughed—a real laugh this time. A deep, rich, and nearly musical sound. It made his pale eyes shine like aquamarines in the moonlight as he tilted his head back and sighed skyward. "Some things never change, I suppose."

I stared at him, studying the hard lines of his defined cheekbones and fierce brow. Hints and traces of the hero I'd seen chiseled into every fountain and marble bust throughout the kingdom were hidden there, like a ghostly whisper on his darkly tanned skin. But more than anything, I saw Ulric, and the thought turned my stomach sour.

I couldn't tell him. This resistance, our small company of mismatched warriors, was already hanging by a thread. Any tug in the wrong direction might snap it. And what then? Maldobar might fall with it. I couldn't risk that. So I swallowed that secret like a bitter pill, and promised myself I would tell him later. I would keep my word, but only when this was all over and done.

Providing we weren't all bound in Tibran chains, that is.

A deep, thrumming growl from Mavrik's throat made everyone pause—dragons included.

Jaevid and I stopped, watching as the king drake unfurled from his resting place and shook the snow from his back, snapping his jaws as his nostrils flared and sniffed the air. The other dragons did the same, clicking and chirping at one another as they bristled. Phevos lowered his head next to me, growing deep in his chest.

My body shuddered with a surge of panic. I looked at Jaevid. "Tibrans?"

His brow furrowed, jaw setting as he studied his own dragon for a moment. "No," he answered. "It seems someone has come to meet us."

"Meet us?"

His frown was as tense as it was ominous as he strode beside me back to camp. The freezing wind whipped through his shaggy ash-colored hair, and one hand rested on the pommel of the scimitar clipped to his belt. "We must gather our party. It's time to leave." I couldn't tell by his tone if this was a good or bad thing.

Back at our tent, Haldor was already on his feet, bow and quiver strung over his back as he put on his riding gauntlets. "There's a disturbance in the camp."

Jaevid nodded. "It's all right. They haven't come to fight. But we should be ready to move out as soon as possible. Go and wake the others." He waved a hand, gesturing for me to follow. "Let's go and greet our guests."

There wasn't time to ask who. Jaevid immediately turned on a boot heel and led the way down the slope. We picked our way along the steep, icy path into the camp where all the other civilian refugees and a few scattered Maldobarian soldiers from Cernheist had dug in for the night. Their tents and wagons were packed full of the young, elderly, or remaining injured. Those who couldn't find a place to sleep out of the wind had hunkered down beside one of the many campfires blazing in the weak light of dawn.

But as Jaevid and I passed by, everyone began to emerge. The camp buzzed with whispers. Children peeked out of the tent flaps. Men picked up anything they could to use as a weapon—old swords, hammers, pitchforks, and hatches— and began to follow. They weren't an army, not by a long shot, but I could only guess that seeing Jaevid made them feel the odds were in their favor if this was indeed some kind of attack.

Jaevid stopped at the edge of camp, facing the miles of frigid wilderness that stood between Luntharda and us. The terrain was thick with evergreens and the first rays of the rising sun painted the snowy slopes and mountainsides pastel shades of pink, orange, and lavender. Facing it all, Jaevid stood firm and tall, his shoulders squared and expression stony.

Whatever he sensed—I couldn't see it. Not yet.

Then the soft blast of a horn carried through the cold,

morning air. My pulse raced. I *knew* that sound.

They appeared like white phantoms under the dark of the trees. Gray elves dressed in full armor, their feathered war headdresses fluttering in the wind, sat astride huge, elk-like creatures. Each one was as large as a draft horse, but their shape was far more slender and dynamic. Their shaggy hides were as white as untouched snow and shimmered like platinum in the morning light. With heads crowned with sloping white antlers boasting twenty or more lethal points, I recognized them at once.

A faundra cavalry.

The rider at the front of the formation wore a grander headdress than the rest, the mask pulled down to cover most of his face. He also carried a pair of duel scimitars belted to his hips and a long cloak of some strange, blue-tinted fur that was striped in black. I was familiar enough with gray elf customs to know that only those of the royal bloodline would ever wear something that ornate. I'd seen this ensemble before, though only at court during formal ceremonies. He was a prince—one of King Jace and Queen Araxie's sons.

The rider stopped less than ten yards from us, throwing a hand up to the rest of his company. They all came to halt behind him, their mounts snorting, stamping, and tossing their heads. My head swam with wonder at the sight of them. I'd never seen a full cavalry like this. There must have been fifty of them at least. The sight of so many noble beasts standing in formation, their powerful bodies wearing fine leather armor and their riders stone-faced and proud, put a surge of adrenaline in my veins.

The prince dismounted, leaving his faundra stag to paw at

the ground and snort as he came striding toward us with his long cloak fluttering at his heels. I knew him—even before he threw back the mask of his headdress to cast a broad smile at Jaevid and me.

His olive skin gave a rich contrast to his deeply set green eyes. They were sharp and quick as they glanced at our pitiful excuse for a camp, his long brown hair catching in the wintry air. The points of his ears were much shorter than the rest of his full-blooded company. They looked more like Jaevid's, in fact. They had the same squareness and robustness tainting their otherwise perfect elven beauty, thanks to his father's human blood.

"Greetings, cousin," he offered with a heavy elven accent. "It seems you're in need of assistance."

"Cousin?" Jaevid's bewildered gaze flickered to me.

Before I could explain, the elven prince gave a deep bow. "Forgive me, lapiloque. I am Judan, son of Queen Araxie. I believe that makes us family, doesn't it? Regardless, I watch the westward jungles. That is my charge as Second Son of Luntharda. After your tree disappeared from our horizon, many warriors began to amass in the royal city, eager to see the Tibrans undone. They rally under my mother's banner and want to join you in the fight. Our scouts have kept us well-informed of your movements." He laughed, flashing me a roguish grin and wink. "You've been very busy. Sieging Northwatch on your own with only a handful of dragons? And here I wondered if the tales of lapiloque's insane bravery were puffed up by storytellers over the years. I'm pleased to be mistaken."

"I'm afraid the siege wasn't so successful, unfortunately,"

Jaevid sighed. "We lost a member of our company there. He's being held captive and stands to make things ... very complicated moving forward."

"So I'm told. My scouts came with harrowing reports of a creature made of rot and bone carrying a rider in Seraph's armor." Judan's smile faded and he rubbed his chin. "When we saw smoke rise from Cernheist, we feared the worst."

"Argonox sent that thing after us," I affirmed. "The city survived, but the people could not remain there. Cernheist is not defensible, not against that manner of monster."

Judan's eyes narrowed as he looked around at our company again. Lines of worry deepened in his brow as his gaze lingered upon the tents, where dozens of children peeked out, their eyes glittering with mystification as they pointed and marveled at the gray elf cavalry. "Where will they go?"

"To Luntharda." Jaevid's answer came firmly. It was not open for debate. "They can't stay in the wilds, and they can't go back to Cernheist. The Tibrans have all but taken the western coast. They need a safe place to wait until this has ended."

"Then we will guide them there." Judan gave a dragonrider salute, clasping his fist across his chest and bowing slightly. "It is not far to the border, but the road is steep. My scouts on shrikes can send word ahead to prepare to receive them."

Jaevid arched a brow. "I haven't seen any shrikes."

That cunning little smirk curled up Judan's lips again, making his green eyes sparkle with delighted mischief. "I should hope not. My father took great care in training all his sons in the arts of subtly and stealth, something he claims to have learned in his early life. In turn, I was permitted to construct and train a very specialized order of scouts who work exclusively at gathering information while remaining undetected. Granted, this war has been the first official test of our skills. I'm pleased to report that so far, we are yielding excellent results."

"You've managed to spy on the Tibrans?" I couldn't keep from sounding shocked.

"Oh yes," he announced with a proud flourish of his hand. "All we required was official order from the queen to begin—something she wouldn't have allowed unless there was enough support amongst the people to engage in this war. Now that we are on the move, I can supply you with information about Tibran legion positions, outposts, supply routes—you name it."

"That," I gasped. "I want all of that. Right now."

"Of course. Did you have any particular region in mind, Princess?"

"We should focus on what might stand between Halfax and us." I glanced to Jaevid, relieved to find him nodding in agreement. At least we were on the same page again.

Judan winked a gleaming emerald eye. "At your service, my lady. And might I just say, you are as fetching as ever. A shame Maldobar has still not learned to appreciate the compelling beauty of a woman who knows her way around a blade."

Heat rose in my cheeks. I wanted to say something, change the subject, but all that came out were breathy choking sounds.

"Some of us have," Phillip's voice growled at my back.

Judan's expression blanked as he gaped up at the towering

figure that stepped in close to my side, arms crossed, feline tail flicking. He reached for the hilt of his blades, hands hesitating as he studied Phillip with mixture of shock and horror. "Paligno preserve us, what manner of creature is that?"

Phillip growled and put an arm around my shoulder. "The kind that can snap you in half if he suspects you're messing with *his* lady."

My neck and ears blazed with embarrassment. "N-now, Phillip, let's just—"

"Phillip?" Judan sucked in a sharp breath, his eyebrows shooting up as he glanced between the rest of us as though searching for an explanation. "*Duke* Phillip Derrick?"

"None other," Phillip rumbled.

Putting his hands up in surrender, Judan managed a nervous chuckle. "You, uh, look a bit different, my friend. I suspect there's a good story attached to this?"

"Perhaps not a good one, but a story indeed," Jaevid spoke up, motioning toward the camp. "We should meet with the rest of our company while the refugees prepare to move. Perhaps your cavalrymen can lend them a hand?"

Judan's proud grin was back full force. "It would be our honor, lapiloque."

ELEVEN

Men like Judan had always confounded me. They cruised the waters of the royal court like sharks in an ocean of polished marble and glittering glass. They were always on the hunt for any advantageous relationship they might kindle there. In that world, Judan's reputation painted him like an elusive stag, strutting through the ballrooms with starry-eyed noble women trailing in his wake. He was the only one of Jace's sons who had never married, although I'd heard he had no trouble lining up options. If rumors were true, then he practically had a queue outside his chamber door just in case he decided to marry, but no one at court could claim to have ever crossed that threshold. Not yet, anyway.

Once, the ladies at court had sneered at the idea of a halfbreed in their midst. Now, men like Judan were a point of intrigue. It was a ridiculous and sad spectacle, watching them all vying for his attention as though they'd lost all sense of self-respect. I'd promised myself a long time ago never to be that kind of woman. No man's attention was worth the price of my dignity—even if he was blessed with a handsome build and more than his share of that half-elven prettiness.

And Judan was *very* pretty.

Swaggering forward to take my hand and kiss my wrist seemed as natural as breathing for him—something I couldn't even begin to comprehend. Phillip seemed to grasp it well enough, though. Or at least, he was wise to Judan's game. He stood beside me like a guarding wall, planting his imposing frame directly between us as we gathered around our campfire to exchange what information we could while the refugees prepared to move out.

Judan was full of useful intelligence his scouts had collected by watching the Tibrans. He admitted they were still receiving more as his men moved further down the western coast, but he could draw some conclusions from what they had already provided about the Tibran movements.

"They struggle with the mountain roads," he explained, gesturing to a detailed map etched into a large piece of hide he'd brought along. "It seems they cannot tunnel through the stone. And without any means of moving in the air, Argonox's forces must clear them of snow and debris before they can maneuver their war machines through. It takes time, so their progress has been slow coming in from the western coastline. Even more so, they struggle through the Marshlands. The deep mud and bogs have slowed their advance to a crawl. The soggy earth and water causes their tunnels to flood or cave in. Even the river has given them great difficulty. The spring storms have swollen its waters far beyond the established banks. The waters run fast and deep, and none of the existing bridges can bear the weight of their war machines. They are forced to wait until the water retreats." His wistful smile was filled with devious pride. "Apparently Maldobar's rugged terrain is not one the Tibrans are accustomed to. It's as though the very land itself has joined the fight to slow their advance."

"They won't stay grounded for long," Haldor murmured. "Not now that Argonox has found a way to force dragons into submission with that foul magic, I'm willing to bet good coin we can anticipate more aerial attacks."

"Then you should go quickly. Ride hard and do not stop unless you must. Here are a few places in the Marshlands where you'll be safe to camp and rest overnight." He gestured to the map, and we all leaned in to study the points. "But you should know, we are not the only ones using stealth to watch our enemy's movements. My scouts have come across many Tibran spies. We've been killing all we can without risking exposure or capture. No doubt those agents are watching the skies for dragonriders very carefully."

"Perhaps we should wait to move at nightfall?" Haldor rubbed the back of his neck, glancing worriedly up at me. "We would be harder to spot."

"Not for a spy of any skill," a deep voice spoke over us. Everyone paused, turning to watch my older brother emerge from our tent.

My heart jumped into my throat.

Dressed in bits and pieces of borrowed armor, Aubren stood with his mouth drawn into a tight, grim line and his body tense—as though he half-expected we might attack him. His shaggy dark golden hair had been brushed back away from his face, revealing deeper lines in his brow and dark, heavy circles under his eyes.

"A good point," Judan agreed quickly, not seeming to pick up on the rising tension in the air. He had no way of knowing what we'd just been through with Aubren.

My brother's fractured gaze drifted to me for a moment before he lowered his head and murmured, "You can't afford to sit here any longer. You should go now, keep above the cloud cover as much as possible."

Something in his voice made my stomach turn. What was he saying?

"You don't intend to go with us?" Jaevid guessed before I could speak.

Aubren wouldn't even look at him. "The fewer extra passengers you take, the faster you'll go. I'd be nothing but a burden to your progress now." He paused, looking past us to the refugees still breaking down camp. "Besides, someone should stay with them. Someone should warn Queen Araxie of the danger now that Reigh is … " His voice faded, expression skewing as he looked away.

"Then we should speak alone." Jaevid stepped toward him, placing a hand on Aubren's shoulder to guide him away from the rest of our group.

My heart ached with every beat as I watched them walk away. What was this about? Was Jaevid going to ask him about what had happened while he was imprisoned at Northwatch? How that defilement had been put on him? Or what Reigh's current situation was?

Deep in my gut, another suspicion arose to gnaw away at

my insides. Was it possible Jaevid knew about how Aubren had intended to betray him? If that was the case, I wanted to be there to speak up in my brother's defense. Yes, Aubren was an idiot for even imagining Argonox could be bargained with—but he wasn't a bad person. Aubren was a good man and nothing would ever persuade me otherwise.

Jaevid *needed* to know that.

I surged up to chase after them, only to be yanked to a choking halt by the neck of my own tunic. I whirled around, scowling up into Phillip's eerie feline eyes as he let go of the back of my shirt.

"You need to sit this one out," Phillip warned in a sharp whisper. "Let them handle it."

"But he's my brother!"

"Exactly. It doesn't take a divine gift to see that he's not in a good mental state right now. He's lucky to be alive. Let him have a little space." Phillip gave my cheek an affectionate stroke. "He'll come to you when he's ready to talk about it."

Phillip didn't understand—he couldn't. He didn't know what had happened in Northwatch or that Aubren had tried to betray Jaevid to the Tibrans.

Stealing a glance over my shoulder, I watched Jaevid and my brother disappear behind a clump of trees. My heart wrenched until I could hardly breathe. Whatever had happened with Argonox and Reigh, I wasn't dumb enough to assume Aubren would just brush off the last words we'd spoken to one another before this.

"We should decide now who else will go with the refugees to Luntharda," Haldor suggested, breaking the awkward tension in the air. He cleared his throat and cast me an expectant stare.

Right. I still had responsibilities here. Time to pull it together. There were still a lot of people counting on us.

"If Tibran spies are going to be tracking us, then we should use our numbers to at least cast as much confusion to their reports as possible. I suggest we split up and choose one of these places to rendezvous after nightfall." I panned a look around at our company, gauging their response.

Eirik raised his hand, and I had an immediate flashback to our fledgling training year. "Can I, uh, make a little suggestion?"

"You don't have to raise your hand. You can just say it." I tried not to laugh.

He blushed. "Right. Well, since I'm officially an unseated dragonrider, maybe it's better for me to go with Aubren and escort the refugees to Luntharda?"

That idiot. Escorting refugees? Did he honestly think I was buying that? All right, so that might have been his secondary concern, but I knew the primary reason—and she was sitting with her aunt within earshot of our war meeting, wrapped up in *his* cloak.

I couldn't resist a cattish grin. "Hmm. Well, I suppose someone should make sure the baroness and her niece arrive safely."

Eirik's flushed as red as a beet all the way to the tips of his ears. "R-right."

"That's rather mundane work for a dragonrider," Judan mused, his gaze flicking back and forth between us curiously. "Even an unseated one."

I waved a hand dismissively. "Oh, well, we must be absolutely certain that our noble families are taken care of and spare nothing but the finest of our warriors for that task. Wouldn't you agree, Phillip?"

"Absolutely." He was grinning, too.

"Then I'll, uh, go with them," Eirik croaked. "Just to make sure she—er—they get to Luntharda safely."

Phillip snickered.

I elbowed him in the ribs on my way to gesture to the map again. "In that case, I'll take a formation with Calem and Phillip. Haldor can fly wing end to Jaevid and take Aedan. We'll meet here at nightfall. Agreed?"

One by one, the rest of our company gave a nod or grunt of confirmation. We had a plan. We had a destination.

Now we just needed the tiniest bit of luck.

The gods were gracious enough to grant us a bleak, gray sky as we rushed through the final checks on all our saddles and gear. Another storm was approaching, bringing with it tall walls of clouds and the distant rumble of thunder over the mountain peaks. Foul weather was good—for us, anyway. In the lowlands it would muddy the roads and make the waters rise in the swamps and bogs. In the mountains, it would mean more snow, high winds, and another good freeze. Both would make things worse for our enemy, who apparently wasn't accustomed to the brutality of Maldobar's seasons.

It didn't take long to gather the dragons together. Jaevid

seemed able to persuade and manipulate them without saying a word, probably because of his divine power. They gravitated to his side like eager puppies, still nipping and taunting one another. Vexi, however, was no longer among them.

When I asked about it, Jaevid confirmed that she'd vanished without a trace sometime in the night. My heart sank a bit. I didn't have to ask where she'd gone. Dragons who chose riders like she had selected Reigh were loyal to a fault. Their loyalty was relentless. He belonged to her now, and I knew better than to think she would abandon him at Northwatch—even after what she had endured already.

I just prayed that Argonox wouldn't capture her again. She seemed clever. Surely she had learned better than to get too close to the Tibrans.

At least, that's what I told myself as I tightened one of the girth straps on Phevos's saddle. I strained and pulled, struggling to wrestle the strap up one more notch. No luck. It wouldn't budge an inch.

"You!" I leaned around to glare at him. "Stop holding your breath! If this isn't tight, you'll be slinging me around all over the place."

Phevos grumbled, snapping his jaws defiantly before he went back to preening the scales on his wing arms.

"Stubborn, scaly donkey!" I cursed as I began pulling again.

Suddenly, a pair of large, gloved hands reached around me and gave the strap a stern yank. The buckle slipped into place with a *click*, and Phevos let out a cough. He swung his head around, eyes narrowed, and ears slicked back, puffing a snort of disapproval.

"Sometimes the cavalry horses do the same thing," Aubren mumbled as he stood back, putting a few feet of space between us.

I didn't know what to say. Before me, Aubren shifted his weight and refused to look me straight in the eye, keeping his right arm tucked in close against his side. The refugees were leaving. They were already setting out for Luntharda, flanked on all sides by gray elf cavalry. I'd just assumed he had already left.

I cleared my throat. "So, you came to say goodbye?" Gods, the question sounded awkward, even to me.

"Something like that," he answered quietly, finally looking up with a despondent, fretful expression.

"Does it hurt?" I gestured to his arm, the one that still bore the defilement. He stood stiffly, still keeping his arm angled out of my direct sight even though it was covered by his clothing and gloves. "I can bear it. Jaevid insisted he would look into it again once this is all over." His voice caught, and his brow drew into a deep frown that made his jaw go rigid. "I ... I told him everything."

"You did?"

Aubren nodded slightly. "He forgave me." Looking down again, he rubbed his neck along the collar of his breastplate. "It's really him, isn't it? He's really here, fighting with us."

Somehow, it didn't seem like he wanted an answer—as though he were asking himself that question rather than me. I quirked my mouth enough to chew on the inside of my cheek and waited for him to get to the point.

"I keep expecting this to be a dream, that I'll wake up back in that *place*." He sucked in a sharp breath and shut his eyes tightly. "Jaevid knows everything I do now about Argonox and Reigh. He'll brief you when you land tonight."

"Aubren?" I dared to take a step closer, just enough that I could reach out and touch his unmarked hand. I could feel the warmth of his palm even through his leather gloves, and yet it still seemed like he was a thousand miles away.

He angled his face so I couldn't see, but I could hear the brokenness in his voice. "Jaevid might be able to excuse my betrayal, but I doubt our father will. And then trying to take your life? Dark magic or not, I don't expect anyone to forgive that easily. But Jenna, please, I am so sorry, I never meant for—"

"There is nothing to forgive!" I snatched his hand tighter, jostling him so that he would face me again. Standing on my toes, I snagged my arms around his neck, gripping him with all my strength as I hugged him tightly. "It wasn't your fault. I know you would never hurt me. Argonox poisoned your mind, and you fought it. You resisted and won. If our father can't appreciate the kind of strength that took, then I'll spit right in his face."

He bowed his head slightly, letting his chin rest on my shoulder. "Regardless, I can't face him yet. I will, when this is over. I will be the one to tell him what I've done and accept whatever punishment he orders without resistance—but not now. There are far more important things that require our whole attention."

"Gods, you stupid, stubborn man," I grumbled as I leaned back and put my hands on his face. "This discussion is *not* over. If I find out you've gone to our father without talking to me first, you will regret it. I can promise you that.

You're my brother, Aubren. I love you—always."

One corner of his mouth quirked slightly, but it was only a ghost of a smile. He leaned in, looping an arm around my neck to give me one last, tight hug in return. "Thank you, Jenna. Please stay safe."

TWELVE

We kept the rest of our farewells brief. It was better, safer for everyone, if we moved quickly and gave the Tibrans less time to respond or catch up to us. Eirik and Aubren rode off with Judan, leading Baroness Adeline, Miri, and the rest of the refugees from Cernheist along the safest road toward the wild jungle of Luntharda.

Sitting astride Phevos, I watched the last of their company disappear along the tangled, twisting mountain pathway through the thin glass visor of my helmet. I prayed that they would make it—that Argonox wouldn't have some nasty surprise waiting for them. If they pressed on hard for the rest of the day and didn't fall prey to the encroaching storm, they might make it in less than two days.

Regardless, there was nothing more we could do for them now.

Jaevid gave the motion to take off, so Calem, Phillip, and I hunkered down to wait our turn. We watched as Mavrik and Turq took to the air first. The rapid, powerful beats of their wings stirred up the snow. I had to wipe it from my visor once they were clear.

They would be taking the western route, following the bristled spine of jagged mountain peaks down to the Marshlands. We would make a wider pass to the east, right along the foothills that sloped down into the Farchase Plains. Our goal was to meet right on the edge of the Marshlands, where the forest turned swampy, and let our mounts rest before we pressed on toward Halfax. Since our path was shorter, we were going to double back a little, just to throw off any Tibran spies that might be mapping our movements. No need to make it too easy for them, right?

If Judan's information was correct, the path would be fairly clear all the way from the Marshlands to Halfax, as long as we stayed above the marshes, where Argonox's war machines couldn't go. We'd approach from the west and pray that my father decided to let us land safely within the walls of the royal city. Jaevid hadn't really considered the possibility that he might turn us away. Maybe it seemed silly to him, considering everything else that was going on, but technically, I was still an exile from the royal city.

My last encounter with my father hadn't been a positive, heartwarming one. Not that we'd had many of those lately. Fewer and fewer after Mother passed away, in fact. That last, fiery debate had been months ago, and I'd received no word from him since. I honestly didn't know how I would be received now.

It wasn't until I felt my dragon's body flex beneath me, filling his wings with the frosty air, that I realized how much that scared me. Would he be furious? Would he banish me from my homeland altogether? Mark me as a traitor for fighting in battles and leading other dragonriders to fight without his permission? Gods, he was well within is right to demand our arrest. I might be spared a traitor's punishment, but Haldor, Calem, and Eirik didn't have the luxury of being the king's only daughter. He might put them all to the sword for taking part in my insane rebellion.

I swallowed against the hard knot of uncertainty in my throat and leaned into Phevos's motions as he pumped his wings harder, soaring toward the bleak open sky. We moved as one, rising with the winds and letting our bodies brush the heavens. Every takeoff, every flight, still gave me that rush that set my heart ablaze. This was freedom. It tasted of the wild, icy mountain air. It felt like the rolling of sturdy muscles beneath ironclad scales. It sounded like a dragon's booming roar, thundering in the deep.

It was only the strength of Phillip's arms around my middle that reminded me who I was. Everything down there, back on the ground, was complicated and painful. Part of me still wished we could just sail away on a wintry breeze and leave it all behind.

Off our right side, Perish dipped gracefully into formation with her white wings spread wide to catch the rising updrafts. Her scarlet eyes flicked around, always watching the air around us as we broke through the clouds to the clean blue sky above. Sitting astride her sleek shoulders, Calem's bronze-plated armor shone like gold. The wing-shaped details on his helm caught in the sun and his sweeping cloak fluttered behind him like a rippling banner of royal blue velvet.

Hours of daylight dragged. Beneath me, Phevos's breathing grew heavier and his wing beats more strained as the day wore on. Carrying two riders was taking its toll. It was a lot to ask of him to take us both so far. Our dragons would need to land, eat, and rest very soon.

As the sun began to dip below the clouds over the western sea, we made our last turn toward our destination and descended low enough to get a good view of the ground below. There, the dense forest flanked both sides of the Marshlands for miles, stretching along the floodplains of the river that ran all the way to the eastern coast. It made for deep, murky bogs thick with brambles and mud as thick as tar. The whole area was known for flashfloods in the spring, when the rains and snowmelt made the river swell beyond its banks.

Usually, it was a place traveled only by the dangerous and desperate. During the Gray War, it had served as a common hideout for bandits and slavers. I'd also heard of escaped slaves, elves mostly, who had tried hiding there to avoid capture. But if rumors were to be believed, there were more dangerous things lurking in that filthy mire than slavers and thieves.

A glint off Calem's armor caught my attention as he flashed his vambrace to get my attention. "*Smoke rising,*" he gestured, using our dragonrider code of hand signals. "*A Tibran attack?*"

Following the point of his finger, I narrowed my gaze upon a few plumes of dark smoke rising from the edge of the forest along the swamp. Strange. They seemed too big to be mere campfires.

"*Let's take a look,*" I gestured back. "*If it's Tibrans, I'm going in hot.*"

"*Lead on.*" Calem gave a salute.

I gave Phillip's arm, which was still wrapped around my waist, a pat before I leaned back to yell over the rush of the wind. "Hang on; we might be in for a fight!"

He didn't reply, or if he did, the wind was too loud in my ears to hear it. Still, his hold on me tightened.

With a twist of my saddle handles, I applied pressure to the underside of my dragon's saddle, letting him know when and how steeply to turn. We banked, flaring, and making a speedy descent toward the smoke curling up from four difference places just within the tree line.

There was no way of knowing what we might be diving into. A Tibran legion trying to burn their way along the swamp to make way for their war machines? That seemed the most likely at first brush.

But as we skirted in close, I could pick out more details. People were running toward the swamp, fleeing from the trees. Women carrying children tripped and staggered through the mud. Men dressed in commoner's clothes were carrying the injured, fleeing as fast as they could over the marshy ground. They were *not* Tibran.

But the soldiers chasing them most certainly were.

From the trees, lines of men dressed in that familiar bronze armor emerged with their shields interlocked. Some used crossbows to launch fire-tipped arrows at the fleeing civilians; others swung slings with miniature versions of the dragon venom-filled orbs we had seen them use in a much larger size at Barrowton. The clay orbs shattered, sending burning venom spraying in every direction. Every time one exploded, it lit up the dusk with orange flame. People screamed, some falling as they were caught in the spray.

I gripped the saddle handles so hard my fingers went numb. My jaw creaked as I ground my teeth. These were not bandits or slavers they were chasing down. These were unarmed civilians. They were butchering families with children.

I'd burn every last one of those Tibran cowards alive for it.

Phevos snarled and bared his teeth, wings snapping in for a rapid rush of the battlefield. Behind us, Perish let out a screeching roar as she followed. We took the first line of Tibrans with a long blast of burning venom, creating a barrier between them and the fleeing civilians. They wouldn't be able to pursue now.

As we swooped low over the ground, low enough I could have plucked a few blades of grass on the way, Phillip suddenly let go of my waist. I twisted around just in time to see him take one of the blades from my belt and leap from the saddle. He landed in a roll and immediately sprang up, running headlong for the nearest Tibran soldier.

Perish dipped in for another sweeping pass, lighting up a portion of the tree line. I wasn't sure why she'd bother—until I saw around a hundred more Tibran soldiers come pouring out of the thickets to escape the fire. She was flushing them out!

They ran straight for me, apparently too panicked to notice the angry purple dragon turning for a second pass. Arrows zipped past my head and glanced off my dragon's scaly hide. They pinged off my breastplate and stuck into the leather of my saddle. My pulse sped with wild fury, every muscle quivering as I leaned down against Phevos's neck. My ears rang with the screaming of men and the roar of flames in between my dragon's thundering roars.

Straight ahead, a Tibran soldier closed in on a young woman clutching a squirming bundle of muddy cloth against her breast. Sword drawn, he reared back as she stumbled and fell, covering her baby with her body as she screamed.

Heat and rage flushed through me, coursing along every nerve and setting my brain ablaze. I unbuckled from the saddle, giving Phevos a quick pat to let him know I was going in.

He chirped and ducked lower, angling himself with one wingtip barely brushing the earth.

I hopped out onto his wing, using it like a fabric slide to land in a crouch less than ten yards from the soldier. Not a second to waste.

Drawing my remaining blade, I rushed and sprang, kicking both feet hard against his back. One swing, swift and relentless, sent a spray of blood through the air. The soldier's body hit the ground with a *thud* and didn't move again.

I landed in a crouch, shaking off the pulsing rush that still hummed through every muscle as I stood. The woman let out a desperate cry as she looked up at me, tears leaving clean streaks down her mud and soot smeared face. "H-help us! Please!"

I threw back the visor of my helmet, revealing my face to her.

Her eyes went wide, mouth dropping open as she stared upward.

I assumed it was because I was a woman. It was still shocking to a lot of people, particularly the common folk who didn't get to see a lot of battle or training firsthand.

I assumed wrong.

Behind me, a resounding bellow shook the ground under my boots. I turned, catching a flash of blue scales an instant before the ground nearby exploded into flame. The blast incinerated a group of Tibran soldiers coming straight for us with crossbows at the ready. They didn't even have time to scream.

"I-is that … ?" The woman gasped.

It was.

Mavrik descended into the thick of the fight, his leathery black wings cupping to form a shield from incoming arrows and orbs as his rider dismounted. When the huge blue dragon rose up again, his saddle was empty. He threw back his head, black horns flashing in the setting sun as he shot a plume of flame straight up into the air. His wings unfurled, and Jaevid Broadfeather strode onto the battlefield with his scimitar in hand.

THIRTEEN

I had to give him some credit, Jaevid knew how to make an entrance. He took to the battle not like a man or even a dragonrider. He was a vengeful god. His eyes flickered, glowing like peridot stars in the failing light of day as he flexed his divine power. A vein stood out against the side of his neck as he raised his free hand toward the line of advancing Tibran troops. His expression sharpened, lips curling in a vicious snarl. The ground shuddered, nearly knocking me off my feet. I wobbled to keep balance and threw up an arm to keep myself between the woman still carrying her infant and whatever was about to happen.

Jaevid closed his fist, sending out a sharp burst of power like a blast wave through the air. The earth flinched again. In seconds, two enormous creatures began twisting and writhing free of the swampy sludge as though they'd been buried there, right under our feet, for a thousand years. A gnarled mixture of rock, root, and dripping mud, the beasts rose up like knuckle-dragging giants. Each one was twenty feet of primal earthen power. No faces. No features. Just two bottomless, glowing green pits for eyes and *very* big fists. One hit would smash a man into jelly—armor and all. Their every step shook the ground, and their bellowing cries made many of the Tibran soldiers break ranks and flee with screams of sheer terror.

From the sky, Haldor and Calem threw down a perimeter of flame, forcing the remaining Tibran ranks into range of Jaevid's two monsters. Our makeshift meat grinders worked with brutal efficiency. While Phevos and Mavrik stood watch, crowing excitedly at the other dragons still circling, I ran the perimeter on cleanup duty. Chasing down any of the soldiers who decided to make a break for it across the swamp wasn't easy. Running through that muck and mire in armor was a challenge—but I wasn't about to let any of those cowards leave our party early.

Suddenly, a frantic scream drew my attention back toward the forest, just in time to spot a lone Tibran soldier dragging a little boy into the tree line. The child kicked and fought, screaming for help. The soldier's gaze flashed upward, meeting mine for an instant. His face paled, eyes wide in horror that reflected the flames of battle around us. Then he clenched an arm around the boy's neck and dragged him further into the tree line.

Not on my watch.

Yanking my blade free of a dead soldier's back, I started after them at a sprint. It took everything I had to keep going, fighting against the slushy mud that threatened to suck the

boots right off my feet. But I couldn't stop. That boy—
someone had to save him.

Suddenly, I was in the air. The battlefield whirled around
me in utter chaos, and then all I could see was the ground
blurring by. I was flying—no—being carried!

"Hang on!" Phillip snarled as he lugged me over his
shoulder. His paw-like feet were speedy over the mud, and
he carried me like I weighed nothing at all.

"There's a boy," I started to shout.

"I know! I saw," he called back. "They won't get far."

Gods, I hoped he was right.

Wrapping an arm around Phillip's neck, I sheathed my
blade and quickly wriggled myself over his shoulders. No
way was I going to let him tote me around like this. Clinging
to his back with my legs around his middle like a child riding
piggyback, I searched the edge of the forest for any sign of the
boy or soldier. There was nothing.

"I smell them," Phillip said with a thrumming growl.
He poured on more speed toward the forest, dropping to all
fours to leap the last twenty yards in one mighty spring.

Darting through the forest, splashing through muck-
filled sinkholes and leaping over fallen trees, Phillip moved
like a panther on the hunt. His padded feet didn't make a
sound on the soft earth, but his growling pants were hard to
miss. My heart hit the back of my throat as he lurched to a
halt, swinging around with his nose in the air and his pointed
ears wiggling. The vertical pupils of his strange eyes widened,
taking in the dim light.

Suddenly, a scream made us both jerk. It was a child's
voice. And it was close.

Phillip squatted down slowly, guiding me down from his back. "Draw their attention," he whispered. "Distract that soldier. I'll move in. He'll never hear me coming."

I nodded.

My hands shook with nervous energy as I crept through the soggy undergrowth. Every step was painfully loud, squishing and splashing or crunching on twigs and fallen limbs. The warm, damp air reeked of silt and rotting leaves. Thick clouds of fog drifted aimlessly and twisted around the trunks of the trees, and the distant rumble of combat echoed through the gloom.

Then I heard it—the soft crying of a child.

Surging forward, I rounded a clump of trees and saw them at the crest of a small rise. The soldier whirled around, his whole body shaking as he gripped the little boy by his hair. He had the sharp end of a long, curved daggered pressed right up against the child's throat.

"S-stop right there," the soldier yelped. "I'll cut him open! By the gods, I swear I will!"

I slowly raised my hands, gesturing surrender. "This doesn't have to end with anyone being cut open."

He coughed out a broken, maniacal laugh. "It does! It will! You think I don't know it will? Do you take me for a fool?" His expression twisted, eyes widening as he looked all around and up toward the limbs of the trees. "We'll all die here. All of us. Cut and burned!"

Alarm bells tolled in my head. Something about this man wasn't right. He looked to be about my age, or maybe a little older—no older than thirty for sure. But his eyes were bloodshot and his cheeks sunken. His whole body twitched and tremored with more than just fear.

I'd seen the horrors of battle break men. It changed people, some more than others. But this was *not* that.

"Your accent is Maldobarian," I observed, careful to keep my tone calm. "Why are you fighting for the Tibrans?"

His gaze darted back to me. For one terrible instant, he seemed to realize what he was doing—the blade in one hand and the child in the other. His brow quivered. His eyes welled with tears.

"Please, just let the boy go. We can talk about this. It doesn't have to end with anyone dying," I coaxed.

Any sense or remorse in the man's eyes vanished, snuffed out like a candle in the night. "You don't understand," he screamed. "I didn't want this. No one wants this. They tell you to fight on. If you fight well, then you can have back everything they take. But it's a lie!" He squeezed the knife until his knuckles blanched. "Death is the only reward—the only freedom from Argonox!"

The soldier's body lurched suddenly, and he fell silent. Second by second, his expression went from crazed to blank. His arms went slack. The dagger rolled out of his hand and landed in the mud at his feet.

My heart jumped with relief. Phillip? Had he come to intervene?

As the soldier slumped forward onto the mud with a resounding *thud*, a man rose up behind him, brandishing a freshly bloodied hatchet.

It was definitely not Phillip.

He stood tall, broad shoulders not bent or bowed with age despite the silver that streaked his black hair and the deep creases in his aging skin. Dressed in a strange mixture of furs, common clothing, and bits of makeshift Maldobarian armor, the man leered at me with pale blue eyes and mouth pinched into a grim frown. "It's useless to talk to them, Your Highness," he warned in a deep, gruff voice.

My mind whirled. Who was this guy? A woodsman, maybe? Or a hunter? And how did he know who I was?

"Grandpapa!" The little boy wailed suddenly, breaking the tension as he ran for the man with arms wide open.

The burly old man slipped his hatchet back into his belt and took the child into his arms. Then he motioned to me. "Let's go. The others will need our help," he mumbled, rubbing his short white beard as his piercing gaze panned over me quickly. I could sense him sizing me up, not that I wasn't used to it. That's generally what men did when they spotted a woman carrying a blade and wearing a dragonrider's armor.

"Tell your monster to come along, too," he grumbled as he strode past.

On cue, Phillip sprang from the undergrowth and let out a disapproving snort as he stood beside me with the tip of his tail flicking. "Not sure I'd toss around names like that. I wasn't the one who just buried an axe in someone's spine."

The man gave a grunt, maybe a chuckle or a cough—I honestly couldn't tell—and kept on walking. He didn't even stop to see if we were going to follow.

Phillip and I exchanged a look and a shrug. Not like we had a lot to lose.

"Just who are you anyway?" I called as I jogged to catch up.

The old man's steely gaze never wavered as he picked his way through the underbrush, still carrying the little boy. His movements were trained and swift, and his every step smooth and calculated. I'd seen that kind of posturing before, many times in fact, but only from Maldobarian soldiers.

"One of many refugees trying to find some hole to hide in until the tide turns," he answered. "But if there are to be introductions, you can call me Roland."

Roland. Where had I heard that name before? It struck a chord in my brain right away, but the memory refused to surface, lodged somewhere just out of reach. As soon as we broke through the edge of the forest and back out onto the open marshes, however, the thought was lost.

The battle was over. Tibran soldiers lay in burning piles scattered everywhere, and most of my dragonrider brothers were helping the scattered refugees regroup at the edge of the forest. By the look of things, only a few had fallen victim to the Tibran legions.

I stopped, my heart dropping to the soles of my boots as I spotted Calem struggling to pull a young woman away from one of the refugees lying in the mud. Even from a distance, it was obvious he was dead. The girl wailed and wept, fighting to stay close to the body and taking wild swings at Calem in the process. Her pale face was smeared with fresh blood and her ginger-colored hair was caked with mud.

I had almost made up my mind to try talking to her. Sometimes it helped for people to see a gentler, more feminine face in moments like this. But before I could take a step, Calem snatched off his helmet and one of his riding gauntlets and grasped her by the shoulders. He whirled the young woman around to face him. Leaning down to look directly into her eyes, he cupped her face with his bare hand. "Look me in the eye so I know you hear me. You must take a breath and listen." His voice was as calm and unfazed as ever.

She stared back at him, her chin trembling as she choked back sobs.

"Your father is dead. You, however, are very fortunate to still be alive. I'm sure he'd want it to stay that way," Calem murmured gently, withdrawing his hand slowly.

"I-I can't just leave him here to rot with them. He should be buried! He should be ..." The girl bawled. Her shoulders seized up as she leaned forward, burying her face against his breastplate to cry.

For a moment, Calem stood stiffly, his brow furrowed as he looked down at the girl as though he weren't sure what to do with her now. She couldn't have been more than sixteen, wearing what looked a lot like a long nightgown and robe. Both were coated in the same smelly swamp mud that was sloshing in her too-big boots.

When his puzzled expression finally panned to me, Calem gave me a few dragonrider signals. *What do I do?*

I rolled my eyes. I'd never seen Calem interact with many people outside our dragonrider circles, especially not young women. It wasn't that he didn't seem to care for them—more like, he didn't know how to relate with people in general. Battle he understood. But sentiment? Affection? That was apparently another story.

"*It's called a hug*," I signaled in reply.

His eyes narrowed. "*That is not helpful.*"

Eh, he'd figure it out. If nothing else, this was a good learning experience. At least he was making an effort.

Continuing after Roland, I counted thirty-two more refugees huddled together like frightened sheep. Most of them were men dressed in the same sort of mismatched clothing and armor Roland was. They were carrying chipped old swords, archaic shields, work axes, or blacksmithing hammers—basically whatever they could use as a weapon. Not exactly an army prepared to rival a Tibran attack.

The women and children hiding amidst them bore haunted, empty expressions on ashen, dirty faces. Their clothes were rags, and many of them were wore nightgowns. Anger rose in my chest like a molten tide. Driving them from their homes, enslaving them, murdering helpless women and children—Argonox was doing this to *my* people.

That would not stand. I would put an end to it or die trying.

"We should move back into the cover of the forest." Roland spoke and immediately had the attention of everyone in the group. The younger men rallied to him, expressions still fierce from battle. Strange that so many of them were halfbreeds, with at least some gray elven blood judging by their slightly pointed ears and olive skin. You didn't normally see so many this far from the border of Luntharda.

"The dragonriders have bought us some time," Roland continued. "But we need to move deeper into the marshes and make camp, tend to our wounded, and restock our supplies as best we can."

"We can help, if you like."

Jaevid's voice made everyone turn—including Roland. As the old man slowly turned to him, all the color drained from his face until his skin nearly matched his bristly white beard. "Jaevid." His eyes went round and his mouth opened slightly, just enough that the name slipped out in a breathless whisper.

Our infamous companion's mouth twitched, hinting at an apprehensive smile. He ducked his head slightly, shoulders drawing up anxiously as he flushed across the cheeks and gave a little nod. "It's been a long time, brother."

My body jolted suddenly as my heartbeat gave a frantic stammer. Gods and Fates—that's where I'd heard that name before. This man was Roland *Broadfeather*! He was Jaevid's half-brother! They'd shared the same brutal, abusive father in their childhood, but while Jaevid had been adopted into the brotherhood of dragonriders, Roland had defied their father's legacy of crafting saddlery for dragons and joined Maldobar's ground infantry.

Well, that explained the old man's finesse with a blade.

When their eyes met, Roland's entire posture gradually went slack. He bent long enough to place the little boy he'd been carrying back on the ground, then took one staggering step toward Jaevid. His breathing hitched, catching as he struggled—and failed—to choke out words.

"I know I'm a bit late," Jaevid fretted in a quiet voice. "But we are more than willing to help you in any way we can."

With a booming, rasping laugh, Roland suddenly surged forward and threw his arms around Jaevid. "It's really you!"

"Yes. It's me," Jaevid wheezed.

"I saw your dragon fly overhead, but we've heard so many stories of wild dragons taking up the fight—I didn't dare to hope!" Roland pulled back and grabbed Jaevid's shoulders to shake him.

All around us, the group of refugees pushed and shoved, ducking and standing on their toes to catch a glimpse of our fearless leader. They murmured to one another in hushed voices—right up until an older woman emerged from their midst. Though the deep bronze skin of her face was aged, she strode smoothly forward, her head held with regal poise and her multihued eyes shining bright. She was a full-blooded gray elf, with far longer pointed ears and hair as white as morning frost woven into many complex braids down to her waist, but she wore Maldobarian clothes. There was an elven-styled bow across her back and strings of colorful clay, bone, and copper beads hung around her neck.

When she drew close, Roland reached out to take her hand and guide her closer to Jaevid. "Delphi, this is my brother."

The elven woman's lips curved into a shrewd smile. "Honestly, Rolly? You think I don't know who he is?"

"Of course, my dear." The rugged man blushed like a scolded child. "Jaevid, this is my wife."

Jaevid's eyes went wide for a blink or two. "Wife?" He blinked a few more times. "Rolly?"

Roland gave a small nod that was eerily similar to the sheepish one Jaevid had given earlier.

"You seem surprised?" Delphi arched a brow, her mouth still split with a grin.

"It's nothing against you, my lady. But the last time we spoke, Roland insisted he had no intention of taking a wife."

She giggled again. "Oh yes. He told me that too, when we first met. So naturally, I dedicated myself to convincing him otherwise. It wasn't difficult. It turns out that sulky exterior is quite thin and easily cracked. I've tamed shrikes that were far more stubborn than he is."

Roland's cheeks glowed like ripe tomatoes over his short white beard. "M-my dear, please."

"At any rate, I'm pleased to see you have returned to us, lapiloque." Delphi gave him a slight bow before gesturing to a group of refugees around her—the ones who looked distinctly half-elven. "These are our children, your nieces and nephews, as it turns out. My sons are Alani and Kaeson, and my daughters Brisa and Daeyli. And of course, their children."

Jaevid's gaze panned the crowd of curious onlookers, mouth open and brows raised. He blinked rapidly, eyes seeming a little watery as he finally stared back at his brother. "You've been … very busy."

"Thanks to you," Roland affirmed.

He didn't reply. Instead, Jaevid bowed his head low enough that his shaggy hair hid his face. It would have been a lot for anyone to take in. I suppose he had to collect himself.

"There are rumors everywhere, lapiloque. It's hard to tell what is true and what is merely wild speculation." Delphi's tone was softer as she moved closer, grasping Jaevid's chin to gently lift his head so she could look him in the eye. "So many are living in terror, being driven from their homes and murdered in the streets, or dragged away to meet an ever-worse fate with the Tibran legions. No one has forgotten what you did for us so many years ago, but I'm afraid you are needed now more than ever."

"I made a promise," Jaevid answered, his jaw clenched and gaze steely. "I intend to keep it."

FOURTEEN

"We evacuated Ivangol when the Tibrans made landfall and Southwatch fell. So many good men died defending it—some I knew. But I had to take my family out of that place. We brought as many friends as we could with us, although we've lost more than half to Tibran scouting forces like you saw today. They roam the countryside looking for good roads to use to expand their reach." Sitting around the campfire, Roland's voice was heavy with exhaustion and sorrow. The light of the crackling fire turned his pale, glacier blue eyes orange as he watched the flames dancing in the dark. "We've done all right until now, keeping on the move and out of sight. But it was only a matter of time before they caught up to us."

"If it's not the soldiers, then it's the monsters," Delphi added as she sat close beside her husband with her shoulder resting against his. "Argonox set loose a horde of strange creatures into the wild—the likes of which I have never seen, even in Luntharda. They appear as some sort of feline, but with fur as black as coal and spines along their backs."

Phillip shifted next to me.

I took his hand and squeezed it tightly.

"There were also hounds. Beastly things. Blood-hungry and wrong in the head," she continued. "I shudder to think of what that tyrant might do to dragons or shrikes. Gods help us if he were able to turn them on us."

"I can't imagine he won't try that," Haldor mumbled. "We've already seen evidence of it."

Jaevid's expression darkened and his jaw clenched.

It was time to change the subject. I cleared my throat to get their attention. "We intend to go to Halfax as quickly as possible. We stand a good chance of making a final assault on Argonox there, if my father will listen to reason."

Roland paled. "Have you ... not heard?"

Oh no. I froze, my heart pounding in my fingers and throbbing in my toes as I held my breath. "Heard what?"

"Halfax is all but surrounded. Argonox has focused all efforts on cutting the city off from the rest of the kingdom. Word is that the people inside the walls are starving," Roland said, his tone like an apology. "They're prepared for dragonriders. You'll be hard pressed to reach it without taking heavy Tibran fire."

Jaevid sat up straighter, his face the picture of quiet ferocity. "What about demigods?"

Delphi's multihued eyes shimmered with vicious delight. "I pray not. And may you kill many Tibrans without mercy, lapiloque, for that is precisely what they deserve."

"Because of the Marshlands, their fortification of the western side of the city is very likely weaker," Roland added. "If you strike from that side, you stand a better chance of punching through their perimeter and making it to the city."

"I think I can buy you the time." From across the fire, Aedan sat forward and began drawing out a rough sketch in the dirt with the pointy end of a long twig. He marked out a rough circular shape—like that of Halfax—and began outlining it with an estimation of how the Tibran forces would be arranged. "Argonox's machines are highly specialized for sieging. His trebuchets and catapults are able to corner and turn quickly to reposition for incoming threats. But if I were to sneak back into the Tibran ranks, I might be able to disable them just before you make your assault. No doubt he has most of them focused on the city, since that's where the bulk of the remaining dragonriders are. I could make them unable to turn to face your approach. I might even be able to compromise some of the net-throwing bows, too."

"That's a lot for just one person to take on," I cautioned. "And if you get caught—"

"I'll go with him," Phillip blurted suddenly.

My mouth went dry.

Before I could even open my mouth to protest, Phillip flashed me a stern look of warning. "I hate to be the one to point out the obvious, love, but out of our group, I am most certainly the one least likely to be taken as a Maldobarian spy."

He was right. Deep in my gut, I knew that. He looked like the work of morbid Tibran engineering because, well, he was one. But that did not make it okay for him to go storming off to sacrifice himself like this. If they found out what he was doing, or even suspected he wasn't one of them … My stomach rolled just to think of it.

"There's more than enough Tibran armor lying around out in the marshes now for us to disguise ourselves. I think we can pull this off," Phillip continued, trying to assure me—as though I would ever be okay with this plan.

"How will you get into the city after it's done?" Haldor asked.

Phillip gave a snort, waggling his claw-tipped fingers. "I think I can climb it rather easily. If we snuff a few Tibran watchmen at the right moment, we should be able to get inside without anyone being the wiser. Providing, of course, you can convince the Maldobarian guards on the ramparts not to shoot us on sight."

It was risky—beyond risky. I didn't like it one bit. But as I studied the faces of my comrades, I could see the same bitter realization rising in their faces that settled over my own heart like a cold stone. We didn't have any other choice. This was our best and only shot.

"All right," I conceded. "Let's do it."

I didn't feel any better about our plan the following morning when we were sitting astride our dragons awaiting Jaevid's signal to take off. Roland insisted that what Judan had told us was true—apart from a few rogue Tibran scouting legions, the western Marshlands were clear and safe to fly. The small legions moving through the area were searching for better paths to bring the larger forces through, and as far as he'd seen, none of them were equipped to deal with a dragonrider assault. They likely wouldn't even fire upon us if they saw us fly over, for fear of giving away their position.

As for how Phillip and Aedan would infiltrate the Tibran forces ... I cringed to think of it. We were putting a lot of faith in that gray elf boy. I prayed he could manage it. We stood to lose a lot if he failed.

The tension must have been weighing on him because Aedan fidgeted and chewed on the inside of his cheek while Delphi gave him a gray elf warrior's blessing before we departed. It had been years since I had practiced the language. Kiran tried to teach us as little children, and I'd caught onto many common phrases—particularly ones like "apologize to your brother" or "don't eat that." But I couldn't even begin to translate what Delphi said to him as she pressed the heel of her hand to his forehead and said those solemn prayers.

With his face hidden beneath a bronze Tibran helmet, I had no way of knowing if her blessing made Aedan feel any better, or at least less nervous about what we were about to do. We wouldn't be able to get close enough to drop them off without running the risk of being spotted. We agreed it would be safer to do it under the cover of darkness, and we'd have gone that night, but the dragons needed rest. Our hope was to get within range of a good drop-off point the next day, wait until nightfall, and then get in as close as we could to deliver them.

So, for the rest of the night, we'd stayed with the refugees. We passed the time helping them set up another makeshift camp. We collected as much dried wood as we could find, set up little shelters of canvas and poles, and even offered up our bedrolls for the women and young children to sleep on so they didn't have to spend another night lying in the mud. It was the least we could do, really. After everyone had settled in, I sat close to Phillip and watched them—the mothers rocking and nursing their babies and the children quietly muttering to one another as they huddled close in their beds. I wished we could do more, but our own supplies were just as limited. The best thing we could do for everyone right now was reach Halfax, convince my father to attack Argonox, and end this war before it killed more innocent people.

Morning brought the relief of sunlight and warmth, and the hunters brought a few wild hares to make into stew to fill the hungry bellies around the camp. Phillip unnerved the refugees, especially the men. I could see it in their eyes when he strode past on his paw-like feet, with skin the color of slate and black tail swishing. They had every reason to be afraid, considering what they'd been through. But he did seem to win a bit of trust when he helped the hunters by smelling out game.

But now we had to leave them behind.

I shivered, not certain if it was from the cool morning air, the hunger wrenching in my stomach, or the fact that we were about to leave all these people defenseless. Sitting astride Phevos on the edge of the forest, we waited while Jaevid said his last farewells. He'd spent most of the night talking rather than sleeping—chatting and getting to know his extended family. Not that I blamed him. It was probably nice to know he wasn't quite as alone in the world as he must have felt sometimes. He still had relatives, people that weren't just adoring fans of his past heroics. Maybe, if everyone came out of this alive, he'd even have a place to go home to and start a real life.

That was my wish for him, anyway.

As he walked amidst the small camp of clustered refugees, Jaevid led a little girl of about three years old by the hand. He was carrying another squirming infant on his hip with the other, smiling like he'd found his bliss as he laughed with Roland. They must have been a few of his great-nieces and nephews. Even dressed in full armor—most of which was borrowed off dead Tibran soldiers—Jaevid made it seem effortless and natural having both children in tow. Parenthood suited him. It was the most joyful thing that had ever broken my heart to see. He was still so young, or at least he looked it; surely there was time for him to start a family of his own. But would he ever get over Beckah? Would he get to have children? Or had that hope died with her?

Handing the infant off to Roland, Jaevid gave his brother a parting embrace, and then knelt to do the same to the little girl. She squeezed him back and patted his cheeks with her tiny hands before he stood and backed away. His brow drew up, skewed with pain he couldn't disguise. His body stiffened, and there was fresh agony in his eyes as he turned away and went to climb into Mavrik's saddle. It tore at my chest like razors through flesh. He'd already said goodbye to his brother once. Gods, I hoped this ended differently than the last time.

Giving us all a signal, Jaevid and Haldor took off

first. Calem and I followed shortly after and fell into tight formation, moving at high speed less than a hundred feet off the ground. The idea was that if we remained below the tree line, we would avoid anyone spotting us from a distance while we scooted in to drop our boys as close as possible to the Tibran lines.

Hugging the border of the forest, we skirted around and turned north at the end of the Marshlands, dropping even lower than before. Jaevid dropped in first, since out of all of us, Mavrik was the largest and the most likely to be spotted from afar. There was roughly forty miles between the royal city and the edge of the forest. A long way on foot, but that was as close as our entire group could go.

We swept in for a speedy landing, and everyone dismounted to gather quickly to go over our plan one more time ... and to say our final farewells.

At nightfall, we had to be ready to move.

"As soon as everything is in place, find an open patch of earth and bury this," Jaevid instructed, pressing an acorn the size of a thumbnail into Aedan's hand. "I'll know it, and we will begin our approach. As soon as they see us coming, I'm sure it will cause a stir. Make sure you find a spot to wait out the chaos until nightfall. With any luck, there will be enough low cloud cover to hide us, but I'm not going to bet on that. It looks like it will be a clear night."

"Can't whip up a bit of cloud for us, demigod?" Phillip teased with a nervous chuckle.

Jaevid shrugged. "I'm afraid my particular brand of miracles is restricted to earthen and living things."

Phillip leaned against me, jostling my shoulder. "We

should complain. Maybe ask for a water or weather deity next time, eh?"

I couldn't join in the jest. My mind raced, searching for a good reason for me to be going in his place. Just the thought of the Tibrans having Phillip again made my insides feel like they were on fire. I couldn't handle it. I couldn't lose him again.

While everyone else confirmed our plan, I ground my jaw and dug the toe of my boot into the dirt. It should have been me. Phillip wasn't even a trained soldier. He'd never even used a blade in combat before Hilleddi tried to hack my head off. And even then, he'd barely been able to—

A warm, strong hand closed around mine. His voice spoke softly against my ear, "I'll be fine, love."

I couldn't look at him. It made my chest burn with pain, like someone was splitting it wide open. Pinching my eyes shut, I looked away. "Don't say that. Don't give me false hope."

Phillip grasped my jaw, turning my face and pressing his lips against mine. I sucked in a sharp breath through my nose. For a moment, my world stood still. Everything was quiet. The war was a distant annoyance. Nothing but the smooth, strong mouth moving against mine mattered at all.

Then he pulled away. My tranquility shattered. As I stood staring up at him, the evening sun made those tiny flecks on his soot-colored skin shine like scattered diamonds. The switchbeast venom had changed so much about him—but the way he looked at me, as though he were seeing the sunrise for the very first time, hadn't changed in the slightest. He still touched me like I was something fragile and stared at me with admiration and awe ebbing from every corner of his face.

"If it's not too much trouble, try and persuade those soldiers guarding the ramparts not to shoot the cat demon scaling their wall, would you?" He was still teasing as he combed his fingers through my hair, tucking a few stray locks behind my ear.

"I'll try." My voice broke, and I swallowed hard.

"I love you, Jenna."

"Don't," I warned. "Don't say that now."

"Why not?"

I turned my face into his hand, kissing his palm before I pushed it away. "Because it feels like goodbye, and this is *not* goodbye."

He laughed. "Very well. I find your presence easy to tolerate, Jenna. Perhaps even somewhat enjoyable. How's that? Better?"

Despite my best efforts, a smile broke over my lips. "That will do, Phillip."

Nightfall came too soon.

Phevos was the darkest patterned of our group, apart from Mavrik, who was too large and would be easily noticed. That meant I had to send both of the boys I loved dearly toward the city. It took no small amount of bribing and sweet-talking from me to convince Phevos to let Aedan and Phillip onto his back. Until that moment, I couldn't remember anyone else ever sitting in his saddle without me in it as well. It wasn't something I cared to commemorate, though—not when every fiber of my being screamed in protest at the sight of them zipping away into the twilight. Phevos flew so low, his wingtips brushed the earth with every flap. He was going as low as possible, making a stealthy approach and drawing no attention. His job, according to Jaevid's instructions, was to get them within range of the Tibran forces, drop them off, and immediately fall back to us. No triumphant roars. No bursts of flame.

We wouldn't know he had pulled it off without being captured until he returned.

Sitting back, my heart pounded until my ribs ached. I wrenched my sweaty hands in the hem of my tunic, squinting at the horizon as more stars winked into view. Jaevid had been correct—it was a clear night. The heavens were alight with countless glittering pinpricks, so bright and perfect it was like you might be able to reach out and touch them.

"I have eight nieces and nephews," Jaevid announced as he suddenly sat down beside me and rested his elbows on his knees. "I can't even remember all their names."

I sighed and let my eyes keep wandering over the night sky. "What about the little girl? The one who held your hand?"

I could hear the smile like a warmth in his voice. "Briella. She asked a lot of questions about dragons. I promised to let her pet Mavrik the next time we meet."

"You're well on your way to becoming her favorite uncle, then, I'd say."

"Hah! I do have a few advantages working for me in that regard, I guess."

"Legendary war hero? Dragonrider? Chosen one of a god? I'd say so." I stole a peek at his face out of the corner of my eye, surprised to find him looking at the sky as well. "I'm sorry you had to leave them behind."

He sighed. "That's the soldier's lot, isn't it?"

"I guess so."

"Forty years and it still feels the same. It never gets any easier, or less painful." He looked down and rubbed his brow with both hands, massaging his fingertips along his temples. "I can feel Reigh's power growing. Whatever is happening at Northwatch, it's getting worse. We may not have much time before Argonox moves to strike."

"Perhaps he means to try and do it before we can reach Halfax?"

Jaevid gave a somber nod. "That was my suspicion, too. But the fact that Reigh hasn't completed his ritual means his power can't be forced beyond a certain point—not without killing him. That may be the only thing holding him back and buying us time."

I hated to think of that boy, supposedly my younger brother, suffering. After what Argonox had done to Phillip, I could only imagine what he might be experimenting with now—let alone what condition Reigh would be in if we saw him again.

"Have you thought any about what you'll say to Felix when we arrive?" he asked.

I mashed my lips together, resisting a few choice profanities. "No," I muttered at last. "I doubt he'll leave me much room to talk, though. What about you?"

Jaevid's mouth flattened, as well. "No."

"Maybe open with a joke. I hear he used to like that sort of thing."

"True, although usually only when I was the punchline." I caught him stealing a glance at me, then a strange squint came to his eyes. "Did he ever tell you about the ballroom dancing incident from our avian year of training?"

"Um, no. I can't say he did."

His brows shot up. "Really? And here I thought that would have been his favorite one of all."

"Perhaps you should tell it, then," I coaxed.

"Not a chance. If I had my way, I'd take that one to my grave," he said with a grin. "Besides, it would probably be much better if he told it."

FIFTEEN

The *thump ... thump ... thump* of wing beats jarred me from a daze. I shot to my feet, scanning the horizon in search of any spot of movement. In the distance, I saw the faintest disturbance against the canopy of stars—a dark shape eclipsing them as it moved toward us. My pulse thrashed wildly, and every muscle drew tight.

Phevos had returned and his saddle was empty.

I ran to him as he touched down, cupping his strong wings, and stretching out his hind legs like an eagle catching a perch. He snapped his jaws, still sulking as I hugged the end of his snout. I got a blast of hot, musky dragon breath right in the face when I rubbed the scales behind his ears. He made low clicking sounds and nibbled at my ponytail—something he *knew* drove me nuts. His slobber would leave my hair crusty for days.

"Rude," I scolded as I gave his nose a swat.

His clicks and chirps softened, and he nuzzled against my shoulder, casting me a pleading, round-eyed stare with his little scaly ears drooping like withered leaves. Ugh. How could I stay angry at a face like that? Not fair.

"Are they all right? Did they make it?" I whirled around, looking to Jaevid—our resident animal mind reader—for answers.

Tilting his head to the side slightly, Jaevid's brow creased as he studied my dragon. Then he breathed a sigh of relief, shoulders relaxing as he nodded. "He was able to drop them off about five miles from the nearest Tibran encampment. No alarms sounded. It seems they have every chance of making it there as planned."

"Then it's up to Aedan now," Haldor murmured, crossing his arms. "Gods, I hope he can pull this off."

"As soon as they give the signal, we have to move. Keep in close, diamond formation, and make a straight break for the castle courtyard. Don't stop or move to engage—we're not there to burn anything. Not yet anyway. We'll stay as high as we can for as long as we can, but the sound of our approach will likely give us away as we descend for landing." Jaevid turned his gaze to me, his hand resting on the pommel of his scimitar. "Once we're inside, we can assume Argonox may strike at any time. He won't want to give us time to prepare for his assault, let alone confer with your father. We need to be ready to act quickly."

I nodded. "Putting aside family sentiments in lieu of duty is practically my middle name."

Calem studied me, his frown the picture of perfect

seriousness. "I thought your middle name was Evangeline?"

Haldor choked, suppressing a laugh.

There wasn't time to explain to Calem the finer points of sarcasm. Clearing his throat, Jaevid rubbed his palm along the pommel of his scimitar and shifted. He flicked me a quick look, brow tense, before he began to speak again. "While we have the time, we need to discuss what's going to happen once we reach the castle. Assuming Argonox will make his strike soon after, we may not have time go over this then."

My skin prickled, picking up on the note of reluctance in his tone. "Is this about Reigh?"

He nodded once. "Even with me fighting at your side, Reigh's destructive capability is ... extensive."

"That's putting it lightly," Haldor grunted. "We all saw what he did at Barrowton."

"If Argonox is manipulating his power, we don't know what we will be up against. I don't even know if I will be able to stop him. Our best chance will be ensuring Argonox does not find the crystal that would aid in completing Reigh's ritual." Jaevid paused, his lips thinning as he seemed to consider his next words carefully. "But I fear that might not be enough. If Roland is right, then even without Reigh, Argonox's forces have cut Halfax off from the rest of the kingdom. Meanwhile, he's destroyed every other dragonrider watch throughout Maldobar and left our forces scattered."

Heat rose in my chest, making my hands draw tightly into fists at my side. "So you're saying it's hopeless, even if we make to the city? We'd just be arriving to make a final, futile stand?" The words rolled out of me, each one sharp with anger.

Jaevid leveled a steely glare at me. "I'm saying that we are going to need *other* reinforcements if we are to win this."

"Other?" Haldor scoffed. "The gray elves don't have a military capable of making any considerable stand against—"

"I wasn't referring to them," Jaevid cut him off. "The kind of help required doesn't exist in this world. I must go into the Vale."

Dread dropped into my gut like a stone sinking in a pond. Gods and Fates, not that awful place again. "What could possibly help us there? I saw only spirits and ... " My voice died in my throat as the memory of Noh pricked at the back of my mind like a poisonous thorn.

"I don't know if I can explain it to you in simple mortal terms," he confessed, his forehead creasing with uncertainty. "If I am unable to stop Reigh's power, then the surest bet to undo it would be to ... call out the source of it. As you know, his power is bound to a deity, just as mine is. But bringing *her* here is very risky."

"Her?" Haldor repeated, his expression sharpening. One brow slowly raised as he tilted his head to the side ever so slightly. "Surely you are not talking about the dark goddess."

"Clysiros," Jaevid affirmed.

I instantly felt sick. We'd talked about her before while we were at Cernheist, but only briefly. I knew nothing about her apart from a few old songs I'd heard bards murmuring at court. Vague references, for the most part, to the one who spun death like a spider's silk and used the dark sins of men's hearts to lure them to a premature grave. Even though that might have been nonsense, it certainly didn't paint a wonderful picture in my mind of what kind of creature we might be inviting into our midst.

"Can you even do that?" Haldor questioned. "Bring a goddess into the mortal world?"

Jaevid shook his head. "I can't risk trying it now. Using my power will certainly draw Argonox's attention. It was enough of a gamble using it in the Marshlands but doing it this close to Halfax or even to help us reach the city might push him to launch his attack. And I cannot do it alone. On my own, I can't even reach Clysiros. But there is another who can. She's living in Luntharda, and I've already prepared her in case this became ... necessary."

"Who?" I demanded.

"Princess Hecate. She is what the elves called the Akrotis—she has the gift of valewhispering. It's extremely rare. I'm not sure it's happened in this millennium."

Wait, was he talking about the same girl Aubren was engaged to? The next in line to be Queen of Luntharda? It took me a moment to wrap my head around that. Gray elf bloodlines were always traced through the mothers, so powerful titles were primarily passed to daughters or granddaughters. Since Queen Araxie had only given birth to sons, she had chosen Hecate to be next in line to take the throne of Luntharda. Years ago, Hecate had been one of several granddaughters for Araxie to choose from. But one by one, all the elder cousins had all passed away. Now I had to wonder ... could that have had something to do with this divine gift?

Before I could ask, Jaevid continued, "Hecate can channel voices and even spirits from those who have passed on. She hears them just as clearly as we hear one another now." He gestured to the rest of us. "It's a complicated talent that has a tendency to overwhelm its user if they don't learn to harness it early. With Paligno's guidance, I gave her some instruction while we were in Luntharda. If she's been practicing, then she should be able to channel Clysiros's voice while we are in the Vale. That's how we will strike our bargain."

"Hecate can walk in the Vale, too?" I asked.

"Well, it's not that simple," he replied with a nervous chuckle. "Physically, no. You'd need Reigh's power to do that. But because of her talent, she won't need to be there physically."

Haldor sank back on his heels, letting out a heavy sigh that made his cheeks puff out. "This feels desperate," he mumbled. "And insanely dangerous."

"Because it is," Jaevid agreed.

I couldn't stop myself. The words tore out of me like an insult before I could check them. "And you honestly think you can negotiate a bargain with an evil goddess of death and convince her to fight for our cause? What's to stop her from just killing everything and everyone—us included?"

"I do have one bargaining chip when it comes to Clysiros." He held up his hand, waggling his fingers. "She needs me alive. Only my blood, given as a voluntarily offering, can complete the ritual that will solidify her bond with Reigh. In short, she needs something from me, and I need something from her. I'm hoping to arrange a trade."

"That's good for you, but it doesn't exactly do much for the rest of us," I fumed. "It doesn't mean she won't butcher the rest of us on a whim."

Jaevid flashed me a sudden, somewhat menacing smirk

that made me stop short. "Oh yes, it absolutely does. If she wants even a drop from me, then I'd better be satisfied with the terms—that includes Maldobar's survival, as well as yours."

"All this assuming you can even bring her here." Haldor was muttering under his breath and shaking his head as he turned away. He strolled back toward his dragon, snatching his helmet and riding gauntlets up on the way. Calem followed him silently, the wind catching through his platinum hair as he stared off into the distance. I couldn't tell if he was even listening to any of this or not.

I started to walk away, too. There wasn't much else to say. Jaevid's plan was insanity, and yet, we'd come to a point now where those kinds of solutions were our only viable options left. I didn't like it—but I didn't have a choice. It was this, or surrender.

Dragonriders did not surrender.

Suddenly, a flash of brilliant green light burst from the ground right in front of me. An explosion? A Tibran attack? I sprang back and threw up my arms to shield my face.

The dragons hissed and recoiled. Phevos sprang over, quick as a cat, and wrapped himself around me like a wall of guarding scales. His deep growl was like thunder in my ears. I had to shove one of his wings out of my way to see what was happening.

It was the seed—the one Jaevid had sent with Aedan and Phillip.

Hovering about three feet off the ground, the seed glowed like a tiny star, filling the air with its brilliant aura. Jaevid strode right toward it, purpose in every step. He stretched out a hand and plucked the seed from the air, carefully closing it tightly in his fist. The green light bled through the cracks between his fingers. It flashed brighter for several seconds before it finally went dark. When he opened his palm again, a fine white mist swirled into the air and vanished without a trace.

Jaevid looked up, fixing me with a hard stare. "They're ready."

"*Remember, do not engage, even if you take fire,*" Jaevid signaled as we tucked into a tight diamond formation around him. "*We need to get to the castle as fast as possible. Lingering will draw Argonox's attention. We don't want to set off a battle we aren't ready for.*"

As tempting as it was to roast every Tibran I saw purely out of spite, he did have a point. There was no way to anticipate how my father might react to seeing us. But I sort of doubted we would be getting off on the right foot if we instigated a final battle for Halfax without giving him any warning. Still, the idea of that scenario brought a sadistic grin to my lips. What could I even say? Maybe something like, "Hi again, Dad, I know you exiled me, but I thought I'd come back, bring your revived war-buddy-demigod-savior along, and start an all-out brawl for the last standing major city in the kingdom!"

Yeah. No way that would go over well. Not without someone getting the axe, anyway.

Dipping into formation off Jaevid's left wingtip, Phevos and I locked into our positions and poured on the speed. They would hear us coming before they saw us, but there was nothing we could do about the noise of our wing beats, after all. Even from a higher altitude, they would hear our approach from five miles out. But with any luck, we'd be moving too fast and the Tibran long-range weaponry, net throwing machines, trebuchets, and orb-hurtling catapults would be disabled—thanks to Aedan and Phillip.

Across from me, Haldor and his dragon moved in flawless synchronization. He leaned with the rippling motion of Turq's spine as the bluish-green beast pumped his powerful shoulders. Haldor's legs flexed in stabilizing bursts against the boot sheaths to keep his weight centered, and his hands gripped the saddle handles with his resin-palmed riding gauntlets fitted perfectly around all but two fingers—the two on his right hand he used for firing his bow. It was the perfect union of strength and precision.

In the rear of our formation, Calem and Perish flew a few feet above us so that we could give some added cover from any arrows that might be fired at us from below. Perish's hide wasn't as thick as most dragons. Her pearlescent white scales were smaller and more delicate. A well-aimed arrow might pierce it and bring her down. Normally, her speed would make her a difficult target for all but highly proficient archers. She was forced to keep pace with us this time, however, so we would be acting as her shield until we got to the castle.

I cut my gaze forward again, watching Mavrik's majestic

body gliding effortlessly through the air at the front of our formation. He was a massive creature compared to the rest of our dragons—more than twice Phevos's size. Once, he'd supposedly been the fastest dragon in all of Maldobar. But he'd grown into a size now that inevitably sacrificed some of that youthful speed. Still, he was no less impressive—or lethal. His eyes glowed like pools of molten gold, scanning the horizon with all his jagged black spines raised. The starlight glinted off his dark blue scales and each flap of his mighty wings sent a concussive boom through the air. Nothing compared to the magnificent, primal beauty of a king drake.

Ahead, the glint of a thousand lit torches caught my eye, taking a shape I knew all too well. My eyes stung and watered. My throat constricted. I bit down hard, trying to keep it all in. It had been over a year now since I'd even seen my home. As my gaze traced the grand keep, rising tall and proud at the crest of the city, I wondered if my room was still the way I'd left it. Or had Father cleaned it out when he exiled me? I hoped not. I hadn't taken Mother's letters with me when I left. Those notes were all I had left of her. If they were lost …

I shut my eyes tightly and sucked in a ragged breath. Now wasn't the time. I had to pull myself together. I could *not* be the wretched little princess who came sobbing back to her father's feet. I'd die first.

As we descended for our final approach, I finally saw them. Tibrans—more legions than I could count—surrounded my city and loomed on the northern horizon like a rising black tide. Their camps dotted the lower hills by the hundreds. The shapes of their towering war machines were easy to pick out under the wash of sterling moonlight. They almost had the city of Halfax completely surrounded. But as Roland had promised, their westward ranks were thinner. Not being able to push more of their forces up from the south and over from the west might have been the only thing still staying Argonox's hand. He didn't seem like the type of man to want to risk everything not going according to his carefully-devised plan.

Phevos snapped his jaws, body thrumming with a growl as we zipped toward the city. No sooner had we come into range then arrows began zipping past my helmet and glancing off Phevos's hide. He snarled and bared his jagged teeth, ears pinned back in anger. Mavrik did the same and, with a few angled flaps of his black wings, dropped lower to act as a living shield for the rest of us to finish our approach. Shouts and horns blared. I caught a glimpse of Tibrans scrambling, panicking as they clamored over their failing artillery devices. Relief poured over my body like cool rain—Aedan and Phillip had done it!

In their panic, the Tibrans were clumsy. Their archers kept firing, but nothing hit its mark. The only trebuchet they were able to angle toward us in time was too far away. The massive boulder hurtled through the air and landed more than two hundred yards short, crunching through a few ranks of their own men before it stopped.

Haldor let out a shout, hefting his bow in the air. I ducked back down again against Phevos's neck, unable to keep from smirking. The coming battle might not be so bad if the Tibrans kept up that sort of nonsense.

As we crossed over the high ramparts of Halfax's outermost wall, hundreds of Maldobarian soldiers poured out of the guard towers and clamored along the battlements. They whooped, waved their arms, and beat their swords against their shields in celebration. In the distance, I heard the battle horn sound, announcing our arrival to everyone in the city. By the time we circled for our final landing in the forward courtyard of the castle, bells were tolling in every corner of Halfax.

Jaevid let the rest of us land and dismount first. I hurried to unbuckle myself from Phevos's saddle and gave one of his ears a gentle tug, urging him to make room. Then, Haldor, Calem, and I stood back to make way for the king drake's arrival.

My father's elite guard, dressed in full armor with the eagle emblazoned on their breastplates and their faces covered by golden masks, gathered around us. They stood at attention, raising torches against the moonlight, and watched as the enormous blue drake descended with a *boom*. Mavrik rose up, long tail curling as he spread his wings and let out a shattering cry. My heartbeat surged and part of me prayed that, wherever he was hiding amongst his vile ranks, Argonox could hear it and would know what was coming. Jaevid Broadfeather had arrived at last, bringing hope and vengeance with him. There wasn't a soldier in Maldobar who wouldn't hear his call to arms and not a single dragonrider who would not rise up now to join him.

Argonox could still prove victorious at the end of all this—I knew that. He might still add Maldobar to his empire and butcher us all down to the very last child. But he would not take my home unfought. He would have to pry it from my cold, dead hands.

SIXTEEN

The instant Jaevid's boots hit the ground in the castle's grand front courtyard, one of my father's elite guards stepped away from the crowd and approached him. Through the visor of my helmet, I glanced at Haldor. His hand was clenched around his bow as he gave me a nod. This was it—the moment of truth. Would we be received as a long-awaited cavalry, or as unwelcomed vigilantes?

The guardsman offered Jaevid a deep bow and motioned to the grand arched doorway at the far end of the courtyard. "His Majesty King Felix Farrow welcomes you. Please follow me."

My shoulders sagged in relief. At least it seemed like we weren't going to be arrested right away. So far, so good.

Jaevid led the way toward the doorway, the guards falling into formation around us so that we were flanked on all sides like a parade march. Only a couple of them stayed behind, most likely to guide our dragons down into the catacombs for the night. No doubt the castle's usual dragon housing, a circular structure we called the Deck, was already at capacity with so many dragonriders called here. My desire to be anywhere other than under my father's disappointed glare was not a recent feeling, and I'd spent a lot of time at the Deck as a child, secretly tucked up alongside the snoozing dragons.

But our dragons wouldn't get to enjoy those cozy chambers. There wouldn't be room. Not that the catacombs under the castle would be terrible. I was certain my father would make sure the dragons housed down there would have every comfort. They'd get a fresh meal of raw meat, and a bed of soft hay to curl up on to sleep off the weariness of our journey. Master Godfrey had been the stablemaster in charge of looking after our horses and dragons for as long as I could remember. He ran a tight ship, and our mounts never wanted for anything.

We had almost reached the massive set of double doors leading into the castle. Every step made my heart race faster until it clashed in my ears and made my fingertips go numb. I clenched my teeth to stop them from chattering. Nearly a year's time hadn't changed this place at all—although it had changed me plenty. Too late, I realized I wasn't ready for this. I wanted to run, bolt back to Phevos, and make a break for ... anywhere else.

Suddenly, the doors before us rumbled and opened wide, groaning on their iron-wrought hinges.

Jaevid stopped. The rest of us did, too.

Felix Farrow, my father and the current King of Maldobar,

came striding out into the courtyard with a flock of men in armor following close at his heels. Most of them I knew, or at least recognized the distinction of their armor. They were men of the court—High Commander Morrig, Infantry General Craig, Duke Brinton and his son, and Vaelin, who had taken over Kiran's office and now represented Luntharda as a royal ambassador.

In fact, my father was the only one not wearing his full court armor. Dressed in a simple tunic, pants, and leather jerkin underneath a black bear hide cloak, the only thing that marked him as king was the simple golden circlet nestled on his head. Even that was one of the simplest, most lackluster crowns he owned. Not that he'd ever been all that fond of courtly clothes, but we'd clearly caught him off guard.

When he saw us, my father stopped short. His light brown eyes fixed on Jaevid and went wide, white brows lifting slowly. Gods, the months had aged him. His face was creased, somber eyes now hooded, and more of his dark golden hair had turned silver. It hung to his shoulders in gentle waves, so gray now it nearly matched his neatly trimmed white beard.

My stomach fluttered as he took another step. His lips parted, and his eyes narrowed as he came closer and closer, stopping only when he was a few feet away from Jaevid. "You," my father murmured quietly, his deep voice thick with emotion. Was it anger? Sorrow? Gods, I couldn't tell.

Jaevid was motionless, standing with his entire body rigid. His fists clenched at his sides and his brow skewed into an expression of withheld panic, our resident demigod didn't say a word. He didn't even blink.

I held my breath. My mind raced, and it felt as though

my heart might have stopped beating altogether.

"Forty years." My father's face twitched, scrunching violently. He squeezed his eyes shut and looked down, expression contorting and chest heaving deeply. "And now you come back."

"Felix," Jaevid rasped as he took a stumbling step forward, "I ... Gods, I am so sorry. Please, I-I ... I couldn't do anything to—"

The King of Maldobar sprang forward faster than I'd ever seen him move before. He seized Jaevid in his arms and nearly snatched the poor man right out of his boots.

Jaevid winced, going as stiff as a dried-out corpse in my father's grip at first. His eyes were as round as moons and his whole face blanched. Then, he suddenly seemed to process what was happening. His expression crumpled, and he hugged King Felix back fiercely.

My father's tearful, barking laughter echoed through the courtyard as the two men gripped one another. I swallowed against the hard knot of emotion forming in the back of my throat and was thankful to still have my helmet on so no one could see the tears welling in my eyes. I couldn't remember the last time I had heard my father laugh like that. It must have been before Mother died, years ago.

"I guess this means it really is the end of the world." My father pulled back, shaking Jaevid by the shoulders a little. "Wait—I'm forgetting something, I think." He scratched at the white beard on his chin and pursed his lips. Then, without warning, he reared back and punched Jaevid in the arm.

"Gods, Felix!" Jaevid staggered back, hissing curses under his breath as he rubbed his bicep. "Seriously?"

My father wore a cattish grin. "You have *no idea* how long I've wanted to do that."

"I'd wager about four decades or so," Haldor murmured as he slid off his helmet and slipped it under his arm. "If we're placing bets, that is."

"Hah!" My father barked another chuckle before he realized who had spoken. As soon as he spotted Haldor, his expression hardened. His brown eyes went as cold as steel and darted through the crowd gathered around him as though he were searching for someone.

Oh no.

I took a quick, careful step and dodged behind one of the elite guards.

"Wait." I could hear rising anger in my father's tone. "Do *not* tell me you came here without my daughter. Jaevid, I love you like a brother, but if you have come here to tell me she fell in battle or was taken by the Tibrans on your watch, so help me, I will—"

"Felix," Jaevid interrupted his rant.

I chanced a quick look around the guard's arm, just in time to see him point right at me. My father turned, following the line of his finger until he spotted me.

Curse it. I shouldn't have looked. Why did I have to look?

Paralyzed with fear, I swallowed over and over against the growing pain in my throat. I cringed underneath my armor and kept my gaze locked on the ground as heavy footsteps crunched across the gravel toward me. The elite guardsman stepped lightly out of the way, making way for the king, who now stood before me. I didn't want to see his face. I couldn't take that look of wrath and utter disappointment—not again.

I couldn't stop trembling as he grasped the sides of my helmet, and slowly pulled it off my head. My long hair spilled out, bolts of dark gold falling across my chest and over my shoulders. Then a warm hand touched my chin, gently bringing it up so I had to look at him.

"Jenna." There were fresh tears in my father's eyes. I saw none of the anger I'd been expecting. Only relief, joy, and … love.

I tried to speak, but only managed to choke on a sob.

Fates, I wasn't supposed to cry. Not in front of all these men! But the more I tried to hold it in, the more the pain wrenched and tore at my heart until I had no choice. All I had ever wanted was his approval. His exciting stories of danger and adventure, his legacy in the Gray War—those things had been what lit this fire in my soul in the first place. I wanted to be like that, to walk in his footsteps, and lead our kingdom further into greatness.

Having him reject all my efforts was unbearable … because, more than anything, I wanted to make him proud.

"Come here," he cooed gently as he reeled me in closer. He kissed my forehead and held me as though I were a little girl again. "Welcome home, love."

"Let me see if I have this right, because this is sounding suspiciously like one of your suicidal, save-the-world plans."

King Felix leaned forward, resting his hands on the broad mapping table. "You want to go into the Vale and broker a deal with the goddess of death, all in the hope that she will honor that bargain and fight for us in the event your power isn't strong enough to stand against whatever Argonox brings onto the battlefield? That about the size of it?"

Jaevid crossed his arms. "Well, of course I'm open to suggestions."

"Oh, and let's not forget about the part where you allowed my youngest child—who I intentionally placed in the deepest, darkest corner of Luntharda where this very thing would *never* happen to him—to fall into the enemy's hands." He shook his head, rolling his eyes as he pushed away from the table to drop into his kingly chair. "Just like old times. Only now we're gambling with the lives of my children instead of just our own. Gods, I should have hit you harder. Or in the face. Maybe both."

"I am sorry about that," Jaevid confessed. "Reigh is as stubborn as any Farrow I've ever met. He wasn't going to leave without Aubren, and I wasn't about to try to convince him to leave his brother behind. There wasn't any other option."

"Of course, there was! You knock him unconscious and drag him out by the ankles," my father grumbled. "When he was born with that ... darkness in him, I knew there was no way he could ever live in Maldobar. You'd promised to return when we needed you again, and to me, that meant something was coming that would require your presence to fix. I didn't want to put any of my children in that kind of danger—least of all him. If his power turned out to be anything like yours, I worried what war might do to him."

"So you sent him away?" I heard myself ask. Shock left my skin feeling cold and tingly as I watched the realization slowly seep into my father's face. He'd just confessed! Reigh *was* his child—and he was my little brother.

"I gave him to the only man I knew I could trust to keep him safe," he confirmed, dropping his head into one of his hands. "Kiran promised to take Reigh deep into Luntharda and keep him there for as long as possible. He also knew how vital it would be for Reigh's existence to a secret kept from everyone. I couldn't allow anyone to try to abuse him for what he could do or twist him into something he wasn't meant to be." He rubbed his fingers along his forehead and sighed. "Reigh wasn't just born a prince, he was hand-chosen by a goddess. Taking that kind of power and using it in malice nearly destroyed our world once. I couldn't let that happen again. I didn't believe he'd ever be safe here."

"You mean the God Bane?" Haldor asked.

My father looked up and nodded. "Our culture has all but made him into a myth. They like to toss it around at the Dragonrider Academy like it's something to boast about, another great notch in the belt of our military. But after the Gray War ended, I was able to track down enough records of God Bane's existence to paint a good picture of what we might be up against if that threat should ever rise again. What I found was ... horrifying."

"We defeated him once, Your Majesty. We can do it again." High Commander Morrig stood on the opposite side of the war table, his sharp gaze still perusing the map of our kingdom laid out on the table.

My father glanced up, blinking in surprise as though he'd

forgotten he had a room full of nobles and military officials all awaiting his decision on what to do next. With another great sigh, he waved a hand and sank back deeper into his chair. "Let's call this meeting adjourned for now, gentlemen. You all have plenty to keep you busy. In the meantime, I'd like some time alone with Jaevid and my daughter. Family business—you understand."

The High Commander gave a dragonrider salute. "Of course, Your Majesty. I'll escort Lieutenants Calem and Haldor to the barracks and have them properly outfitted immediately. We will be battle-ready and ready to mobilize on your orders."

"And I'll see that my boys on watch don't shoot your … cat monster and his gray elf friend when they climb over the wall," the Infantry General added with a grin. "If that elf boy is as useful as you say, he might have a lot of vital information on our enemy's positions outside the wall."

I managed a cursory smile as the general turned to depart. I'd intentionally left out the part where the "cat monster" was actually Duke Phillip Derrick. Somehow, that seemed like one of those things they would have to see to believe. That, and I wasn't sure if Phillip would want them to know. Of course, my father would recognize him eventually—his demeanor and inflections were the same, after all. But if Phillip didn't want his condition proclaimed to every corner of Maldobar, then I'd respect that. It was his choice to make.

"Well, then. I suppose I owe you some gratitude. You saved my eldest two, after all. Returned one to me, even." King Felix pushed himself back up with a groan, stretching his neck from one side to the other before he waved for us to follow. "I've got something for you, Jae."

Jaevid flicked me an uncertain glance, as though silently asking me what this was about. Why? It wasn't like I had any special insight into their ancient friendship.

All I could do was shrug.

My father led the way from the mapping room deeper into the castle, a place I knew all too well. The fact that it hadn't changed much since I left made my heart ache for my private quarters and everything familiar I'd been missing. My bed. My clothes. The letters from my mother that I kept tucked into the drawer in my night table.

Mother must have known her pregnancy with Reigh would be too much for her to survive because she had taken the time to write me letters, arranging for them to be delivered one-by-one much later—after she was gone. I'd received one every week while I was at the academy for training. They told stories of my childhood, things she remembered and adored about me, reminded me of how much she loved my brother and me, and declared how proud she was of me. I hadn't taken those notes with me when I left, too afraid of being forced to leave them behind in the burning ruins of some battlefield. They were my most precious treasures. I couldn't bear to lose them like that.

The royal wing of the castle was off limits to anyone apart from direct family members and extremely special guests. Jaevid qualified as both, since my father had formally adopted him into our family years ago. There was even legal documentation to prove it. On paper, Jaevid was a Farrow, not a Broadfeather, although I didn't know that he'd ever used our family name. It would have certainly turned some heads.

Passing through the gilded doors flanked by more elite

guards, we entered the grand foyer that boasted two elegant sloping staircases leading off in either direction. The bannisters were carved so that each one looked like a man with a sword clutched at his breast. The newel posts were engraved in the shapes of dragons raising up on their hind legs, leering down to the center of the room, where a broad blue velvet carpet covered most of the white marble floor. Overhead, an iron-wrought chandelier held three hundred lit candles that filled the room and shone off the polished mahogany walls.

To the right, my room quarters were up the stairs and down the hall—directly across from Aubren's. To the left was where my mother and father had lived in the most luxurious part of the castle. I wasn't sure if my father had slept there in years, though. At least, not after Mother passed away.

"Is that supposed to be me?" Jaevid asked suddenly, his head tilted to the side as he studied the enormous embroidered tapestry hanging on the back wall—right between where the two staircases met. It was thirty feet long at least, spanning from the ceiling all the way to the floor with an intricate design of a dragonrider seated on a snarling mount, driving the point of his scimitar at a skeletal-looking monster.

I blushed. Countless hours of my childhood had been spent sitting before that tapestry, admiring every detail of the rider's armor, his handsomely shaped features, fluttering blue cape, and compelling gaze. It was like a glimpse from a fairy tale, the glorious hero throwing down the villain in an epic battle—essentially everything an imaginative princess might dream of.

Jaevid stopped short and snapped a puzzled scowl at my father. "You hung a picture of *me* on your wall?"

"Well, if you remember, you essentially reduced this castle to rubble at the end of the war. I had to come up with some new décor. You were a popular topic of conversation at the time," King Felix wafted a hand dismissively.

"And you couldn't come up with anything else to put there? It had to be me?" Jaevid rolled his eyes. "Fates preserve us. That doesn't even look like me!"

I covered my mouth and bit down, trying not to laugh. I wondered what he'd think about being featured in every town square's fountain sculpture, as well. To be fair, he was right. The images didn't look like him all that much. They made him seem far bigger, brawnier, and older than he was.

Jaevid rubbed his brow and grumbled under his breath, "Jace hasn't seen this, has he?"

"Uhhh, well ... " My father shifted and cleared his throat.

"Great. Just great." Jaevid shot him another venomous glare as he turned away. "That thing is ridiculous, and so are you for hanging it." He thumbed back at the tapestry.

There was a glint of mischief sparkling in my father's dark eyes as he passed by, leading the way up the left staircase toward his private chambers. "*Pfft*, just wait till you see the one hanging in the throne room."

"*WHAT?*"

SEVENTEEN

J aevid was still muttering like a madman when we entered my father's private study. Three entire walls of the large space were covered completely by bookshelves, crammed tight with tomes, scrolls, and ancient texts. The third was an entire wall of windows made of intricately-cut colored glass that formed the shape of Maldobar's royal seal—a golden eagle against a field of blue, gripping swords in its claws. Along the edges, green vines with vibrant red roses twisted around a golden border. It filled what would have been an otherwise dank space with radiant shafts of colored light whenever the sun struck it.

On a large, claw-footed desk right in the center of the room, papers and books were stacked around piles of parchment, and a golden inkpot held a crisp silver feather. My father wasted no time diving into the middle drawer, raking things around until he pulled out a thin wooden box. It didn't look all that special—plain and dusty, like it had been tucked away there for a long time.

Without a word, he handed it to Jaevid.

I stepped in closer, peering over his shoulder as he opened it. For a few seconds, Jaevid didn't make a sound. He didn't move. He stared down into the box with his expression blank. Then, with a trembling hand, he reached in and took out two trinkets. The first was a necklace strung on a woven cord. The teardrop-shaped pendant seemed to have been carved from bone and polished smooth before intricate, tiny elven engravings were added. The second was a very old, ragged handkerchief. By the look of it, it had seen a lot of use. Parts of it were stained with what looked like spots of blood. The edges were torn and tattered. But in the very center, stitched in blue and black thread, were the images of two dragons. They faced one another, their tails intertwined, and necks arched so that the negative space made the shape of a heart.

That was a woman's token—something usually given to a loved one before battle.

Jaevid sucked in a breath, his brow furrowing as he ran his thumb across the stitching. Pain crept into the corners of his features like an encroaching stormfront, darkening his gaze and making his mouth go tense. He was breathing heavily through his nose when he looked back up at my father.

"You know she's back," he seethed quietly, the words hissing through his teeth.

King Felix shook his head. "No. Whatever you saw was not her, Jaevid. Maybe it looked like her. Maybe it even sounded like her. But the Beckah we knew—the one you loved—would not turn against us. She would die before she joined with someone like Argonox. You know that as well as I do."

Jaevid lowered his gaze again, saying nothing as he closed his hand around the handkerchief.

My father stepped toward him and planted a hand on his shoulder to give it a firm squeeze. "He'll pay for it, Jae. Make no mistake. You and I are going to make him pay for every person he's hurt and every life he's taken. He came here looking for a fight—and by all the gods, we will give him one he'll never forget."

Servants brought us a light meal as we sat together in the lounge area of my father's chambers. As the crown princess, now returned to her home, I should have eaten with delicate restraint and poise while seated properly on one of the elegant, tufted chairs. Hah! As if I had patience for that after what I'd been through over the past few weeks.

I still reeked of swamp mud from the Marshlands and my hair was in a thousand knots as I stormed the table of delicacies like a barbarian. Heaping cheese-stuffed pastries, herb roasted lamb and potatoes, and a handful of my favorite candied figs on to a porcelain plate, I plopped down on the sofa and stuffed my face as fast as I could. It had been days since I'd had more than a handful of dried meat or nuts from riding rations. I couldn't remember food ever tasting so good.

I felt a little less self-conscious about it when Jaevid did the same, taking up a seat on the couch beside me. Part of me had to wonder if that was intentional, like he might be trying to ease the tension in the room. He snuck a quick glance in my direction, smiling around a cheek full of cheesy pastry goodness.

Okay, fine, so the demigod war hero was growing on me a bit. I respected him, yes. How could I not? But I also sort of ... liked him now. Not like *that*, of course. But Jaevid was steadily becoming less of the legendary figure and childhood hero I'd aspired to be like and more of a genuine friend. I understood now why my father had gotten along with him so well.

"So, Aubren has gone to Luntharda." My father exhaled deeply as he passed by all the bottles of imported wines and rich meads to pour himself a goblet of spiced apple cider. I didn't know why, but he never drank alcohol. "I suppose it's the best place for him now. Ever since he was a boy, he's always been softer and more like his mother. That strong empathy sometimes rules his head too much. I worried what war would do to him. Nothing is worse than watching the world crush your children's innocence like that, knowing there's nothing you can do to stop it. Now he's a man and I can't protect him like that anymore." The sofa lurched as he sat down on Jaevid's other side. "He's always seemed to be searching for something—himself, or meaning, or a cause, I don't know. Whatever it is, perhaps now he'll find it."

"I think we all do some of that, in our own way," Jaevid agreed. "Searching for our purpose, that is."

My father chuckled between sips of cider. "Yeah. And we generally start looking for it in all the wrong places."

The roaring of flames in the hearth filled the silence as we sat and ate. I couldn't stop thinking about Aubren as I chewed. Had he and the other refugees made it to Luntharda with Judan? Were they safe now? Trapped here in the city, with more and more Tibrans surrounding us every minute, there was no way to know.

"I'm sorry, Felix," Jaevid blurted suddenly. "I should have been here when Julianna died."

My father leaned forward with a groan, putting his empty cup onto the coffee table and letting his elbows rest on his knees. The light of the fire danced in his eyes, reflecting sparks of memory that made the wrinkles in his skin seem to deepen. "I don't blame you for her death, Jae. It wouldn't have mattered if you had been here. Her fate was my fault, not yours. Nothing you could have done would have saved her from it."

Jaevid frowned. "What do you mean?"

His lips thinned as his gaze fell to his right hand, where an old scar made a gnarled line right across his palm. "It happened here, during our battle in the throne room. You went off dealing with bigger issues, and I was … being me. Reckless. Stupid. Anything to win." My father's eyes closed as his fingers curled in, making a fist around that scar. "I cut my hand on that black crystal, not knowing what it was. From that moment, Julianna and Reigh's fates were sealed— because of a dumb accident. There was nothing anyone could do to reverse it, not even you. I'd given the dark goddess a blood offering and I didn't even know it until years later."

I sat up straighter, forgetting about my mostly-empty plate of food. "You knew about the starium crystal? You've known all this time? And said nothing?"

My father nodded grimly. "After Reigh's birth, it was obvious he was going to be … *different*. I'd been around Jaevid's brand of bizarre long enough to know divine power when I saw it. My only hope was that someone had left behind texts or at least documented stories about whatever was afflicting Reigh. But until I found them, I knew he could not stay here. Most of the royal archives were destroyed during the Gray War, so it took years to track them down. When I finally did, I prayed they were wrong or just making wild guesses."

"To be the Harbinger of Clysiros is a costly blessing," Jaevid muttered, his voice hardly more than a whisper.

My father gave a snort, like that was a bad joke. "Some might call it more of a curse. In fact, most of these divine gifts seem to be double-edged swords. But in Reigh's case, because of my dumb accident, he is now a part of the legacy of the most hated figure in Maldobar's history—the God Bane."

"It wasn't your fault, Felix. You didn't know. Neither of us did. How could we?" Jaevid put a hand on his shoulder.

"What does that even mean? Who was God Bane?" I had to stop and take a breath. My heart was pounding so hard it was making my eardrums sore. "I mean, we all heard the stories about the old war, about how the dragonriders were forged in the flames of that battle against God Bane, but who *was* he?"

There was a harrowing sense of hopelessness in my father's eyes as he gazed back at me. The light from the hearth cast heavy shadows, making his cheeks seem thinner, raw-boned, and deepening the puffy circles that hung under his eyes. "He was Clysiros's last Harbinger."

Panic turned my body cold. I stole a glance at Jaevid, hoping for some reassurance, but he seemed just as stunned as I was. His expression tightened, and his jaw went rigid as we sat waiting for my father to continue.

"None of the documents I found could trace his origin, only his path of destruction after his ritual with the crystal had been completed. An initial offering of blood triggers it, but the goddess chooses her Harbinger from that person's bloodline, not necessarily the one who gave it. That's why you and Aubren were spared." My father reached over, around Jaevid, and settled one of his heavy, leathery hands on my arm. "A life must also be given to bring the Harbinger into the world, because he must be able to walk here and in the realm of spirits. Two souls, one body, one shared mind. Reigh's twin was the one who paid that price."

"Twin?" I gasped.

His gaze swung back, fixing on the hearth before us once more. "Julianna—your mother—was so fragile during that pregnancy. We assumed it was because of her age. Carrying twins is difficult enough on its own, but for one of them to be the Harbinger was too much. As soon as Reigh was born, he cried out like he was in agony. He … consumed the soul of his brother. It happened so quickly. There was nothing we could do. He'd taken his first victim and his first breath simultaneously." My father closed his eyes and bowed his head. "I was horrified. I couldn't even bear to touch him. But it was my fault, not his. I made him into this."

All the tension in Jaevid's face dissolved, gradually falling back into a look of shared sorrow. He shook his head and looked away with a heavy exhale.

"What's he like?" Father's voice was quiet, barely audible above the crackle of the flames. They danced in his eyes, reflections of some memory that seemed to carry him far away.

"Who?" I asked.

"Reigh." He stirred in his seat, brow furrowing in an uncomfortable frown. "What does he look like? Does he seem … happy?"

I wasn't sure what to say. I'd only been around Reigh for a short time at Barrowton, and during that time I hadn't known he might be my brother. Aubren had only told me a little about him then.

"Happy and twice the fighter you ever were. He had a good life in Luntharda. Kiran raised him well." Jaevid assured him. "He's got Julianna's hair. It might even be redder than hers, if you can believe it. But he's got your eyes and—I'm sorry to say—your sense of humor."

My father gave a snort and a bemused half-grin.

"He's got the Farrow stubborn streak, for sure," I added. "He was chosen by a dragon."

Father's eyes went wide. "A wild one?"

I couldn't resist a proud smile. "One of Mavrik's hatchlings. She's as green as a tree snake and so beautiful. He named her Vexi."

There was regal pride in the way he sat up straighter, squaring his shoulders. "What did Kiran say to that? Shocked, I bet!" he asked with a laugh.

Oh, gods. He didn't know. Stealing a quick look at Jaevid, I took in a steadying breath. "Father, Kiran is gone."

His smile began to fade, draining away little by little until only a pale, hollow-eyed expression of shock remained. "What?"

"He fell at Barrowton. H-he fought well, but … " I struggled to keep my voice steady, but the words were poison. Cringing, I turned away.

"He did not suffer," Jaevid finished for me. "And he died bravely."

My father's proud stature shrank again, seeming to wither away right before my eyes. "He was a good man, one of the best I've ever known. I hope the Gods give him rest."

"He found peace in paradise," Jaevid confirmed. "Now it is our duty to make sure that his sacrifice was not in vain."

King Felix lowered his head, as though the weight of a kingdom and the lives of thousands of people were resting on his brow.

Jaevid didn't give him a moment to dwell, though. "What else have you learned about God Bane?"

"He came here with the exact intentions of Argonox— to enslave not just every person in this world, but also all the gods. Hence the name," my father replied. "Owning the mortal world was not enough. He hungered to rule the divine one, as well. He'd spent decades scouring the earth for every trace of godly power he could, and amassed plenty. He came for Paligno's god stone but knew he would have to get through Maldobar to claim it. But we had one thing God Bane didn't."

"Dragons," I breathed, recalling the story the instructors

told every new class of dragonriders when we began a new year of training at the academy.

"They are completely unique to our kingdom, apparently," my father confirmed. "They don't exist anywhere else in the world. God Bane had never seen anything like them. And they were the last thing he ever saw, as it turns out. Dragons chose human soldiers as their riders for the very first time on that battlefield. Then, as one, they tore down God Bane's ranks and sent what was left of his forces scurrying back to the shadows."

"And now they've returned," Jaevid concluded as he rubbed the back of his neck.

"I honestly don't know if Argonox is the same man as God Bane. All accounts say that man was killed. But he was a fully manifested Harbinger, able to bend the laws of death. Who's to say he isn't the same person, now stripped of his own divine power?" Father patted my arm and sat back again. "At last I had to face the reality that it doesn't matter who Argonox is—his vendetta is the same. He wants to control every source of divine power he can get his scheming hands on and I have what is quite possibly the most powerful artifact of them all. I had to do anything and everything to make sure he never got it. I can't allow him to set foot in this castle, no matter what the cost."

"So that's why you recalled all the dragonriders here," Jaevid guessed as he stood, putting his plate aside so he could pace and rub his chin thoughtfully.

"Naturally," he replied. "And I couldn't tell anyone else about it, not even the people I loved most of all. Tibran forces had already begun taking prisoners along our borders.

The only advantages I had were dragonriders and the fact that Argonox didn't know the crystal's location. Based on the number of Tibran soldiers rallying outside my gates, I'd say that last one is forfeit now."

"You could have told me all of this," I scolded as I reached over Jaevid's empty seat and gripped my father's hand. "You should have trusted me. I would have understood—I would have stayed! But you exiled me like a heretic! I thought you hated me for choosing this path!"

His brows rumpled and drew up in a smile that made my heart wrench like someone was tearing it in two. "My sweet, brave girl, there is nothing you could ever do that would make me stop loving you. That's the hardest part of being a parent; realizing that your hopes for your children's futures, everything you ever wanted for them, are not within your control or right to decide."

Tears stung my eyes. I had to look away. "Well, it is *your* fault. You made me this way. All you ever talked about was the glory days and what it was like to ride on a dragon."

My father laughed loudly and gave one of my cheeks a pinch. "Oh, is that what you think? I beg to differ. You'd have heard those stories with or without my help. You can't throw a cat in this kingdom without hitting a statue of this idiot." He tipped his head toward Jaevid, who now stood staring at him with a red-faced look of horror.

"Statues?" Jaevid growled. "There are *statues*, too?"

My father ignored him, his eyes still fixed on me. "You are a dragonrider because you were chosen, not because of anything I did. That beast saw something in you, something worthy of his eternal loyalty. So don't you dare try passing credit for that off to me, understood? I may not have liked it, but only because the idea of losing yet another one of my children to a power I can't control is … infuriating, to say the least. Regardless, embrace it, be proud of it, and never apologize for it. My daughter is a dragonrider, and I couldn't be prouder."

Heat exploded through my chest in a burst that left me breathless. It was as though all the strangling chains of shame that had held me captive my entire life snapped at once. I hadn't chosen to be the polite, dainty princess he wanted. But he was still proud of me. He still loved me.

I couldn't stop the tears. They welled up, rolled down my face, and dripped from my chin. I hid my face in my hands, too embarrassed to even look at him.

Then I felt his arms around me.

I hugged him back, burying my face against his shoulder as he petted the back of my head. "Sending you away from here was the hardest decision I've ever made, Jenna," he whispered gently. "But it was all I knew to do. I couldn't stop you from fighting, but if the hammer was destined to fall here and Argonox overwhelmed this place, I didn't want you anywhere near it."

"Gods, you're so stupid for such an old man." I sniffled.

"No argument there," Jaevid muttered. Peeking over my father's shoulder, I found him standing with his arms crossed, brow locked into a deep, bitter scowl, and lips pursed angrily. "Did you really build statues?" he demanded.

"Oh yes," Father snickered. "*Hundreds* of them."

EIGHTEEN

Phillip and Aedan's arrival had the castle buzzing before noon. The servants dashed about, filling the hall with anxious whispers and jittery energy as everyone gathered in the great hall to receive them. Meanwhile, the elite royal guards watched Phillip closely through the eyeholes in their golden masks, hands always hovering somewhere near their weaponry. It was clear they didn't like the look of him, not that I could blame them. He towered over everyone, a monstrous mixture of man and beast with skin the color of stone, paw-like hind feet, glowing silver eyes, and a long flicking tail. His powerful build tested all the seams of his clothes, and the claws on his feet clicked against the marble as he strode into the great hall.

Beside him, Aedan was half his height with only a little bit of short white fuzz beginning to grow back in on his shaven head. His pointed ears and multihued eyes were all that marked him as a gray elf, and he still wore the bronze armor he'd disguised himself in. With the Argonox's brand burned into the side of his neck, he still looked like any other Tibran slave-soldier we might have plucked from their ranks.

Only, we knew better.

My father choked out loud at the sight of them, his gaze darting back and forth like he wasn't sure which one was more bizarre. Phillip won in the end, of course. He flicked a dubious glance at Jaevid before clearing his throat and attempting to compose himself. "We are, uh, pleased to have you both back safely," he said in the same kingly tone he liked to use when addressing the court. "I believe introductions are in order."

"Aedan, formerly of Brine's Hollow in the Farchase Plains." He gave a deep bow, his eyes never leaving the floor. I wondered if that was out of respect or fear. Perhaps it was a bit of both.

"He assisted in our rescue of Jenna from Northwatch," Jaevid explained. "He's proven himself to be quite the proficient spy and has certainly earned our trust."

Aedan blushed until even the tips of his long, pointed ears were as red as cherries.

"I was so injured I couldn't walk," I added. "Aedan carried me out on his back."

"I see." My father regarded him again, his expression softening. "Then I believe I am in your debt."

"Oh! N-no, Your Majesty, not at all!" Aedan stammered. "I was honored to help."

I gave one of his pointed ears a playful tug. "He's just

being modest. He's quite capable with a blade, too. Perhaps you should knight him?"

Father combed his fingers along his short beard thoughtfully. "Not a bad idea. Unless, of course, he'd prefer to be a dragonrider."

Aedan didn't reply. He seemed to shrink lower and lower, cowering with the ends of his ears still glowing red.

"You should have seen him talking circles around those Tibran officers. He's a clever kid, I'll give him that," Phillip added. He patted the top of Aedan's nearly bald head with a chuckle. "He would do better in the noble court, if you ask me."

Hearing Phillip speak made my father tense and go still, staring back up at our monstrous-looking companion with a puzzled frown. He tilted his head to the side slightly, eyes narrowing as though he couldn't figure out why that voice sounded so familiar. Then his eyebrows suddenly shot up. His eyes went as wide as teacups and his mouth fell open. "Gods and Fates, is that ... Phillip?"

I immediately stepped between them. "Father, it's not his fault. Argonox took us both prisoner, and he did this to Phillip. I know he looks different now, but his mind is unchanged. He's still the same person."

A warm, heavy hand came to rest on my shoulder. I knew his touch, strong and steady, without even looking. "You don't have to explain for me, Jenna," Phillip scolded gently. "It's all right."

"H-how?" Father stopped and cleared his throat, as though he were trying to collect himself. "How did this happen? I mean, how did he do this to you?"

It took a while to explain. Jaevid had to do most of it, since he had a much more intimate understanding of how the venom worked. But the basics of it were fairly simple. The switchbeasts' bite contained a venom that slowly turned you into one of them. Most didn't survive the agonizing process, and Argonox had been experimenting with a way to make a hybrid—a person with the physical strength and abilities of the switchbeast that could still take orders like any other soldier. Phillip was the first successful subject and, as far as we knew, the only one.

"He's stable now," Jaevid assured everyone. "The venom is no longer active in his body, so he won't get any worse. But he also won't improve. What has already been changed can't be reversed."

"Well that's … unfortunate. I'm sorry to hear about this, Phillip." My father cast him a look of earnest sympathy.

"I know I'm difficult to look at. I'm still not quite used to it, myself," he admitted with a little shrug. "Please don't worry, Your Majesty. I have every intention of resigning my noble title after the war ends. As far as anyone else knows, I perished in Barrowton. Perhaps it should stay that way."

My heart sank, disappearing beneath the depths of my silent panic as I stared up at him. Did this mean he would not return to the court at all? What about us? Would he try to leave again? He couldn't—I wouldn't allow it!

My father opened his mouth, but after a second or two, closed it again without saying a word.

"Felix, maybe it's not my place anymore to be doling out orders, but I think we should start preparing," Jaevid interjected. "I'll need a little time to get things ready on my end. I'm sure our friends would like a chance to catch their breath before we do this."

"Right, of course. I agree," my father agreed, his gaze slowly panning from Phillip to refocus on the task at hand. "Take whatever time you need to prepare. Triple the guard on the ramparts. I want all eyes on Argonox's front line. If he makes a move, I want to see it coming." He turned to begin walking away, then paused to study Aedan for a few seconds more. "And for the love of all the gods, someone get this boy some Maldobarian armor!"

Stepping into my bedroom felt like going back in time. Everything was exactly as I'd left it. The maps I'd used in dragonrider training were still spread out on my desk in the study, covered in markings to show the progression of the Tibran forces across my kingdom. All my books on aerial battle techniques were stacked on my bedside table, right beside my bottle of lavender and vanilla oil I used to help ease my restlessness and anxiety. Little dabs behind my ears or a few drops on my pillow sometimes helped.

I knew it was stupid and an inefficient use of time, but I wanted a bath. There was reeking swamp mud caked on my skin and in my hair, blood smeared and splotched all over me, and the stickiness of old sweat squished under my clothes. I was about to ride into battle, maybe for the last time in my life, and I just wanted a moment to be alone and think. My soul craved it—a few minutes of quiet, to let the world stand still. I wouldn't have long; minutes at the most.

Outside the bathroom, my chamber servants were already spreading out my armor and padding, making sure every piece was polished to perfection. My eyes lingered on it as I passed, wondering if this would be the last time. Would I die in that armor tonight?

While the servants drew the bath, I rummaged through my night table until I found all my mother's letters tucked at the back of the middle drawer. There must have been thirty of them, all neatly folded and tied into a bundle with a purple ribbon. I took the bundle into the bathroom and sat, reclining back in the steaming water, to read them all one by one.

Every tiny, carefully-printed word soaked into my mind like rain into the earth. She had been proud of me. She knew I could do anything I put my mind to. She believed I was strong enough to do anything I set my mind to. She envied my bravery. She admired my strength and hoped I would be happy.

Droplets hit the crinkled, yellowing page I held—but it wasn't from the bath. I wiped my eyes and put the letter safely on the floor outside the tub with the others. Pain ground and grated through my chest like two rough stones scraping together. I missed her. I needed her. Somehow, I had to be that person she believed I could be.

I jumped, sloshing the bathwater as someone knocked on the door. "Jenna?" His voice came softly, wrapping around my heart like an old, threadbare blanket worn by years of offering warmth and comfort.

"What is it, Phillip?" I struggled to keep my voice steady. "Is it time? Is Jaevid ready to start the ritual?"

"No, it's not that, I just ... " He paused, taking a deep breath as though steeling himself. "Can I come in?"

Oh, Fates. My pulse flourished, kicking hard against my ribs as my entire body flushed with embarrassment. This *again*?

I sank lower in the deep marble tub, barely peering over the edge. "Why?"

"I ... I just want to ... " His voice caught, and he hushed again. It was okay. I didn't need to hear the rest. He wasn't coming in for *that*. Something was wrong.

"Okay."

The knob twisted, and the door clicked open. Phillip stood in the doorway, his expression a mixture of apprehension and concern. His gaze traveled around the room, seeing the letters on the floor and me hiding, hunkered down in the water so he couldn't see anything but my face and neck. Switchbeast strength aside, I'd still punch his teeth in if he tried anything funny. Now was not the time for any of his absurd attempts at romantic gestures.

Without a word, he walked over and sat down next to the tub with his back against the side. He picked up a few of the letters and started to read, silver eyes skimming the delicately printed lines one by one.

"You miss her a lot, don't you?" he murmured at last.

I waded closer, leaning against the edge of the tub so I could peer over his shoulder at the page in his hand. "All the time," I whispered. "Somehow, whenever everything feels like it's spinning out of control, hearing her voice in my head makes it feel like I can survive."

"I understand." One corner of his mouth twitched at a smile. "That's how you've been for me."

My pulse skipped, and I forgot how to breathe. "M-me? Why?"

"You still don't understand, do you?"

"Understand what?"

Putting down the letters, Phillip turned around. His face was mere inches from mine, and his strange silver eyes searched my face for a long, quiet moment—almost like he suspected I might be making fun of him. He sighed at last and shook his head. "I've never been in love with anyone else, Jenna. It's only ever been you."

My stomach fluttered. Somehow, I knew I'd never get used to hearing him say that.

"I meant what I said," Phillip murmured as he angled his face away. His frown put little wrinkles between his brows. "I will have to resign my place as Duke of Barrowton. I can't be a noble, not like this."

There was something else—something more he wanted to say. The fact that he was holding back, biting down hard against the words as though he hated every single one, was terrifying. I swallowed hard, dangling in the gap of his silence while I waited for him to continue.

"I recommended Aedan be given the position," he continued, muttering as he turned to rest his back against the side of the tub again.

"Aedan? But he's awfully young, isn't he?"

Phillip gave a small shrug. "I wasn't much older when I took the position. He's proven himself time and again to be someone worthy of our trust. Besides, your father does owe him quite a lot now. It seems appropriate to have the first full-blooded gray elf to take a noble title in Maldobar be at Barrowton." He bowed his head, propping his elbow on his knee as he spoke. "I offered to stay on in secret and act as his advisor—just until he's comfortable. I believe he'll do well. He's clever, humble, and seems to have more sense than most men twice his age. He'll be a hero amongst the gray elves and humans alike after this. Well, providing we all survive the next twenty-four hours, that is."

That wasn't it. Phillip was still holding back. I could sense it, like pressure building against a dam. Drop by drop, second by second, that heaviness was mounting. It would break, and so would he.

I shrank back, using the moment of silence while his back was turned to stand up and wrap myself in a towel. I climbed out of the bathtub and sat down next to him. The marble floor was cold against my legs and my hair dripped a puddle between us.

Suddenly, Phillip's expression tensed. His jaw went rigid and his eyes squeezed shut. "Jenna, you are the Crown Princess of Maldobar. The chosen heir to the throne," he blurted at last. "You are going to be queen! And I ... "

"What?" I urged.

"The man you marry will become the next King of Maldobar." His shoulders curled forward, as though he were trying to fold into himself and hide. "How could that possibly be me?"

"Because it can't be anyone else," I said. "I love you. Only you."

"But, gods, can you imagine it? My face hanging in the

hall of portraits? The looks on the faces at the coronation parade? At balls? At ceremonies? I-I can't even give you an heir anymore." His voice broke and he covered his face with his hand.

My breath caught, watching him crumble before me while those words carved fresh wounds on my heart. "You mean—?"

"I'm sterile, Jenna," he confessed, tone raw with anguish and rage. "Because of the venom and the way switchbeasts reproduce, I can never have children of my own now. Jaevid said he could sense it but there was nothing he could do. Whatever small chance there still was of your father letting me marry you won't stand, not if I can't even give Maldobar an heir."

All I could do was sit in complete shock, gaping at him. I'd never considered something like this might happen—or what it would mean for us. From where he was sitting, it must have seemed like Argonox had taken absolutely everything from him, even his hope for a family.

But that wasn't true.

"I won't consider anyone else as my husband," I announced firmly. "It's you or no one."

He shot me a dubious glare. "Have you lost your mind? That would mean—"

"Refusing the crown," I finished for him with a smile.

"Jenna, no, I can't let you do that. Not for me. It's not worth it. If Maldobar survives this war, it will need a strong figure at the helm, guiding it into restoration."

"They'll have it," I assured him. "Aubren is still alive. Reigh is also. And Jaevid is technically a member of the family. There are plenty of other heads that will fit under that crown, but mine belongs next to yours."

"But we'll never have a family," he rasped frantically. "Don't you want children?"

Taking one of his hands in mine, I scooted close enough to kiss his knuckles. "Of course I do. When the time comes, we'll figure it out." I pressed his warm, rugged palm against my cheek. "Until then, stop looking for excuses to leave me. I mean, do you even realize how horribly backward this is? I've spent the latter half of my life dodging your affection and now I'm terrified if I look away, you'll vanish."

He choked out a nervous laugh. "I suppose it is a little backward. I can't help but look back on who I was before and hate myself now. Before, I was ready to be the man I thought you would need me to be, to stand beside you and make your family proud to have me in their lineage. I believed I had enough to offer to make it worth your time. Now I have nothing. I am nothing. All I have to offer you are the broken pieces of the man I used to be. Is that really enough?"

Grabbing the sides of his face, I yanked Phillip in to press my mouth against his in answer. Of course it was enough. There was nothing Argonox could do to him that would change that. He would *always* be enough for me.

Before Jaevid could perform his ritual and cross into the Vale, we had to be absolutely sure that everything else was in place.

According to him, this act would give away his position to Reigh, and by extension, Argonox. An attack would almost certainly come right after, so we had to be ready. It put thick tension in the air as we met with the rest of my father's war council in the mapping room to go over the final details one last time.

"We can't know the full extent of what Argonox has in store for us this time," Jaevid warned. "But we do know we will at least have Beckah and Icarus to contend with."

"The dragonriders stand ready," High Commander Morrig declared. "The men have been briefed on the possible threat. If any dragons, living or dead, make an appearance to fight for the Tibrans, they will have to get past us first."

"You can expect war beasts, and lots of them," Aedan said, gesturing to the map. Sporting a brand-new, navy-blue infantry uniform trimmed in gold and a broad, black leather belt with matching vambraces, he looked much more at home. If not for the brand on the side of his neck, plainly visible above the collar of his tunic, it was easy to forget he'd ever been in the Tibran ranks. "You need to find the storage wagons and take them out. That's where they'll be keeping all the dragon venom orbs until the battle begins. The wagons are ironclad and heavily guarded, but that just makes them easier to spot. If you can send a dragon or two around the perimeter and attack them, it would significantly cut down on the amount of incoming fire the walls take."

"We can handle that," the High Commander agreed.

Jaevid fidgeted with the bone-carved pendant now hanging around his neck as his gaze darted across the map. "Once Mavrik and I make our appearance, I suspect we'll have Argonox's full attention. We need to find Reigh as quickly as possible. The sooner we find him, the easier it will be to bring Clysiros forth and let her destroy whatever Reigh's been forced to create."

"Provided she keeps her word," my father pointed out. "Forgive me for my lack of enthusiasm, but a *lot* is riding on your ability to blackmail the Goddess of Death into evening this fight out for us. I've seen you do some insane things before, but this would certainly set a new bar."

"She'll do it." Jaevid ground his jaw, eyes flashing like moonlit steel.

"But in the meantime, we need to hold the Tibran lines and keep as many of them as we can from ever reaching the city," the Infantry General pointed out.

"This is going to be ugly," Jaevid warned. "I will try to bolster your advances and cover flanks with earth golems and anything else I can muster. Paligno's will is with us. But many good men are going to die in this battle."

The High Commander straightened, his expression resolute. "They know the risks—just as they know what they are fighting for."

"We will not falter," the Infantry General agreed.

"When I find Hecate in the Vale, I will send word with her to warn Araxie of what's about to happen. I can't promise Luntharda's warriors will be able to mobilize in time to help us, but it's something." Jaevid pushed back from the table, glancing around at everyone one last time. "What happens next will change everything. It isn't just Maldobar looking to us for deliverance. The eyes of the world are upon us. If Argonox falls, we stand to topple his empire. Kingdoms long subjugated under his banner will need our help in rebuilding what he has torn down. Thousands of enslaved soldiers will suddenly feel their chains break, and it's up to us to determine their fate. You see their armor, helmets, swords, and shields, but I can sense what lies beneath. Many of them are terrified. They long for their homeland and have lived in a constant state of fear and survival since they were taken from it." He paused a moment, shifting his gaze to my father. "I hope we can be merciful and not end lives unnecessarily."

King Felix gave a steady nod. "Tell our men that any Tibran who lays down his arms voluntarily will be shown mercy."

The High Commander and Infantry General saluted in unison. "Yes, Your Majesty."

There was a heavy sense of finality in the room as we all stood back, staring down at the map together. The meeting was over. Our plan was fixed. Our soldiers and dragonriders stood waiting for the order to strike. There was only one thing left to do, and only one person in the room who could manage it.

Jaevid Broadfeather wore a determined frown as his eyes narrowed upon the map, irises flickering with a hint of eerie green light. In his mind, I imagined a deity raging like a lion against a cage—pacing, restless, hungry. "Very well then," he growled through clenched teeth. "Let's end this."

PART THREE

REIGH

NINETEEN

Through the delirium and darkness, a face stared down at me.

At least, I thought it was a face. The fresh agony thrumming through my body, slowly tearing me apart from the inside out, sort of threw everything into a haze. I couldn't tell if I was conscious or trapped in a relentless nightmare. All I knew, all I could think about, was the pain. It had to stop at some point. Either by being set free or dying—there had to be an end coming. I didn't even care which one it was anymore.

"It's gonna be okay, Reigh," a tiny female voice whispered against my ear.

"Enyo ... " Her name left my lips as a thin, rasping prayer. Was it her? I blinked, but nothing got clearer. I couldn't make out any details apart from the curve of a feminine cheek catching in the torchlight.

"No. I'm afraid not." She sounded genuinely sorry about that. "It's still Phoebe."

Involuntarily, my body seized up and cringed away. That voice—it burned in my head like the touch of a red-hot dagger point. I tried in vain to will myself to struggle, to try to get away. But it was no use. Even if she cut my bonds, I'd never be able to climb off the table on my own, let alone find my way out of ... wherever this was.

"P-please," I begged. "Kill me."

"Shhh. Don't say that. There's always hope. Always." She pressed something to my mouth and cold, wet liquid dribbled against my lips. "Here, drink this. It's only water."

Every sip burned my throat like acid. But I couldn't stop—my body lurched forward against the shackles binding my arms and neck as I gulped down as much as she would allow.

At last, Phoebe stood back and took the waterskin with her. My head slumped back down against the stone slab where I'd been chained for, well, honestly, I had no idea how long. Days? Weeks? The absence of anything but wavering torchlight made the room feel cavernous, as though we were deep underground, but I didn't know that for sure, either.

Not that it mattered. I was going to die here, in this room, strapped to this table, and there was nothing I could do to stop it. No one was coming for me. I'd given up that hope a long time ago.

"W-where's Aubren?" I managed to croak.

Phoebe bowed her head without a word, expression bleak. They'd left not long ago—my brother and that *thing*. Argonox had poured my blood and magic into them and sent them on their way. How long had they been gone? Were they coming back? Was Aubren going to be okay? Would he ever be the same again?

Or had my power destroyed him forever?

With her ginger hair pulled into two chaotic-looking ponytails right behind her ears, Phoebe glanced up at me. Wide, frightened eyes the color of sunlight through raindrops met mine. I wasn't a good judge of character, but it didn't seem like she was enjoying this any more than I was. Granted, she wasn't the one chained to a table and being tortured. But still, she didn't seem to get any pleasure out of it.

Or so I wanted to believe.

"He wants me to try again," Phoebe murmured, brushing some of her tightly curled bangs away from her face.

My throat constricted. On impulse, I pitched against the bonds and shrieked. No—gods, please, not again. I yelled and fought, begging her not to go through with it. I couldn't do this again!

I couldn't hold back my desperate sobs and screams as Phoebe came back to the tableside holding a mask made of cold, dark metal. The inside was coated in something like black glass with little panes of it set into the eyes. I didn't know what it was, or where it had come from. Argonox had called it the Thieving Mask, and when she buckled it around my head, I couldn't see anything through the black glass eyeholes. The instant the cold mask touched my skin, my body started to tremble. I sucked in frantic, shallow breaths and tried to pray. *Let it kill me this time. Anything to make it stop. Please, Paligno— Clysiros—anyone! I can't do this anymore! Jaevid, help me!*

Then it didn't matter ... because I was drowning in the dark again.

Everything came into focus as I crawled out of the Well of Souls, my lungs stretching as I sucked in gulps of the stale air. Around me, the familiar grayscale of the Vale made my heart sink. I was back. But why? Why would Argonox or Phoebe want to send me here?

I wanted to look for Noh or call out for him. He had to be here somewhere, right? If anyone could help me get out of this, it was him.

As soon as I thought to move, my body jerked a different way—totally out of my control. My body got up, standing shakily, and turning in a slow circle. I wiped my hair from my eyes and glanced back at the well behind me, its dark waters deceptively serene on the surface.

Then I saw it.

The reflection in the water wasn't mine—it was Jaevid's.

It only lasted a second, a single glance. That was all it took, though. Somehow, the Thieving Mask had put my consciousness inside Jaevid's body. I could see through his eyes, see and hear everything he did, but I had no control over him.

I was a spy in his head.

"You," a familiar voice hissed suddenly.

Jaevid whirled around, staggering a bit when he found himself nearly nose-to-nose with Noh.

"You are not supposed to be here. The Vale is *my* domain," Noh seethed quietly. Standing motionless, Noh had his arms folded into the sleeves of his long silver and black robes.

"I didn't come here for a holiday," Jaevid snapped back. "I came because your other half is in trouble. I would think you'd be aware of that."

Noh's eyes narrowed, and his nose scrunched as he curled his lip. "Am I to believe Paligno's champion has come to offer me help? Hah!"

"Believe whatever you like; it makes no difference to me."

"How? How did you manage pass through the well? It should be forbidden to you," Noh interrogated, eyes glittering with distrust.

"Unless it is *her* power that brings me here," Jaevid countered. "I have the crystal in my possession. I used its power to bring me here, just as I used the defilement's pull to send Jenna through before."

Noh's expression went slack. His eyes popped open wide and his lips parted just enough for a few breathless words to hiss out. "You ... you have it?"

"Yes. It's safe—for now. But if you want it to remain that way, then I'm going to need your help." Jaevid took a step away from the well, water sloshing in his boots. "Reigh is running out of time. He won't last much longer."

Well, at least someone else agreed with me on that point.

"What can you possibly do for him? He is beyond even my reach now."

I wished I could have control of Jaevid's body just long enough to sock Noh across the jaw. *Stop mouthing off and help him, moron!*

"Mine as well. But not hers." Jaevid marched forward, scaling the grassy knoll that overlooked the bleak stone city.

Hers? Wait a second, he wasn't seriously thinking about asking ...

"Clysiros?" Noh gasped the name as he trotted to catch up. "Are you mad? You cannot speak with her! She is imprisoned in Desmiol! Not even I can hear her speak. Reigh is one of the few who can."

"One of the few, yes," Jaevid countered. "But not the only one. Now, if you're finished with your interrogation, take me to the Sivanth. We need to do this quickly." He gestured to the city and waited.

Noh studied him with a sulky scowl, his mouth pursed as he licked the front of his teeth. "Fine. Have it your way. But I do not think you'll find Clysiros eager to help your cause."

"We'll just have to see, won't we?"

"Indeed." Noh snorted as he led the way down the hill. "We shall see if life can bargain with death."

The nearer we drew to the Sivanth, the more spirits appeared around us like shimmering, translucent figures. Some whispered and stared. Others seemed totally oblivious to our presence. Noh could pass through their crowds like a ghost. His body became a fine black mist instead of crashing into them, and effortlessly reappeared as solid on the other side.

Jaevid didn't seem to have that same ability. He dodged and ducked through the huddled crowds of spirits, jogging to keep up.

Overhead, a dark cloud gathered on the horizon. The encroaching thunderhead, massive and snapping with bolts of lightning, rolled in slowly. Every time a bolt would pop nearby, zapping a rooftop, the spirits would wail and huddle in closer with their forms quivering in fear.

"What is that?" Jaevid asked.

"As you said, Reigh is running out of time," Noh replied dryly. "Whenever the power of the Harbinger is used to a great extent in the mortal realm without the completion of the ritual, it threatens to tear the Vale apart. Desmiol will inevitably consume it, and soon after, the mortal realm as well. With no means of passing into the afterlife, spirits will roam wild in the mortal world unchecked. The dead will walk. The ancient evils Clysiros bound within the earth in the first age will break free." He paused long enough to flash Jaevid a cold glare over his shoulder. "In short, the world will end."

"I see." Jaevid sounded unfazed, which I had hard time believing. Maybe he was just keeping his responses in check, fortifying his reactions for what was to come. "Then it sounds like fixing this as soon as possible is in *everyone's* best interest."

Noh didn't reply. In fact, he seemed to get more anxious the closer they moved to the swelling storm cloud in the sky. Weaving through the streets and around clumped crowds of spirits, Jaevid's gaze flashed back and forth between Noh's back and the sky, as though he wasn't sure which one was more unsettling.

It was a toss-up for me, too.

Darting around a corner, Noh came to a halt in the middle of a long, straight avenue. Enormous statues of white stone, more than twenty feet tall, flanked each side of the road like pillars. Each one was identical, appearing like a woman garbed in a flowing white robe. The figures stood with heads bowed toward the road between them and hands covering their eyes.

Noh walked down the center of the street, passing between the statues without giving them a second look. Jaevid seemed more impressed, or maybe unnerved, because his gaze continually turned up to study them as they passed.

Not a single spirit stood in this road. If anything, it almost seemed abandoned. Weird. Didn't some spirits want to seek the afterlife? Surely some did. Then again, the huge dark cloud hanging over the street was probably a deterrent. It rumbled and buzzed with chaotic energy, lashing out with tongues of lightning that snapped off the tops of some of the statues.

At the far end of the avenue, an even larger pair of statues stood on either side of a raised stone pedestal. A graceful, arching stairway led up to it, and walking there would inevitably leave a person standing right between those two figures. At first glance, it was hard to see. The farther we went down the street, the more the air seemed to grow dim and suffocating, as though we were sinking gradually into a bank of fog. It was so subtle, I hardly noticed at first. Then Jaevid started jogging faster and squinting to try and keep Noh in sight ahead of us.

When we caught up to him at last, we were standing

at the base of the staircase. The statues on either side of it were monstrous—towering like silent giants. One was made of stone as dark as onyx. The other was a pearly, milky white. But apart from that, both were identical.

And both were dragons.

With their necks arched and wings folded close, the pair of dragons gazed down at the pedestal between them with tranquil indifference. Nothing about them seemed threatening, apart from their size and the fact that, you know, a dragon that size could eat a person in one bite.

Jaevid regarded them for a moment, and then stared back at Noh. "The Fates are dragons?"

"That is the mortal word for them," he replied with a shrug. "Here, they are called Viepol—*those who see all.*"

"Are they any relation to the dragons in Maldobar?"

The corners of Noh's mouth curled slowly into a secretive little grin. "We're all related in one way or another, lapiloque. But it does make you wonder, doesn't it? Do the dragons who choose riders do so by random chance? Or is it because they can actually *see* something in that person no one else can?"

Jaevid muttered an elvish curse under his breath. I guess he wasn't a fan of Noh's mind games, either.

"At any rate, this is the Sivanth," Noh gestured up to the stairs and pedestal. "Souls come here to face the judgment of the Viepol and accept whatever reward they've earned, be it paradise in the kingdom of the gods or banishment to the prison of stars. This is as close to Desmiol as anyone can get without actually passing into it."

"Good," Jaevid muttered under his breath as he began up the stairs. "Let's hope it's close enough."

TWENTY

Lightning sizzled through the air, popping off the ground mere feet away as Jaevid ascended the staircase. The two dragon sculptures never moved, and yet it felt as though their eyes were following him the entire time. At the last step, he hesitated. The wind from the storm churning and boiling overhead teased through his gray hair. I couldn't fathom what he must be thinking. This was madness. He had no way of knowing what was about to happen. The Fates—Viepol—whatever they were called, might send him into the afterlife. And what then? Who would be left to help Maldobar? Who would stand against Argonox?

And me … who would prevent me from destroying everything I'd ever loved?

There was nothing I could do to stop it, though. With one final step, Jaevid stood on the circular pedestal between the dragons, his gaze flicking back and forth between their monstrous heads. Thunder cracked and shook the ground.

"All right, Hecate," Jaevid whispered. "You can do this. I know you can."

Hecate? Wait, was she coming here, too? How? That didn't make any sense; how could she get into the Vale without Noh or me helping her? Was it even safe for someone with her abilities?

No time to hash it out now—not that I could. I got the impression Jaevid had no idea I was watching, seeing everything through his eyes as it was happening. The Thieving Mask had that effect, although the first four times Phoebe had tried putting it on me, Noh had been adamant in resisting it. The result? Pure agony—like my head was a melon being squeezed in a vice while both Noh and the mask battled for control.

This time, Noh hadn't even put up a fight when Phoebe put the mask on me. Had using so much of our power weakened him? Or was he just giving up? Either way, I doubted that was a good sign. Jaevid was right; I was running out of time.

Raising his gaze to the cloud overhead, Jaevid stretched his arms wide and closed his eyes. Everything went dark. And then there was light—blinding, searing, white-hot light that sent a jolt of pain and panic through my body like I was being lit on fire. I couldn't move, couldn't resist, or pull away from it. The heat tingled through every part of me, rising like a mug filled with boiling water. I tried to stop it, tried to break the mask's hold, but nothing worked. I was stuck in Jaevid's head. Death or unconsciousness were the only ways out of this, and I couldn't force either.

Jaevid opened his eyes, looking to the sky again. Suddenly, a giant head eclipsed his view. On either side of the pedestal, the dragon statues quivered and twisted, writhing free of their spots to spread their wings and stretch their legs and long tails. The black one craned its neck to stare right at him with eyes of bottomless, blinding light.

Pain roared through me again, more intense than before. Could it see me? Sense my presence somehow?

The creature blinked owlishly, stone nostrils flaring as the flashes of lightning sparkled over its onyx scales. Then the other dragon moved in to inspect Jaevid, as well. Except for their differing colors, they were perfect mirror images of one another down to the very last detail.

"*Who is it?*" a voice asked, its tone piercing through me like a molten spear. I wanted to scream, to get away, but there was nothing I could do.

"*Alive,*" another voice grumbled. "*Not for judgment. He does not belong here. We must send him back.*"

"Wait!" Jaevid protested, throwing his hands up toward the dragons. "I am the chosen of Paligno. I carry his essence, and I have come here to seek council with Clysiros!"

The dragons blinked, their stone faces eerily indifferent and unchanging as they loomed over him. At last, one of the voices confirmed. "*The lapiloque.*"

Jaevid nodded. "Yes."

"*No one can speak to Clysiros,*" the other voice snapped. "*She must never pass beyond Desmiol.*"

"I don't need to bring her here," he clarified. "There is another way to speak with her. The Akrotis can help me, if you allow her consciousness to enter the Vale. Surely you can sense it. She's looking for a way in and a willing host to lend their voice. Please, allow her to speak through you."

Once again, the dragons fell silent. After several grueling seconds, the black one recoiled and snapped his mighty jaws. *"We cannot allow it. No one else may enter the mind of the Viepol, for therein hides secrets that surpass the ages, the lies of a thousand kingdoms and the truths of the ancients."*

"Then she can use me," Noh spoke up suddenly. "All we will require of you is to bring forth the gateway to Desmiol, so the goddess can reply. Is that something you'd allow?"

Turning, Jaevid watched in silence as Noh ascended the staircase to stand right next to him. With his arms still folded beneath his robes, Noh kept a sharp scowl focused on the Viepol. I couldn't believe it. He was *helping*? Things must have been bad if Noh was volunteering to do something useful that didn't involve killing anyone.

The two dragons considered in tense silence, and I got the creepy feeling that they were somehow able to debate with one another without having to say a word. At least, not one that we were able to hear. Finally, the white one let out a blasting snort that blew Jaevid's hair back and turned away.

"We will allow it."

Jaevid's shoulders dropped in relief. "I am grateful."

"I would suggest saving the gratitude until you are standing safely back in the mortal realm," Noh snorted.

Jaevid didn't even look at him. "I am. That's why I didn't thank *you*, yet."

Ouch. I felt that burn from worlds away. Noh didn't retort, though his lips thinned, and he shot Jaevid a brief, scathing glare. I wondered if wrinkling my nose made my scar crinkle like that, too. Probably, since Noh and I were identical.

"*Mortal eyes must turn away,*" the dragons warned in unison as they stirred, snouts turning to the empty air behind the pedestal. "*None but the dead may gaze upon the maw of Desmiol or risk being pulled to it.*"

"That would be you, lapiloque," Noh added.

Jaevid was already turning around. "I gathered that."

An instant before his back was turned and my view was lost, the two dragons opened their jaws wide and drew back, blasting the air with a sudden burst of power like a plume of white fire. It made a huge circular portal appear. Then I couldn't see anything. Overhead, the cloud rumbled louder. Searing pressure rose in my body, squeezing harder and harder at my already frazzled mind. My vision spotted and dimmed—or was it Jaevid's? No, it had to be mine. Something about that portal was putting a strain on the mask. It was too much. Already, I could feel its hold beginning to slip like sand through a sieve.

I was going to lose it, or die, or maybe both.

"*Jaevid Broadfeather. I've been expecting you. A shame it's always the handsome ones who dare to keep a lady waiting,*" a woman's voice whispered, purring like a lover in his ear.

It was Clysiros—her voice was coming from Noh's mouth!

Her voice hit me like a knockout punch straight to the nose. My vision flashed, going dark for a few seconds. For an instant, I was back in hell, with cold chains biting into my skin and dry screams in my throat. Phoebe must have been somewhere close because she was whispering to me frantically, assuring me it was going to be okay. It was almost over. Just a few seconds more.

"Unfortunately, this isn't a social call," Jaevid replied, keeping his gaze trained upon Noh.

"*It never is,*" she replied. "*You've been so very busy, just like before. Not that I'm complaining; I always did enjoy watching you work. And to find the Akrotis, too? I am thoroughly impressed.*"

"Then you know why I've come," he guessed. "Things cannot remain the way they are."

"*Naturally,*" she snickered. "*But then, they were never meant to be this way in the first place. Stones and nonsense running about, bathed in blood. This reckless chaos was inevitable. I tried to warn them. It's far too clumsy. You mortals are a clever lot. But reason and truth become lies if spoken from an unpopular throat.*"

Jaevid took a deep breath. "Well, I'm not here for popularity. There is more at stake than Maldobar's future if Argonox remains unchecked and Reigh's power is twisted until it destroys the Vale. The balance must be reset, and that can't be done without your help."

Clysiros laughed again, which was especially creepy since Noh's expression never changed from a blank stare. "*Of course.*"

Every word grated on my brain, adding just a little more pressure. More heat. More pain. I couldn't take it much longer. I was going to break.

"I have the crystal, and I'm willing to help, to give you what you need to see this done," Jaevid declared as he held up one of his hands, staring down at his open palm. "But Paligno and I have terms."

"Oh, I'm sure you do. My brother always did love a good bargain," she purred excitedly. *"Every drop of sweat and blood has a price. So, what is yours, lapiloque? What will it cost to free me from this starry cage?"*

The connection broke so suddenly; I didn't understand what had happened at first. Darkness swallowed me, snatching my consciousness from the Vale and dragging me back into Argonox's torture chamber. I thrashed against the chains, my cries muffled by the mask until Phoebe began unbuckling it.

"Shh, it's okay. It's over now," she cooed as she pulled the mask away. "You did so good, Reigh. I think that will make him happy this time."

My body throbbed; every muscle fiber was raw as I went slack on the table. The cold sweat beading on my skin made me shiver. But it was no relief to the searing heat in my mind. It felt like my eyeballs might melt right out of their sockets. Something warm oozed from my nose and eyes, dribbling down the sides of my face. Blood?

"P-please," I begged hoarsely. "You h-have to make it stop. K-kill me."

Her cheeks flushed until all the hundreds of little freckles along her cheeks, nose, and forehead became invisible. Her delicate features drew into a shattered look of regret. Tears welled in her eyes as she stood over the table, looking childish and tiny in a leather apron that was far too big for her. "Don't say that. There is hope. There *has* to be hope," she said. "Someone will stop him. I think maybe Jaevid can. I know Lord Argonox has never faced anyone like him before."

"R-right," I growled, letting my eyes fall closed. It hurt too much to keep them open, and I couldn't stand to look at her for another second. "Cause you'd want that, right? Y-you're helping him destroy the world, making all these things for him, torturing people. You're just as bad as he is!"

I couldn't see her face. I didn't want to. And yet I could hear the brokenness in her voice as her footsteps began to retreat. "Not every cage is made of metal. Some are made of whispered threats."

I knew what she meant. Phoebe was as much a prisoner here as I was. Sure, Argonox hadn't bound her to a table, but she had to do his bidding. There was no telling what he'd threatened her with, or what he'd done to her already. The Tibran soldiers called her "Miss Artificer" like it was something precious, but they always locked the doors behind them whenever they came and went from this place. She was not free to leave.

Remembering that while she was experimenting on me with various artifacts was difficult, though. She could kill me. I wanted it. Anything was better than spending what was left of my days in chains being stretched and drained until my power or my captor killed me. She could do it now and make it quick and painless. Maybe then I could forgive her for what she'd done to Aubren, Vexi, me, and so many others.

"D-don't you get it? If you l-let me live, everyone will die. N-not just me, or the people h-here in Maldobar," I fought to growl through ragged breaths. "Argonox d-doesn't want me—he wants the world, and the l-lives of everyone in it. Whatever d-deal you struck with him only lasts until he d-doesn't need you anymore."

The lurch and clank of the door lock made my eyes fly open again. Someone was coming in. In an instant, Phoebe reappeared at my side and stashed the water skin under her apron. Her face was pale, and I could see her trembling as she stood close by, eyes like two big raindrops watching the door.

"Miss Artificer," the voice of a man addressed her from the doorway—a soldier, judging by the faint clinking of his armor. "Lord Argonox would like your report on the most recent test."

Phoebe's smile was as haunted as it was forced. "Oh, yes. I've only just finished. I'll just need some time to write up the results."

"That won't be necessary." The soldier's footsteps came closer. "He wants you to deliver the report personally. He's already on his way."

"Lord Argonox is coming here?" she squeaked like someone had stepped on a baby rabbit.

"He will arrive momentarily. I was sent to give you notice and to assist in moving the prisoner to the bleeding stocks."

Horror gripped me like a snagwolf to the throat. I couldn't move—couldn't speak or even breathe.

"Oh, but I'm afraid he's much too weak to withstand that procedure right now." Phoebe's voice trembled. "Perhaps if we waited a day or two—"

"I'm afraid that won't be possible," the soldier interrupted. "Orders have already been passed down. The legions are mobilizing. Lord Argonox intends to strike tonight, as soon as the final bleeding is complete."

"F-final … ?" The question died in her throat and she swallowed hard.

"Don't fret, my little bird," another deep, masculine voice spoke over them. It echoed from the direction of the doorway, smooth and even, with a calculating edge I'd come to recognize. Just the sound made my pulse thrash in my ears.

It was Argonox.

The last time he'd come to pay me a visit, the result had come the closest of any of Phoebe's experiments to successfully killing me in the most painful way imaginable. It had also resulted in reanimating yet another deceased war hero—only this one was not a demigod or supposed to be alive again. Well, if you could even call *that* being alive.

There was no mistaking who she was. I'd never seen her in person, but Kiran had told many stories about the bravery and grit of Beckah Derrick, the first woman to ever ride on a dragon. Defiling her grave and reanimating her remains … I didn't want to think about what kind of punishment that might earn me in the Vale. But Argonox wanted his own champion in a dragonrider's saddle. And now, thanks to me, he had one.

The state she'd been in reminded me more of a whirling tornado—destructive, powerful, and directionless if left to her own devices. She was beyond dangerous and without any sense of her spirit to guide her, she couldn't be reasoned with by anyone except the one holding her leash—which was Argonox.

What my power had done to that girl was wrong on too

many levels to count. Noh had resisted reanimating her remains every inch of the way, and the process had almost ended my suffering. But I wasn't that lucky. Argonox understood a lot more about Noh's power and how to manipulate our bond than I'd expected. He'd used it to corrupt Aubren, bind my dragon, and so much more. I doubted even Jaevid knew the extent of it. He'd find out soon enough, though.

I just prayed I didn't live to see it.

"How did the session go? Were you able to learn anything more?" Argonox asked evenly, as though he might as well have been asking about the weather. The metallic tinge of old blood and sweat in the air paired with the musk of scorched metal and ash from Phoebe's crafting didn't seem to bother him at all.

"Yes, My Lord." Phoebe was still shivering as she stood by the table right next to my head. She blinked rapidly, chin quivering as her eyes followed his movements. "The one who serves Paligno has reached Halfax, just as your agents reported. The conversation indicated that he ... " Her voice caught, and her eyes darted down to me for the briefest instant. "He doesn't have the crystal. It must be at Halfax, still guarded by the king, and most likely somewhere in the castle."

My heart thumped so hard I could feel it in my throat. That wasn't what Jaevid said—Phoebe was lying. But why?

"Excellent. Then our timing is perfect. Perhaps they still do not know how to complete the ritual or hope to rescue their friend before they do. They may not even know what it is they harbor there at all." A strong hand grabbed my jaw suddenly, turning my head so that I was looking squarely into Argonox's piercing gaze. He studied me like a tigrex considering an injured fawn, dark eyes glinting with delighted malice. "I must apologize to you, Phoebe. I did have some doubts that your skills would be enough to salvage this situation. He's not been as useful as he might have been with the crystal's ritual already completed. Even so, you've proven yourself once again to be the finest artificer in the world."

Phoebe didn't reply, shying away from the table when he came close. She nibbled on her bottom lip, wringing her hands against her apron as her gaze darted back and forth between him and the direction of the door—as though she were contemplating trying to flee.

"One final bleeding should be enough to secure the dragons and shrikes we've acquired," Argonox went on. He let go of my face and wiped his hand on the front of his jerkin. "Then I want my armor prepped."

"My Lord, I, uh, I should mention that it is very unlikely he will survive another bleeding right after the Thieving Mask session," Phoebe whimpered. "Perhaps we should let him rest a moment, even a few hours might—"

Only Argonox's eyes moved, flicking immediately up to her. She made a panicked squeak and went silent, cringing as she ducked her head. "Phoebe, my bird, I realize this must be … *difficult* for you, but we cannot lose focus now. Surely you haven't forgotten the terms of your role here?"

"N-no, My Lord."

"Good girl. It's extremely important that you remember what we've discussed." He pointed down to me. "*This* is not a person. Anyone chosen by these so-called gods are not people anymore. They're only vessels, like clay pots. You're simply finding the best way to crack them open and draw out the treasure inside."

She bobbed her head frantically. "Only pots. Yes, My Lord. I remember."

His expression slid smoothly into a venomous smile before he turned away, walking out of view. "I knew I could count on you. Hurry now. There isn't much time. Take whatever you can from him and send it with the Captain."

"Yes, My Lord." Her brows crinkled upward as she glanced down at me. "And if he survives the bleeding?"

Argonox's footsteps halted, as though he'd stopped to consider that for a moment. "Then chain him for relocation," he decided. "He'll make a fine adornment for my chariot."

PART FOUR

JENNA

TWENTY-ONE

The battle horn sounded, rumbling in the deep and sending pangs of adrenaline like cold fire through my veins. It echoed through the granite halls and corridors of the castle, resounding through the throne room, and wailing against the gathering dusk. That sound could only mean one thing: our enemy was stirring at last. The time had come. Tonight, Maldobar's fate would be decided, written upon the pages of history in the blood of its fallen soldiers.

Jaevid's ritual was complete. He'd walked in the Vale, counseled with death itself, and now all our hopes hung on those negotiations. All that remained was to strap our boots on, don our helmets, and heft the blade of war one last time.

I stood alone on a long carpet of deep blue that spanned the length of the floor of the dimly lit hall. Overhead, the vaulted ceilings were all but invisible without the chandeliers lit. In fact, the only light came from two ornate braziers burning on either side of the alabaster platform where the figures of three golden dragons made up my father's throne. With two of the beasts forming the arms and legs on either side of the seat, the third rose up right at the center. The dragon's wings were spread wide and its head craned down to watch the long room with ruby eyes.

But that wasn't what caught my interest now.

I studied the glittering dark crystal set in the center of that middle dragon's head. I must have seen it more than a hundred times growing up here. That crystal, as black as obsidian, had never meant anything to me until now. I'd seen it as some frivolous adornment. A strange design choice—but nothing more. Now the sight of the brazier light wavering over its glossy surface made my body tense under my dragonrider armor. It made my blood run cold and my hands clench inside my riding gauntlets. How long had it sat there, watching kings come and go? Whoever had placed it there must have known what it was, or at least had some idea. Was it meant to send a message, like some trophy of war?

I suppose it didn't matter now. The only message it sent to me was one of impending doom. Argonox was coming for it, and the fate of our world depended on keeping it from his grasp.

"I remember the last time I was here." Jaevid seemed to appear out of nowhere, standing beside me with a distant expression as he considered the crystal, too. "I stood right here in this same spot and your father was, well, right about where you are now, actually."

"You killed Hovrid, the imposter king, and stole back

the god stone," I recalled. "That story is one of my father's favorites, I think. He likes the part where he single-handedly killed a company of elite guards *and* a giant boar. Interesting that he left out the bit about cutting his hand on a cursed divine artifact, though."

We stood together in the light of the braziers, not saying a word as we stared up at the throne while the war horn continued to wail in the night. For a moment, it felt like the world stood still. Then I felt his gaze turn to me like sunlight breaking through a storm. "Are you ready for this, Jenna?" he asked.

I smiled. "Is anyone?"

He chuckled. "Probably not."

"I am ready." The words broke out of me with a force that quaked my soul to its foundations—as though they'd been trapped there, caged, and confined, since the day I was born. Now they were free, and so was I. Unashamed, no longer an exile, I could ride into battle without an ounce of regret.

"Good." Jaevid stepped past me, ascending to the throne with confidence in every step. I watched, half in dread, half in hope, as he reached up and plucked the black crystal from its resting place on the golden dragon's head. It wasn't much larger than an apple, resting innocently in his hands as he stepped back down from the throne. His pale blue eyes studied it, defined brow furrowing and mouth tensing into a straight line. The different jagged edges, jutting in all directions, showed tiny reflections of his face. With a heavy sigh, Jaevid tucked it away into the leather satchel strung over his shoulders.

My father had obviously provided him something else to wear, which was good. Dressed in full dragonrider armor, he looked much more the hero our soldiers were undoubtedly expecting. The silver breastplate, helm, gauntlets, and greaves were adorned with intricate details of various animals. The creatures wound all over the metal, flowing with the shape of each piece, and were inlaid with gold.

Most complex of all was the dragon on his helmet. It had been carefully crafted to look like Jaevid's face emerged from the dragon's open maw, with a ridge of spines and horns sweeping back regally along the top and sides. When he slid the visor down, slits of green glass that made the dragon's eyes allowed him to see. I'd never seen a helmet quite like it.

We wore the same dragonriders' cloak buckled to our shoulder pauldrons, lengths of vibrant blue cloth sweeping behind us as we walked out of the throne room. But where mine was lined with the traditional white fox fur around the neck, Jaevid's had been crafted from the silvery pelt of a faundra stag. Hints of his gray elven heritage were sprinkled throughout his armor—a faundra stag's head on the center of his breastplate and the pommel of his scimitar, curled elven writing scrolling along the edges of his gorget, vambrances, and gauntlets.

Father had really outdone himself this time. No doubt he'd paid some lucky blacksmith a fortune for its commission. I had to wonder how long he'd had it stowed away, just waiting for Jaevid to return. Years?

We passed groups of servants and elite guards rushing through the castle halls. Most of the staff had already taken cover in the undercrofts beneath the castle. Those that remained were barricading doors, dousing candelabras, and pulling curtains and draperies over the windows. If the castle was sieged, we didn't want to make things too easy for our enemy. They'd have to find their way around in the dark, through barred doors, all while meeting hidden groups of elite guards and soldiers at every turn.

We took the tunnels from the castle's central keep into the narrow passes of the north wall. There, the infantry forces usually housed within the city had been forced to make room when the dragonriders arrived. Quarters were cramped and, according to my father, supplies were beginning to run scarce since the Tibrans were cutting off all attempts to deliver more by encircling the city's outer walls. Things were not ideal for the soldiers here, but I had to give them credit. As we walked the narrow hallways, weaving our way upward toward the nearest turret, everything was spotless. Bedrolls were neatly folded into corners or stacked out of the way, the floors were clean, and the armories were organized. They were making the most of a bad situation.

When we passed, the line of infantrymen waiting to receive their freshly-sharpened swords from the armor masters stood straighter. They watched us with wide eyes, never saying a word. A few of the younger recruits scrambled to salute, and Jaevid gave them a small nod.

"They look scared," I whispered as we passed through a pair of large, iron-reinforced doors that led into the northernmost turret.

"They have good reason." Jaevid's expression darkened as his gaze grew distant.

I was getting familiar with that particular look. It meant something bad was likely coming our way. "What is it? What do you feel? Is it Reigh?"

He flashed me a troubled glance. "Yes. They're moving this way."

"Who?"

He let out a shuddering breath, cringing and setting his jaw as though something was causing him pain. "I'm not sure. It's hard to put into words," he said, his deep voice going quiet so only I could hear. "I feel Reigh's power growing, as though it has been used to infect a great many things. It's hard to determine what they are from this distance, but it feels similar to Aubren's defilement." He shook his head. "Everything is so frenzied. I should be able to sense more when we get closer."

"He's still alive?" I heard myself ask, although the question left me so numb, I couldn't bear to look at him while he answered.

"Yes," Jaevid murmured. "At least, I think so. Jenna, please understand; I can't promise anything at this point."

My gut soured at those words, and I bit back hard against the taste of bile in my throat. What, by all the Fates, was Argonox doing to *my* little brother?

The turret was packed thick with infantry archers. They clustered around their sergeants, gripping their bows tightly as they listened to their final orders. Elves and humans, men and women, stood together with mixed expressions of pasty horror and stony determination. While it was still frowned upon in Maldobar for women to join the ranks, that hadn't kept a few from choosing that path. And with gray elven culture blending gradually into ours, ladies learning the craft of archery and swordplay was no longer unheard of—especially if you happened to have pointed ears. Ironically, the rumor floating around the barracks was that gray elf women were far better archers than any human man could ever dream of being.

The air grew colder with every step as we made our way to the second highest floor of the turret. There, more infantrymen stood guard at the iron-wrought doors that led out onto the ramparts. They saluted when they saw us and hurried to open one of the doors, so we could pass through. A blast of bitter night air hit my face, catching in the loose locks of my hair that had already slipped free of my braid.

Two steps out the door, I stopped short. My breath caught in my chest, held in suspense by the company that was waiting for us just outside. Four hundred dragonriders in complete battle dress stood at attention in two long rows on either side of the passage. They stretched from one turret to another, packed in tightly without so much as a foot of space between them. With helmets under one arm and the other clasped in salute over their breastplate, each one stood before a snarling dragon bearing a saddle. Some of them had been painted for battle with swirls of blue over their scales, and others had battle notches carved along their horns—a mark for every kill.

I spotted Perish first. Her white scales stood out against the rest, like a glowing cross between angel and monster.

Before her, Calem was watching us with his handsome features as sharp and bare of emotion as ever. Haldor and Turq were right next to them, ready to receive orders.

The sight of those men, two riders who'd become like family to me, filled my heart with blooming heat and the gnawing desire to be right there beside them. Rank and status separated us now, and that left a sour taste in my mouth. I was supposed to be Jaevid's wing end in this fight, so all I could do was wait, hope, and pray that I would see Haldor and Calem again when it was over.

When we appeared upon the rampart passageway, every dragonrider turned at once to face us. My heart thumped wildly against my ribs, and I chanced a look at Jaevid. His pale eyes were round, face flushed except for that faint scar over his cheek. A vein stood out against the olive skin on his neck and his jaw was tense, although I couldn't tell if it was from embarrassment or the overwhelming sight before us. Maybe a bit of both.

"My Lord Jaevid Broadfeather," High Commander Morrig called out to us as he strode up, passing between the two lines of dragonriders. His own silver armor was polished to perfection, reflecting the night sky like mirrors. "Four hundred and seven of the finest Dragonriders of Maldobar stand with you tonight. We are honored to have you in our company. Is there anything you would like to say to the men?" The Commander paused a moment and flashed me a quick, approving smile. "And women, of course."

"I'm not much of a speechmaker." Jaevid was certainly blushing now.

"Nor am I," the Commander laughed. "But I'm sure

they'd rather hear you stammer through one than me."

He did have a point there. The heroic tales of the little halfbreed who was chosen by a wild dragon and rose to become Maldobar's greatest hero in the Gray War were known by everyone who set foot in the academy. I had no doubt every man standing before us had heard them all at least twice. Now he was here, fighting alongside them, in a battle that would decide the fate of our kingdom. Speechmaker or not, we were all looking to him now.

This moment was his.

I stood back, watching alongside the High Commander as Jaevid Broadfeather faced the assembled dragonriders. He was taller than most of them, and there was no disguising those sharp elven features even with his helmet covering his ears. With his visor pulled back, it was easy to pick out the hints of uncertainty that crinkled his brow. Then all at once, that apprehension disappeared behind a stern look of fierce resolve.

"Dragonriders of Maldobar, tonight we stand on the edge of the abyss." He squared his shoulders, eyes the color of glacier water scanning the crowd. "At this very moment, the eyes of the world are upon us. Every man, woman, and child left stamped into the mud, crushed beneath the wheels of the Tibran Empire, waits to see if we will suffer the same fate." He paused, taking a breath. "We stood against this evil once. We knew it by a different name then, and just like now, victory seemed impossible. But we knew we had to try. *Someone* had to try. And the ferocity of our spirit, our determination to stand unshaken in the face of that evil, shone so brightly that not even the wild dragons could look away. They were drawn to it—drawn to us—and joined us not as servants, but allies. Now we stand together, unified, forged as one by the bonds of blood and duty to oppose anyone who would dare threaten us with the chains of bondage!"

A cry like the thrumming boom of thunder roared overhead, accompanied by the burst of giant wing beats. Mavrik rose up, blue scales flashing and yellow eyes glowing in the night. He landed atop the turret behind us with a *boom* that shook the wall and made the rest of the dragons growl and stir with excitement. They flapped and chirped, trumpeting at their king.

"That is why, tonight, we don't fight for Maldobar. We don't fight for kings or crowns, for borders or blood," Jaevid snarled over the noise. "We fight for our brothers and sisters, to resist the chains of bondage, and to set our people and many others free. We will send Argonox, and every other tyrant who would dare to set foot on our shores, a message that will echo through the ages." Jaevid widened his stance, drawing his scimitar to raise the point to the night sky. The length of his cloak caught in the wind, rolling at his heels and billowing around his armored form just as it did in those countless sculptures and draperies. "If there is even one dragonrider left to carry the flame, we will *never* submit! Ours is a spirit that will *never* be broken! Ours is the spirit of the dragon!"

A chorus of cries, yells, and cheers went up through the ranks as the Dragonriders of Maldobar drew their blades and raised them to the night sky. Behind every one of them, a dragon joined in with a trumpeting roar and burst of flame. I couldn't resist. Before I knew it, my own blades were in my hands and I was screaming my war cry along with the rest of them, my heart thrashing in my ears and dragon fire blazing through my veins.

Jaevid didn't say another word as he turned away, sheathing his blade and giving me a distinct nod to follow. I did, but not before stealing one last look at Calem and Haldor. I had to believe they would be safe, and I would see them again. To think anything else was … unbearable.

Jaevid led the way back into the turret, up the last flight of stairs, and onto the rooftop, where archers and spotters for the catapults were already in place. Granted, they were all making a wide berth around a certain king drake, who snarled and snapped his jaws at the sight below.

Our enemy was moving closer. As far as my eyes could see, an endless ocean of torches, armor, and bronze shields were gathered. They moved closer and closer, like an encroaching tide, pushing their war machines into range to the deep booming of war drums.

We only had minutes left.

"Here we are again, my old friend." Jaevid greeted his dragon with a broad smile, wrapping his arms around the creature's head.

Mavrik closed his eyes and made low chirping sounds, his ears perking toward the sound of his rider's voice.

"Do you remember our bargain? The one we made when we first met?" Jaevid closed his eyes as well, resting his forehead against the dragon's. "I promised I'd never make you do anything you didn't want to do, and that when our war was over, you would be free to return to the wild place they took you from." He pulled back slowly, a sad smile touching his lips as he scratched Mavrik behind the ears. "It's still your choice. If you want to ride with me again, let's make this a fight to remember."

The king drake gave a snort and growl, lifting his head and pointing a savage snarl at the encroaching Tibran army. At least—I thought it was the army.

I was mistaken.

The shape of a monstrous black dragon, silhouetted against the starry sky, landed atop a rocky hill amidst the Tibran ranks. With scales glittering in the torchlight like polished obsidian, the beast let out a roar that vibrated my breastplate and made my insides flutter. Icarus had returned.

From high atop the turret, the rider seated in his saddle was plainly visible, bathed in the glow of torches and ambient starlight. Her black armor was still adorned in golden painted wings, and a long red cloak swept from her shoulder pauldrons to flutter in the night wind. Though her face was hidden beneath a golden-painted helmet, I knew who she was ... and what she meant to the young man standing next to me.

Beckah Derrick was the only person I suspected might make Jaevid falter. He would have to face her again. But this time, if he hesitated to do what was necessary, it wouldn't be Cernheist at risk of burning. If Jaevid could not make that killing blow, then Maldobar would fall, and with it, every person I had ever loved.

Mavrik unfurled to face the imposter king drake, his teeth bared and black spines bristling along his back and head. His tail whipped, and his plated chest heaved with furious breaths. Burning venom drizzled from his open maw, hissing as it hit the stone. Feral wrath blazed in his yellow eyes as he looked back to us, as though silently demanding we hurry up.

Jaevid's expression twitched. He turned slightly, glancing over one shoulder as two more dragons circled and landed next to us. Phevos and Vexi crawled in closer, dipping their heads in respect and chirping at us anxiously. I hesitated, studying the pair. That couldn't be right. Vexi was wearing a saddle—and there was someone sitting in it!

Gods, had she done it? Had Vexi rescued Reigh already?

My heart leapt, swelling with hope. But when the man threw back the visor of his helmet to grin down at us, it wasn't Reigh. My father, King Felix Farrow, was sitting casually astride the green dragoness in an ensemble of dragonrider armor I'd never seen him wear before. It was old, tarnished in places, and a little too small for him around the middle.

Oh no. Surely that wasn't his old dragonrider armor from the Gray War. He hadn't worn it in ... well, probably sometime before I was born. That must have been well over twenty years ago!

"You didn't honestly think I'd let you run off to have all the fun without me, did you?" He chuckled when he caught me gaping.

I blinked, just to make sure I wasn't hallucinating. I sort of hoped I was. "But, I thought Vexi chose Reigh to be her rider? H-how did you manage to convince her to let you ... ?"

"I can be very persuasive," he said, puffing his chest out proudly.

Jaevid rolled his eyes. "Felix, you had nothing to do with

it. I, on the other hand, spent two hours talking her into this. And she only agreed to do it if we made rescuing Reigh our first priority."

My father wafted a hand. "Details, details. The important part is, we're back in the sky causing trouble again. Just like old times, eh? You and I, impossible odds, the fate of the world, and nothing but a bit of dumb luck on our side."

"Just try and keep up," Jaevid taunted, a little smirk playing on his lips as he grabbed ahold of Mavrik's saddle and climbed into place. "I did warn her to take it easy on you. Being forty years out of the saddle, I'm sure you'll appreciate a *gentle* reintroduction."

Father's lips pursed with any annoyed scowl. "If I'm not mistaken, you've been out of the saddle a while, too. Only difference I see is that you still can't grow a beard. Just try me, Jae. We'll see who's really out of practice."

Jaevid was laughing as he slid the visor of his helmet down, covering his face. That was my cue to get ready.

Gripping the saddle handles, I hauled myself onto Phevos's back with one swift motion. My legs slipped comfortably into the boot sheaths on either side of his strong neck, and my fingers flew over the buckles as I strapped myself in. My hands shook with nervous energy, teeth rattling as I fumbled with my helmet. In my rush, my sweaty fingers slipped over the slick, polished metal. My helmet went tumbling. I flailed to catch it, but it was too late.

A swift, slate-colored hand, glinting with tiny white specks along the wrist and fingers, appeared out of nowhere, snagging my helmet out of the air before it could hit the ground.

Phillip stood right beside us, staring up at me with his silver eyes shining in the starlight. His wavy black hair blew around his face, nearly hiding the smile that showed the points of his incisors. He stepped in closer and handed the helmet back up to me. "Nervous?"

"No," I lied.

"I thought I should come see you off," Phillip said, glancing around at Jaevid and my father. Both were watching us. "I'll be helping hold the wall. The men are terrified. We're outnumbered twenty to one. But I won't let them falter—not when your life depends on it."

My heart hit the back of my throat. Suddenly, I wished I wasn't already buckled into my saddle. I wanted to hug him, to kiss him one last time. Gods, if this was the last time we ever saw one another, I had to tell him, to make sure he knew how much he meant to me.

"Phillip, I—"

He shook his head, pressing a finger to his lips as he backed away. "No goodbyes. Not tonight. Go on, love. When it's over, you know where to find me."

TWENTY-TWO

The Tibran ranks advanced, marching with a pace that resounded like thunder, with hundreds upon thousands of soldiers carrying their crimson banner ever closer to our city walls. Every block of troops stood beneath the golden eagle standard, bronze shields interlocked, and bloodshot eyes fixed upon us. What came next was inevitable. Like the calm before the rush and chaos of a storm, a moment of silence hung in the air as though the whole world had stopped to hold its breath.

Only one question lingered, caught in the mind of every man and woman on the battlefield: who would draw first blood tonight?

The answer came in a cacophony of shrieks and bellowing roars. Like ghosts from the moonless night, the shapes of creatures sailing through the air toward Halfax took form.

They came at varying speeds, some as fast as a shrike, others more steadily like dragons—because that's precisely what they were.

I recognized a few of the dragons right away. Once, they were proud and honorable beasts. They'd fallen in battle at Northwatch, defending it to their last breath, only to be left upon that battlefield with their deceased riders still belted into the saddles. There was no way to go back for the bodies so that they could receive the proper burial rites. Argonox did not honor ancient battle customs. He chose to use the corpses for fouler things.

Like this.

The creatures were in the same state as Icarus—reanimated, rotting corpses brought back to some semblance of life by Reigh's divine power. Whatever honor they had possessed before was gone. Tonight, they were our enemies.

Biting back my revulsion, I steeled myself as best I could. This was only the first of Argonox's horrors. No doubt he had many more in store for us.

As the flock of monsters soared past, Icarus let out a rumbling cry, spitting a plume of white-hot flame into the night. The monstrous black drake reared onto his haunches, sweeping tattered wings open and diving forward into the air to lead the charge. That was all the motivation they needed. The Tibran army shuddered into motion, advancing straight toward us.

On our left, Mavrik stirred and hissed, ears slicked back, and jagged teeth bared at his imposing rival. Jaevid barely had time to signal to us, *"You two find Reigh. The dragonriders will hold their sky assault. Mavrik and I will deal with Icarus."*

My stomach dropped. He was going after them alone? Oh no—not this again.

There was no time to reply or argue as Mavrik kicked off the turret and surged forward, aimed directly to intercept Icarus and Beckah's path. With Haldor's words of warning still ringing in my ears, I had no choice but to signal to my father and take off. Phevos and I took point, taking to the air and immediately bolting upward to get out of range of the Tibran ground fire and net-throwers.

From the air, it was easier to map out the true immensity of the Tibran forces. Blocks of legions moved as one, responding to the cadence of drummers to tell them where to go. Lines of cavalrymen came after, their steeds straining to haul the first of their war machines, huge metal ladders, toward the city walls. Each one was tall enough to reach the ramparts and armed with grasping hooks to anchor them in place. It took no less than four horses to haul them forward, and the beasts were well-guarded by the soldiers clustered around them.

Behind them came more legions, different blocks brandishing different styles of weaponry—some of which I'd never seen before. Masses from around the world, enslaved and spurred to fight for this madman, carried all manner of devices and dressed in strange styles of armor. Some rode on the backs of beasts, creatures like giant boars as big as bulls, and hefting double-headed axes. Others were dressed in gleaming silks, brandishing curved scimitars as they rode in chariots hauled by stallions with pelts that shone like scales and cloven hooves.

An entire line of war beasts like the one Hilleddi had

ridden into Barrowton stomped and bayed, swaying beneath platforms of bone and steel. Moving slow, twelve of the beasts tromped across the earth behind a leader whose scaly hide was as red as ruby. Its body was studded with spines and horns, like a cross between lizard and porcupine. Seated on one of those raised platforms, snapping the long chains anchored to the creature's stocky forelegs, was a figure I could have sworn I recognized. No—that was impossible. It couldn't be.

I steered Phevos a bit lower, doing a swift pass just to be sure.

Gods and Fates and all things holy … it was *her*!

Hilleddi stood atop the platform of that spiny creature, her eyes milky and skin as pale as a corpse. Some sort of iron collar had been fixed around her neck, most likely to put her head back where it was supposed to be, and she looked out across the battlefield with her mouth drawn into a sneer.

A thousand questions ran roared through my brain like a surge of electrical current. Had Reigh's power been used to revive her corpse, as well? When? How? Why would Argonox defile the body of his own sister that way? Did he have no sense of morality or honor at all? If not even his sister's body was sacred, then what else had he revived to send against us?

A sudden shriek from Vexi drew my focus away. The green dragon pitched her head, snapping and yelping as we passed the army below. She fought my father's directions, flapping and snarling as she tore away from our formation and past the line of war beasts Hilleddi was leading.

Suddenly, I saw why.

Behind them, flanked by legions pushing countless trebuchets and catapults into range, was a grand chariot. Lord

Argonox himself stood at the front of the carriage, draped in a long dark cloak that looked as though it had been cut right from a dragon's scaly hide. Clever, if not completely barbaric. A dragon's own hide was the only thing that couldn't be melted or burnt by their venom.

Bound to a long draft pole by iron-wrought chains were two dragons, each harnessed by the same cruel muzzle device that had been used on Vexi. From where I sat, it looked as though their wings had been cut—leathery membranes sliced away entirely so they stood no chance of ever flying again. The sight made my eyes well and anger burned in my chest as hot as hellfire. My vision swerved with fury. Beneath me, Phevos let out a roar of disgust. How *dare* he disfigure them that way!

But that was not what had Vexi pitching wildly in the air like an unbroken horse, trying to buck my father out of her saddle.

Tethered between the two dragons, his arms held wide by shackles bound to the muzzle of each of the beasts, was Reigh. The sight of him, slumped and nearly naked, his limp body dragging over the ground between the dragons like a prize, was too much. I couldn't bear it.

A scream tore out of me, so primal I didn't even recognize it. Rage and grief boiled up from my soul. With all the gods as my witness, Argonox would *pay* for this.

Vexi cried out again, shaking her head and spinning wildly as my father fought to keep her at bay. Now it all made sense. She wanted to go to him—her rider. She wanted to set him free.

"*Let her go,*" I signaled to my father, who was struggling

just to stay in the saddle. "*That's him! That's Reigh!*"

Father immediately released the saddle handles and leaned down, pressing his body flat against her neck for stability. The young dragoness dove straight for Argonox like a tongue of lime green lightning. I urged Phevos to take up the chase, and he bellowed in agreement. There was no way we would let her do this alone.

The battle began like a mighty wave breaking upon an ancient seaside fortress.

Dragons and shrikes collided in the air above countless Tibran soldiers, plumes of flame flashing in the night as dragons spat their burning venom and catapults launched orbs that smashed against the city walls. Mavrik and Icarus collided in midair like two eagles, rear legs and talons extended and jaws snapping. The night was a riot of men shouting, swords clashing, bowstrings snapping, and the *swoosh—boom* of trebuchet fire. The acrid smell of dragon venom mingled with the metallic stench of fresh blood.

Before they could reach the outer wall of the city, Argonox's cavalries were interrupted by the sudden appearance of a hundred enormous earthen golems. They writhed free of the ground, resembling the ones Jaevid had summoned out of the Marshlands before. Only these were larger—*much* larger. Their bodies were crafted of stone and root rather than mud and rot. They lumbered forward, smashing through enemy lines with boulder-fists flying.

Enemy fire from the ground howled past me in barely discernable blurs. Arrows glanced off my armor. Spears zoomed passed my head, missing by inches. A net snagged at the edge of one of Phevos's wings, but he was able to shake it off and continue his rapid dive toward the ground.

We'd trained for years on how to make an assault like this. It was our primary mission—to lay down fire and clear the way for ground infantry. Vexi, however, had never seen a single day of official training. She was still wild and didn't know how to work with a rider in battle. So, the instant the young dragoness touched down, Phevos and I moved as one to hold the perimeter so that my father could dismount. It was safer for him to get as far away from her as possible. His life wasn't the one she was interested in saving, after all.

He unbuckled quickly and kicked free of the saddle, hitting the ground in a roll before springing up to run headlong toward Reigh with his sword drawn.

Argonox saw him coming. He unfurled a long, nine-tailed whip and drew it back to strike, snapping the tip off the rumps of the grounded dragons hauling his chariot. The beasts screeched in pain and bucked as Argonox pulled back on the reins, undoubtedly wrenching those pinch bits into their soft tongues. The dragons responded with a spew of burning venom aimed right for my father.

Fire exploded into the night. I had to look away, shielding my eyes from the bloom of intense light. When I looked back, there were only flames. I couldn't see anything—no sign of my father.

"No!" I shrieked and whipped the saddle handles, giving the command to pursue. There was still time. I could make it! I would not let my father die this way!

A figure unfurled from the flames. Two broad, birdlike wings spread wide, their feathers as bright and colorful as gemstones as they beat once. The flames instantly died out, snuffed by the rush of wind off those feathers.

How was that possible? Nothing could douse dragon fire!

I gaped, barely able to keep myself upright in the saddle as a creature rose from where it had wrapped itself protectively around my father. It had appeared out of nowhere, but now it stood like a riot of color amidst the churning darkness of battle. It was a bizarre mixture of bird and fox, with feathers as bright as a jungle parrot's and eyes that glowed like fiery emeralds in the night. It was almost as big as a dragon, although far stranger than anything I'd seen before—outside of paintings and tapestries from the Gray War, anyway.

I gasped. It was a foundling spirit.

On slender birdlike feet, the creature crept around my father, its large pointed ears perked forward, and vulpine snout wrinkled in a snarl. Throwing off his helmet, my father stood and aimed a broad grin up toward Argonox. He was alive! And without so much as a singe mark anywhere that I could see.

As Vexi sailed in from the sky, her sides swelling with the distinct deep breath that preceded a spray of fire, King Felix drew his sword. He rushed for the chariot, swinging wide with a furious shout I heard clearly over the roar of battle. "*Give me back my son!*"

PART FIVE

REIGH

TWENTY-THREE

My body was so numb I couldn't feel my own breathing anymore. Everything was cold, as though I were suspended under ice water, drifting while my last few seconds of consciousness slipped away. Was my heart still beating? Was I even alive?

No—I had to be alive.

I could still feel the dull sensation of iron shackles biting in to my wrists and the scrape of the earth under my legs and knees as I was dragged forward and across the ground. Phoebe had tried to bandage my arms after the bleeding. I didn't understand why. And it didn't matter now. The shackles reopened the wounds, and that small amount of discomfort somehow made it through the haze of raw power humming through my body—just enough to keep me conscious. But where were they taking me? What was happening? I was slipping, falling into the cold darkness again. This time, I didn't resist. I couldn't. My strength was gone.

I just wanted it to be over.

The muffled roar of beasts—dragons and Tibran monsters—spun through my frayed mind like echoes of an invisible nightmare. The rumble of explosions, blasts of fire, and cries of men came from every direction. The world seemed to shake around me, smelling strongly of ash and brimstone. But I was too far gone to be afraid. Why? What was the point? Death was the only way I would ever escape. Argonox would never let me go.

A voice boomed over the noise, so loud I could feel it rattling in my skull. "GIVE ME BACK MY SON!"

My arms went slack as though someone had cut the chains bound to my wrists, and suddenly there was nothing there to force me upright. My legs buckled. I fell, too weak to even try to catch myself, and hit the ground face-first.

What was happening? Who was that? My ears rang, and I strained to hear that voice again.

Bellowing howls and thunderous booms shook the ground under me. The sound of snarls, snapping teeth against scales, and shrieks of pain seemed to come from every direction. I recognized the deep inhale and throaty hiss, followed by the roar of flames. A dragon was spitting its fiery venom so close by I could smell the acidic tinge of it lingering in the air. The low hum of something huge swooshed right over me, probably missing me by inches. A tail? Wings? Gods only knew. But I couldn't even lift my head to see.

The brawl seemed to end as abruptly as it had begun. No more roars. No more flame. A break in the commotion with only the distant sound of the battle to fill the silence.

A soft whine and series of pops, clicks, and chirps resonated against my ear and a hot blast of musky breath blasted over my cheek. I felt it. Something huge was looming over me. But I couldn't move or open my eyes.

A rough shove rocked my senses, rolling me over so that I flopped onto my back. More hot breaths blasted against my face. I didn't have to see her. I knew it was Vexi.

It took every ounce of strength left in my body to will my eyes open. The end of her big green nose was right in my face, smelling me and whining. She licked at my forehead, one big swipe of sticky dragon spit up the bridge of my nose all the way to my hairline.

"H-hey there," I managed to rasp weakly.

She chirped, huge blue eyes blinking down at me with concern. Curling her scaly body around me like a protective living barrier, she laid her head on the ground right next to mine. Her ears perked toward me and nostrils puffed in deep, as though she could sense I was in bad shape.

Too late, I realized that leaving her, trying to send her away, was by far the stupidest thing I'd ever done. That's saying something, I know. Doing stupid stuff was basically my life's hobby. But Kiran had told me about the loyalty of dragons many times. And right after Vexi chose me, Jenna had said something about it, too. She'd said that our bond was special—that Vexi would stick by me no matter what, even in death. At the time, I hadn't understood what that meant.

Now I did.

"I-I'm sorry, Vexi," I croaked, not sure if she'd even

understand. I'd have given anything just to touch her, maybe pet her head a little or give her ears one last good scratch.

My dragon tucked herself in tighter around me, sniffing through my hair and wrapping her wings around us. It muffled the chaos. It made me feel safe. Nuzzling her big head under my arm, she lay still and stared at me, the deep rhythm of her heartbeat right in my ear. I'd never heard anything so soothing in my entire life.

"I found him! He's here!" a woman shouted nearby, her voice familiar even muffled by Vexi's body around me. That was ... I mean it sounded like ... Jenna.

"Where?" a man yelled back. It wasn't Argonox, Jaevid, Aubren, or Phillip. No, this was someone else—a voice I didn't recognize.

Vexi's body tensed around me. She hissed, unfurling somewhat to lift her head and growl.

"Easy there, girl. I know he's hurt. He needs our help. Let me see him, all right? I'll be careful," the man crooned. "Just let me take a look."

Vexi hissed louder, snapping her jaws, and gave a strong blast through her nose as one last threat. Then she leaned away.

And I saw him.

A human man bent over me, his light brown eyes the same color as mine. They seemed kind; gentle, somehow. Staring into them was bizarre, and the more I studied him, the stranger I felt. Why was his face so familiar? His stony, rugged features were crinkled with age, and his wavy, dark golden hair was streaked with gray that was the same color as his short beard. At the sight of me, his thick brows lifted, and his mouth opened. Only one word escaped. "Reigh."

He knew me? How? I didn't recognize him at all. Was he Tibran? Surely not. His armor looked like a dragonrider's ensemble.

Before I could muster a reply, the man was ripping off his riding gauntlets and rushing toward me. He fell to his knees and gathered me into his arms, squeezing me tight. His breathing hitched. Was he crying? Why?

"You've got to get him out of here," Jenna spoke over us suddenly, appearing like an armored angel of vengeance. "Phevos and I can't stay here. Argonox abandoned the chariot and we lost him in the ranks. I don't know what he's up to, but he's on the move and the war beasts are advancing this way. They will be upon us in minutes! I can't cover you any longer; we have to rejoin our formation."

The man didn't respond.

She growled louder. "Father! Did you hear me? You have to get out of here now!"

Wait—*Father*? This man was … ? So that meant he was my … ?

I wanted to look at him again, to check his features over for any more traces of a resemblance. But the next thing I knew, the man was hefting me into a dragon's saddle and climbing on behind me. It was only after he'd started buckling us together that I realized this saddle was on Vexi. Since when did she wear a saddle? Was this Jaevid's doing?

With one arm wrapped around me and the other gripping a saddle handle, he gave her a nudge and Vexi spread her wings. She bounded skyward with a shrill cry and a wild rush of wind. The earth fell away. My head lulled, and for an instant all I could see were the stars overhead. Countless. Brilliant. Only now when I looked at them, all I could think about was the dark goddess taunting me from behind that glittering barrier. The cold of her power had all but consumed me. I was hanging by a thread, waiting for the snap and fall into a restful abyss.

Vexi leveled off with a few hard beats of her wings and I slumped forward, resting against her neck with my cheek against the warm, smooth surface of her scales.

Through the haze and delirium, something else caught my eye. Far below, there was more light, but no stars. No, this was something far worse. A scene of unspeakable horror spread out below us. Halfax was under siege. And from where I sat, it was as though the entire world was burning in the night.

There were Tibrans on the ramparts. They'd pushed their metal ladders to the wall and were climbing, one right after another, to clash against the Maldobarian infantry waiting there. The land all around the city was boiling with the motion of thousands of soldiers—all converging upon the city walls. Swords flashed. Shields bashed. In the air, dragons and shrikes collided in aerial combat with plumes of burning venom. Trebuchets hurled orbs that smashed against the walls and turrets, exploding with a force that blew soldiers to their doom far below. It was like watching burning oil being poured over an anthill.

And in the thick of it all, I saw Jaevid.

Granted, when it came to picking people out in the thick of a battle, Jaevid Broadfeather was easy to spot. Mavrik was one of the two largest dragons on the field. The other—well—I knew that monster far too well. It was the one Argonox had forced me to reanimate. The first experiment. Now that abomination was writhing on the ground, white bone peeking through its rotting hide. The two king drakes kicked and rolled, snarling and snapping like two enormous feral cats. They crunched over any soldier who was stupid enough to get too close.

Nearby, Jaevid had his blade drawn, locked in combat with *her*.

Beckah Derrick.

My brain throbbed at the sight of that black and gold armor, and acid burned at the back of my throat. Even from a distance, her presence made my head swim and my body quiver with a rising swell of cold. So much power had been poured into her, but in the end, it had only brought back her body and maybe a few fragments of her muscle memory— enough to make her a contender in a fight. But there was nothing else inside her except raw, crackling dark energy. No spirit. No soul. No essence of who she'd been before.

I just hoped Jaevid realized that.

From where I was sitting, it didn't look good. Beckah had him on the defensive, bearing in hard with a pair of strange white blades that looked familiar. Crap—those were my kafki! I was sure of it; those were the same white elven blades Hilleddi had taken off me when Aubren and I were captured on our way to Barrowton! Argonox had given her *my* weapons? And now she was using them against Jaevid? Of all the sick, twisted—

Beckah suddenly lunged in with a brutal assault, swirling the white blades with an effortless grace. Every movement was precise, steps in a deadly dance, as she swung wide. Dipping and feinting, she darted around him in complex strikes that would have forced even a seasoned fighter to put up their guard.

Jaevid, however, was just as fast. He had size and reach on her but didn't seem to need to use either as he met every strike like they'd rehearsed this beforehand. They dueled like demons, their armor reflecting the glow of dragon fire and exploding orbs, and their faces twisted with similar expressions of rage. But where Beckah's seemed more disconnected and violent, Jaevid's was riddled with grief.

With an abrupt surge of energy, Beckah rushed him with a swing of those white, scythe-shaped blades and sent him reeling backward. The slice missed his neck by centimeters. He rocked back, off balance for less than a second. But that was all the time she needed. Faster than a viper's strike, Beckah planted a boot right in the center of his chest. The kick sent him flying with a burst of dark power. He skidded over the ground, losing his grip on his scimitar, and rolled to a halt flat on his back.

I felt my pulse return with a vengeance, thrashing in my ears with a rush of adrenaline and fear. Jaevid couldn't lose. Not now—not like this.

Beckah spun the blades over in her hands as she prowled forward, her spine rippling with confidence in every swaggering step. Jaevid sat up on his elbows, staring at her with brows crinkled upward as he shouted at her. Whatever he said, I never heard it. The words were lost to the rumble of the battlefield.

She stopped over him. I cringed, every muscle instinctively drawn tight with dread as she brandished my razor-sharp kafki. This was it.

All of a sudden, Jaevid's eyes began glowing like two emerald stars. He snapped a hand forward, clenching a fist in the air. At the same instant, three huge vines burst out of the ground and snaked around Beckah's body, pinning her arms to her sides and anchoring her to the earth. They held her fast, suspended so that she was eye-level with Jaevid when he got to his feet.

His eyes still shone through the night as he approached her cautiously, his mouth moving. What was he doing? Reasoning with her? Couldn't he tell there was no trace of her spirit in that monster Argonox had forced me to create? That was *not* the real Beckah!

Jaevid bent down, fingers wrapping around the grip of his scimitar. When he straightened, his eyes were pinched shut and his mouth screwed up as though he were in pain. He didn't look at her again, even when he rammed his scimitar to the hilt into her chest.

Beckah's milky, lifeless eyes went wide. Her jaw went slack, and then so did the rest of her. My blades slipped out of her hands.

It was over.

Jaevid slid his scimitar back, head hung to his chest as he turned away. I couldn't see his face until he slowly turned back to her. With broad shoulders curled forward, his expression shattered into anguish. His eyes welled, and his chin quivered, hand shaking as he grasped the back of her head and let his forehead rest against hers. He stood like that for a second or two, and then brushed his fingers over her face to gently shut her eyes.

Jaevid stumbled back away from her, his whole face twitching and expression skewing. He let out a horrible, broken cry as he crumpled to his knees before her and buried his face in his hands. He couldn't see the figure in spiny black armor approaching through the ranks of soldiers.

Oh no.

Clenching my teeth, I gave Vexi's neck a pat to get her attention. "T-there. We h-have to warn him," I rasped. "Hurry!"

She chirped and flashed me a disapproving glare. Fine, so she had a point. I wasn't exactly in prime shape for a fight. This probably looked a lot like a grand gesture of suicide. But my focus was on warning Jaevid. I had to. This was a fight he couldn't win.

"Trust me, okay?" I forced a weak smile.

She snorted, looked away, and made a swift, spiraling descent toward Jaevid.

The dark figure was getting closer. Twenty yards away. Through the toiling hordes of soldiers, no one else seemed to notice him. But I couldn't look away. I had to stop this. Jaevid didn't know!

"What are you doing?" The old man sitting behind me protested. Father or not, he didn't seem to like what was going on and pulled me back from Vexi's neck, restraining me against his chest.

I didn't have the strength or time to explain. I was already on borrowed time. That dark figure in armor was drawing closer, and as far as I could tell, Jaevid still hadn't seen him.

He didn't know what was coming—what I had been forced to create.

Vexi laid down a broad perimeter of her burning venom to clear a landing path. She hit the ground at a trot and loped in as close as she could without getting caught in the fray of the dueling king drakes. With a gale-force rush of wind, the two beasts kicked off the earth and took their fight back into the sky. With the undead drake making speed toward the city, Mavrik took up the chase with a shriek of wrath.

Vexi ducked as they howled past, her emerald hide shivering. She chittered anxiously and looked all around as the Tibran ranks began to converge on us from all sides, armed with net-throwers and spears. I guess they'd been instructed to stay clear of Beckah and Jaevid—but we were fair game.

I had to hurry.

Shoving away from the man, my father, I hurled myself off Vexi's back and hit the ground like a dead fish. I lay there for a moment, mustering the will to crawl across the dirt as far away from them as I could.

With a desperate, final breath I yelled back at my dragon, "GO!"

She screeched in dismay, and the man on her back shouted at me again. There was no time to debate it. Jaevid was in trouble. I had to stop it. He had to know—that man, the armor—whatever happened, Jaevid could *not* attack him!

TWENTY-FOUR

"Jaevid!" The cry left my lips a second too late.

A deep laugh resonated over us like the rumble of thunder.

Jaevid and I looked, moving in unison, just in time to see the figure of a man clad in black armor step forward out of the line of awestruck Tibran soldiers. With a black cloak of dragon hide draped over his shoulders, every inch of his body was fortified behind armor that made my mind scream in panic and protest. I felt its presence like a white-hot brand pressing at the base of my skull. It pierced the numbness, the cold, and threatened to burn me alive from the inside out.

I opened my mouth to scream, but nothing would come out. My breath—my voice—hung in my throat as my body convulsed on the ground.

That armor was more than a defilement or abomination.

Every inch of that dark armor had been crafted especially for this moment, etched in runes and forged with *my* blood infused in the metal. Basically, if evil had a garment of choice, Argonox was currently wearing it.

Jaevid was already staggering to his feet. His nostrils flared with deep, enraged breaths as he fixed Argonox with a focused stare. With his hands curled into fists at his side, he strode forward to meet him. Emerald light bloomed from his eyes once again, sparking to life at the same instant two white feathery wings unfurled from his back. Each feather seemed to be crafted from shining mist, piercing through the haze of combat like guiding starlight. Sweeping white horns like those of a faundra stag grew from Jaevid's head right above his pointed ears. His skin shimmered with a pearlescent hue like scales along his cheekbones and brow.

With lips curled back into a snarl, he flared his white wings and drew back a hand.

NO!

I dug my hands into the dirt, trying to claw my way in closer. I had to warn him! *Stop! Don't do it, you idiot!*

Jaevid launched his assault with a thrust of his hand. The ground shuddered, cracking open like an eggshell along the path of a bolt of green power that hurtled toward Argonox. The green comet collided full force against his breastplate with a flash of blinding light and a gusting blast wave.

My spine went rigid. Pain coursed through my body, setting every nerve on fire. I could feel it in my bones, the electrifying power like acid in my marrow. It rattled in my teeth and sizzled over my skin.

"Reigh!" Jaevid called out to me.

I couldn't reply or do anything at all except lie there, my vision tunneling in and out, until the pain passed.

As the light faded and the dust began to clear, Argonox let out a booming laugh. "Hah! It seems that didn't quite kill him. Care to try again?" He stepped from the swirling smoke, sliding off his helmet and tossing it onto the ground between them. He prowled closer, a satisfied grin curled across his face. "Perhaps your next strike will save me the trouble. Did you really think I'd bring him here if he could be so easily rescued? His power—his very essence—is tied to me now. Every strike you make will seal his fate."

Jaevid stared at me, his glowing eyes wide and expression devoid of any emotion. Not exactly the most hope-inspiring look, considering the circumstances. Didn't he have a plan for all this?

"It's pathetic, really," Argonox sneered as he stepped in closer, tipping his chin up in confidence. "I mean, him, I get. He's a sniveling child, too stupid and naïve to know his place in this grand symphony. But I expected more from you. Not that it matters. You'll both die on this battlefield, mired in your own blood and filth, while I claim every prize this kingdom has to offer. There's a far more powerful artifact to be had and I won't have to worry about keeping some sniveling whelp alive to use it. This power, this divine rite, after centuries of waiting and searching ... I am finally *myself* again." Argonox's laugh crackled in the cold air. "I am the only Harbinger this world deserves."

Jaevid bowed his head to his chest, obscuring his face behind clumps of sweaty ash gray hair as he turned to face me. His arms moved, and I sucked in a sharp breath.

I was the problem. If he killed me, it would be merciful. Then he could deal with Argonox without having to listen to me scream the entire time until one of his powerful blasts finally finished me off. He could end my suffering now.

He moved like a blur, so fast I didn't even have time to brace myself. Throwing back his dragonrider cloak, Jaevid grabbed a small leather satchel that was strung across his back and reached inside.

The ambient glow of torch and starlight made the dark crystal sparkle in his hand. As he drew it free of the satchel, my mind erupted with a chorus of whispers that sent cold shivers through my body. I couldn't look away. Every jagged point and glittering inch of that crystal made my body tremble and quake with power, bubbling up from somewhere deep inside.

What … what was that thing?

"Is this the artifact you had in mind?" Jaevid asked, his voice laced with spite as he kept his face hidden.

Argonox's eyes grew wide and desperate. "It's mine! Give it to me!" He roared and surged in for a charging assault.

Jaevid snapped his gaze to meet mine, and I saw a tiny hint of hesitation quirk across his brow. His hand flourished over the crystal, jerking strangely. I could have sworn I saw blood drizzling over one of the jagged points of the crystal.

In a single heartbeat, everything around me stopped. Every second became a decade. I was suspended, weightless, … free. My mind was as quiet as the stillness of the deepest winter freeze. There was no more pain as I pushed myself up to my knees, staring around at the eerily silent and frozen chaos around me.

Everywhere I looked, Tibran soldiers stood like statues, caught in the middle of their strikes and parries with Maldobarian infantry. Overhead, dragons were suspended in the air, locked in combat with shrikes or others of their kind. Everything was frozen in time.

In fact, the only one still moving besides me was Jaevid and …

"*Hello, Reigh. About time we met face-to-face, isn't it, my pet?*" The woman before me loomed like a giant, eight feet tall at least. She was like a living statue, larger than life and bathed in ageless beauty. With skin as white as milk and lips of ruby red, she studied me with eyes that glittered the same way that dark crystal had—black, bottomless, and eternal. "*A gift of pure blood is a difficult thing to come by. But the blood of the lapiloque? Well, there's nothing purer unless it came from the veins of the foregods. But I doubt they'd be so accommodating. After all, they were the ones who built my starry prison. Lovely, isn't it?*" Her laughter crackled in the air as she gestured upward, to where the stars shone more brightly than ever, seeming to flicker and pulse.

I staggered to my feet as she began to come closer, bolts of her wavy black hair flowing down to brush the ground at her bare feet. The length of her black robe slid off one creamy-white shoulder and didn't seem to be made of any kind of earthly material. Every movement made the bolt of fabric ripple and shimmer, as though millions of tiny dark crystals were embedded into it.

"*Don't be afraid, my darling,*" she crooned in her smooth, breathy tone as she stopped before me and bent down, crouching so that we were looking eye-to-eye. "*I've waited a long time for this moment.*"

"Clysiros," I managed to croak her name.

Her smile was electric and staggeringly beautiful. It pulled me in like a single candle burning in a dark cave. I wanted to go closer. To hear her speak. To know her. Something told me being in her embrace would be peaceful—restful, even.

She stretched out a hand and brushed her fingers along my cheek, each one so big she could have mashed my head like a grape. "*An eternity trapped in a cage, imprisoned with the damned and despised, with only my trusted Harbinger to be my eyes and hands in this world. And then the lapiloque comes to me with a bargain. So many favors in exchange for a fresh start.*"

"Favors?" I glanced back over to where Jaevid was watching, his expression fixed in a tense frown.

"Terms," he clarified, his expression sharp and ominous. "We spoke of this before. Paligno and Clysiros require some form of manifestation on earth for their powers to remain effective. Formerly, that was the stones. I shattered Paligno's and became a vessel for his essence instead. But your crystal remains." He paused, emerald eyes flickering to Clysiros and narrowing. "It must also be destroyed. A new balance must be struck—a new way for the gods to manifest."

Right. I did remember that discussion, although at the

time I hadn't envisioned we'd be reopening the topic in front of an actual deity. "You have an idea?"

Clysiros's pouty red lips curved into another alluring smile. "*He proposes we resume our presence on earth as it was in the old times. No more silly stones in need of mortal speakers. But with the added agreement that should either of us seek to dominate the other, a most terrible punishment would befall.*"

"What kind of punishment would a god fear?" I almost didn't want to know.

"*The thing all gods fear, my darling.*" She traced a cold fingertip down the bridge of my nose. "*Mortality.*"

"The god found guilty of overstepping his or her bounds would suffer a lifetime of mortality—devoid of any divine power," Jaevid concurred. "Hopefully such an existence would be as educational as it would be humbling."

"*I doubt if anything could humble my brother,*" Clysiros scoffed with a taunting grin.

Jaevid gave a snort. "I pray we never find out."

"*At any rate, these terms are agreeable to the three of us. But we need an accord of all parties for this to work. As long as this agreement is acceptable to you, as well, then we have only one small matter to attend to.*" She drew back slightly, licking her lips as she stared at me like a hungry she-wolf eyeing a meal. "You must complete the ritual and become my Harbinger."

My mind raced. Standing in that frozen eternity, my gaze darted from the Tibran soldiers, Maldobarian infantry, dragons, and war beasts to the blood-caked mud under my feet, the vines Jaevid had summoned, and the men who had already fallen to a blade, arrow, spear, or flame.

Then, of course, there was Argonox. My lip curled. Anger

swelled in my already frazzled brain, making a coppery taste rise in my throat.

I set my jaw and looked back to the goddess. "What about all things he did with my—er—your power? Can it be undone?"

She grinned. "*Of course. He was such an unruly child. It was never enough, all the power I gave him. He always wanted more.*"

"And my abilities? Those will be gone, too?"

"*Don't look so disappointed, darling,*" she crooned again. "*What we had was beautiful while it lasted.*"

My stomach tensed. "What about Noh?"

Tilting her head to the side made Clysiros's hair brush against her porcelain-hued cheek. "*Is that a hint of concern I hear? Are you worried for your dear brother?*"

"I think he deserves better than dying alone in the Vale. I don't understand him, but he was dragged into this mess because of me. I can't just turn my back on him."

She studied me with those bottomless black eyes. Something about them reminded me of the Well of Souls— as though they were churning with the same chaotic force and I might drown in them if I stared for too long.

"*I will still need a faithful guardian to guide the spirits there and shepherd them on to their final rewards. He may remain, if he chooses, and hold that position. You have my assurance that he will be well taken care of,*" she agreed. "*Is that your only request? Lapiloque has already demanded much of us.*"

I looked past her to where Jaevid stood, silently observing our debate. What else would he have possibly asked for? At that moment, I was doing good just to comprehend what was happening. I didn't keep a wish list of potential favors to ask from deities tucked into my back pocket.

"I-I, uh, I suppose it is." I glanced back to Clysiros. "I just want this to end, for all our sakes."

Her silky, coy laugh hung in the air. *"You mortals are all the same! Always fretting over the present, barely able to perceive all that's come before you and all that will come after."* Combing her fingers through my filthy, tangled hair, she took a lock of it and teased it with her thumb. *"Everything ends, my love. Then it begins again. Cycles upon cycles, the spheres of time are endlessly turning. Not even the gods can stop it. So, try to appreciate the now. Nothing else is guaranteed, my love."*

"Then let's end it. How ... how can we complete my ritual?" I almost didn't want to know. Somehow, I doubted it would be anything pleasant.

Her face drew in closer, only a breath away as she stroked a single, cold fingertip from my forehead, down the bridge of my nose, to my lips. *"With the kiss of death. Come now. It's rude to keep a girl waiting. And we have left much to do."*

PART SIX

JENNA

TWENTY-FIVE

It took less than two minutes to join in with another dragonrider formation. They were already preparing to intercept Hilleddi's company of monstrous war beasts, something I had a little experience with. Irony like ash soured on my tongue as Phevos and I fell into position. Ahead, I spotted the glimmer of Perish's white scales shining like a pearl against the night. Calem was in this formation. Perhaps Haldor was, too, although I couldn't see him anywhere.

We made four clean passes and broke the enemy line, bathing the battlefield in waves of burning dragon venom to stop the war beasts' advance. Separated and dazed by the fire, they would be far easier for our troops on the ground to contend with.

Three of the creatures fell, overwhelmed by the flames. Four more began bucking and swinging their massive heads, pitching against their chains and trying to flee. A portion of our dragonrider company immediately split off in pursuit, while the rest of us stayed the course and prepared for another pass on the remaining line.

Gritting my teeth, I steered Phevos into position at the point of one of the formations. My pulse clashed in my ears, and my palms sweated under my thick leather gauntlets as I gripped the saddle handles so tightly my knuckles ached. I'd already seen what one of those beasts was capable of at Barrowton. Halfax was far less fortified, even with the dragonriders to guard it. We could not allow them to reach the outer wall.

We banked in hard for our approach, lining up through the hailstorm of assaults coming from the ground. We veered and weaved sharply, dodging hurling nets and flying orbs of venom. Arrows pinged and clanged as they glanced off my armor. A few passed so close to my head I heard the scrape of the metal arrowheads against my helmet.

A dragon's panicked cry screamed out over the roar of battle. I turned just in time to see the dragonrider off my left wingtip begin to fall, his mount's body hopelessly tangled in one of the Tibran nets. Both dragon and rider plummeted, pitching and whirling toward the ground. My heart hit the back of my throat, and before I could think, I signaled to the rider on my right to take over point.

Then Phevos and I dove after our fallen comrade.

With his wings snapped in tight, Phevos zoomed toward the ground. We only had seconds. We were body lengths away. Then yards. Then feet. The ground rushed up, beckoning death on impact.

No—not if I could help it.

Phevos let out a hiss and stretched his hind legs out at the same moment he spread his wings wide. He caught the falling dragon by the tangled net with his claws. His powerful wings filled like ship sails, braced in the wind to break the force of the impact.

We hit hard—but not as hard as it would have been in free-fall. My brain rattled against my skull and my vision spotted. I wheezed, my chest so tight I couldn't breathe as I hit the saddle and Phevos's neck. It took a second or two to shake it off, peel myself back upright again, and figure out who had survived.

The snared dragon wriggled out from under us. Already his rider was cutting away the net and signaling me his gratitude. They were both alive. Thank the gods for that.

Phevos shook himself and snapped his jaws. He craned his big head around to glance at me, as though checking to make sure I was still okay. I gave his neck a pat. "Still here, big boy! Let's get off the ground!"

He chirped his agreement and crouched, prepped for takeoff.

Light exploded in my vision.

In an instant, I was flying again, my saddle straps snapping like threads. Flung free of my saddle, my body pitched wildly, skidding over the ground like a stone over water. Phevos gave a sharp cry—a noise I'd never heard him make before.

I landed in a heap, dazed and breathless. Heat and agony bloomed through one of my shoulders. Sitting up, I threw off my helmet and sucked in a desperate breath of the cold wind. Without that metal bucket to buffer the sound, the rumble of battle was nearly paralyzing. I blinked through the bright spots still flashing in my vision.

Gods—I was sitting in the middle of a cauldron of pure pandemonium. The sky was alive with fire and the screech of dragons locked in combat. The ground around me boiled with soldiers, both Tibran and Maldobarian, and the air rang with the metallic *clang, smash,* and *scrape* of blades upon shields.

Phevos? Where was my dragon?

The sight of purple scales drew me to my feet, cradling my left arm. It was dislocated, maybe worse. With my armor on, I couldn't tell exactly. Regardless, it was useless now. I couldn't even hold a blade with it.

"Phevos!" I screamed for him as I staggered toward him. No reply.

Faster—I had to go faster. I had to reach him. He needed me!

Yards away, Phevos lay motionless while a Tibran soldier approached his head with sword in hand.

Rage blazed through my body like hellfire. I ran, screaming as I drew my blade with my only usable arm. He would *not* touch Phevos.

I launched for him, leaping the last few feet to kick the Tibran soldier's knees out. He fell, too stunned to retaliate, and I landed on him in a rabid frenzy. Before the soldier could even move, I sank the point of my sword into the chink between his pauldron and breastplate. He shrieked under his helm and went still.

"Phevos!" I screamed again.

He still hadn't moved, lying on his side in a motionless heap. But his sides—they were moving. He was breathing!

As soon as I got to my feet, my legs threatened to buckle. I wobbled, barely able to stand, as my body flashed hot and cold. My head spun as I looked up, setting my jaw to begin a desperate stagger toward my fallen dragon.

Behind me, a monstrous roar shook the ground. It knocked me back onto my rear, and I gaped up in horror at the war beast tromping toward me. Its every step made the earth flinch, and its bellowing cry sent the soldiers around us scattering in terror.

That's what had hit us—a blast of electric energy from that creature's maw. It was the same stunt that had almost killed us at Barrowton. Now the beast loomed over me, a behemoth ready to crush me underfoot.

From the iron and bone-wrought platform on its back, Hilleddi's ashen face was twisted into a sneer. Her milky, glazed eyes stared right at me as she snapped the chains, ordering the monster to run me over. With another booming cry, the beast obliged. It reared, pawing the air, and came down with one foot aimed right for me—howling through the air like the fist of the sky god.

There was no escape. I couldn't run. I couldn't even stand. Death bore down, and I closed my eyes to meet it.

But death never came.

Over the constant storm of battle, a familiar shout found my ears. I opened my eyes and gasped, heartbeat stalling at the sight of a man standing over me. With legs braced and arms locked overhead, Phillip had a grip on the war beast's enormous foot and refused to let it fall. His body shook, back and arms bulging against the crushing force that bore down from above.

"Get out of the way!" He snarled through fanged teeth.

I tried to breathe and choked. Where had he come from? How, by all the gods, had he found me in this ocean of chaos?

"*Now!*"

I snapped free of my daze, seized my sword, and immediately kicked into an evasive, sideways roll. I clenched my jaw as the pressure of the maneuver set my injured arm and shoulder ablaze with pain again. No time to fret over it now.

Back on my feet, I ran, tripping and stumbling, to get out of the way.

The second I was out of range, Phillip let out another primal cry. I whipped around just in time to see him give the giant's foot one violent shove before he ran after me. He ran like an animal, leaping and bounding, and snatched the blade of the Tibran soldier I'd killed. His fangs flashed, eyes glowing like platinum fires as he charged for the war beast at full sprint.

And he wasn't alone.

Overhead, the rush of wind off the wings of a dozen dragons hummed like thunder. They bathed the creature in flame while Phillip, dodging and dancing to avoid the spray, used his clawed hands and feet to climb the creature's hide. Reaching the platform, I glimpsed his silhouette through the flashing flames as he drew back and made a vengeful strike right at Hilleddi's neck. She fell one way and her head rolled the other, separated once again.

Phillip tossed the blade aside and sprang skyward with his arms outstretched, burning venom licking at his heels. Right on cue, Turq and Haldor made a low pass right over him.

The dragon caught him by the arms and broke skyward. He might have a little singed fur on that tail of his, but Phillip was alive.

Alive—and more incredible than I ever could have imagined. I'd never seen anyone fight like that.

Hilleddi's war beast fell as the flames rose higher, so intense I had to shield my face from the heat. It hit the ground with a deafening *boom*, and the impact blew me backward and knocked my sword out of my hand. I landed on my rear again, spitting out rubble and wondering which deity I'd pleased enough to help me dodge certain death so many times in one day.

Whoever it was, I prayed they'd grant me one last favor as I limped toward my fallen dragon as fast as I could. Phevos stirred the instant I touched his snout, rubbing my hands along his cheek and neck. His big yellow eyes opened, blinking and rolling until his pupils narrowed with focus.

Tears sprang to my eyes as I pressed my lips against his scaly nose. He gave a snort of disapproval. Now wasn't the time for that. We had to move. There were still more of those war beasts to contend with, and while Phillip had a head start, I wasn't about to let him drop another one without me.

I couldn't see any visible injuries or wounds as Phevos gathered his legs beneath him and shook the rubble from his back. My saddle, however, was in shambles. Being torn out of it like that had compromised the seat. The girth straps were in shreds.

Dread sank to the pit of my stomach like a cold stone. My saddle was useless.

And with my left arm injured, unable to grip onto his

scales and spines in flight, so was I. I couldn't ride him bareback—not in this state. If the tingling and pain in my shoulder was any indication, I could only guess it was dislocated. It might have even be broken.

I took a deep, steadying breath, and made a decision. Drawing a dagger from the side of my boot, I cut the remaining straps and let the saddle slide off. It landed with a thud on the ground beside me. It was nothing but dead weight now, anyway.

Phevos growled and blasted my face with furious puffs of hot breath as I quickly cut some of the leather straps off. "Oh, stop fussing, you big baby. I'm fine," I said as I pushed his head away.

It only took a minute or two and a few strong leather straps to secure my wounded arm against my body. Phillip and Turq had given me an idea. If I couldn't ride, then Phevos was going to have to carry me.

Suddenly, we were out of time.

Tibran soldiers surrounded us—too many for me to even bother counting. Despite their numbers, they advanced slowly, uncertainty in every step. Their hands shook on their weapons and their eyes flashed to my dragon. They were right to fear him.

Phevos curled himself around me with a growl, shielding my body with his. He bristled his spines and opened his jaws, showing rows of jagged teeth that dripped with burning venom.

Carrying me this way would slow us down. We would be easy prey for the net throwers and archers. It was the only way, though. I knew better than to hope I could talk Phevos into leaving me behind.

"We must fall back to the wall," I murmured against his ear as I stepped back, close against his side. "You have to carry me."

Phevos gave a snort of confirmation.

I took a deep breath, never taking my eyes off the Tibran soldiers encircling us. "Go!"

TWENTY-SIX

With a spray of flame and a rush of wings, Phevos launched off the ground. He showered the Tibrans with a long blast of burning venom, blinding them long enough to snatch me up in his clawed hind legs and hoist us both skyward. Our flight was awkward and off balance. I dangled like a dead sheep in his grasp, gripping onto his eagle-like toes as tightly as I could.

In a rush of wind and heat, the ground fell away. The battlefield spread out before me, a tapestry of anarchy mottled with fire, blood, smoke, and steel. Hanging from my dragon's grasp, it was nearly impossible to make out anything specific as we rose beyond firing range of anything from the ground. Phevos wasn't taking any chances.

The roar of another dragon nearby drew my gaze. I still couldn't see much, but a flash of white scales was all it took.

Calem and Perish were with us. From his saddle, Calem's gauntlets flashed as he waved his hands. He was trying to signal to me. In my current state, however, there was nothing I could do to answer.

Phevos landed carefully, releasing me less than two feet off the ground as he touched down on a secure area of the ramparts. I lay on my back, arms still crossed over my breast, breathing in the smoke and acrid smell of venom. The pain in my shoulder made it hard to move. I couldn't sit up.

A pair of familiar, worried yellow eyes appeared over me. Phevos sniffed at my face, sucking my hair into his nostrils and smacking his lips against my cheek like a curious horse.

"Jenna!" Calem appeared over me suddenly, ripping off his helmet and shoving Phevos's head out of the way. Maybe it was just delirium from the pain, but I could have sworn I saw relief in his eyes. "I thought—gods, woman—I thought you were dead!"

"Sorry to disappoint you," I rasped as he helped me sit up. "My arm is … " Pain throttled the words out of my throat before I could finish.

Calem moved quickly, dismantling my crude attempt to secure it against my body. He untied the straps and unbuckled my breastplate and shoulder pauldron, never looking away even as Maldobarian infantrymen rushed all around us. They were shouting orders, lugging shields and extra quivers packed full of arrows, and rolling carts loaded with heavy stones—ammunition for the catapults.

"The shoulder is dislocated, and your collarbone might be broken," Calem pronounced as he fastened my armor back in place. "We need to get you to the medics. You're done."

I cursed under my breath. This is not how I wanted my fight to end.

An earsplitting *whoosh* sent Calem diving over me, shielding my body with his as something enormous sailed overhead. Incoming fire from a Tibran trebuchet? It had to be.

The boulder passed like a moon overhead, missing us by mere feet as it hurtled by and smashed into ramparts. Men screamed. Shards of stone, ash, and twisted bits of metal flew in every direction.

"Calem!" I choked, struggling to wheeze through the dust. "We have to move! We need to get off the ramparts!"

No reply.

I jostled him as best I could with my one working arm. Shakily, he pushed himself off me, and sat back onto his knees. His movements lurched, unsteady as he struggled to get to his feet. Something wasn't right. His face was blanched, stark and pasty against the blood beginning to seep through his lips. He fixed me with a stare—and I knew.

"C-come on." He grabbed me under my good shoulder and hoisted me up. Together, we shambled across the crumbling ramparts toward the nearest turret. Our dragons circled, chirping their concern, but unable to land again. It was too risky. All the enemy's fire was focused upon these walls—on us.

"Almost there," I wheezed with every step. "Just a little farther. Almost there."

He didn't answer. His breathing rattled through clenched teeth as he staggered beside me, gaze focused on the turret's open door.

We were going to make it.

Calem fell just inside the threshold. He crumpled forward, taking me with him. We landed in a tangled heap of armor not far from the doorway. Wrestling myself free, I whipped back to try to get him up again. We weren't safe—not yet. Another one of those hurtling stones could easily smash right through this tower. The only difference was now we wouldn't see it coming.

"Get up!" I shouted as I crawled to him.

Lying on his front, I could see three, no, four coin-sized holes in the back of his plackart—the portion of his armor that was supposed to shield his torso from harm. The jagged tip of a metal shard stuck out of one of the holes, glittering wickedly in the gloom.

Fear tore through me like a mountain wind.

I fought to roll him over, heaving his heavy, armored body onto its back. One glimpse of his face stole the breath from my chest.

Blood oozed from the corners of his mouth, staining his cheeks and sticking in his corn silk hair. His eyes were wide, fixed straight ahead, and as empty as a starless night.

A cry tore out of me—half sob, half scream. My body shook as I gripped him fiercely. It wasn't real. It couldn't be. It wasn't supposed to be this way. If he hadn't thrown himself on top of me, if he hadn't been so stupid, then it would have been me lying there.

It *should* have been me!

His skin was still warm when I pressed my forehead against his, cupping the sides of his face. I kissed his brow and closed his eyelids, my tears peppering his blood-smeared cheeks. There was nothing more I could do. Over the boiling rumble of battle, I heard Perish roar as though she were looking for him.

But Calem was gone.

My ears were still ringing as I sat on the edge of an examination table, staring out across the white canvas tent. Medics and healers rushed around me, calling to one another as they raced to treat the injured brought in from the battlefront. I couldn't remember how I'd gotten here exactly. A medic team sweeping the ramparts for the wounded had found me, but after that ... everything was a haze of shouts and the distant roar of combat.

Sitting with most of my armor stripped away to the padded garments I wore underneath, my body felt cold and exposed. How long had I been here? Minutes? Hours? What about Calem? Had they left him behind?

A thunderous boom shuddered the ground, so loud and close I could feel it echo in my chest. Everyone stopped. All eyes turned upward and for a few seconds, no one made a sound. Gods and Fates, what was happening outside?

"It's going to hurt, Your Highness," the young medic warned as she prepped to wrench my shoulder back into place. She couldn't have been more than fifteen, and her hands trembled as she probed around my shoulder.

"Just do it," I growled.

A twist, pop, and release of pressure brought tingling

feeling back to my fingertips. I let out a shuddering sigh of relief. Flexing my arm, I tested squeezing my fist and wiggling my fingers. Every movement still sent a sharp bolt of pain across my chest, but it was bearable. At least I could move now.

Good enough.

"Wait a moment! Please, my lady, you're not fit to fight," the medic protested as I stood and gathered my gear. "Your collarbone is most certainly fractured, possibly broken. You should not be lifting anything—"

I spun on her with a frown. "Who is in charge here?"

"Medic Captain Evined," the young woman sputtered, paling as she pointed across the room full of groaning, wailing patients. Most were far worse off than I was and far more deserving of her attention.

I thanked her and left, buckling my sword belt back around my hips as I stepped through the maze of bedrolls on the floor. The air was thick with the smell of blood and medicinal herbs. In a far corner, body-shaped lumps covered in white sheets were piled out of the way. I grimaced and looked away.

Medic Captain Evined was in an absolute frenzy. The plump woman rushed about, sleeves rolled to her elbows and sweat dotting her forehead as she doled out medicines and materials. With just a glance, it was easy to tell she was at her wit's end, with far more patients pouring in than one official could manage. Fresh blood speckled her white robes and apron from wrist to elbow. It was caked in the creases of her hands and smudged across her face. She gaped at me for a second, her warm, hazel eyes wide and frantic, when I asked where I could find the nearest officer's post. Of course, she didn't know. And in this mess, who could blame her?

I was on my own.

Somehow, I had to find my way back to the battle. With my arm mobile again, I would be able to hang onto Phevos. We could resume the fight, even without a saddle. Providing I could find him, that is.

I left the surgical tent at a jog and was immediately surprised—I recognized this place. I was deep in the undercrofts of the royal castle; possibly the only safe place left in the city now. It was an excellent place for the medics to work without fear of being crushed by incoming fire from the trebuchets. But, gods, it was a long way to get back to the city walls. Dangerous as the ramparts were, that would undoubtedly be the best place to spot Phevos.

Setting my jaw against the sharp pain in my collarbone, I sprinted along the corridors and dashed up flights of stairs. Maldobarian soldiers rushed by me in groups, their armor and swords spattered with blood, as I wound my way higher and higher in the castle. The fastest path I knew to get to the ramparts meant crossing the main courtyard. Risky, considering it was out in the open and where my father had positioned several of his largest catapults to return fire over the wall.

I was running low on choices, however.

Darting through one of the narrow servants' passages, I burst through a small door hidden behind a line of prickly shrubs. Before me, the courtyard burned and boiled. An exploding orb of dragon venom hurled from Tibran lines had already smashed one of the great machines and left it in cinders. Soldiers surrounded the two that remained operational, working the cranks that aimed the arm and coiled rope along the winch. More soldiers rolled massive stones from the backs of wagons into the firing bucket.

I crossed the courtyard in a mad dash, seizing the arm of the first soldier I could reach. "What's happening out there?"

The man turned to me, multihued eyes betraying his elven heritage even behind his helmet. "We're supposed to keep firing!" he shouted back over the *whoosh—snap—boom* of the catapult fire. "They say reinforcements from the north have broken the Tibran lines; a cavalry of faundra led by Prince Aubren!"

My brother was out there? Riding with the gray elves?

I clapped a hand on his shoulder as a gesture of thanks and kept running. There was an entrance to the wall passageways at the far side of the courtyard. Providing no one had barricaded it before the battle, that would be my fastest way up onto the ramparts. From there, I prayed I could find Phevos. Surely, he was nearby, looking for me. I had to believe that he was still—

I skidded, tripping and nearly falling as a sudden surge of wind and a flash of gleaming white and purple scales dropped from the sky before me. Perish and Phevos landed side by side, craning their huge horned heads to peer at me expectantly. The soldiers manning the catapults panicked. They called out to me, waving their arms, and ordering me to run. I couldn't blame them. Without my dragonrider armor, I looked like a common infantry foot soldier at best.

Not the sort to be wrangling a pair of dragons.

Phevos chirped insistently, snapping his jaws, and swiveling his ears. Perish responded with a hiss, lashing her tail and leering at me with eyes like pale rubies. She crawled closer, her tapered snout wrinkled with a twitching snarl as she flattened herself before me.

Was that … an invitation?

Phevos gave a grunt of approval.

Knees shaking, I edged toward her. Before Calem, it was common knowledge that she'd killed riders for doing this very thing. Why now? Why me?

Perish answered with a look, her scarlet eyes steely and brimming with intelligence. The anger and anguish in her gaze mingled with my own. This wasn't a choosing. I wouldn't be permitted to do it again. But for the honor of her fallen rider, for vengeance, she would allow it.

I climbed into Calem's saddle with my eyes tearing and my chest burning with agony-driven rage. His secondary weapon was still buckled to the back, and I quickly clipped the short sword to my belt before securing the straps that would hold me in place. Phevos watched with his golden gaze ardent. He prowled around us, bristled and anxious, as Perish stood and coiled for takeoff. Maybe he didn't quite trust her not to kill me. Honestly, I wasn't sure I did, either.

It was far too late to second-guess things now, though.

Perish coiled her legs and sprang skyward with a graceful leap, arching her back and flapping her white wings swiftly. I gripped the saddle handles, my pulse throbbing in my palms and clashing in my ears as I leaned into her movements. Her flight was as fast and brutal as it was effortlessly smooth— much different from what I'd gotten used to with Phevos over the years. She moved with exacting speed and sharp precision, conquering the dark, war-torn skies with a challenging roar.

Phevos flew close behind, his eyes never leaving me as we surged above the city walls and spiraled higher. I squinted through the wind, scanning the battlefield for some idea of what was happening. In the distance, the low tone of Gray Elven war horns helped me to spot their advance.

The line of mounted cavalry moved like a wave of silvery white, smashing into the bronze shore of Tibran shields. Each of the monstrous faundra stags was the size of a draft horse, sixteen hands to the withers, and around a thousand pounds. That, paired with the crown of razor-sharp white horns on their heads, made for a formidable beast when it was charging at full speed. Many of the Tibran soldiers broke and ran. The ones who stood firm were easily trampled or impaled on those brutal horns—if they survived the flawless aim of the elf archer on its back, that is.

At the front of the line, Aubren's physique was easy to pick out even from a distance. He wasn't as slight or petite as the elves, and he wore human armor beneath a rippling cape of gold and blue—Maldobar's colors. Hefting his sword high with one hand, he gripped the reins of his stag in the other as he led the charge. My heart raced at the sight, and I steered Perish toward them. Perhaps we could offer some help clearing the path for their advance.

Suddenly, a sharp explosion like the crack of a whip burst through the air directly below us. Perish shrieked in dismay and behind us, Phevos gave a cry of warning. Was it another one of those Tibran orbs exploding? Or a dragon crashing to the ground? I leaned to get a look.

My eyes went wide. A panicked breath caught in my throat, lodging before I could make a sound. My blood seemed to freeze solid in my veins.

Gods and Fates … what had Jaevid Broadfeather done?

PART SEVEN

REIGH

TWENTY-SEVEN

The wheels of reality ground back into motion with the sounds of war raging like a dark symphony in the night. I staggered back, putting some distance between the goddess and myself as she rose back to her full height. From a few yards away, Jaevid sent me one final, earnest look before he raised the black crystal above his head.

This was it. I knew it. He knew it.

There was no turning back.

I held my breath.

At the last second, Argonox seemed to catch on. His eyes darted between the three of us before he pitched forward wildly, his expression twisted with frantic rage. "NO!"

A horrible *crack* pierced the air. It bored into my ears and rattled my bones.

Jaevid smashed the crystal against the ground at his feet.

It fractured on impact, splitting in half, and sending black shards, like slivers of obsidian, flying in every direction.

I fell to one knee, wheezing and gripping my chest. Heat blazed through me, prickling and spreading with every heartbeat, until it raged from my ears all the way to my toes. My lungs expanded, stretching to their fullest as I sucked in a deep breath of the cold night air. Warm serenity washed over me—a soul-deep calm and strange emptiness I could barely comprehend. It tingled through every finger and shivered down my spine. I could feel it with every thundering thump of my heart.

The chains of death and divine power I'd toiled under for so long had finally been broken. Life rushed back in to breathe new energy into every weary muscle, filling me up like a wild spring wind. I wasn't the Harbinger anymore.

I was … free.

Too bad there wasn't much time to savor it.

Clysiros let out a shrill laugh of pure delight and spread her arms wide, body arching as three sets of black-feathered wings unfurled from her back. Each one was mottled in intricate designs of silver in flecks like tiny diamonds, and horns of spiked black crystals crowned her head like a tiara. With one beat of those six wings, she hovered over the battlefield, robes and hair floating as though she were weightless.

Argonox skidded to a halt right before her, eyes wide and mouth agape. Even dressed out in his wicked armor, the goddess towered over him. I guess he hadn't planned on meeting an actual deity today. Bathed in ambient starlight, her skin glowed and the silver designs on her wings sparkled as she regarded him with a bemused grin.

The battlefield around us fell silent. The lines of Tibran soldiers all around stood frozen, their faces pasty at the sight of Clysiros and their reigning tyrant facing off. It was as though they were all waiting to see who would prevail before they decided whether to strike or flee.

With a sharp scrape and ring of metal on metal, Argonox drew a straight-bladed sword from his belt.

Clysiros moved like a blur, vanishing like a wisp of smoke and suddenly reappearing mere inches from Argonox's nose. He flinched, shrinking back, but much too late. Her fingertips traced the sharp edge of his sword—totally unfazed by it. Mortal weapons were useless here. She studied him, her bottomless dark eyes gleaming with pleasure as the metal began to rust and decay, rotting away to ash in his hands until he was left with nothing except an empty hilt.

I had to give him some credit; he was a sick, deranged, tyrannical maniac, but Argonox was as fearless as anyone I'd ever seen. That, or I'd just never encountered the level of stupidity it took to attack the Goddess of Death. Maybe he was still assuming that armor would protect him?

I gaped as he threw down the useless hilt and snatched the morning star—a club with a spiked ball on one end— that was hanging from the other side of his belt. He reared back to swing, and Clysiros vanished again. His club howled through the air and hit nothing but empty air.

Stumbling forward with surprise, he whirled in a frantic circle, his gaze darting all around for some sign of the goddess. Argonox's bloodshot eyes searched the crowd of soldiers and the skies in vain before finally settling on Jaevid. His jaw set, expression sharpening and lips drawing back over his teeth in a snarl, as though he'd found an acceptable substitute.

But Jaevid didn't move. He didn't even blink.

The fight wasn't over.

Before Argonox could take a single step, a huge, pale hand reached from behind and grasped his throat. His whole body went rigid and all the color drained from his face.

Clysiros reappeared behind him, her chin on his shoulder so that her red lips brushed his ear with every word. "*Tsk tsk tsk. You've made quite the mess, haven't you, little man? You smeared my magic on the unworthy. You defiled my name.*" She stretched one finger up to stroke along his jaw. "*Whatever shall I do with you?*"

"Your time in the mortal realm is over," he growled through clenched teeth. "I am the only true Harbinger. Your power is mine. This world belongs to me."

"*Oh my darling,*" she purred. "*My time has only just begun.*"

Her pale fingers tightened upon his throat as her eyes fluttered closed. One euphoric smile from those scarlet lips sent a shudder through the air like a burst of frigid wind. It radiated out from her, expanding and touching every soul standing on that battlefield.

I reeled, thrown back on my heels as it tore through me. Jaevid braced, leaning into it with jaw tight, hands clenched, and eyes still burning like fiery emeralds.

Overhead, a sharp screech came from Beckah's reanimated king drake. Mavrik hesitated, instinctively drawing back. The massive creature twisted, howling and spitting erratic plumes of burning venom before it froze, hovering in the air directly over us as motionless as a statue.

Suddenly, its glowing red eyes went dark. Rotting flesh and naked bone melted into the air, turning into flecks of ash, and curling black smoke. In seconds, it was completely gone.

One by one, the rest of Argonox's monstrous creations— soldiers, dragons, shrikes, and other creatures he'd forced me to drag back from the abyss—began to dissolve, as well. Empty suits of armor hit the ground with a *thunk* and clatter. War machines groaned to a halt. Ash from a hundred undead dragons fell from the sky like snow.

Clysiros's laugh tolled over the masses, as harrowing as the bells of doomsday. She stood, Argonox writhing in her grip as she snatched him off the ground like someone picking a carrot. He pitched and kicked, screaming as she held him at arm's length, her huge fist still closed around his neck.

"*There is nothing you own I cannot destroy, nowhere you can hide to escape my kiss. I curse you, Argonox, God Bane, and every firstborn of your bloodline.*" She giggled, her tone dripping with delight. Her dark eyes flashed, glinting with pleasure, as the wicked armor on his body began to dissolve, too. "*A life to repay each one you took while defiling my name.*"

With his armor gone, Clysiros dropped Argonox into a heap at her feet.

My breath caught. Was that it? She wasn't going to end it? End *him*? Why? Why would she possibly let him go after—

Argonox sprang to his feet and tripped all over himself as he backed away from her, trembling with terror. He spun, turning to bolt. He didn't make it two steps.

Argonox ran straight into the point of Jaevid's scimitar.

Argonox choked, eyes wide as Jaevid bore in, driving the blade into his body all the way to the hilt.

"Never again," Jaevid growled. His lip twitched back in a snarl, expression caught between disgust and wrath as he gave the blade a brutal twist before yanking it free. He planted one swift kick to Argonox's torso and laid him flat. His body hit the ground with a *thud*.

It was over.

Clysiros looked on, swiping her tongue hungrily across her bottom lip, as Jaevid stepped back. The end of his blade dripped red and his body heaved with deep, swift breaths as he stared up at her. I held my breath, too afraid to move, as the goddess gave him a final, coy smile. She blew a kiss in my direction. Then she vanished without a sound.

The living Tibran soldiers stood still, staring at their dead ruler in horror, their faces smudged with the ash of their fallen monsters. Some of them cried out and immediately threw down their weapons as they dropped to their knees in surrender. Others began to flee. They wouldn't get far, though. Seeing the sudden change in the tide, the Dragonriders of Maldobar were already throwing down perimeters of flame in an attempt to hem in the deserters.

Plenty more Tibran soldiers, however, were either too determined or too far gone to realize what was happening. They charged.

Sucking in a ragged breath, I glanced back to meet Vexi's worried stare. She gave a whine as King Felix climbed down off her back. He forged toward me, sword drawn and shield at the ready.

Jaevid stepped forward to meet him, and they took up the fight, standing back-to-back, their movements a perfect balance of lethal speed and brutal force.

I darted across the ground in a mad sprint, seizing my kafki blades and spinning into position to fight alongside them. No sooner had I fallen into rhythm, dealing blow after blow to the onslaught of crazed Tibran soldiers, then a dragon with scales as white as fresh snow dropped from the sky. I'd seen that dragon somewhere before—Barrowton, maybe?

Suddenly, it didn't matter. The dragon crouched long enough for a familiar female figure to climb off her back, sword in hand. Princess Jenna had blood spattered on her face and a storm in her eyes as she whipped in to join the fight.

The ground quaked as Mavrik let out a booming roar. Every dragon on the battlefield answered in a united call like a roll of thunder—a cry that shook the very foundations of my soul. Vexi and the white dragon joined their king in the air, soaring with a group of dragons to deliver blasts of flame on every Tibran war machine still standing.

My ears rang with the clash of blades and cries of the men who fell to my blades. Sweat soaked through my clothes and streaked down my face. But I wouldn't stop. This was it—the moment Enyo and Kiran believed would come. I was not a monster. I wasn't a beast or a demon. I was no longer the Harbinger of Clysiros.

I was Reigh Farrow, Prince of Maldobar, and I would not fail.

TWENTY-EIGHT

The end of the battle came as the sun began to rise. The red horizon revealed a canopy of black smoke curling up from the cinders of Tibran war machines, fallen dragons, and more dead men than anyone could have counted. But the city of Halfax still stood, the tattered blue and gold banners of Maldobar waving in triumph from the castle spires. Horns sounded from every corner of the ramparts, declaring our victory.

The Maldobarian soldiers, dragonriders, and cavalry raised their blades high and shouted in triumph. But as I stood amidst the bodies of slave soldiers and smoldering dragon venom, I couldn't join in. The smell, that horrible acrid stench of death, burned my eyes and caught in my throat. I gagged.

This victory tasted like ash.

I leaned over, hands aching as I let go of my kafki blades and struggled to catch my breath.

"Reigh! Are you okay?" Jenna called out as she jogged toward me. "Are you injured?"

I shook my head. A few nicks, cuts, and shallow sword slices didn't count. "All good," I panted. "Where's—?"

Jenna hugged me before I could get the words out, gripping me so hard it was as though she was afraid I might disappear. "Gods, you stupid … reckless … "

"Farrow," someone finished for her.

Pulling back, Jenna and I stared together as the King of Maldobar approached, the length of his cloak rippling behind him. In the light of the rising sun, I got my first good look at his face. His light, amber-colored eyes studied me, too. The more I looked, however, the harder it was to see because my eyes welled with tears. I could see *myself* in him. His eyes, the shape of his jaw, the crooked way he smirked as he brushed his hand through my hair.

It wasn't a trick. This wasn't my imagination. He really was … my father.

"Reigh," he spoke softly.

I cringed. He knew my name? How? Had Jaevid told him?

"I suppose I have a lot of explaining to do," he murmured with a sad smile.

No kidding. Emotions like a tangled briar patch writhed in my chest, pricking and stabbing with every breath I took. He'd thrown me away like I was garbage, hadn't he? Why? I deserved an explanation—and yet, I was terrified that if he gave me a good one, I would be obligated to forgive him, and move on like nothing had happened. My mouth screwed up, chin trembling. I clenched my teeth and looked away, fighting to keep it in. I couldn't do this, not yet.

"When you're ready, we'll talk about it," he said. "For now, just know that you are my son, and I love you."

I swallowed hard, and held my tongue.

"Father, look!" Jenna broke in suddenly, seizing him by the arm.

Not far away, Jaevid was picking a careful path across the battlefield toward the mass of vines he'd summoned to ensnare Beckah. It had continued to grow, weaving and twining together like reeds in a basket, to form a huge sphere. My heart thumped against my ribs as he stopped before it, hand clenched around the hilt of his scimitar.

What was he thinking? Would he hack his way through them? Surely, after what Clysiros had done to the other reanimated monsters and soldiers, there wouldn't be anything left of her now.

Jaevid's blade hit the ground with a clatter.

"You promised," he begged, his mouth locked into a desperate, shaking frown. "You gave me your word."

Jenna and I exchanged a confused glance. Who was he talking to?

Suddenly, warm, golden light blazed from inside the sphere. It shone through the cracks between the interwoven vines, glowing like a netted star. I shielded my eyes, struggling to squint through my fingers to catch a glimpse of what was happening.

The vines moved, twisting and curling away, as a single, slender hand emerged. It reached out from within the light, and Jaevid stepped closer without hesitation. He seized the hand, lacing his fingers through those delicate digits.

With a sudden powerful flash, the sphere of vines burst, shattering into fragments that instantly dissolved into mist. It was so bright, I couldn't bear it. The instant before my vision blanked, I could have sworn I saw the shape of a creature rising from the light. A stag, maybe? It was too brilliant to be sure.

Then, as I blinked away the glare, I saw *her*.

The young woman standing where the sphere had been, lifted her head slowly. She still held onto Jaevid's hand, staring at him with eyes the color of evergreen needles. Her fair skin was freckled over her cheeks and nose, and her dark hair was pulled back into a loose braid that hung down to her waist. The cool wind teased through the length of her pale blue gown, billowing over her lean frame and bare, freckled shoulders.

No one said a word as she and Jaevid stared at one another in total silence.

Then, as softly as a spring rain, the girl breathed his name. "Jaevid?"

His voice cracked and halted, as though he could hardly get the word out. "Beckah."

She blinked, a crinkle of confusion on her brow as she took a tiny, shaking step toward him. "I-I don't understand. I was … gone. I lost you. How did you bring me back?"

"There is nowhere, mortal or divine, I would not go to find you," he said. "I love you, Beckah Derrick. In that life, in this one, and until the end of our days."

With a yelp of joy, Beckah leapt at him. Jaevid snagged her in his arms and lifted her off her feet. He planted his lips firmly against hers in an earnest kiss.

Beside me, King Felix gave a chuckle and smacked a hand on my back so hard I almost fell forward. Jenna chocked back a sob, covering her mouth with her hand as she watched them embrace. Other Maldobarian soldiers who had gathered around to watch began to applaud.

How he'd done it, I'd never understand. During our brief exchange, I recalled Clysiros mentioning that Jaevid had demanded a few favors in exchange for his help. Be that as it may, I felt certain that gleaming white stag I'd spotted rising out of the light wasn't anything sent by Clysiros.

It was something else—something greater.

"This is going to call for some new tapestries, I think," King Felix mused with a mischievous grin. "Perhaps a few statues, too."

Jenna flashed him a teary-eyed glance and gave his arm a playful shove. "Oh, stop it. You're terrible."

"No worse than you," a deep voice interrupted.

Wait—I knew that voice!

King Felix, Jenna, and I turned at once. We gasped in unison. From the back of a proud faundra stag, Aubren led a group of gray elf cavalry in full battle dress. The brightly colored feathers of their war headdresses fluttered in the wind and their mounts stamped and bleated, still riled from battle.

Right behind Aubren's mount, however, was a creature I knew all too well—and it was no faundra. A foundling spirit with colors as vibrant and vivid as a parrot stood, tall ears swiveling and bushy tail swishing. Seated on the spirit's back, her fingers clenching earnestly to its silky fur, Hecate panned a teary-eyed smile in my direction.

"I suppose it runs in the family. Bad luck for you, Reigh. You had your fun frolicking around in Luntharda, but now you're stuck with this sorry lot." Aubren smiled, giving me a wink before he passed his shield off to the nearest soldier and climbed down to meet us on foot.

Jenna hit him like a charging bull, knocking him flat on his back in a frantic hug. He wheezed and laughed as she yelled at him for making her worry. A few of the soldiers around us started laughing, too.

"He's right, you know," King Felix murmured as he stood close at my side. With his arms folded over his ornate breastplate and his fingers stroking at his short beard thoughtfully, he cast me a curious sideways glance. "This is your home. I won't force you to stay, but you are welcome—and wanted—right here."

I swallowed hard and took a deep, steadying breath. "I'll consider it. But only on one condition."

He lifted a brow. "Yes?"

"I get to call you Father."

King Felix laughed and grabbed me by the shoulder, wrenching me into a gruff hug. "Don't you dare ever call me anything else, boy."

TWENTY-NINE

The war was over. Argonox was gone. And as word spread from Saltmarsh to the boundary like wildfire, cities and villages throughout Maldobar celebrated with tolling bells and parades through the streets. They were already toasting to our names and telling our stories. Once again, Jaevid Broadfeather was a hero and a legend for the ages.

But this time, so was I.

I tried not to think about that as I lay in a soft, lavish, four-poster bed in Aubren's wing of the royal castle. I didn't feel much like a hero at the moment. Being kept as a Tibran prisoner for so long had left me badly injured, dehydrated, and so weak I could barely stand. Not being the Harbinger anymore helped, of course, but it didn't do much to speed the healing of my physical body.

Aubren had lent me a room in his quarters to rest and

recover. Not that I wasn't grateful, but it was weird and a little uncomfortable to hear the servants and healers calling me "Your Highness" every time they came in to bring me a meal, draw a bath, or change my bandages. That would take some getting used to.

After a week, I was well enough to get up and walk around without help, although the medics and healers still warned me not to do any heavy lifting or dragon riding just yet. It was good timing, because I wanted to attend the funeral ceremony for several of the dragonriders that had died in the battle for Halfax.

One of them, I'd learned, was a close friend to Jenna and had even been her wing end. I couldn't imagine not being there for her during that event. She'd been through a lot, and while she did a good job of not to letting it show, I could tell watching the procession as they carried his body to the pyre was almost more than she could take. Her whole body remained stiff and rigid, dressed in formal battle armor and scalemail that gleamed like gold in the light of the setting sun. Her expression stayed locked into a somber frown that didn't waver the entire time. After it was over and his ashes had been locked away in a majestic granite vault alongside many other fallen dragonriders, I watched from a distance while she and the rest of her comrades gave him one final salute.

That image stayed burned into my brain as I made my way back to my room in Aubren's wing. Every step ached as I hobbled through his private library, lounges, and parlors. I could walk without limping too much, but it still hurt. Walking this far always left me sweaty, sore, and exhausted by the time I flopped back down onto the bed.

"Have a nice stroll?" A familiar voice snickered from the chair at my bedside.

I floundered upright, gaping at the dark, ominous figure who sat there casually, his arms crossed under black, silken robes. "Y-you!" I rasped.

One corner of Noh's mouth curved into a half-smirk. "Relax, brother. I'm not here to cause you any trouble. Not today, anyway."

I eyed him over, body tense and hands shaking as I clenched the sheets with trembling hands. "Why are you here?"

His expression smoothed, and he flicked his gaze away. "I came to thank you," he answered simply. "And ... to say goodbye."

"Goodbye?" I didn't understand.

He nodded slightly. "I am to remain in the Vale as its guardian. It is unlikely I will ever return to the mortal world again."

"Oh." A hard knot formed in the back of my throat. For some reason, hearing that made my chest feel tight. He was leaving. We'd never speak again—after having his haunting presence living in my head literally since birth.

"You asked Clysiros to spare me." He stared at me again, with eyes the color of rubies catching in the candlelight. "I thought you should know that, regardless of how we began and what transpired, I have never thought badly of you. I've never blamed you for what happened."

I opened my mouth to reply, but nothing except for a few choking sounds would come out.

"I did envy you, though. I still do, in fact. You will go on to share your life with your family—*our* family. And I find myself wishing I could do the same." His brow creased slightly, as though he were uncertain. "Please do not take it the wrong way when I say I look forward to their deaths. I ... I look forward to meeting them."

With a heavy sigh, I sat forward on the edge of the bed and let my elbows rest on my knees. "Well, as it turns out, our father is *really* old, so you'll probably get to meet him soon. Maybe even sooner, if he keeps commissioning statues of Jaevid."

Noh's expression split with a mischievous grin that made his scarlet eyes shimmer. "I will miss you, brother," he added with a chuckle. "Though I realize the sentiment may not be mutual. I know our encounters were never easy for you."

"No, they weren't," I agreed. "But that doesn't mean I won't miss you, too."

His face went blank, mouth opening slightly for a moment as his brows lifted in surprise.

"Take care of yourself, okay? And if you do get a chance to come back here to the mortal realm, don't be a stranger." I managed an unsteady smile, gritting my teeth against the stiffness in my throat.

Crap. I was really going to miss him.

Noh rose from his chair and regarded me with a smile that seemed almost as unsteady and forced as mine. His brow and chin trembled a bit as he stretched out a hand to shake mine. "Until death reunites us again."

I took it and clasped firmly. "Until then, brother."

He dipped his head in a small nod and winked one of his crimson eyes. Then his shape quickly dissolved into a fine black mist that dissipated without a single sound.

I realized about two seconds before my giant, green, scaly, overexcited dragoness landed on top of me that I was probably about to die. Crushed to death by my own mount. Great.

I threw up my hands, yelling at the top of my lungs.

She didn't listen.

Vexi smacked into me like a charging faundra—a huge wall of muscle and scales that sent me flying like a ragdoll across the grass. I wheezed for breath as I hit the ground under her massive body. Thankfully, she didn't squish me for long. Wrapping her tail around me like a giant python, Vexi swiped her long, sticky tongue up the side of my head. She chirped and squawked with delight, purring as she rubbed her horned head against mine.

"Y-you're crushing me!" I managed to rasp as she blasted my face with a puff from her huge nostrils.

She loosened the grip of her long tail and I slumped to my knees to gasp and cough for breath. I'd almost recovered when my face and hair got a second coating of gooey dragon spit.

I gagged. "For crying out loud, would you stop that?"

"Aw, look. She loves you!" Jenna giggled as she stood back at the far corner of the courtyard, watching and making no attempts to rescue me. "How sweet."

After another week of rest and rehabilitation, I was

almost back to my old self again. The pain in my muscles was nothing more than a dull soreness now. I could manage walking the castle on my own without having to stop to catch my breath. My wounds were well on their way to healing, and I was able to get by without needing any sort of pain medicine. Although, after this, I'd probably need something for bruising.

"Maybe she needs to love me a little less," I grumbled as I tried wiping my face on my sleeve.

Now that I was able to walk the castle grounds, I usually wound up with company for my afternoon strolls. Jenna and Aubren seemed to be taking turns, alternating days to follow me along the white stone paths through the gardens or through the cavernous castle halls while we talked. I'd be lying if I said it wasn't a little awkward. They were my siblings—my older brother and sister—and I knew almost nothing about them. Most of the time, I had no idea what to say because there was so much I wanted to know. What had our mother been like? Did we have anything in common? Did I have grandparents? Aunts? Uncles? Cousins? Would I get to meet any of them, too?

Jenna was a little easier to talk to than Aubren, if only because of what had happened in Northwatch. He'd begun wearing long, black leather gloves all the time, and while it usually suited the rest of his princely attire, I knew the real reason he wore those gloves. He didn't want anyone to see the marks *my* power had left on his hand.

Guilt soured in my gut like poison every time I saw him. Would that feeling ever go away? Or would there always be this weird tension between us? As much as I wanted to apologize to him for basically ruining his life, every time I tried, the words lodged in my throat and I couldn't even look him in the eye. Anything I said sounded pathetic whenever I rehearsed it in my head.

Thankfully, today was Jenna's turn. Besides being more affable, she was almost as socially awkward as I was. Maybe that was a family trait, too.

"It's interesting, isn't it?" She mused as she walked over to run a hand across Vexi's lime green scales. "Jaevid said the Fates look like dragons. I've never heard of such a thing. But it makes me wonder if our dragons really are descended from them somehow."

I shifted, lowering my gaze and avoiding her eyes. Thinking about that moment dredged up painful memories of being forced into the Thieving Mask. "I'm kind of hoping I can just forget about everything I ever saw or heard in the Vale, to be honest."

Her expression dimmed as she nibbled on her bottom lip. "If only it were that easy."

No kidding. Jenna and I had shared a lot about our experiences during the war. She'd mentioned going into the Vale to rescue Aubren, although she'd been very careful to dance around the details of exactly what happened there. Not that I blamed her. I'd kept my own recounting of my experiences there brief, too. Eventually, I might be up to having that discussion. Not yet, though.

"Reigh, can I ask you something in confidence?" Jenna's hushed tone caught me off guard.

I leaned around Vexi's neck to get a better look at my older sister. She was still nibbling away at her lip and staring down at the tops of her boots with a fretful frown crinkling her brow. "Sure. Of course."

"If you knew something—a secret that you promised to tell someone—but you knew telling might cause that person a lot of pain and sadness, would you still do it?" Her keen blue eyes darted up to search my face for a second or two. "Would you still share that secret, knowing the hurt it might cause?"

I had to think about that. She was being awfully vague. But if talking about the Vale had somehow brought this question up from the depths of her heart, then I could guess what this might be about. "It's Jaevid, right?"

Jenna drew back slightly, her jaw tensing. She wouldn't look me in the eye.

"You can trust me," I assured her. "I won't say anything to him."

She stood rigid for a moment. Then, little by little, her shoulders sagged. Jenna let out a small, defeated sigh. "I met someone in the Vale when I went there to rescue Aubren. I met ... Ulric Broadfeather, Jaevid's father."

My mind blanked. "The traitor? The one who started the Gray War?"

She nodded. "He ... he wasn't at all like I thought he would be. He was nothing like the stories said. And the way he talked—" She stopped short, quirking her mouth as she chewed on the inside of her cheek. "He said he was waiting there for Jae so he could apologize because he'd never meant for any of that to happen."

"And that's the secret?"

Jenna nodded again. "He wanted me to tell Jaevid that

he was sorry for all of it. I … I promised that I would. But I can't seem to find the right time to tell him. I don't even know if I should."

I rubbed the back of my neck. "Well, maybe Ulric should just tell Jae himself."

Jenna's expression crumpled, collapsing into a grimace before she turned her back. Her shoulders shook some as she sucked in a trembling breath as though she were trying not to cry.

"Jenna? What's wrong?" Pushing Vexi's neck out of the way, I stepped over to take my sister gently by the arm. "What happened?"

"He's gone, Reigh. Ulric sacrificed himself; he gave up his spirit to save Aubren." She bit the words through clenched teeth. "That's why he made me promise—because he won't be there now to tell Jae himself."

The wind rushed out of me like I'd been punched in the gut. No wonder she was struggling with this. Ulric probably hadn't considered what that kind of promise would do to her. She probably felt like it was her fault somehow, even if it wasn't.

"Does Aubren know?" I kept my voice quiet.

"No."

"Good. Don't tell him. He can never know."

Jenna looked up, meeting my stare through tear-filled eyes. With her lips pressed into a tense line, I saw agreement slide over her features like a stony mask of resolve.

"He's been through a lot already. Knowing he's only alive right now because someone gave up their entire spiritual existence would destroy him." I put an arm around Jenna's shoulders and drew her in, hugging her tight. Despite being a few inches taller, she still felt fragile as she gripped me back. "It wasn't your fault, you know."

"I keep thinking if I'd done something different, if Jaevid had gone into the Vale instead of me, then he would have been able to say goodbye," she sobbed against my shoulder. "How can I tell him? What do I say?"

"You don't have to say anything," a deep voice interrupted suddenly.

Jenna and I turned, gaping, to where our father, King Felix, stood nearby. I had no idea how long he'd been there, watching us and listening in. The wind caught in his gray-gold hair and snagged in the lengths of his long, dark blue cloak as he strode closer. I spotted my reflection in his light amber eyes as he stood over us, considering Jenna and me for a moment before he spoke again. "I'll tell him."

Jenna protested, "But, Father, I was the one who—"

He raised a hand to silence her. "It doesn't matter. Ulric has always been a difficult topic for him to talk to anyone about. He should hear it from me." King Felix's expression softened, the hard lines around his mouth, eyes, and along his forehead smoothing slightly as he smiled down at us. "Besides, soon I'll be passing the crown to you and all the many burdens that come along with it. It would be my honor to carry this burden for you."

I swallowed hard. I'd had a lot of visits from Jenna and Aubren while I was recovering. But King Felix, my father, had only come to see me once. I was pretty sure it wasn't because he didn't care about me, though. It seemed more like … he didn't know where to begin. I didn't either. We were strangers.

And even as he'd sat at my bedside and told me about my birth and how he'd voluntarily given me over to Kiran for safekeeping because of my dark birthright, I could hear the guilt and sadness in his voice.

I could see it in the depths of his eyes now, too.

My father hadn't thrown me away like garbage. He'd given me away to the only person he believed he could trust to watch over me because he hadn't believed he could keep me safe. As much as I wanted to be angry and hold a grudge for being passed off like that ... I had to admit, it was probably the right thing to do.

The only issue now was figuring out how to pick up the pieces of our shattered lives and use them to patch together something good. I had to figure out how to be a Prince of Maldobar. And he had to figure out how to be my father. Easier said than done. I'd yet to really talk to him about how I felt. We still didn't know each other, and every encounter seemed more painfully awkward than the last.

"It'll be dark soon." King Felix cleared his throat and flicked a quick glance between us. "I ... thought maybe we could have a meal together. All of us. Like a proper family. Seems long overdue, doesn't it?"

Jenna and I exchanged a look. She let out a breathless laugh, tears still in her eyes as she smiled. My heart thumped sloppily as I tried to find the words. That sounded ... amazing.

"I think that would be wonderful." Jenna smirked as she brushed past our father, grinning at him tauntingly on her way back toward the castle. "Will dear Uncle Jae be joining us, as well?"

King Felix let out a deep, cackling laugh that almost

made me jump out of my boots. "Of course! How else am I going to show off the newly-embroidered table runner and matching painted plate chargers? I'm sure he's going to *love* the designs I chose."

Jenna joined in, giggling all the way back into the castle. I gave Vexi a parting scratch under her chin and followed along behind her. King Felix fell in step right beside me, planting one of his large hands on my shoulder. My heart wrenched deep in my chest, torn somewhere between a nervous breakdown and pure, unbridled joy. I stole a glance up at my father's face, jolting a little when I found him staring right at me again.

"Everything all right?" he asked.

"I was just thinking," I murmured in reply, half hoping Jenna wouldn't hear. "I'm ready to have that talk you mentioned."

His heavy brows rose. "Oh?"

"Yeah, well, if I'm going to hang around here, then I should probably get to know you better." I shrugged, trying to play it off like I was indifferent. I guess he knew better. Maybe an inability to make a convincing bluff was one of the things I'd inherited from him.

"Very well, Son," he chuckled as he ruffled my hair. "We'll talk after dinner."

I couldn't resist a smirk. "Sounds good, Father."

THIRTY

"I-I can't breathe," Jaevid wheezed as he paced back and forth, tromping through the sand. "What if she doesn't come? What if she changes her mind? It's been a long time, hasn't it? Things are so different now. I-I'm not even sure I'm the same. If she changes her mind, then—"

"Calm down," King Felix sighed as he drummed his fingers and leaned against the wooden podium set up right in front of the shoreline. "She loves you. Of course she's coming; don't be ridiculous. And stop pacing like that. You'll wear a trench in the aisle."

Jaevid stopped next to me but didn't stay still. Dressed in a formal dragonrider uniform, complete with a silver ornamental breastplate and matching vambraces polished to sparkling perfection, Jaevid shifted his weight from one foot to another. He fidgeted with the embroidered collar of his tunic and the fingers of his black velvet gloves, occasionally flashing me a wild-eyed look like he might run screaming down the beach at any moment.

"Maybe three months wasn't enough time," he muttered under his breath. "I should have given her longer to adjust. There's so much she—we—don't know. The house isn't even finished yet. I should have insisted on waiting until after Jenna's coronation."

My father groaned and rolled his eyes. "You're hopeless."

I couldn't dispute that, although Jaevid was right on a few counts, too. The past three months had flown by, packed with a mixture of memorials and celebrations that made everything sort of run together. Jenna was set to take the throne as Queen of Maldobar soon, although she had our father's assurance she wouldn't be tossed to the wolves and left to scramble on her own. He was still going to help and advise. Well, as much as she allowed him to, anyway.

Even with extra help, I didn't envy her whatsoever. The idea of wearing the crown was terrifying on its own. Pair that with the prospect of trying to put all the broken pieces back together—not only of our kingdom, but also the dozens of others that were now in shambles thanks to the conquest of the Tibran Empire—and you were left with a mountain of problems and responsibilities that looked insurmountable. Jenna had her work cut out for her. But if I had to bet on who could pull it off, I would have put all my money on her.

For now, we had a small break in our chaotic schedule—a quick moment to breathe. Standing on the beaches of Saltmarsh, I watched the dragons chasing one another through the waves and wondered if this was the first time so many had been welcomed in attendance to a wedding— as guests instead of an accessory or honor guard. Vexi and Phevos yipped and chattered, darting over the surface of the rolling ocean. Nearby, Turq and Perish dove down to snag fish from the sandy bottom.

Only Mavrik was lounging on the beach, a mountain of blue and black scales, sleeping while he basked in the sun. Next to him, a foundling spirit named Pasci was also reclining in the warm sand, preening her brightly colored feathers. She seemed particularly fond of my father, who confessed he'd taken a liking to her after the Gray War. She came and went as she pleased but could usually be found snoozing in the rose bushes outside his private courtyard. She'd made a few trips back to the wild jungle of Luntharda, of course—most recently to answer Princess Hecate's call to arms.

According to Aubren, Hecate's role as the Akrotis had allowed her the ability to speak to foundling spirits. She'd rallied many of them to join the fight, including Pasci. But now, thanks to Jaevid's bargain, none of us had to worry about divine gifts any more. Hecate was free, too.

The dragons and spirits weren't Jaevid's strangest guests, though, just the largest. Phillip towered over everyone by at least a foot. He looked … a little *different* from the last time I'd seen him at Barrowton. Jaevid had explained the basics of what had happened to me, and while Phillip was terrifying to look at, with his beastly features and eerie silver eyes, his personality seemed pretty much the same. It still spooked a lot of the servants and staff around the castle. Fortunately, his bizarre appearance hadn't done anything to slow him down in the romance department because he and Jenna were practically inseparable. I wasn't sure how that had happened. The last time I'd heard anything about them was at Barrowton before the siege and from what Phillip had said, it sounded hopeless for him.

Now, the only thing hopeless about that situation was the hopelessly mushy way they looked at one another while they walked the halls holding hands. Our father had already given his blessing for Phillip to officially court her, but I had a feeling it was going to be the world's shortest courtship ever. He'd probably already acquired a ring and was just waiting for the right moment to propose.

Phillip stood alongside Haldor, Roland, and me at the front of the gathering as part of Jaevid's patron court, waiting for the ceremony to begin. Human weddings were already proving to be a much more complicated and formal affair than gray elf ones. Jaevid had insisted on keeping it "small," which wound up being around two hundred and fifty guests. I guess it added up quickly with so many extended relatives and new friends to account for. I was still struggling to learn all their names, but a few were easy to pick out.

King Jace and Queen Araxie stood alongside Hecate, beaming with pride. They'd also brought along their own sons, the three princes of Luntharda, with their spouses. Aubren and Jenna stood together, each holding a squirming baby—some of Jaevid's great-nieces and great-nephews, most likely, since Roland had brought his *entire* family. Next to them, Miri and Eirik were a couple I'd only met a few weeks ago, although Eirik looked somewhat familiar. Maybe I'd seen him in passing at Barrowton? I couldn't remember.

Aedan was next to them, and he gave me a broad smile and nod when our eyes met. I still owed him one for getting us into Northwatch to save Jenna.

There might have been more people I knew, but before I could scour the audience for more familiar faces, King Felix straightened and cleared his throat, nodding further up the beach. Right away, Phillip bowed to the crowd and stepped away with a secretive smile, his strange feet leaving paw-like impressions in the sand. When he returned, he was leading Beckah by the arm.

The sight of her made Jaevid suck in a sharp breath. He stood stiff, eyes as wide as saucers, while his face and pointed ears blushed bright red. I was a little concerned he might've stopped breathing until I saw him let out a long, shaky exhale of relief. He blinked rapidly, eyes watering and hands shaking at his sides as he watched her approach as though he were counting down every step that brought them closer.

Beckah was radiant in a simple white gown that dragged along the sand behind her. The corset bodice fit her slender frame elegantly, and her dark hair had been woven into an intricate crown of braids dotted with pearls and tiny white flowers. Behind her, two older ladies wore crowns of flowers and carried baskets of flower petals, sprinkling them in her wake. Judging by their dark hair and green eyes, I decided they must be her sisters. It was beyond strange to think that they were actually her *little* sisters, even though they looked about forty years older—chalk that up to divine happenstance.

Phillip escorted Beckah to Jaevid's side, passing her arm over to him with a quick kiss on her cheek. He looked a little misty-eyed too when he came back to stand next to me. I bit back a smile and passed him the handkerchief from my pocket. He immediately wiped his eyes and blew his nose into it. Gross. He could keep it.

"As many of you know, the ceremony of marriage is one held in highest esteem among dragonriders," my father began to speak over the rush and roar of the surf. "Today, I'm honored to be performing this sacred rite, not only because it will be one of the final acts of my reign as King of Maldobar, but because, as many of you know, these two have … incredible significance to me. They're more than friends. They're more than legends. They're family."

In the crowd, Araxie was already crying against her husband's shoulder, and the pudgy little baby squirming in Jenna's arms let out a coo of delight. They were wonderful sounds, though. Those were the sounds of family—of the people that loved them.

My heart ached, carried far away for a moment as I thought about Enyo. She was doing an excellent job looking after my clinic in Mau Kakuri, working her fingers to the bone so I could be here. I'd written her dozens of letters but had yet to actually steal enough time to fly back and visit. The distance put a knot in my chest I knew wouldn't go away until I was back on that doorstep, gazing into her beautiful, multihued eyes.

"When a Dragonrider of Maldobar marries, he offers his chosen bride a token—a gesture of his eternal vow. We call it a square-cloth, and it is a tradition passed down in our brotherhood since its founding," King Felix continued. "He cuts a small piece of the cloth from his cloak, the very same cloak given to him when he took his oath at the feet of the king and became a true dragonrider. He gives that square of cloth to his bride because it represents the piece of himself that stays behind with her whenever he must leave for battle."

Pausing, my father's expression tensed for a moment as he gripped the sides of the podium where he stood. Half a minute passed before he seemed able to go on, his tone heavy. "When she dies, that piece is placed in her hand and buried with her. Jaevid, I know your original cloak is lost. Gods only know where it wound up. But I still have mine. Hopefully you won't mind that's already missing one piece."

Reaching under the podium, my father took out a long, royal blue cloak. The length unfurled smoothly, brushing the ground as he tied it around Jaevid's shoulders. The neck had a plush mane of soft white fur, and a diamond-shaped hole was cut right below the neck on the left side. Drawing an ornamental dagger from his belt, King Felix cut another diamond of cloth out directly beneath it, and then placed it in Jaevid's hand with a smile.

Only when he stepped back behind the podium again, dabbing at his eyes and clearing his throat, did I realize why that was so significant. The other hole in that cloak, the one my father had mentioned, must have been from the square-cloth he'd given to my mother.

And she had been buried with it.

The rest of the ceremony went smoothly. They repeated a few vows, swearing by the Gods to remain faithful and to cherish one another until death. Jaevid placed the square-cloth on Beckah's palm, closing her fingers around it and pressing his lips to her knuckles. By the time they finally embraced for a kiss, there weren't many dry eyes left in the audience.

Everyone cheered and threw petals in the air, thronging around them with congratulations and well wishes. I found myself squished between a bunch of Jaevid's relatives as they rushed in from every side. It took some wrenching and squeezing before I managed to squeeze free of the crowd. My heels sank in the sand and I wobbled backward, tripping and smacking against someone's chest.

"Easy, there." Aubren grinned as he steadied me. "And here I thought a boy raised by elves would be used to a lively gathering."

I dusted off my tunic, and straightened my collar. "I am. But there's a lot more smooching and hugging going on around here than I'm used to. I gotta get out of here before anyone else tries to—"

He ruffled my hair. Ugh. I'd almost killed myself and helped save Maldobar, and still people kept petting me like I was a puppy. Aubren laughed off my scowl and nodded toward the beach. "You're not the only one plotting a stealthy escape." Somehow, Jaevid and Beckah had managed to slip away. They were walking the shoreline together, hand in hand, the waves lapping at their feet.

Once again, I found myself envying him and wishing I were somewhere else. "You think they'll be upset if I don't stick around for the reception?" I asked.

Aubren rubbed the back of his neck as he studied me out of the corner of his eye. "Got somewhere else to be?"

I chewed the inside of my cheek and looked down at the sand clumped on my boots. There was a fair amount scraping around inside them, as well. "More like someone else I'd rather have doing all the kissing and hugging," I admitted quietly. "Not the petting, though. That's got to stop. Seriously, I'm gonna start biting people."

He smiled and gave me a nudge with his elbow. "Give it the rest of the night. It's a long journey back to Luntharda from here. No sense in making it on no sleep and an empty stomach."

"True," I conceded and nudged him back. "It would be a shame to miss out on free cake."

"Not to mention the gifts," he added, his tone ominous. "Just wait until you see what Father has done."

THIRTY-ONE

King Felix gave them a house.

I should say a chateau, I suppose, because the drawing of it he presented to the happy couple was extravagant to say the least. It was one of the few that had survived Tibran occupation and only needed minor repairs.

"It's been in the family for years," he explained as he passed Jaevid the document bearing the official royal seal. "My mother used it as a summer home. It's been empty for so long—seems only fitting someone make some good memories there. And since I did legally adopt you into the family all those years ago, no one can argue that it isn't staying under the Farrow name."

Jaevid was frozen, his mouth hanging open in shock, while everyone gathered around to get a good look. It was no secret Jaevid had been working on his own "house" the past few weeks—a small cottage somewhere in Mithangol. This was about fifty times bigger and came with tracts of wide-open land that bordered the coast just outside Eastwatch, deep in wild dragon territory.

"Felix, this is too much," he managed hoarsely.

Father waved a hand and snorted. "Don't start with that nonsense. You've saved Maldobar twice. You're just lucky I don't wrestle you onto the throne to take my place."

"You can thank me for talking him out of that." Jenna leaned over to nudge him with her elbow. "No way was I going to let him pass this mess off to you."

Jaevid's shoulders sagged, his expression drooping with genuine relief. "T-thank you."

"Oh, don't thank me yet," Jenna added with a laugh. "I plan on enlisting your *veteran* expertise for advice whenever I need it, Commander. There is a lot of work to be done fixing what Argonox destroyed."

Everyone got a good chuckle out of that. Well, except for Jaevid. He was scowling at her with his mouth scrunched and his face flushed several shades of red. He'd dodged the crown, yes, but my father wasn't going to let him sail into the sunset worry-free. The title of Academy Commander might take him some time to get used to, though.

While Jaevid and Beckah stood close together, taking well wishes and compliments from their guests, the great hall filled with the sounds of laughter, music, and excited conversation. According to Jenna, Haldor's family had insisted on hosting the reception banquet at their home. They were renowned merchants who owned a fleet of trading ships that came in and out of the port at Saltmarsh. Their home wasn't enormous, and it had suffered some Tibran abuse, but it was packed full of exotic curiosities from all over the world. Their great hall was large enough to host a great, albeit cozy, reception, and had been decorated with wreaths of flowers and colorful ribbons.

Inviting aromas floated from long buffet tables lined with fancy cakes, pastries, and pies of every flavor imaginable. I guess Jaevid had a special passion for pie, because every time I spotted him through the crowd ,he had a new piece on his plate. Not that I was going to judge. I couldn't resist stealing a slice of flaky, buttery, peach-and-cinnamon-packed goodness, either.

I was still licking the sugary juices off my fingers as I wandered through the hall. Servants stood by the corners of the room offering refills from bottles of bubbling ginger and fruit ciders. Queen Araxie had also brought along quite a few bottles of sweet wine—a gray elf delicacy—for everyone to share.

After the feasting came the dancing, and I drifted to the back of the room close to the door. I still hadn't quite gotten the knack of human-styled dancing, but it was still fun to watch. Couples twirled under the warm candlelight, clapping and dancing to the rhythm of the music. Girls dashed by in groups, giggling and tying ribbons around their wrists and in their hair. Every now and then, one would stop to ask me if I wanted to dance and I stumbled through an awkward explanation of why I didn't know how. That wasn't the *real* reason, of course. There was only one person I wanted to dance with … and she was miles away from here.

Everyone cleared the dance floor when Jaevid and Beckah

began to waltz to a gentle tune. From where I lurked the doorway, I watched them glide past with their expressions the picture of total infatuation. It was the kind of happiness you could almost taste, like the subtle hint of honeysuckle floating on the summer breeze outside.

Jealousy twisted in my chest, squeezing at my heart. I had to look away. My mind knew three months wasn't that long, but my heart begged to differ. I wanted to go home.

I wanted to see Enyo.

While everyone was still transfixed by Jaevid and Beckah's wedding dance, I slipped out the door and into the night. The night wind carried the stalky, fishy scent of the harbor nearby. The tall masts of the ships groaning and swaying at their moorings barely peeked over the rooftops as I made the short walk back out to the beach.

Vexi was waiting there, preening her bright green scales, and nuzzling along Mavrik's side like a kitten craving attention from an older, much more dangerous cat. As soon as I called her name, she perked up. Little ears swiveled in my direction and she let out a screech, swooping over the sand and landing so close it sent a spray of sand all over me.

Great.

"Are you kidding me? Now I'll be itching all the way back to Luntharda," I grumbled as I tried to shake the sand out of my hair and blow it out of my nose.

"Leaving so soon?" someone asked. I tensed and slowly turned around. Jaevid stood behind me with his arms crossed and a strange, almost wistful smile on his face. "Still not an animal fan, I take it?"

Vexi lowered her head right next to mine and puffed

heavy dragon-breaths right in my ear. "Not really. This one is growing on me, though." I gave her chin a scratch and she purred.

"They do that." His smile widened. "So, you were planning on running away? Without even saying goodbye?"

"I, uh, well, um … " I couldn't come up with a good excuse—other than the truth, anyway. "So much has happened. I need to go back. I need to see her again."

The wind tousled his ash-colored hair as Jaevid gazed out at the ocean.

"I will come back," I clarified quickly. "I know I've got responsibilities here."

"Like attending dragonrider training at Blybrig Academy?"

I hesitated as my thoughts blurred through the realization of what that meant. Now that I'd seen first-hand what it truly meant to be counted as one of them, and what that might mean for me in the future, I could appreciate what that meant. Jenna had been right—being a dragonrider wasn't something to take lightly. It wasn't just zipping around in flashy armor, drinking in the envy and admiration of everyone in the kingdom. There was a legacy in their name, a tapestry stitched by the lives of hundreds of men who had taken that oath.

But was I ready to be a part of that?

The answer rose up in my chest, blazing like a raging firestorm. "Yes."

"I won't go easy on you," Jaevid warned with a smirk. "Prince, Harbinger, and all that aside—you'll be just another fledgling."

I shot him my best challenging grin. "I wouldn't have it any other way, Commander."

"Good."

"Still friends though, right?" I just had to check.

"Of course."

The rumble, boom, and hiss of the surf filled the silence as Jaevid and I stared at one another. The light of the moon glinted over his polished breastplate, putting shadows of bold relief over the design engraved across his chest: the head of a stag. An interesting choice for dragonrider armor, considering that was the symbol of gray elf royalty. But then again, he was an interesting guy. And, hey, it did match his scimitar.

"So, it's really over? No more lurking dead twins or whispering goddesses for me?" I rubbed the back of my neck and found a few more bits of sand stuck inside my shirt collar.

He glanced toward the heavens and the millions of twinkling stars. "That was the agreement. They get to walk the mortal realm again, and we don't have to carry their essence as our burden anymore. No more harbingers, lapiloques, akrotis, or otherwise will be necessary."

I couldn't resist a smile. "That's good news."

"Hopefully," he agreed.

"I never thanked you for helping with Noh—and, well, for everything else."

Jaevid tensed and met my gaze with his brows knitted. "Reigh, you should know, I ... when you get back to Luntharda you might ... " His mouth hung open, as though he were going to finish that thought, and then suddenly snapped shut. He shook his head. "Never mind."

I raised an eyebrow. "Isn't there a big party you're supposed to be at? Something to do with a pretty girl in a white dress?"

He laughed and waved a hand. "Have a good trip, Reigh. We'll see each other again soon."

I stood alone on the sand, watching Jaevid disappear back into the dark city streets with his long blue cloak fluttering at his boot heels. Beside me, Vexi let out an anxious chirp. I couldn't agree more—it was time to get going.

My chest tingled with excitement as I climbed into the brand-new saddle fixed to her back. The dark chestnut leather was oiled to perfection and the brass saddle handles shone like gold in the moonlight. Slipping my feet down into the deep, boot-shaped compartments on either side, I strapped the securing harness around my waist and gave her neck a pat. More and more, we'd been practicing learning how to fly together and to communicate in the air. Now, sitting in that saddle while she flared her wings for takeoff felt as natural as breathing.

I loved every second of it.

We charged skyward as one, veering over the city and harbor before we set our noses to the wind. Luntharda was a long flight away. We'd probably have to stop to rest somewhere in the Farchase Plains. But every long hour in the cold wind with my rear end sore from the saddle would be worth it. Luntharda was home—and half my heart was already there.

Vexi touched down at the boundary line between Maldobar and Luntharda in a few graceful wing beats. Tired, hungry, and sore from flight, we both groaned in unison as I climbed out of the saddle. I stretched my back and shoulders while she did the same. My knees creaked and ached as I walked around her, unloading the rest of my gear from the saddle. There wasn't much, just my kafki and a bag of supplies and personal items. I didn't need much else.

Now came the hard part.

"Okay, Vexi, we went over this. Jaevid went over it. Mavrik, too. So, no fits this time, all right?" I warned as ran a hand down her snout. "I'm coming back, I promise."

She narrowed her sky-blue eyes, nostrils puffing in an irritated snort.

"Think of this as a vacation for you, too. Go back home and visit the family. Tell them all about the scrawny kid you're about to drag through the most brutal training in the kingdom."

Vexi swiped the side of my head with her tongue, leaving a foul-smelling, sticky trail behind.

"Yuck! Come on!" I wiped the side of my head, only to wind up having to peel my sleeve off my face when it stuck to her spit.

Lowering her head again, my green dragoness bumped her nose against my chest. I ran my fingers along the horns on her head, scratching behind her ears, and brushing over the places where the muzzle Argonox had put on her left scars in her hide. The sight of them threatened to take me back there, a flash of dark memory that could yank me under at any moment.

I clenched my teeth and looked away, but not before giving her chin one last scratch. "I'll see you soon, pretty lady," I promised.

She yipped and sprang backward, leaping into the sky with a rush of wind that nearly knocked me on my back. With a flash of green scales, Vexi spiraled out of sight, heading straight for the eastern coastline where her wild kin lived. After watching her at Saltmarsh, it was easy to imagine her there, dancing over the waves and grooming herself on the ledges of the steep cliffs. She'd get to enjoy a few weeks of freedom before we had to return to Halfax for Jenna's coronation.

Right now, however, all I could think about was making it to Mau Kakuri. There was still at least a two-day journey for me to reach it through the jungle. I wasn't about to wait a single minute to start.

I found an encampment of scouts less than a mile inside the jungle boundary. Fighting in the Tibran War and being the Harbinger of Clysiros had earned me a little distinction amongst the gray elves—or at least, enough that they let me borrow a shrike, so I could make good time getting back to Mau Kakuri. Zipping through the vivid green maze of the jungle, past the towering giant trees with their interwoven branches, massive fern fronds, vibrant flowers, and wandering banks of fog, I drank in all the familiar smells of home. Every breath of the moist, cool air felt like taking in a healing elixir. And yet, the closer I got to the city, the faster my heart raced. I couldn't sit still. My sweaty hands squeezed and wrenched on the saddle.

Suddenly, the thick jungle greenery opened to a rocky,

moss-covered valley, where towering waterfalls spilled down the side of a steep cliff, pooling and filling the narrow canals that flowed all through the city. The falls filled the air with fine mist that hung and sparkled like diamonds. It was like I'd never left.

I urged the shrike to land, touching down right at the city gates. All around the square, shopkeepers were just beginning to open for the day. Merchants unfurled their carpets and opened their stands. Bakers and blacksmiths lit their fires. Shepherds and faundra breeders guided herds along the cobblestone streets.

As much as I would have enjoyed standing there to drink in every detail of this place I had missed, there was somewhere I had to be.

I coaxed the shrike onward at a casual speed, buzzing down the market district where the clinic stood. We landed at the base of the front steps, and for a moment, all I could do was sit there with my heart hammering in the back of my throat. I was home.

I tripped twice scrambling down from the saddle and totally forgot to tie the shrike, so he didn't wander off. It didn't matter. I had to get to that door. *Now.*

Running up the steps, I screeched to a halt with my hand hovering over the knob. My heart hammered in my ears like war drums. Wait—should I knock? It was my house, right? But I'd been gone for so long. Maybe I should, just in case Enyo—

The door swung open.

The old, stiff-looking gray elf man standing on the other side didn't say a word at first. His multihued eyes studied me from head to foot, mouth set in a hard line, as though he were looking for obvious signs of damage. His brow furrowed deeply in parental disapproval.

I couldn't take offense, though.

Kiran looked at everyone that way.

My heart stopped. All the wind rushed out of my lungs as I trembled in front of him, too stunned to make a sound. Tears welled in my eyes until I couldn't see him anymore. My chest heaved, bursting with emotion I barely understood. A strangled sound tore out of my chest—something between a scream and a sob.

It wasn't possible. It couldn't be. How? When?

"Enyo," Kiran called back over his shoulder. "He's here. Better draw a bath. He smells awful."

"K-Kiran," I managed to croak through wheezing gasps.

A corner of his mouth lifted, curling into a familiar half-smile. "Jaevid sends his regards."

That sneaky … secret keeping … JERK!

I lunged forward, grabbing Kiran and squeezing my arms around his neck in a rough hug. I half expected to find nothing but empty air—that this entire moment was nothing but a hopeful dream. But it wasn't.

Kiran put his arms around me and laughed, holding me tight as he patted the back of my head. "It's all right, Reigh."

Behind him, I spotted Enyo leaning around the corner from the sitting room. Her eyes crinkled with a broad smile as she wiped a tear from her cheek. She'd been keeping this from me, too. I'd have to think of a good way to get revenge later. For now, I burned my face in his shoulder and tried to catch my breath. Every inhale filled my nose with his smell—

the scent of the herbs he used for medicines and damp jungle soil. It was the same smell I'd known since childhood.

"I'm so sorry," I blurted. "Kiran, I-I—"

"There's nothing to be sorry for," he said as he stepped back, motioning for me to come inside. "But I wasn't joking about the bath. Don't sit on anything until you've washed." He leaned in to give my head a sniff, then cringed back and made a face. "Is that … dragon spit?"

I flushed. "I-it's a long story."

He and Enyo exchanged a knowing smile. "I look forward to hearing it, then. Welcome home, Reigh."

ACKNOWLEDGEMENTS

Whew! Another series in the books (*rimshot*)! Reigh's adventure took me to some unexpected places. But I hope you're as excited and eager to see what will happen next in the world of the dragonriders as I am!

BUT FIRST …

I'd like to extend a big thank you to all my readers and fans around the world who have been so supportive of and enthusiastic about the Dragonrider books! The most encouraging thing an author can hear is how their books have impacted someone or touched their heart in some way. Being able to share Jaevid's story has certainly impacted my life, and I'm so pleased and honored to hear that it has affected so many others as well.

Here's to many more adventures, battles, and dragons!

THUNDER & PILSUNG!

NICOLE CONWAY

Nicole Conway is the author of the international bestselling series, THE DRAGONRIDER CHRONICLES, Nicole Conway is originally from North Alabama. A graduate of Auburn University, she now lives in Tucson, Arizona, with her family and enjoys a full-time career in writing. When not working on a new book, Nicole loves spending time with her husband and son, traveling, and playing video games. A coffee addict and active bookstagrammer, she has also recently begun teaching free writing classes to local youth in the community.

Learn more about Nicole Conway and her future book releases on her author website:

https://www.authornicoleconway.com

Introducing

HUNTER

Book 1 in
The Dragonriders Trials Series
(Unedited Sample Chapters)

by Nicole Conway

ONE

I startled awake to the smell of smoke and my father shaking me.

"Thatch, get up!" He shouted over me. "Hurry!"

I fell out of bed, tripping over my own feet as I scrambled to yank on my boots. "What's going on?"

He didn't have to reply; the answer was written all over his face. With his eyes wide and face blanched with panic, my father shoved a lumpy saddlebag into my hands and spun me around, roughly steering me out of my tiny bedroom into the hall. "Go to the stable; run!"

Terror sent a jolt through every muscle in my body. What was happening? Was it the Tibrans? That was the only reason I could think of. For last few months, our kingdom of Maldobar had been under attack by a foreign enemy. The Tibran Empire had come with war machines and numbers beyond counting, and they only had one goal—to conquer and kill. So far, they'd done a good job of it, even here. City after city fell to their hordes of soldiers, and not even our prestigious dragonriders, the finest knights in the king's entire army, had been able to hold them off.

Not yet, anyway.

"Go!" Father roared at my back.

I took off at a sprint. Pumping my legs as fast as they would go, I darted down the hall to the narrow staircase that led into the stable below. We'd lived in the loft directly above it for as long as I could remember.

The horses were panicking. They whinnied and bucked, kicking at their stalls as smoke and embers swirled in the air. Was it on fire? Wait—it wasn't just the stable. My legs locked up, bringing me to a screeching halt before the open door.

Outside, every building up and down our street was swallowed in roaring flames that licked and crackled against the night sky. Men shouted. Women screamed. Children wailed. Horses ran wild in the streets, dragging burning wagons as they searched for a way out.

Gods and Fates, what was happening?

My father appeared as though he'd materialized out of thin air. He gripped the reins of our buckskin mare and snatched the saddlebag out of my hands to fling it over her back. "Get on, now."

"What about you?" I slipped a hand into one of the stirrups and swung my leg over the saddle.

His eyes squeezed shut, jaw clenching as he shoved the reins into my hand. "I'll be right behind you. Go. Ride to the North River Bridge. Don't stop. Do you hear me, Thatch?"

"B-but Father—"

He grabbed the sides of my face, yanking me down close enough to press his mouth to my forehead. "Do as I say, son. Go!"

My father smacked the mare on the rump. She bucked, pawing at the air before bolting out of the stable at a frantic gallop. We burst into the fire-lit streets with hooves thundering over the cobblestones.

I gripped the reins for dear life. My heart thrashed in my ears as I leaned down against her neck. My body shook. My mind blurred, tangled with panic and worry. What was going on? Why wasn't Father coming with me? We should have left together!

There were burning heaps of something—maybe debris—piled on the streets and sidewalks. My mare skirted around them and jumped the ones she couldn't avoid. It was only when we rounded a corner, heading for the North River, that I realized those heaps weren't debris.

They were people.

Fear throttled the breath from my lungs as I sank my heels into my horse's flanks. She shrieked and poured on more speed. Ahead, I spotted something blocking the road through the plumes of black smoke that poured from buildings on either side of the street. A barricade? No. The closer I got, I could pick out the shapes of men—men dressed from head to toe in heavy bronze-colored armor. They brandished swords that dripped with fresh blood. Their broad shields were spattered with it, too. Marching together shoulder-to-shoulder, I realized the soldiers at the front of the line were holding up torches. Occasionally, they would toss them through the window of a building they passed, setting fire to whatever was inside.

Tibrans.

They spotted me. My body seized up, my blood going cold in my veins.

I pulled hard on the reins, bringing my mare around in

a sharp turn that nearly flung me out of the saddle. Arrows zipped past my head, pinging off the cobblestones all around me. We bolted back the way we'd come, zigzagging through narrow alleys and avenues. I had to find another way out of the city. My horse puffed, her mouth dripping with foam and her flanks shining with sweat as we crested a steep road into a small square. Here, nothing was on fire yet, but people were still pouring out of every building in droves. They were all fleeing toward the North River—toward the bridge. It was our only way out.

Hope gave me new strength. I squeezed the reins harder. We could make it. Just a bit further.

I heard the *twang* of a bowstring—no, not a bow. It had to be something else. The sound was much sharper and more abrupt.

An arrow caught right in my mare's chest. She crumpled, legs instantly buckling.

I didn't even have time to scream.

I flew over my fallen horse's head and hit the street hard, bouncing off it like a stone across a pond. My head cracked off the stone, and my arms and legs flailed until I finally landed in a heap, sprawled on my back.

For a moment, all I could do was lie there. My vision faded in and out. My ears rang. No. I couldn't pass out. Not now.

I had to get up. I had to get out of here.

I clenched my teeth and forced my body to move. Rolling over onto my stomach, my arms shook as I pushed myself to my hands and knees. Something hot and wet ran down my face, making my shaggy hair stick to my skin.

My mare lay on her side a short distance down the street, but she wasn't moving. The arrow sticking out of her breast had hit with so much force, it was buried all the way to the black-feathered fletching. She was gone.

Now I'd have to run for it on foot.

* * *

Shambling to my feet, I staggered toward the nearest alleyway. My head spun, and bright spots winked in my vision. I stumbled, still dazed from my crash landing, and caught myself against the side of one of the buildings. Maybe if I could just rest for a moment, my head would clear, and I could—

"He went this way," a man's throaty voice growled. "I already winged him for you. He won't go far. Best hurry, before the Tibrans steal the kill."

Spinning around, I met the glittering eyes of two big men as they stepped into the alley behind me. Their dark silhouettes were ominous against the faint moonlight and orange glow of distant flames. Oh no.

Run—I had to run!

The heel of my boot snagged on an uneven stone. I fell backward and landed on my rump.

One of the men barked a laugh. "There's an easy mark for you, pup. Look at him, helpless as a newborn fawn. Pathetic."

My body shook, paralyzed as I watched them prowling closer and closer. They both wore an ensemble of black—

black leather armor, cloaks, and boots. Something like soot was smeared across their faces, just a single swipe to cover their eyes.

The shorter, stockier one of them carried a large, black crossbow slung over his shoulder. He stroked the trigger fondly with one finger as he grinned wickedly down at me, still chuckling under his breath.

The other man was taller and more leanly built. In addition to the dark streak across his eyes, a black handkerchief tied over his nose and mouth covered his most of his face. I couldn't see much more than the whites of his eyes and his shaggy, dark hair ruffling in the wind.

He stalked toward me, polished black boots crunching on the gravel. Reaching for the hilts of two long, curved scimitars, he drew them both from the sheath across his back. The metal hummed, singing in the dark as he lurked just a few feet away from me.

Oh gods. He … he was going to kill me.

Every inch of my brain screamed for me to flee. Get up! Go! Get out of there, stupid!

But fear turned my muscles to mush. I couldn't move. I trembled as I sat, staring up at the man brandishing those long, flawless scimitars.

Tears welled in my eyes. I didn't want to die. Who were these people? Where was Father? Mother? What was happening?

"Hurry it up! We don't have all night. Those Tibran dogs will be here any minute! We've got orders, you know," the man with the crossbow snarled.

"P-please, I just want to go home." My voice came out in

a broken, breathless sob. "You don't have to do this."

The warrior in black raised one of his blades, fingers tightening their grip. His eyes narrowed into lethal, emotionless slits.

I sucked in a breath. I waited for that blade to fall. For pain. For death.

But he didn't move.

The hand gripping that raised blade began to shake. His eyes went round, brow skewing with an expression I didn't understand. What was he waiting for?

The other man yelled louder, his voice cracking over us like the snap of a whip. "I said, hurry up!"

In one fluid motion, the guy brandishing the scimitar whirled into a spin and hurled his weapon through the air. It sailed down the alleyway, wind howling over the blade.

I squeezed my eyes shut.

Someone, or something, made an awful gurgling sound like someone choking on water.

Only, it wasn't water.

Peeling my eyes open, I sucked in a gasp. My heart dropped to the soles of my feet. The other warrior in black dropped to his knees. His crossbow clattered to the ground. Then his body fell one way, limp and lifeless. But his head rolled the opposite way.

I gagged. Bile burned in my throat. My eyes watered. I couldn't bear to look anymore. If I was next, I didn't want to see it coming. But I couldn't tear my eyes away.

The remaining warrior stalked toward his fallen comrade, picking up his thrown blade and tucking both weapons back into the sheaths strapped against his back. He snatched up the crossbow and stormed back toward me. Was he going to shoot me instead?

"Take this and go," he growled, his deep voice muffled by the handkerchief covering his mouth. He sounded young, like maybe he wasn't much older than I was.

I eyed the weapon. I didn't want to touch that thing. I'd never held a sword, crossbow, or any other kind of weapon in my life! I was a farrier's son—not a fighter. I didn't even know how to shoot it! "B-but why?"

"Listen to me, kid." He growled as he seized the front of my nightshirt and dragged me to my feet. "Your home is gone. Your family is most likely gone, too. The Tibran army is moving on the royal city of Halfax. You have two choices: either run and maybe you get out of here alive, or you stay and die. What's it going to be?"

My pulse roared in my ears as I stared at the crossbow, then back up at the guy holding it out to me. Why was he doing this? He could have killed me—he was supposed to— but he'd saved my life instead. I didn't understand it.

"Why didn't you kill me?" I managed to wheeze.

One of his eyes twitched. "Are you dense? I said get out of here *now*."

"What about you? Where will you go?"

His brows snapped into a sharp scowl. He shoved the weapon against my chest hard enough to make me stagger and almost fall over. Then he turned away and began to leave.

"Hey! Wait up!" I staggered to my feet and wobbled after him, my knees still shaking.

He didn't look back or slow down. "Get away from me. I told you to run."

"But I don't have anywhere to go. If the Tibrans are attacking Halfax tonight, then—"

He stopped so suddenly I crashed into his back.

"Don't you get it? This is it. This is the end. The Tibran Empire is going to raze this whole kingdom to the ground. There won't anything left. And if you stay here, you'll end up dead in a ditch somewhere along with everyone else." He snapped each word as though it were bitter on his tongue. "The king is making his final stand at the royal city right now, but it won't matter. A few dragonriders against the entire Tibran army? They won't last the night."

It was true, then. I shivered, staring down at the sleek, elaborate crossbow in my arms. It was heavy. The wood had been stained until it was black. Someone had even taken the time to cover it with intricate silver scrollwork and designs. It was wickedly beautiful—you know, in a "murdered-my-favorite-horse-in-a-single-shot" kind of way.

But I didn't want this thing. I hated it.

"You don't know that." I heard myself mutter. My face was so numb I couldn't even feel my lips moving. "The dragonriders could still win."

"Don't be stupid," the warrior in black snapped. With a growling curse under his breath, he started off toward the street again.

Then he froze.

More of those soldiers in bronze armor were storming the streets directly in front of us. There must have been hundreds of them. The noise of their synchronized marching was like the droning rhythm of war drums. It thundered in my ears until I could feel my teeth rattle. The only other sound, the one that never stopped, was the screaming. Townspeople—the ones who hadn't run when they had the chance—were being dragged from their homes.

Suddenly, the warrior slammed an arm across my chest. He flattened me against the side of the nearest building and stood with his back to it, completely motionless. A group of soldiers passed right in front of the alley where we were hiding in the shadows. One of them glanced right at me.

My heart stopped.

I held my breath.

He paused, blinked twice, and then glanced away. The soldier moved along with the rest of his group without ever looking back.

He hadn't seen us.

As soon as they were gone, my whole body sagged back against the wall. I wheezed and fought for breath, wiping away some of the blood that was still dripping down my face from a deep gash on my forehead right at my hairline.

"It's too late." The warrior growled quietly under his breath. "The streets are being patrolled, meaning they've got the city surrounded. There's no way to get past them now without being seen."

"Well, what do we do?" I whispered, almost falling over as he moved his arm away.

The warrior pulled the black handkerchief down away from his face, revealing features that were surprisingly young. I'd been right. He wasn't much older than me. Taller, sure, but maybe eighteen at the most. His thin mouth was set in a grim, focused frown and his gaze darted around the alley. Every move he made was quick, sharp, and aggressive, as though he were ready to cut someone else's head off at a moment's notice.

I just hoped it wasn't mine.

"Come on." He pushed away from the wall, moving fast to the far end of the alley.

I ran after him, lugging the crossbow with me. "Where are we going?"

He glanced back at me, but only for a second or two. The glow of the fires caught over his sharp features, revealing bands of gold and green hidden amidst the amber color of his eyes. "I know a way out."

TWO

My father had always joked that I was a terrible judge of character. He'd said that I only saw what I wanted to see in people—good things—even if they weren't really there. He'd warned that I couldn't believe every sob story someone told me. If I did, I'd wind up swindled, robbed, and left for dead on the side of the road someday.

As I watched the warrior in front of me, dressed out in black leather armor with his blood-spattered weapons sheathed at his back, I wondered if this was that moment. I had no reason to trust this guy. He'd murdered someone, most likely one of his own comrades, right in front of me. And if his skill with those blades was any kind of evidence, then it was a safe bet that this probably wasn't the first time he'd killed someone.

But right now, he was my only shot of making it out of the city alive.

A few old wooden crates were scattered around the back of the alley, empty and long forgotten. He began stacking them one on top of the other until he'd made a teetering tower. It was just tall enough to reach the eaves of the roof.

… If you jumped for it, that is.

He scurried up first; scaling the tower in an instant and springing like a cat to catch the edge of the slanted roof. In one smooth motion, he hoisted himself over the ledge and crouched on the rooftop—all without making a single sound.

I swallowed hard.

"Come on. Hurry up." He turned around, holding out a hand.

I took a few steps back, trying to mentally prepare myself for what I was about to do. I could make the climb. I might even be able to catch the edge of the roof when I jumped. But hoisting myself up like that? Not a chance. This guy, whoever or whatever he was, had clearly gone through some rigorous physical training. My physical training amounted to moving boxes of supplies for my father around the stable, trimming hooves, and occasionally weeding the garden.

Gods help me.

Threading the thick leather strap on the crossbow over my shoulders, I took a deep breath. I charged forward, clamoring up the tower of crates. At the last second, I jumped. My arms stretched, reaching for the roof. The air rushed out of me as my fingers brushed the edge.

Then I started to fall.

I wasn't going to make it.

Before I could scream, the young warrior lunged out and caught me by the wrists. With his heels braced on the edge of the roof, he cursed through his teeth and steadied himself with my weight.

I dangled over the alley, helpless, staring up at him with desperation. It took everything I had not to yell or freak out. If he dropped me, it was all over. The soldiers would hear it when I crashed into the crates. They would find me in an instant.

"You are useless," the warrior grumbled as he dragged me up. With one last, incredibly-powerful yank, he hauled me over the edge and dropped me onto the roof next to him.

I lay there sprawled on my stomach, panting, trying to figure out why I wasn't dead.

The reason was simple, though … and currently glaring at me. "Get up," the warrior commanded.

Shakily, I clamored to my feet again and took off after him. We ran the lengths of the rooftops, racing up and down the sloped pitches and leaping the gaps between buildings. Every step made my body burn with fatigue. My lungs ached. My heart felt like it might punch right out of my chest. I couldn't keep this up for much longer.

All around us, the city blazed in the night. The air was filled with smoke, flames, embers, and screams. Occasionally, the ringing and clanging of metal-on-metal, the clashing of swords and shouts of combat, broke over the noise. Some of the townsfolk were resisting. But it wouldn't be enough.

As we skidded down another steep incline, the warrior cut a steep path to the right, sprinting the narrow ledge all the way to the very end. He kept stealing quick glances back at me, as though he were making sure I hadn't fallen behind. Or maybe I was hoping I'd fall, die, and then he wouldn't have to worry about me anymore.

I wobbled after him, barely able to keep up. Every move he made was so solid, sharp, and precise. He never stumbled, never lost his balance. When we got to the end of the roof, he jumped, executing a perfect spin in the air to catch the ledge with his hands and then drop into a crouch on the balcony below.

Nope. I couldn't do that. Not going to happen.

Shambling to the edge, I sat down and eyed the drop to the balcony where he had landed. It had to be ten or fifteen feet, at least.

Oh, gods.

"Don't go stiff. Land on your feet. Keep your legs loose, bend to adjust for impact," he called up to me. "And quit stalling. The longer you wait the more you give yourself a chance to panic."

Right. Okay, but I was *already* panicking.

I set my jaw and tried to focus. This was going to hurt.

Maybe if I just eased down slowly …

Suddenly, my hands slipped. I lost my grip on the roof. I fell, kicking and flailing, as I dropped like a rock toward the balcony.

THUD!

I landed flat on my stomach—right on top of my warrior friend.

"I hate you," he groaned, his voice muffled as he lay face down beneath me.

"S-sorry," I wheezed as I scrambled off him.

He muttered a few more curses as he got to his feet and dusted off the front of his black silk tunic and elaborate leather breastplate. Everything he wore was crafted with excruciating care and detail, and seemed to have been made specially to fit his frame. Every piece matched, fitting seamlessly against his tall, wide-shouldered frame. The only thing that wasn't black was the single silver-plated cuff he wore over the vambrace on his right arm. It shone like platinum in the pale light of the moon, and the relief of a snarling wolf's head had been engraved into its surface.

It was a little strange that he only had one. He wore a black leather vambrace on this other arm, too, but there was no cuff to match. Had he lost the other one?

"Okay, you know what, you're going to wait right here." He decided suddenly.

Panic shot through me and I took a reflexive step closer. "What? Wait, please don't—"

He shot me a glare of warning. "I'll get this done faster on my own. Just wait here. I'll be back."

There was no arguing it.

The warrior unclasped his black cloak and threw it in my face before he prowled to the edge of the balcony. "Stay down. Don't make a sound," he ordered as he crouched low and sprang over the railing. He must have landed somewhere below, but I never heard it. His clothes didn't even rustle.

Draping his black cloak around my shoulders, I sat down to wait. There was nothing else I could do. The balcony itself was about four stories up, and the house it was attached to seemed like it had already been abandoned. But at least it wasn't on fire. I decided to count that as a blessing.

My mind immediately snapped back to my father. Where was he? Was he still alive? Had he made it out of the house? Why hadn't he come with me?

I had no answers. No hope of getting them at the moment, either. My only hope for even living to see daylight again was that warrior in black, somewhere in the city.

And that was if he did come back for me …

* * *

Minutes passed. About the time I had made up my mind that my mysterious warrior-friend had left me there for dead, the clatter of metal against stone made my whole body go rigid. I peeked out from under the cowl of the cloak, shaking as my heart pounded in my ears.

The warrior had returned—with an armload of what looked suspiciously like blood-spattered Tibran armor.

"Here," he said as he shoved a breastplate and helmet in my direction. "Put this on."

"Where did you get this?" I squinted at the crimson speckling the metal. "Is this blood?"

"It's tomato juice."

I blinked. "It is?"

He shot me an exasperated glare. "Of course, it's blood, you idiot. Put it on."

I tried. Sliding the crossbow off my shoulders, I picked up the breastplate first. My shaking fingers fumbled over the clasps and buckles. I'd never put on armor before. I'd never had a reason to. Being a farrier's son meant I was a commoner. I ran errands and helped my father around the shop. I looked after horses, swept the stables, mucked stalls, tended to our small garden out back. Nothing about my life had ever been violent. I'd never fought anyone, or even wanted to.

Now, I sort of wished I had. Maybe then I wouldn't be so useless, or could at least put on a breastplate without looking like a complete moron.

It was a sloppy job and I knew it. The straps weren't right. The metal front of the breastplate hung off me crookedly. I looked like a poorly dressed scarecrow.

With a grumble and a huff, the warrior stomped over to help. He'd already snapped his own outfitting into place right over the leather armor he already wore. Breastplate, pauldrons, gauntlets, even greaves—he'd put them on in a matter of seconds.

"For crying out loud," he hissed through his teeth as he stormed over and began adjusting all the straps. "What good are you?"

"Not much," I admitted. "Not when it comes to things like this. I-I'm sorry. You spared my life and I can't even ..." My voice died in my throat. I couldn't even look him in the eye.

He puffed a sharp sigh and stood back, giving me one last appraising look from head to toe. "Look, not everyone is cut out to be a fighter. But if you want to survive this, then you need to do a good job faking it. The Tibrans have the city locked down. They've closed off the bridge and roads to everyone except their own forces. So if we want to get across, then we have to look like them. Got it?"

I nodded.

He didn't look convinced. "What's your name?"

"Thatcher," I replied, swallowing hard. "Thatcher Renley."

His eyes narrowed, studying me for a second before he gave a satisfied nod. "I'm Murdoc."

"No family name?" I asked.

He turned away. "No."

Okay, that was a little odd. Then again, he wasn't exactly normal. In size and age, we didn't seem to be all that far apart. He was taller, and obviously a few years older, but somehow standing next to him made me feel like a frightened little kid by comparison. I didn't know how to handle anything that was happening. If he left me behind, I wouldn't last five minutes.

"We're going into the street now. You need to prepare yourself. It's bad out there," he warned. "Try not to look. Just keep your eyes on me and do what I do. We'll get out of here and make a break for marshes."

I stared back at him, silently wondering why my body had begun to feel cold and heavy. My fingers tingled. My ears were ringing again.

"Hey!" He snapped his fingers in front of my nose.

I cringed back.

"Stay with me, Thatcher." Murdoc handed me the Tibran helmet. I tried not to notice how much blood was on it. "Stay close. Keep the visor down and don't look anyone in the eye."

Swallowing against the growing tightness in my throat, I forced myself to nod. Then I slipped the helmet over my head and pulled down the visor so that it covered my face. A long narrow slit cut across the face of it gave me a limited view—but it was enough to see. I could follow him. I could do this.

Picking up the crossbow again, I held it tight against my chest. I didn't even know how to fire or load it. But if Murdoc was right, if I at least looked the part, then maybe I stood a chance.

Maybe I'd get out of here alive.

THREE

Murdoc was right. Leaving that house was like walking into the darkest pits of the abyss. Everywhere I looked, Tibran soldiers marched in small groups, searching the rubble for survivors. Anyone they found was either slapped in chains or murdered on the spot if they were too old or wounded to be useful. The horizon glowed red against the night because of the fires. The air was thick with the smell of smoke and blood ran in the streets like rainwater.

Gods and Fates, how were we ever going to get out of here alive?

"Stay right with me," Murdoc whispered suddenly, jostling me as though to get my attention. "If anyone stops us, let me handle it. They are only looking for civilians now. And with the bulk of their forces being slave-soldiers, you can bet they aren't trained thoroughly enough to second-guess anyone wearing their armor."

I met his fiercely determined stare through the eye-slit cut in my helmet. How did he know all this?

"Who are you?" I whispered.

He flicked his gaze away and didn't reply.

I tried to tell myself it didn't matter. He was helping

me. I shouldn't question him. He could have left me on that balcony, or killed me on sight, but he hadn't. I should just be grateful.

Murdoc led the way into the war-torn streets, stepping smoothly into formation with a group of soldiers marching past. I scrambled in beside him. We kept with that group until we reached another city square. Then, as quick as a shadow, Murdoc whirled out of the line of soldiers and into a shadowed corner between two shops. I clambered after him, almost tripping over my own feet.

His eyes panned the square like a hawk surveying its territory—fast and focused. Then he nodded toward another group of the Tibran soldiers approaching. They weren't marching, just strolling along more casually, while leading a string of captured Maldobarian townsfolk all tethered to a heavy iron chain.

I tried not to look at their faces. I was afraid I'd recognize someone.

What if I saw my father?

With one wide step, Murdoc assumed a position at the end of the line of prisoners—as though he were making sure none of them escaped. I jumped in after him. As we rounded the square, the formation departed down a large avenue to the right. We veered to the left, making our way toward the northern side of the city.

Step-by-step, minute after grueling minute, we moved in and out of Tibran formations like phantoms. I was getting better at it. I didn't stumble or stagger. I tried to march like they did, with my shoulders back and my head high, hand resting on the grip of the crossbow like I knew what to do with it. But if someone had confronted me, I'd have probably resorted to hurling the whole weapon at them rather than actually firing it.

Thankfully, that didn't happen.

We were getting closer. The bridge wasn't far now, only a mile or so from where we'd stopped in another darkened alley to wait for a chance to join another formation. Reaching up under my helm, I wiped the sweat from forehead. It kept running down, mixing with the blood dried onto my skin, and dripping into my eyes.

"Almost there," Murdoc whispered.

I nodded.

A thundering roar shook the ground under my boots. It rattled the cobblestones like chattering teeth. That sound—I knew that sound.

At the same instant, Murdoc and I glanced skyward just as two huge, scaly bodies zoomed past. They were flying low, barely above the rooftops. I sucked in a breath. My pulse raced, thrumming wildly in my ears. Just the sight of them set my blood ablaze with awe.

Dragons.

Outside our hiding place, crowds of Tibran soldiers began running past with their weapons drawn. Suddenly, a column of fire exploded through the street before us. It blasted through the ranks of soldiers and sent them flying in every direction. The wave sizzled over my body. It stung my eyes through the slit of my helmet. Something reeked like acid.

Dragon venom.

Murdoc and I staggered back as two more dragons

whooshed overhead. I spotted the glint of firelight off the armor of a rider. It wasn't just dragons—the Dragonriders of Maldobar had come. But weren't they supposed to be defending the royal city? What were they doing here?

"The tide has turned." Murdoc's voice was low and ominous as he ripped off his helmet and threw it aside.

"What?"

"They must have overtaken the Tibrans at Halfax. They're winning. That's the only reason they would split their forces and mobilize elsewhere."

"T-that's good, though, isn't it? That means they've come here to retake the city?" I guessed.

His expression darkened, hard lines creasing across his brow. Something was wrong. I didn't understand at all.

Then it was too late.

* * *

"You there! Drop your weapons and get down on your knees!" An enraged voice shouted from the street.

I looked up, straight into the faces of two Maldobarian soldiers. They advanced towards us, blades drawn, still yelling at us to disarm and surrender.

Murdoc bristled, baring his teeth like a wild animal. What was he doing? These guys were on our side, right?

Behind the soldiers, a large, scaly head suddenly blocked the entry to the alley with a pair of piercing green eyes. My body went numb. I froze. The crossbow slipped out of my hands and to the ground at my feet.

The dragon snarled, its lips curling back over jagged black fangs and its cat-like pupils narrowing to slits. Its huge body rumbled with a growl and its ears slicked back.

"You won't be given another chance! Surrender now or face our flame!" From the dragon's back, a figure, clad from head to toe in gleaming armor barked down at us.

I dropped to my knees immediately.

Next to me, Murdoc bit angry curses under his breath as unbuckled his scimitar sheaths and tossed them aside before coming to his knees as well. He put his hands behind his head and shot me a meaningful look. I quickly did the same.

None of it made any sense. Why were they treating us this way? They were our allies. Why would they …?

Oh gods—the *armor*! Murdoc and I were still dressed like Tibran soldiers. We looked like the enemy.

"We aren't Tibrans!" I cried as the two soldiers stalked toward us, one holding the point of his blade at our faces while the other roughly bound our hands behind our backs. "Please, you haven't to believe me. We're from Maldobar. We were just trying to—"

"Silence!" The soldier tying my hands planted a boot right in my back and kicked me the rest of the way to the ground.

I lay, wheezing and coughing under my helmet, as they dragged Murdoc toward the street first. They didn't forget about me, though. After snatching me to my feet and ripping off my helmet, they patted me down for any more weapons before shoving me toward the street. As I staggered ahead of them, my eyes locked upon the dragon still crouching right outside the alleyway entrance. Its huge green eyes followed me, tracking me for any false moves, as its snout twitched at a challenging growl.

The dragons of Maldobar had quite a reputation. They were powerful and highly intelligent creatures, but also notoriously spirited and temperamental. And while their lean, muscular bodies weren't much larger than a big draft horse, they had strong, leathery wings attached to their front legs like those on a bat. They also breathed plumes of flame— or rather, they could spray sticky acidic venom from their mouths. The venom caught fire whenever it was exposed to air, and couldn't be doused by water. I'd only heard about them from stories told around the city. I'd never seen one so close before. We were miles away from Southwatch, the nearest fortress where the dragonriders were posted, so they didn't come around this area very often.

The sight of the creature made my whole body shake with primal fear. Every shred of sense in my brain begged me to run—not that it would have helped. You didn't run from dragons. All it would take was one wrong step, one breath, and my life would be over. I'd be nothing but a black scorch mark on the ground.

"Wait," the rider sitting astride the creature's back called out.

The soldiers paused, jerking me to a halt between them.

The dragonrider dismounted with a flourish of his long, dark blue cloak. I'd heard they all wore cloaks like that; it was part of what distinguished them on the battlefield if they weren't in the saddle. The edges of it were trimmed in gold, and the collar was adorned with a mane of white fox fur.

I'd never owned anything that nice. And at this rate, I never would.

The dragonrider stalked toward me, a towering man in full battle armor with that cape rustling at his heels. He slid the visor of his helmet back, revealing a scrutinizing scowl. "You're sure this is a Tibran?" He didn't sound convinced.

"They've been taking locals from every city they conquer and slapping them in armor. They force them to fight under threat of death or torture," one of the soldiers explained. "No doubt these are two of them."

"They didn't even take the time to brand or shave these," the other soldier scoffed. "That tyrant Argonox must have thought hurling every fighter he had at us would help tilt the odds in his favor."

The dragonrider's frown deepened, as his gold-toned eyes looked me over from head to toe. "Put them with the others, then, and see they're sent to Halfax. We'll let the king sort them out." He waved us off.

I started to protest—to insist they had it wrong. We weren't Tibran soldiers. We were just pretending so we didn't get killed!

No one listened.

"You're wasting your breath," Murdoc grumbled as they tossed us into the back of a large armored wagon. The door was barred and locked tight with a thick iron crossbar. You couldn't hope to open it from the inside.

I floundered around to sit up, which wasn't easy with my hands still tied. "What'll they do to us?" I panicked.

He snorted. "If we're lucky? Lock us away as traitors with the rest until we rot in some prison cell."

"A-and if we're not lucky?" My voice hitched with terror.

He flashed me a meaningful glance, his jaw cocked as though he were gnawing on the inside of his cheek. "They put us to the sword along with the rest of the Tibrans."

My stomach dropped, and I lost my breath again. My body flashed cold and I stared at him, hoping for some sign of hope. There had to be something we could do, or some way we could prove we weren't really Tibrans.

Through the bars of the prison wagon, I watched the dragonrider climb back into his saddle. His beast, a powerful monster with black stripes mottling his turquoise scales, gave another bone-rattling roar before it launched into the sky. A blast of wind off its wings hit my face.

I sat back, watching them soar into the night sky and join with another formation of riders cruising over the city. Murdoc was watching them, too. I noticed his sharp features were drawn into a grim, almost resolved frown when his gaze panned back to me. "Do you know anyone here who could vouch for you?"

"I don't know. My father is … he stayed behind. I don't know if he's still alive."

"What about in Halfax?"

I shook my head.

He let out a sigh. "Then we'll just have to wait."

The wagon lurched into motion, rumbling over the uneven stones, and taking us out of the city. It joined with other wagons, packed with the blood-spattered faces of Tibran soldiers. Some of them were even younger than I was.

I tried forcing myself not to look for too long at all the carnage we passed. I was afraid I'd see my father amidst the flames and tangled bodies. But I never did.

Resting my head against the bars, I let my eyes roll closed as I listened to the *clop, clop, clop* of horse hooves and the groaning of the wheels. My chest ached as my heart wrenched. Part of me kept hoping this was a nightmare. Maybe I would wake up back in my bed to the smell of hay, oats, and the musk of the horses from the stable below. Father would scold me for sleeping late. I'd get to work with my daily chores. None of this awfulness would be real.

But then again, I'd never been that lucky of a guy.

And I had a feeling the worst was yet to come.

OTHER MONTH9BOOKS TITLES YOU MIGHT LIKE

Find more books like this at http://www.Month9Books.com

Connect with Month9Books online:
Facebook: www.Facebook.com/Month9Books
Instagram: https://instagram.com/month9books
Twitter: https://twitter.com/Month9Books
Tumblr: http://month9books.tumblr.com/
YouTube: www.youtube.com/user/Month9Books
Georgia McBride Media Group: www.georgiamcbride.com

DRAGONRIDER CHRONICLES 1

Fledgling

NICOLE CONWAY

DRAGONRIDER CHRONICLES 2

Avian

NICOLE CONWAY

DRAGONRIDER CHRONICLES 3

Traitor

NICOLE CONWAY

DRAGONRIDER CHRONICLES 4

Immortal

NICOLE CONWAY

DRAGONRIDER · LEGACY · I

SAVAGE

BESTSELLING AUTHOR OF THE DRAGONRIDER CHRONICLES

NICOLE CONWAY

DRAGONRIDER LEGACY 2
HARBINGER
BESTSELLING AUTHOR OF THE DRAGONRIDER CHRONICLES
NICOLE CONWAY